"Are you still bad to the [bone]?" [she] couldn't resist teasing, [and] flirting.

"I must not be too bad if you're standing out here in the dark with me."

He stepped closer, and Marilee froze. She felt her breath catch in the back of her throat. His face was only inches from hers. He was too handsome for his own good, and for one wild and insane minute she thought he was going to kiss her. Instead, he reached around and opened her door.

"Good night, Marilee," he said. "Don't forget to use the chain on your door until I can fix it."

She realized she was holding her breath, and when she let it out, hot air gushed from her lungs with such a force it made her light-headed. She swayed slightly.

Sam caught her, a look of concern crossing his face. "Are you okay?"

"F-fine," she said, annoyed that she had been so taken in by his good looks that she'd almost swooned. Swooned, for heaven's sake! Nobody did that sort of thing anymore.

"You looked mighty nervous there for a moment. You didn't think I was going to kiss you, did you?" An easy smile played at the corner of his lips.

Charm and sensuality oozed from him. Yes, he was as bad as they came, at least where women were concerned. "You're still a scoundrel, Sam Brewer."

Without another word, Marilee hurried inside and closed the door, securing the chain with trembling hands. On the other side, she heard Sam laugh softly.

Watch for the newest novel from
CHARLOTTE HUGHES
And MIRA Books

Coming September 2002

# A NEW ATTITUDE

## CHARLOTTE HUGHES

MIRA

**MIRA**

ISBN 1-55166-863-7

A NEW ATTITUDE

Copyright © 2001 by Charlotte Hughes.

Visit us at www.mirabooks.com

**Printed in U.S.A.**

This book is dedicated to Mary Lois Nash Coons with love.
Thank you for all the love and laughter.

Many thanks to Curt Copeland, Copeland Funeral Home.

# *One*

Marilee Abernathy had planned her suicide to the last detail. She'd gotten up at dawn, showered, and made up her face with the Mary Kay samples she'd won playing Tuesday-night bingo at church and saved for special occasions. Then she'd put on the beige linen suit and matching pillbox hat she'd bought at the Style Mart. It wasn't Saks Fifth Avenue, mind you, but it was the only place in Chickpea, South Carolina, that didn't have bright orange or lime-green polyester pantsuits hanging from a half-price rack at the back of the store.

She wore her mother's pearl choker—you simply couldn't go wrong with pearls—and the smart, two-tone, beige-and-white high heels she'd never even taken out of the box until today. She knew her shoes were inappropriate. Labor Day had come and gone and dark brown spectator pumps would have been more in keeping with the season, but Marilee had chosen style over tradition. When folks came to her funeral, she wanted them to stand back and take notice.

And say what a shame it was that Reverend Grady Abernathy had abandoned wife and church for some slut with implants and big hair.

As for Josh, Marilee couldn't even think of her son without getting a lump in her throat the size of a turnip, and the absolute last thing she needed to do was start crying again. Someone might think she'd been crying over Grady, and she simply would not have it. Not after he'd turned their fifteen-year-old child against her and moved the boy right smack into the best little whorehouse in Chickpea. That her son had gone so willingly had been the lowest blow, and the closest Marilee had come to having a coronary.

She should have seen it coming. Josh had accused her of smothering him more than once, wanting to know where he was at all times, sticking her nose in his business, just being a regular pain in the butt as far as he was concerned. Marilee had to admit she'd become something of a nag and a worrywart. As a result, she'd ended up alienating him—which explained why Josh was now living in Tall Pines Trailer Park with his father and a waitress by the name of LaFonda Bonaire.

The scandal had rocked the town and the church where Grady had preached for the past ten years. His dismissal came with a notice to evacuate the house provided by the church. A stunned and humiliated Marilee had packed their belongings in record time and put everything in storage. She'd been hiding out at her poor deceased parents' house for the past three days, hoping and praying she would wake up and discover it had all been a bad dream. But it was real. One minute she'd had a family and a life, the next minute it was gone. It was as though a giant tornado had come through and sucked up everything she'd ever known and loved.

But none of that mattered now. What mattered was finding a way to end the pain. And she had thought she'd found it when she had pulled her car into the garage and closed the door with the engine running.

It had seemed like the perfect way to die: sit inside a closed garage with the engine running until she nodded off. Marilee didn't know squat about carbon monoxide poisoning except that it was supposed to be painless. Like falling asleep.

So why in heaven's name was she still alive?

She gazed about her vintage Ford. She still held her son's baby blanket and the rubber duck he'd loved as a toddler. Life had been so much simpler then. Marilee had gotten pregnant on her wedding night. Grady had sent a dozen red roses to the hospital after she'd given birth, even though he was still in seminary school and they were barely making ends meet. She remembered as though it were yesterday the day they brought their newborn home.

Marilee remembered nursing Josh in the middle of the night, when the house was silent and all she could hear were the suckling noises he made. Even now she could close her eyes and conjure up the way he'd smelled, the feel of his downy hair against her cheek. And later, when his eyes lit up each time she walked into the nursery, his chubby arms reaching for her. She had been his world, his universe.

Now he no longer needed her. Funny how one could dismiss another human being so easily.

Marilee's eyes flooded with tears, and she swiped at them and tried to concentrate on the task at hand. The engine wasn't running. She peered over the steering wheel at the gas gauge. The needle pointed straight up to half a tank. Marilee sighed wearily. Somehow, in all the rigamarole, she'd forgotten about the faulty gas gauge. It had caused her to run out of gas several times over the past six months because she'd thought she had enough fuel to get her home.

Obviously, it had happened again.

Wasn't that just her luck!

Marilee wrenched open the door to the car and climbed out. There were still enough noxious fumes that she might be overcome after all, but she couldn't count on it. She needed fuel. She paced a moment and then spied a dull-red gas can sitting in the corner of the garage. She paid a boy to cut her parents' lawn twice a month. With any luck she'd come up with enough gas to get her to a service station.

The gas tank was empty, and Marilee had to bite back the four-letter word on her tongue. She would not resort to foul language. She planned to leave this world with her morals and dignity perfectly intact. Years from now folks would comment on what a lady she'd been, right up to the bitter end. Marilee noted the lawn mower and hurried over to it. She unscrewed the cap and looked inside. It was full! Her joy was short-lived, though, as she pondered how to get the gas from the lawn mower into the gas can so she could pour it into her tank.

Dang! This suicide business was not as easy as she'd thought it would be.

She walked around the garage, searching. A dusty garden hose was coiled on a shelf at the back. She examined it, but there was no telling how old it was. Her father had never thrown anything away in his life. Still, it should do the job. She went inside the house for a knife so she could slice off a three- or four-foot section. A few minutes later, Marilee was trying to siphon gasoline out of the lawn mower. She swallowed a mouthful, then spent the next few minutes coughing and gagging before she gave it a second attempt. Grady had made it all look so simple the time he'd done it. Once the gas started coming, she quickly moved her end of the hose to the tank, but in her rush, dropped it. She grabbed for it but was a split second too late. Gas spewed everywhere, dousing her hair, face and eyes. It felt like someone had set her eyeballs on fire.

"Hellfire and damnation!" To hell with dignity and morals! Marilee dropped the hose and raced blindly inside the house to the bathroom, where she bathed her eyes in cold water, ruining her perfect makeup and hairdo.

There went all her plans for a fashionable funeral. Irby Denton, who owned the local funeral home, would take one look at her and insist on a closed coffin. Marilee sat on the edge of the tub and wept. *And here she thought she'd used up all her tears.*

Where had she gone wrong? What had she done to Grady to make him hate her so? How could two people who'd once been so much in love, who'd vowed to God and themselves they'd never part, suddenly find themselves in such a mess?

It had to be the flannel nightgowns she wore to bed. And the floppy socks that kept her feet warm during the night. It was no wonder he'd left her. She'd failed her husband. She'd let herself go. Chased him right smack into the arms of another woman.

LaFonda Bonaire was probably allergic to flannel.

Finally, Marilee composed herself. She returned to the garage and shook her head at the sight. What a mess. Leaning against her car and feeling defeated, she could just imagine what Grady would say.

"Marilee," he'd say, "if you had a brain you'd have to wear a warning label."

Grady had never talked to her like that in the early years. He'd referred to her as his Sweet Pea. "Sweet Pea," he'd say, "you are a sight to behold in that new dress," or "Sweet Pea, what did you think of my sermon today?"

Now she was just plain old Marilee, who was rewarded with a weary sigh from him when she asked the simplest question. "Marilee, I don't have time to worry about the Easter pageant. That's your job." Sigh. "Marilee, why are you bothering me with questions about the Christmas cantata when you know I have to prepare my sermon?" Another sigh. Or, "Marilee, why on earth would you serve taco salads at the senior citizens' dinner when you know elderly people can't eat spicy food? Have you any idea how many complaints I've received? I swear, Marilee, if you had a brain, you'd have to wear a warning label."

There were times she felt she couldn't do anything right, no matter how hard she worked. What about all the seniors' dinners that had been successful? And had Grady forgotten just how many visitors they had at Easter and Christmas? Of course she wanted everything to go right. Some of those visitors became members.

She shook her head sadly. Maybe Grady was right. What did she know about anything? She gave a sniff. Not that Grady was some kind of genius, mind you. Otherwise, he wouldn't have gotten kicked out of the church for sleeping with a woman who had a tattoo on her fanny that read Easy Rider. At least that's what Darlene Milburn claimed, and she should know since she taught water aerobics at the YMCA. Darlene had "excused" LaFonda from class for wearing a thong bikini, of all things.

*Another woman.* That was the absolute last thing she had expected of him.

Marilee wondered if Grady's recent diagnosis of high blood pressure had something to do with the change that had come over him. Seemed he was always tired and out of sorts or feeling under the weather. Her mother had long ago accused him of being a hypochondriac and although Marilee had defended him, there'd been times she'd thought the same thing. Lately, he'd become so moody she'd found herself tiptoeing around him. Then one day, right out of the blue, he told her he planned to leave the ministry.

Looking back, Marilee was surprised she hadn't tried to kill herself sooner.

With a heartfelt sigh, she stood and walked into the living room. The place was gloomy and musty from being closed up for so long, and she hadn't had the heart to do anything about it the past few days, hadn't wanted to remember how warm and inviting the house had been when her parents were alive. Grady had wanted her to sell it once her mother passed on; he resented the utility bills they received every month for a place that had been closed up for two years. "You'll never find closure until you let go of that house," he'd said more than once. But Marilee had resisted. She'd planned to put it on the market later, when property values went up, then use the money to send Josh to college.

Sheets covered the furniture and the old piano where she had once practiced her scales under the tutelage of Mrs. Sadie Habersham until her behind felt as if it were growing into the piano bench. The wooden floors wore a thick layer of dust. Heavy brocade drapes locked out the early-morning sun. Lord, but they were ugly, what with those thick cords twisted together like a bunch of snakes in mating season. The tassels looked as though they belonged in a bordello. What had her mother been thinking? They'd obviously been on sale, because one thing Hester Brown had never been able to pass up was a K mart blue-light special or a clearance table.

*Wait a minute... Cords?*

Marilee stepped closer and examined them. Three nylon strands were braided to make one thick cord. She tugged hard. The fabric was still good and strong. She glanced up at the beam that ran beneath the raised ceiling, her mind working frantically. Her answer was right in front of her.

She would hang herself!

Marilee hurried into the kitchen, to the junk drawer where her mother had kept everything that would fit and crammed in those things that hadn't. She found a pair of scissors and went to work. Each cord was about five feet long when she pulled the drapes open. She cut four lengths from the living-room drapes before making her way into the master bedroom and guest rooms, where the same drapes, different only in colors and degrees of ugliness, hung. It was no easy task cutting through the cords, and by the time she finished, she wore a blister at the base of her thumb. Gathering them together, Marilee realized she had enough cord to hang a gang of outlaws.

Grady had underestimated her. He figured since she'd never earned a college degree that he was the smarter of the two. It didn't matter that the reason she hadn't earned a degree was that she'd had to work two jobs to support them while he went to seminary school. Not that she'd minded. They were a team, working toward a future. Even when Grady sometimes felt he wasn't meant to preach, she would reassure him, bolster his self-confidence. Wasn't that part of being a wife and team member?

Once he'd become a pastor, she'd devoted her time to church activities. She'd been good at it too, or so she'd thought, until Grady began complaining about every little thing she did. It only made her more determined to work harder. Even if Grady found her lacking, others claimed she was the veritable backbone of Chickpea Baptist Church.

A lot of good it did her now.

Marilee sat on the sofa and began tying the cords together. The frayed tassels clashed with her outfit something awful, but she had no choice. An hour later, she had a sturdy, if gaudy-looking, hangman's noose. She spent the next ten minutes trying to throw the noose over the beam, and was about to give up before she remembered the ladder in the garage. It could also be used as her jumping-off place.

Heavens, but she could be brilliant at times!

Marilee dragged the ladder inside the house and placed it beneath the beam. Holding one end of the cord between her teeth, she began climbing. Okay, so the ladder was a little wobbly. She suddenly remembered her fear of heights and became angry with herself. She didn't have time to fret about *every* little thing.

Pausing halfway up, she attempted once again to throw the noose over the beam, all the while struggling to hang on to the ladder. Finally! She tied it so it wouldn't pull free. Marilee knew how to tie just about every kind of knot there was, thanks to Josh's stint in the Boy Scouts.

Crouching at the top of the ladder, she slipped the noose around her neck. Her hands trembled. She had no idea how much it was going to hurt, but the pain could be no worse than what she was feeling inside.

With an angry burst of determination, Marilee stood straight up. And banged her head on the ceiling beam with such force she almost fell off the ladder. In fact, she would have, had she not grabbed the beam to steady herself. The room spun wildly beneath her and she felt her eyes cross. Her skull throbbed. Afraid she'd given herself a concussion, Marilee stood there, trying to clear her head. The floor seemed miles away. It felt as if she was standing on top of Chickpea's water tower, where she and Grady had sneaked up the night she'd turned sixteen. They'd kissed under the stars and promised to love one another forever.

*Forever. So why, at age thirty-five, was she all alone in the world?*

Marilee swallowed the lump in her throat. Well, she wasn't really alone. She had friends who loved her, people who were probably worried sick about her this very moment. And she had a son. He might not like her right now, but what if he—heaven forbid—ended up blaming himself for her suicide? Josh would have to spend his entire life living with it.

What if he was just going through a stage and didn't really hate her? What if there was the slightest chance of reconciliation?

What was wrong with her? Hadn't she seen enough suffering in her life to know that everybody got a dose of it now and then? Parents died, kids rebelled, husbands cheated. And here she was, standing on top of this shoddy ladder with a noose around her neck and what could possibly be a serious head injury. Not only that—her best outfit and makeup were ruined, her shoes were all wrong and she smelled like a Texaco station.

She was being weak and selfish, Marilee told herself. She needed to stop wallowing in self-pity and start working on her problems, namely getting her son out of that den of iniquity. She needed to clean up her parents' house, find a job and show folks that she was made of tougher stuff than this! And she *was* tough, dang it. As a minister's wife, she had sat with the dying, comforted the bereaved and brought smiles to nursing-home patients who felt neglected, of no use to the world and wanted to die. "The Lord has a purpose for us all," Marilee had told them. "He will bring us home when he's ready. Until then, we must have faith."

She was glad those poor people couldn't see her now, those who were old and sick and in pain. She was young and healthy and had every reason to live. It didn't feel that way right now, but tomorrow she might see things differently.

Tomorrow. She suddenly realized she wanted to wake up to another day, no matter how bleak the future seemed at the moment.

But first she had to get down this ladder in one piece.

Her mind made up, Marilee tried to decide the best way to descend without ending up in a wheelchair and sporting a handicapped sticker on her car. Working up her last nerve, she oh so slowly knelt at the very top, trying to balance herself like a seal on a large ball. Her high heels proved a serious hindrance, and she decided she had to remove them. Somehow. Still perched precariously, Marilee tried to slip

one off, but the ladder gave a shudder and veered right.
Quickly she leaned in the opposite direction but overcorrected. Dang, she thought, only a split second before she lost
her balance and toppled.

She had been so intent on getting down she had forgotten
to take off the noose. Now it snapped tight around her neck.
She was only vaguely aware of a noise overhead, and then
it sounded as if the whole house was crashing down around
her. *Poor Josh.* It was her last thought. Something hit her
on the head, and then there was blackness.


Sam Brewer was in a foul mood. As he grabbed a shovel
from the garage and carried it to his mother's flower bed,
he could only imagine what the neighbors were saying as
they peered out the windows at him. Without a doubt, Edna-
Lee Bodine from across the street had her nose pressed flat
against the windowpane this very moment, watching and
fogging up the glass.

"There goes Sam Brewer digging in his mother's flower
bed again," she'd tell her husband, who kept his own nose
buried in a newspaper. "No telling what that old bat has
gone and buried this time." There were times Sam wished
his mother would bury Mrs. Bodine in the flower bed. "And
just look at him," Edna-Lee would say. "Why, he looks
like a derelict. No telling when he last shaved or combed
his hair."

Sam knew he looked like hell, but how was he supposed
to groom himself when almost everything he owned was
buried? His mother had set out to make a point, and she'd
done just that. After all, her great-great-grandmother had
buried the family silver to protect it from the Yankees during
the Civil War; Nell Brewer had decided it was up to her to
protect their belongings from "Nurse Ratched," as she referred to her latest caretaker, whom she claimed was stealing. Sam had to admit the retired nurse had the personality
of a troll, but his mother had managed to run off several of
her "companions" over the past six months. This latest one

had stormed off the minute she caught wind of the accusations against her, just as his mother knew she would.

Now he was saddled with the chore of finding someone new, despite claims from his mother that she was perfectly capable of taking care of herself. That hadn't been the case six months ago, when she'd insisted she was going blind and losing her mind and needed him there. He'd sold his construction company in Atlanta and moved home to Chickpea so he could personally look after her. Truth was, he'd been looking to leave the rat race behind and find a simpler life anyway. Now he was building single-family dwellings with an old high-school buddy, and Sam rather liked it that way.

Except that his mother was driving him crazy.

Why did women have to be so difficult?

That reminded him of what a royal pain in the butt his ex-wife was. It didn't matter that they'd been divorced five years now. Shelly still called him for every little thing and was constantly borrowing money, despite the healthy alimony check he sent every month.

Seemed there was no way to win, especially where the opposite sex was involved.

With a muttered oath, Sam searched for a fresh mound of dirt that might produce his electric shaver and the iron he needed to press his shirt before he met with an architect in an hour. He drove the shovel into the soft ground and struck something solid. He pulled a plastic bag from the dirt. Ahha! He'd found his electric shaver, perfectly intact. At least his mother was thoughtful enough to wrap everything before sticking it into a hole in the ground. Nevertheless, it had to stop. Yesterday it had been his combs and toothbrush, which was why he looked like the world's biggest slob.

He stabbed the dirt once more, just as a piercing scream ripped through the late-morning air, jolting his already strained nerves. Dropping the shovel, he lunged toward his house before he realized the sound had come from the Browns' next door. He stopped, shook himself and turned in the opposite direction.

Sam jumped the hedges separating the properties and raced across the lawn like a marathon runner, skirting bushes and a large cast-iron pot that had gone to rust. He'd assumed the house was vacant. At least, he hadn't noticed anyone coming or going. But it was of little concern to him as he took the front steps in one leap. He crossed the porch and knocked. No answer. The door was locked.

The scream still echoing in his mind, he knew he had no choice but to break down the door. He braced himself and rammed it hard. Pain ripped through his shoulder, radiated down his arm and arched across his back, but he didn't have time to worry about it. He slammed against the door once more, and the sound of splintering wood told him he'd succeeded.

Stepping inside, Sam crossed a small foyer and stood there for a moment, staring blankly at the sight before him.

The woman on the floor appeared dead. Sam stumbled toward her prostrate body, stepping over Sheetrock as he went, his mind uncertain of what he was actually seeing. He noted the noose around her neck, made of what appeared to be a dozen multicolored tassels. The woman's face and clothes were dusted in white, as though someone had just dumped a sack of flour on her head. He glanced up and saw that a portion of what was obviously a fake beam had been torn away. Had she hanged herself? Sure as hell looked like it.

Without wasting another second, Sam dropped to his knees, loosened the noose and performed CPR. He felt her stir and raised his head, inhaling deeply as he prepared to blow more air into her lungs.

Marilee opened her eyes, taking in the man before her, and her heart sank. From the looks of his unshaved jaw and wild black hair, she could only assume she'd died and landed in hell. She suspected angels took better care of themselves.

She tried to speak, but her throat hurt. "Excuse me," she managed in a hoarse whisper. "Are you the devil?"

Sam stared at the woman for a full minute, trying to make sense of what she'd said. She was obviously delirious. Her face was pale. No telling how long that noose had been around her neck. Could very well have blocked desperately needed oxygen to her brain. "Where's your phone?" he asked hurriedly. "I need to call an ambulance."

Marilee's eyes widened. Phone? Ambulance? She was alive! Relief flooded her, and she wondered again why she'd ever considered ending her life in the first place. To think she'd almost succeeded! Wasn't that just her luck? Just when she'd found the strength to go on living, she'd come close to killing herself by accident.

She bolted upright, trying to disentangle herself from the cords and tassels. "Please don't call anyone," she said, too embarrassed to look at the stranger, even as she wondered how he happened to be there. "You have no idea what I've already been through."

"You need medical attention, lady." And a damn good psychiatrist, he thought. This woman made his mother's antics seem normal.

"I'm fine, really." Marilee scrambled to her feet but swayed, no doubt from the two head injuries she'd received. He caught her up before her legs, which felt as if they were made of mashed sweet potatoes, folded beneath her. The noose, still around her neck although no longer constricted, was an annoyance, but she was more concerned with the sudden pain in her ankle as she tried to steady herself. "I think I twisted my ankle," she said. "I must've landed on it wrong. Other than that, I'm okay." Well, not really, she thought. Her head throbbed. It felt as though the state of Texas was sitting on top of her skull.

All at once, Marilee realized the man was still holding her in his arms. The way Grady had held her when he'd carried her over the threshold on their wedding night. Oh, this was all wrong, she thought. It was simply not done. Why, it reeked of impropriety, and Marilee Abernathy had been raised a lady. Her poor mother was probably rolling over in her grave at this very moment.

"Please put me down, sir," she said in her best well-bred voice.

He eased her to the floor. "Can you stand?"

"Why, I certainly can." She pulled free of him and drew herself up primly, dusting off her clothes and taking care not to put all her weight on her sore ankle. "My, I must look a mess. You'll have to excuse my appearance."

Sam looked on in disbelief as she hobbled about, holding her head as though afraid it would fall off and trying to walk out the soreness in her foot. The still-attached noose dragged a piece of the ceiling beam after her. "It would probably be easier for you to get around if you removed that noose from your neck," he said, sarcasm creeping into his voice. His initial fear had waned, now that he knew she wasn't going to be carried out in a body bag, and he suddenly felt like shaking her.

Marilee regarded him as she fumbled with the tassels. "There is no cause for rudeness. I'm obviously ill-prepared to receive guests at this time, so perhaps we can meet again under more favorable circumstances." Yes, that's what she'd do. She'd whip up her special chicken salad and cucumber sandwiches and invite him to a little housewarming gala once she managed to get the place in shape. But she could not worry about that right now. She had more important business to take care of.

Sam gazed back in pure astonishment as realization hit him. "Marilee Brown," he said, wondering why he hadn't recognized her the minute he'd laid eyes on her. She was still as pretty as she'd been in high school. Her hair, the color of ripened wheat, was shorter, barely touching her shoulders and turning under slightly at the ends. Her eyes were the same sparkling blue, and she hadn't lost the figure that had looked so good in a cheerleader's skirt and the gown she'd worn when she'd been crowned homecoming queen.

"And I'd appreciate it if you'd stop looking at me as though I'm crazy," she went on. "I'm perfectly sane, and I wouldn't be in such a predicament had I not been pushed to the brink. The absolute brink,'' she added, waving her arms dramatically as she almost shouted the words. She paused abruptly. He knew her maiden name. "Have we met?''

He wasn't surprised that she didn't remember him. "I grew up next door. We went to the same high school.'' His mouth took on an unpleasant twist. "We didn't exactly run with the same crowd.''

"You're Nell Brewer's son,'' Marilee said at last. "Sam.''

"So you remember.'' He wondered just how much she remembered.

Marilee had a sudden image of a good-looking adolescent with dark hair and what mothers had called bedroom eyes in those days. Those brown eyes, heavily lidded with thick, dark lashes, gave him a lazy, come-hither look that had lured more than one high-school girl into the back seat of his car. "Stay away from that boy,'' her own mother had warned. "You so much as walk on the same side of the street with him, and you can kiss your reputation goodbye. And you can't blame his parents. They're decent, God-fearing Christians.''

His father had died in Sam's senior year, and the teenager had quit school in order to support his mother. Marilee vaguely remembered he'd worked construction. Somehow, though, he'd still managed to get into one scrape after another. Then, like a bad wind, he was suddenly gone. The town of Chickpea assumed he'd been sent to prison.

"Yes, I remember,'' Marilee replied, thankful she had packed her mother's silver and put it in a safe place long ago. "It's, uh, nice seeing you again, Sam. As you must have surmised by now, my life has taken a turn for the worse since I last saw you. Nothing I can't handle, of course, but thanks for stopping by just the same.''

*He was being dismissed.* Was she crazy? She had just attempted to hang herself, and now she acted as though it was an everyday occurrence and he was in the way. Sam raked his fingers through his hair, wondering what he should say or do. The situation felt unreal, as though he'd just landed in a scene in one of his mother's favorite soaps.

"Look, Marilee, I don't know what your problem is, but I think you need to talk to someone. Nothing is worth ending your life over."

"I realize that now," she said with disdain, still trying to free herself from the noose.

"Here, let me help you with that," Sam offered. He struggled with the tassels. She obviously knew her way around knots. Finally, he pulled it free and tossed the makeshift rope aside. He leaned closer and sniffed. "Do I smell gasoline?" he asked. "Please don't tell me you were planning to set yourself on fire."

"Do I look deranged?"

He arched one dark eyebrow but decided not to answer. The noose had chafed the tender skin at her neck. She brushed plaster dust from her face, and he couldn't help noticing her complexion was still youthful and unblemished, as if she belonged in one of those skin-care commercials. It unnerved him to think just how close she'd come to dying.

Marilee noticed he was staring. "What's wrong?"

"There's a red welt on your neck."

"Trust me, it's not the worst thing that's happened to me in the past few days. I'll deal with it, okay? Just...please go." She was near tears, and the last person she wanted to see her cry was Sam Brewer, who didn't seem to like her very much in the first place.

"You're lucky to be alive, you know. If that beam hadn't collapsed, you'd be dangling like a puppet right now with your eyes bulging out of their sockets."

"What?" Marilee drew back. The mere thought horrified her.

"You obviously don't know what a hanging victim looks like."

"Well, no."

"They mess their pants, and their tongue hangs out and turns purple." Sam wondered what had made him go and say something like that, but he was annoyed with her. Pissed off, actually, now that the initial shock of finding her had worn off. "What the hell were you thinking?"

Marilee shuddered at the mental picture he'd drawn for her, and she was doubly glad to be alive. "I wasn't really going to go through with it."

"Sure you weren't."

She glared at him. Did he think she did this sort of thing on a regular basis? Could he not see that she was coming apart at the seams? He had no right to pass judgment on her. "Look, you've done your good deed for the day, so why don't you run along now. I can pay you for your trouble if you like."

She had a mouth on her, and that surprised him. She'd always seemed so prim and proper, always doing and saying the right thing. "What do you suppose your life is worth, Miss Brown?"

"At this moment? About ten cents. And my name is not Miss Brown. It's Mrs. Abernathy."

"Ah, yes, you married that Grady fellow. He was into sports, right?"

She gave a rueful smile. "He is still something of a sportsman."

"A football player, if I remember correctly." He remembered well. The Golden Boy, they'd called him. Folks in Chickpea could speak of nothing else his senior year. "Wasn't he offered a full scholarship to Duke University?"

"Yes, but he went into the seminary instead."

"I see."

"He's quite popular with some members of his flock," Marilee said, offering him a tight-lipped smile. "You might say he takes a hands-on approach to those who are most troubled." Sam nodded as she spoke, as though trying to make sense of the situation. But how could he possibly understand? "Uh, look, Sam, I'd really appreciate it if you'd keep this little matter between us. You know how it is, small town and all."

"I wouldn't think of embarrassing you. But how do I

know you won't stick your face in the oven the minute I walk out the door?''

"I'm a grown woman, and I can take care of myself," she replied stiffly. She paused to get a grip on her emotions. He had probably saved her life, and she should be grateful, but she needed time to gather her thoughts. The experience had been harrowing. She took a deep, shaky breath. "I promise not to hurt myself again."

"I hope you're sincere," he said at last, offering his hand to seal the bargain. Marilee paused before taking it. It was big and warm, the palm toughened by the work he did. They shook. "We've got a deal," he said. "I expect you to honor it." He was surprised by the self-deprecating smile that touched her lips. She had always seemed so confidant, so self-assured. Who had hurt her so badly? he wondered, feeling oddly protective of her.

He released her hand. The last thing he needed to do was get involved in her troubles. She was a married woman, and he had his hands full trying to keep up with his mother and a new business. That reminded him of the architect who was supposed to drop by later. "I'd better go." He made for the door, paused and turned. "Uh, Marilee?"

"Yes?" Her gaze locked with his, and for a moment she felt completely disoriented. She blinked, trying to make sense of the strange sensations sweeping through her. What was going on here? Had she killed off some brain cells when the noose tightened around her neck? Or perhaps she did have a concussion and didn't know it. Either way, she was suddenly acutely aware of him as a man, the tall, athletic physique and broad shoulders. She couldn't seem to stop staring at his eyes. They were observant. Was he aware that she was looking at him *in that way?* No wonder the girls at Chickpea High had followed him around like puppies. She cast her own eyes downward, certain that no decent woman would stare so blatantly at a man. And her married to boot!

"I know this is a bad time," he said, "but do you happen to have an iron I could borrow?"

At first she thought she'd misunderstood. "An iron?"

He nodded. "I've misplaced mine. I wouldn't ask if it weren't important."

She couldn't imagine anyone making such a request at a time like this, but from the looks of his clothes an iron was exactly what he needed. Not to mention a hairbrush and razor. "Yes, of course. Just give me a second to find it." Marilee hurried to the utility room, thankful for the reprieve. She had to gather her wits about her or the man would sure enough think she had lost her mind.

The iron was on a shelf next to the spray starch and laundry detergent. Marilee leaned her head against the shelf, feeling as though she needed to bang it hard and clear the muddle inside. In all her married life she had never once looked at another man. Well, not the way she was looking at Sam Brewer.

Lord help her.

Marilee took a deep breath, raised her head and reached for the iron. She dusted it off and retraced her steps to the living room. "It hasn't been used in a while," she said, her voice sounding stiff and unnatural. She had to get him out of there if it was the last thing she did. "I hope it still works."

"I really appreciate this."

He looked so grateful that Marilee wondered if there was a shortage of irons in Chickpea. "You're welcome."

"I'll return it as soon as I'm finished."

"Keep it as long as you like," she said quickly, in no hurry to face him again after what had transpired.

Sam was reluctant to leave her, but he had no choice. "I'm, uh, just next door if you need something."

"Thank you." Marilee walked him to the door, noting the damaged trim. "Oh my."

"I'm sorry," he said. "When I heard you scream I broke in. I can fix it. And the ceiling beam."

"No, please, you've done enough." In a matter of minutes he'd turned her upside down and inside out. That was more than enough after the kind of day she'd had.

"Well then, I'd better get going." He started down the

front walk, glancing over his shoulder for one last look. She stood at the door, watching him. He wondered if she remembered visiting when his father died. She and her mother had taken food over, offering their sincere condolences. They'd even attended the funeral. Both of them had been so kind to his mother, and Marilee had sought him out in the crowd and told him how sorry she was. She had done her best to console him when all he could think of was how angry he felt at losing his dad. He had never forgotten her caring nature.

Sam waved and crossed the yard to his own property.

Marilee closed the door and breathed a sigh of relief. If she didn't get a grip on herself she was going to suffer a bad case of the vapors, just like her grandmother used to do when the worms ate her tomato plants. Here she was, ogling her sexy neighbor as if he was something out of a box of Godiva chocolates, when what she needed to be doing was deciding what to do with the rest of her life.

# Two

Marilee had been cleaning nonstop for several hours when the doorbell rang. She hesitated before opening the door, afraid that it was Sam Brewer, returning the iron. She was a mess, having changed into old gray sweats and sneakers, and she smelled of disinfectant. Marilee would almost prefer giving Sam the dang iron, just to keep from facing him again. In fact, she was tempted not to answer the door at all, but after three rings she realized she had no choice. When she opened it, she found her best friends, Clara Goolesby and Ruby Ledbetter, standing on the other side.

"Marilee, you have a lot of explaining to do," Clara said, frowning so hard her black eyebrows touched in the center, as though someone had drawn a straight line across her forehead with a black marker. Her short hair, dyed black as crow's feathers to hide the gray, stood in tufts, a sure sign that she was upset, because she had a habit of plucking the ends when she was anxious about something. The town librarian, Clara was usually quiet and reserved, the exception being when she discovered food spills or dog-eared pages on her beloved books. Then she was a menace.

"Darn right she owes us an explanation," Ruby echoed, crossing her arms over her breasts. She was a diminutive blonde, no bigger than a minute but a formidable opponent when riled. As owner of Classy Cuts Hair Salon, she was a shrewd businesswoman who tried to stay one step ahead of her competition, Martha Grimes, who ran The Hair Affair.

"What in heaven's name were you thinking, Marilee?" Clara insisted. "How could you just disappear on us like that, without telling us where you were going? If it hadn't been for my exceptional memory, we'd never have found you."

Ruby looked at Clara. "Your exceptional memory? Hell's bells, Clara, we searched for almost seventy-two hours before you thought of coming here."

"That may be true, Ruby, but I'm the one who remembered how Marilee couldn't bear to sell this place after her poor sweet mama died. And you don't have to resort to foul language to get your point across."

Marilee looked from one woman to the other. "Is something wrong?"

Both women gaped at her. Clara drew herself up and sniffed as though she smelled something foul. "Did you forget you were supposed to play the piano at the Grace Blessing Home benefit luncheon on Saturday?"

Marilee gasped. "Oh, no!"

"Oh, yes! We had more than two hundred women show up from six counties who paid twenty bucks to eat overdone roast beef and listen to you play Mozart on Richard Griffin's baby grand piano." She paused to catch her breath. "And after all we went through to get that piano inside the school auditorium and pay to have it tuned. Well," she added in a huff, "Alma Jones ended up playing hymns, and the poor thing is so old she's tone deaf. Marilee, how could you!"

"Yes, how could you!" Ruby seconded. "We had a devil of a time getting that piano back to Mr. Griffin. Not to mention having to pay for another tuning."

Clara nodded. "And that's not the half of it. We collected almost a thousand dollars selling raffle tickets, but guess who still has the pure silver antique candelabra in the trunk of her car?"

Marilee paled instantly. Not only had she forgotten about the benefit luncheon, she hadn't remembered that she held the prize for the winning raffle ticket. She felt a wave of panic wash over her. And just when she'd decided to get her life in order and start afresh.

"You can just imagine how mad Esmerelda Cunningham

was over the whole thing,'' Ruby said. ''Especially since she donated that dumb candelabra and claimed it'd been in her family since before Jesus was born.''

''Ruby!'' Clara frowned and shook her head, then turned her attention back to Marilee. ''Esmerelda said we had twenty-four hours to collect the candelabra or she was going to have you arrested.''

''Arrested!'' Marilee cried. ''Does she think I stole it?'' Her heart began to beat faster. After all that had happened, the last thing she needed was to go to jail.

Clara shifted her gaze. ''We didn't know what to think. Especially with Grady getting fired from the church over some...well, you know.'' Clara paused, as though trying to come up with the right word.

''Two-bit whore?'' Ruby offered.

Clara cut her eyes at the woman. ''Honestly, Ruby, the things you say.''

''Esmerelda said you probably hocked that candelabra and hightailed it out of town,'' Ruby said. ''Not that anybody'd really blame you, after all you've been through.''

Clara gave an embarrassed cough. ''Perhaps we shouldn't go into that right now, Ruby.''

Marilee was still hurt over Esmerelda Cunningham's accusations. Esmerelda was Chickpea's wealthiest citizen and the closest thing to royalty the town had ever seen. Marilee, who'd been involved with the fund-raiser since its conception, had personally asked the woman for a donation and had discovered she was not only a snob but stingy as well. Esmerelda had agreed to part with her beloved candelabra, but she'd been none too pleased about it.

Her first thoughts were of Grady. He could handle Esmerelda. But no, Grady was no longer in the picture. It was up to her. *Her.* She suddenly realized just how many problems Grady had taken care of in their sixteen years of marriage. Now they were her problems. Her moment of truth hit her in the face like a lead pipe. She was now solely responsible for her own life. That in itself was enough reason to pawn the candelabra and leave town.

Clara plucked at her hair. "No Mozart, no raffle prize. Can you imagine how utterly ridiculous we felt?"

"And Benson Contractors walked off the job this afternoon for nonpayment," Ruby told her. "Bobby Benson said he wasn't going to make any more repairs to Blessing Home until he was paid—in full."

"What about the roof?" Marilee asked frantically.

Clara shook her head sadly. "The money we raised won't come close to covering it. Bobby nailed plastic over the holes in the roof and left without so much as a fare-thee-well."

"We'll never be able to come up with that kind of money," Ruby said. "Not legally, anyway."

Marilee sank into the nearest chair. "I am so sorry." She was close to tears. They had been working for weeks to raise funds for the unwed mothers' home, and she had let everybody down.

"Do you have any idea how difficult it is to find lodging for twelve pregnant girls in a town this size?" Clara asked, tapping the toe of her shoe impatiently. "My place is no bigger than a shoebox, and I've had two seventeen-year-old expectant mothers living with me for weeks now. Then, today, they get into a catfight, and one of them packs her bags. Which reminds me—"

"I would gladly take the girl in," Ruby interrupted, "but my place is smaller than Clara's."

Marilee jumped up from her chair and started toward the kitchen. "I'll call Bobby Benson right now and explain."

Clara turned to close the door, then paused at the sight of splintered wood. Instead of saying anything, she merely shook her head, as though nothing would surprise her at this point.

Ruby followed Marilee. "Bobby left town this afternoon for a weeklong fishing trip."

"How could you do this to us?" Clara repeated. "I'm so mad I can't stand it. Why, I feel like slapping somebody."

"Slap Marilee," Ruby said, "if it'll make you feel better."

Marilee stepped closer. "Go ahead. It certainly beats having my head chewed off."

Clara drew herself up proudly. "I happen to be a lady, and I prefer to act like one, even if you did let us down."

"Enough, already!" Marilee cried, feeling as though she might pull her hair out any minute. "You've made your point. I blew it!"

Both women stared at her openmouthed. "Dear, you don't have to shout," Clara said. "There is absolutely nothing wrong with our hearing."

Marilee planted her hands on her hips. "I know the two of you are going to find this hard to believe, but I've been preoccupied the past few days. My life has completely fallen apart, so I'd appreciate it if you'd cut me some slack."

"What Grady did was despicable," Ruby said gently, only to have Clara nudge her hard. "Oh, Clara, stop it. We have to talk about it. We can't just pretend it never happened." She walked over and hugged Marilee. "Honey, how did you find out?"

"Grady told me," she said calmly. "Said he had feelings for another woman and was tired of living a lie. Said he didn't belong on the pulpit. Josh overheard the whole thing. By the time Grady met with the church board and received his dismissal, Josh had packed his father's clothes, as well as his own."

"Oh, Marilee, how awful for you," Clara said.

"You must've started packing as well," Ruby said. "By the time Clara and I heard the news, you'd already up and gone."

"I was too embarrassed to stay. All I could think of was coming here."

Clara's look softened. "I wouldn't really have slapped you." She paused. "Marilee, what happened to your neck?"

"What I want to know is what happened to that ceiling beam?" Ruby said, glancing up.

Marilee gave a grunt of disgust. "I tried to hang myself."

Clara gasped. "Marilee, how can you say such a thing?"

Ruby shot her a dark look. "That's not a bit funny. Not one bit."

"Hang yourself, indeed," Clara quipped.

Marilee realized she'd gone too far. She must be hysterical. "I'm sorry. Truth is, I have termites. As for my neck, I think my mother's pearl choker caused a rash." She was surprised how easily the lies slipped from her lips.

"That's the very reason I don't wear jewelry," Clara announced. "It makes me break out every time. As for those termites, you'd better have someone take care of it right away. I've heard what kind of damage they can do. You wouldn't believe what happened to my cousin."

Ruby frowned and shook her head. "Hush, Clara. The last thing Marilee needs to hear is one of your horror stories about what happened to somebody in your family. Can't you see the poor girl has enough on her mind? Her husband has dumped her for a woman with tangerine-colored hair, and her son wants nothing to do with her. Why, folks can talk of nothing else. I don't know how poor Marilee will ever be able to show her face in public again. I think she can wait a couple of days before worrying about stupid termites."

Marilee's look was deadpan. "Thank you, Ruby. I feel much better now that you've put it all into perspective for me."

"You're welcome, honey."

"I suppose we shouldn't have been so hard on you because you forgot the benefit," Clara said. "I wouldn't be so upset if Esmerelda hadn't caused such a ruckus. And then those pregnant girls had to get into a snit with one another. I had to break it up. Which reminds me—"

"Grady has lost his mind," Ruby declared. "It's that blood pressure thing. The minute a man has health problems he has to go out and prove to himself he's still got what it takes. You ask me, I think the scare brought on his midlife crisis. Either way, he'll come around."

Marilee hitched her chin high as she thought of all Grady had put her through the past few days. She had been so hurt at first she couldn't stop crying. Well, the hurt and self-pity were gone. Now she was mad as hell.

"He'd better not come around here. He's going to rue the day he moved my son into that...that trollop's mobile home."

Clara nodded, but she looked distracted. She fidgeted with her hair again. "Uh, Marilee, we have a small problem."

"He's vermin," Ruby continued. "Worse than vermin. And everybody knows LaFonda Bonaire is white trash. Why, that's not even her real name. Her real name is Betty Clump, but she paid to have it changed because she thought it would give her class. Ha! She's still trash, and the only reason Grady fell for her is because she'd let him eat anything he wanted whenever he came into the Tick-Tock. And here you were trying to see that he ate a healthy diet and got plenty of exercise."

"Ruby, what are you talking about?" Marilee asked, her face masked with confusion.

"LaFonda was stuffing him with pecan pie behind your back."

Marilee's look turned to disbelief. "Are you telling me that my husband walked out on our marriage because another woman fed him pecan pie? That's the most ridiculous thing I've ever heard."

"Well, that's *part* of it," Clara replied. "My friend Janie Gilbert who works at the *Gazette* said it was almost sickening the way LaFonda carried on around him. Janie said LaFonda had been giving Grady the come-on for weeks."

"A man can only take so much temptation, Marilee," Ruby said. "Even a fine, upstanding minister like Grady."

Marilee felt foolish that everybody in town had known about her husband and LaFonda long before her. "Why didn't the two of you say something?"

"Because Grady was a man of God," Clara said. "I thought he was way above that sort of thing."

"Ruby's right," Marilee groaned. "I'll never be able to show my face in this town again."

Clara waved the comment aside. "Stop talking like that. You haven't done anything wrong."

"Marilee's in a lot of pain right now," Ruby said, "and rightly so. You're probably still in shock, too, honey," she added, patting Marilee on the back. She lowered her voice to a whisper. "Listen, sugar, I've got a pint of whiskey beneath the seat of my truck. I'll grab it if you like. One good swig will calm your nerves."

Clara gasped. "Why, Ruby Ledbetter, I don't believe what I'm hearing. I would never have figured you for a drinking woman. And you a Southern Baptist of all things."

Ruby seemed to take offense. "Don't you go questioning my spirituality, Clara Goolesby. I may be a Baptist, but I have had my share of stress. And there's nothing like a good shot of whiskey to ease the jitters when you don't have time to whip your vehicle over to the side of the road and pray."

"I hardly think it's necessary to resort to blasphemy," Clara said stiffly.

Marilee looked from one to the other, wondering if the two women would come to blows. How they'd managed to remain friends all these years made her wonder. "Okay, let's calm down," she said. "I'm sure we can work this out. I'll call another roofer first thing in the morning."

"And pay him with what?" Ruby asked. "Clara's good looks?"

Clara glared at her. "That was a low blow, considering you cleaned out your savings account last year on an eyelift and tummy tuck." The ring of the doorbell prevented Ruby from answering. "Oh, that must be Winnie," Clara said. "She fell asleep in Ruby's truck on the way over, and we didn't have the heart to wake her, poor thing."

"Who's Winnie?" Marilee asked.

"You remember, Winnifred Frye from Blessing Home." Clara didn't wait for a response. "I've been trying to tell you since we arrived, but Ruby wouldn't stop yammering. Winnie has been staying at my place, but she and the other girl got into a big fuss. You're going to love her, Marilee."

"I am?"

"I guess I'm going to have to answer the door, since neither of you look so inclined," Ruby said, making her way from the kitchen. "You go ahead and break the news to her, Clara."

"What news?" Marilee asked.

Clara seemed hesitant. "Winnie has no place to stay. I was hoping you'd put her up until we figure out what we're going to do about Blessing Home."

"Me? Clara, are you out of your mind? I can't take care of anyone right now. My life is in shambles."

"So is Winnie's. But you have a roof over your head, don't you? Not to mention a warm bed. That's all poor Winnie needs. Until we can make further arrangements," she added. "Besides," she added with a whisper, "you owe me for not forcing Grady to take one of the girls in when we first started looking for temporary housing."

Marilee was still embarrassed that Grady had not offered to house a girl while Blessing Home was being restored. True, he'd supported Blessing Home in other ways, taking up separate collections, asking for clothes and nonperishable food, but he'd balked at having an unwed mother in the house. He thought it would be a bad influence on Josh. Marilee wanted to laugh at the irony.

"Which girl was Winnie?" Marilee whispered to Clara. "Was she that petite redhead with the pixie face?"

"I'm Winnie," a husky voice said. "And I've never been petite. Not even when I was born."

Marilee turned in the direction of the voice and froze at the sight of the tall black woman. She was at least six feet tall, and her shoulders filled the doorway. "Oh." She forced a smile. "How nice to meet you, Winnie. I'm Marilee Abernathy."

Winnie responded by blowing a big bubble with her chewing gum. It popped, and she sucked it in. "I know who you are. Didn't your old man just walk out on you?"

Marilee blushed. Was there anyone in Chickpea who hadn't heard about her problems? "Well, yes."

"You don't have to be ashamed," Winnie said. "My man left me too. After he knocked me up, that is."

"Oh, how awful. You must've been devastated."

"Yeah. Killing him would be too good for him, but I'm going to do it anyway if I ever lay eyes on him again."

Clara suddenly looked anxious. "Please don't talk like that, Winnie dear. We're Christians." She paused. "You don't…uh…have any weapons on you, do you? I don't believe in carrying guns."

"I don't need a gun. I've got my bare hands."

All three women were quiet for a moment. Finally, Marilee spoke up. "How far along are you, Winnie?"

"Five and a half months. I've got a while."

"Have you eaten?" she asked, wishing she had more to offer the girl than a sandwich. She hadn't figured on needing many groceries.

"Nope. I'm starving. You got any Twinkies lying around?"

"I'm afraid not. But I have bologna and cheese and a whole loaf of bread."

"Long as you don't put those nasty bean sprouts on it," Winnie said, rolling her eyes. "Clara is big on bean sprouts."

Marilee looked at Ruby, who was dwarfed beside the young woman. "Would you mind making Winnie a sandwich while I have a word with Clara?"

"Sure." Ruby turned for the refrigerator.

Marilee grasped Clara's hand tightly and led her into the bedroom, where she closed the door. "Clara, what on earth are you thinking? I can't take in this girl."

Clara shook free. "I was thinking I might get a little peace and quiet, if you want to know the truth. She and the other girl fight constantly. But you wouldn't know anything about that, because you haven't been down in the trenches like the rest of us."

"What are you talking about? I'm the one who had to knock on mean old Esmerelda Cunningham's door and beg her to give us something for the raffle."

Clara went on as though she hadn't heard her. "Oh, you don't mind making a few phone calls to ask for donations or playing Mozart in front of the ladies to show off your skills as a pianist, if and when it's convenient for you. But *heaven forbid* you have to actually open your home to some poor pregnant gal who has absolutely no one to turn to."

Marilee plopped onto the bed. "That's not fair, Clara. You know I'd help if I didn't have so much turmoil in my own life. I have to find a job. Do you know how long it has been since I've worked? All I know how to do is sing and play the piano. And bake cakes."

"Winnie won't be any trouble. She goes to school every day, and she's a straight-A student. Plans to attend right up 'til the baby comes, and as soon as she graduates she's going to the community college here." Clara paused. "Marilee, Winnie has never been in trouble in her life. She's a good girl. Her only mistake was getting involved with a smooth-talking man who hit the road the minute she became pregnant. And her parents—" Clara pursed her lips in annoyance "—God-fearing Christians they are, they kicked her out the minute she told them. Honey, she has no one."

Marilee pressed the palm of her hand against her forehead. What next? she wondered, half-afraid to ask the question in the first place, in case she was in for another shocker. Her family had left her, they'd been kicked out of the church, she'd missed playing for the benefit luncheon, Esmerelda Cunningham was threatening to send her to jail and now Clara wanted her to take in an unmarried, pregnant girl.

And to think that a few days ago her life had been relatively normal.

"Oh, Clara," she cried, shaking her head.

"Listen to me, Marilee. You know what it's like to be rejected by those you love. That's exactly what Winnie's feeling right now, although she'd cut her tongue out before admitting it. She's just a kid. Seventeen years old. Not much older than Josh."

Marilee wanted to hide her head under a pillow and not have to think about it. How could she help someone else's child when she hadn't been able to help her own? How could she not? "Well, I suppose I could take her in for a couple of days," she said at last. "Until other arrangements can be made. You realize I can't make any long-term plans right now."

Ruby appeared in the doorway. "Winnie said to thank you for the sandwich, but she had to be on her way. She took her sandwich with her."

Marilee looked up. "On her way where?"

Ruby shrugged. "She didn't say."

"And you let her get away?" Clara cried.

"What was I supposed to do? She's twice my size."

"She can't just leave," Marilee said, jumping from the bed. "She has no place to go."

Clara made a *tsking* sound. "I should have known something like this would happen. That girl can be downright ornery. Come on, Ruby, we'll have to go after her."

"I'll go," Marilee said, hurrying out of the room. She slammed out the front door. A moment later, she spotted Winnie; it would have been hard to miss her considering her size. "Winnie, wait!" she cried. "You can't go." The girl continued on. Marilee sped up. "Winnie, please don't go."

The girl turned as Marilee caught up with her and stopped so abruptly Marilee almost slammed into her. "What do you want?"

"Please don't leave."

"Look, lady, I may be black, broke and pregnant, but I'm not stupid, okay? I can tell when I'm not wanted."

"I'm sorry if I hurt your feelings."

"Hurt my feelings?" Winnie gave a snort. "You can't hurt my feelings. Nobody can. I've got a thick skin, but I'm thin on patience. And I don't feel like listening to some white woman bellyaching 'cause her husband left her. I've got my own problems, thank you very much." She turned and began walking again.

Marilee stood there, aghast. Here she'd been trying to help the girl, only to be insulted. "Excuse me," she called out, "but I am *not* grieving over my husband. I'm upset because my son left *with* him. And don't talk to me like I'm some kind of wimp, because I'm not. I'm a lot stronger than you think." She was only vaguely aware that the day had turned cold and a fine mist was falling. "Hello," she called out angrily.

Winnie turned. "Listen, I'd love to stay and chat, but I've got to be somewhere."

"Today? Right this minute?"

"It's important."

It was starting to rain. "Perhaps you could stay the night. You need to get out of this wet weather. It can't be good for the baby."

The girl seemed to ponder it. "Okay," she said with a great deal of reluctance. "I suppose I can stay one night, but I definitely have to be somewhere tomorrow."

"Fine. You can spend the night, and tomorrow I'll drive you wherever you need to go."

"As long as you don't start crying again. I can't be around negative people in my condition."

Marilee tried not to take offense at the remark as they started back for the house. "Do you like hot chocolate? It'll chase the chill away."

"Yeah, and may I have another sandwich? I'm not crazy about bologna, but I'm eating for two now, you know."

Marilee nodded. "Yes, certainly."

Winnie nodded. "Okay, then. I'll sleep at your place tonight, but I'm outta here first thing in the morning."

"First thing," Marilee agreed.

"But not too early," Winnie said. "Tomorrow's Saturday, and I don't have school. I'll probably sleep till about ten o'clock."

"Ten o'clock then."

"And I like to drink juice and read the funnies before I start my day."

Marilee wasn't about to tell her she didn't get the newspaper and there was no juice in the house. Besides, she didn't have time to worry about it; she had to concentrate on getting along with Winnie until another home could be found.

It wouldn't be easy. The girl had attitude.

Nell Brewer took a bite of her spaghetti, gagged and spit a mouthful into her napkin. "Sam, this is the worst spaghetti sauce I've ever put in my mouth."

He regarded his mother. "Don't beat around the bush, Mom. Tell me how you really feel."

"How can you mess up something straight out of a jar?"

"It tasted bland so I added spices."

She was making faces. "Tastes like you dumped a cupful of oregano in it."

"You don't have to eat it."

"Well, that's a relief."

With a disgusted sigh, Sam stood. He picked up both plates and carried them to the kitchen sink, where he dumped the contents into the garbage disposal. He flipped on the switch and waited for the ruined dinner to disappear. The disposal ground to life, wheezed and died.

Nell hurried over. "Well, would you look at that? Your cooking is so bad it broke the garbage disposal."

"My cooking has nothing to do with it. I just need to press the reset button and it'll be okay." Sam opened the cabinet door then reached beneath the disposal and located the reset button. He pressed it, but nothing happened.

Peering over his shoulder, Nell gave a grunt. "I knew we should have ordered takeout."

Sam rose quickly and collided with his mother, almost knocking her to the floor. He reached out to keep her from falling, his patience lost. "Mom, would you *please* get out of my way!"

She crossed her arms. "Don't you raise your voice to me, Samuel Brewer. I'm still your mother, whether you like it or not. I'm just thankful your father isn't here to see how you treat me."

"Mom, please move."

"You refuse to let me cook in my own kitchen, despite

the fact you haven't the slightest notion how to go about it. It's a wonder we haven't both died of ptomaine poisoning. You won't even allow me to take a bath by myself. Well, I'm tired of being treated like I don't have the good sense God gave me.''

Sam closed his eyes and mentally counted to ten. The woman was driving him crazy. He opened his eyes and forced a smile to his face. "Look, Mom, we're both tired. Why don't you go into the living room and watch TV? I'll have this disposal fixed in no time.''

She shook her head. "We should call a plumber. Someone who knows what he's doing. You'll only end up making it worse.''

"Thanks for the vote of confidence," he muttered as she left the room.

Sam grabbed a broom and stuck the handle into the disposal, turning it counterclockwise. While he worked, he listened to *Jeopardy* in the next room. He liked the show, and the answers, at least most of them, came easily to him. He figured that wasn't bad for a man who'd waited until his mid-twenties to get his GED. But he'd had a hankering for knowledge as long as he could remember, and despite staying in trouble most of his high-school years, his grades had been high. He supposed it was because he'd always enjoyed reading.

Construction work had been grueling, leaving a man—at least him—too tired to sit in bars and try to pick up women, as his buddies had. He got to where he preferred going home to a good book. He'd read most of the classics because he thought it was important. He'd studied history and politics and economics. Since he hadn't the slightest idea what a portfolio was, he'd read everything he could about investments. Sam didn't believe in luck. He believed a person had to earn their way in this world by using their brain. After twenty years, he could retire right now and never worry about a dime, but he enjoyed what he did. He was not afraid of hard work.

Sam pressed the reset button and the disposal ground to

life. Smiling, he called out to his mother in the next room. "Told you I could fix it." There was no response. No doubt she was still angry that he'd raised his voice to her.

Sam began cleaning the kitchen. Thankfully, his mood had improved by the time he finished. He knew he owed his mother an apology, so he walked into the living room with one on his lips, but paused in surprise when he didn't find her in her recliner as he'd expected. It wasn't until he switched off the TV set that he heard the sound of running water. Muttering an oath under his breath, he hurried to the bathroom door and tried the knob.

It was locked.

# Three

Whenever she was anxious, Marilee baked. That explained the two lemon pound cakes, the chocolate torte and the loaf of banana bread cooling on the kitchen counter. She knew it had something to do with being a minister's wife for sixteen years. One simply did not visit the sick or bereaved without a cake in tow. And then there were the numerous bake sales and bazaars held every year to raise money for choir robes or the new van to accommodate seniors and the handicapped. Seemed cakes were the veritable frameworks of a thriving church.

Sixteen years of baking cakes.

Sixteen years living with Grady.

You got to know a man pretty well after spending that much time with him. She knew what Grady looked like when he opened his eyes in the morning, and she knew which side of the bed he preferred sleeping on. She knew he liked wearing navy blue because he thought it set off his blond hair. She knew he'd wrestled with the idea of becoming a minister, when what he'd really wanted to do was go into broadcasting. He'd dreamed of having his own radio or TV talk show. He was a born entertainer, he'd told her back in high school. Marilee had to admit he had stage presence—he'd even been selected for the leading role in every school play. But his parents had balked at the idea of him going into broadcasting. After all, he'd grown up in a family of ministers, and he was expected to carry on the tradition.

Grady had played the dutiful son and enrolled in seminary school, then convinced Marilee to elope with him. It had caused quite a stink with his family; even though they approved of Marilee, they thought the couple far too young to marry, and wanted Grady to complete his education first. In the beginning, Marilee wondered if he'd asked her to marry him just to get back at his parents for forcing him into the ministry, but Grady had seemed so much in love with her that she'd pushed the thought aside. After a while, Grady no longer complained about being in the ministry, and Marilee assumed he was as happy as she.

It was only recently that he'd begun to second-guess his vocation. Had he kept it to himself all these years? Had he merely pretended to love her? There were so many unanswered questions. Would she ever know the truth?

That was the past, she reminded herself. As difficult as it was, she had to concentrate on rebuilding her life. Part of that meant Josh. His place was with her. It would be so much easier to hate Grady, but for the life of her she couldn't. Sure, she hated what he'd done to their family, and she was terrified at the prospect of facing the world alone. Well, she wasn't entirely alone. There was Winnie to contend with. The girl was presently sprawled on the sofa in the living room watching *Jeopardy*. She called out her answers, then yelped each time she got them right, causing Marilee to start.

Her nerves were shot. She felt as if she was about to jump out of her skin. Perhaps if she tried to take it one day at a time—one *hour* at a time—instead of looking toward the future, which seemed pretty bleak at the moment, she would manage.

Marilee stared at the chocolate torte cake. She could not keep it in the house or she'd end up eating it. Like that time three years ago, when she thought she was pregnant and went on a chocolate binge. Even then she'd known things weren't right between her and Grady, but she'd ignored the signs. Anyway, the church kept her so busy she didn't have time to think about it. There was always something to do, costumes to sew for the Easter pageant or Christmas play, a wedding rehearsal, or a funeral to attend. In the midst of it all, Sunday-school teachers became ill, volunteers for vacation Bible school backed out at the last minute or extra hands were needed to see that the shut-ins received a hot meal each day. It didn't matter that her husband's blood pressure had skyrocketed, that he was unhappy with his calling or that her son was rebelling. Marilee was expected to pick up the pieces when things fell apart at Chickpea Baptist.

In the meantime, *her* life had fallen apart.

Marilee heard movement and glanced up. Winnie stood in the doorway, shaking her head sadly. "Look at the mess in this kitchen. How many cakes are you planning on baking tonight?"

"I'm going to bake until I run out of ingredients." That wasn't likely. She had gone to the grocery store once Clara and Ruby left and had enough baking items on hand to start her own bakery.

Winnie continued to stare at her. "You're having a nervous breakdown, aren't you?"

Marilee sighed. "No, I'm not having a breakdown. I just prefer staying busy when I have things on my mind. Would you like a slice of pound cake?"

"No. I figure I've had enough junk food today, and I really need to start eating healthy. You know, for the baby. I hope you don't expect me to clean up this kitchen, because I need to soak in a hot tub. My back is killing me."

"I don't expect you to clean up after me," Marilee said a little too sharply. She softened her tone. "By the way, do you know your baby's due date yet?"

"Christmas."

Marilee smiled. "No kidding?"

"I wish she would come during my two-week break so I don't have to miss as much school. I've had perfect attendance for three years straight."

"Good for you. You're a senior?"

Winnie nodded. "And I plan to graduate with my class come hell or high water. Of course, I need to line up somebody to watch my baby, but I'm sure my friends will chip in. Once I graduate, I plan to study accounting. I've always been good at math." She paused. "You really ought to

freeze those cakes or I'll just end up eating them. My doctor
warned me about gaining more weight. See, diabetes runs
in my family so I've got no business eating sweets, and that
chocolate cake is crying out for me.''

Marilee decided she definitely needed to get it out of the
house. She suddenly thought of Sam Brewer and wondered
if he would enjoy the torte. Surely she owed him something
for practically saving her life. And maybe if they met under
different circumstances he wouldn't think she was a raving
lunatic. She assumed he was married and had children. They
would probably enjoy the cake, and in future she would
avoid making such tempting desserts.

"I think I'll take it next door," Marilee said, "to repay
my neighbor for doing me a favor this morning."

Winnie eyed the cake ravenously. "Better hurry."

Marilee left the house a few minutes later, cake in hand,
and crossed the lawn to the Brewer house, patting her hair
in place as she went. She hadn't thought to run a brush
through it or apply lipstick. Okay, maybe she *had* given it
a passing thought, but she wasn't going to primp for any
man, married or not. Besides, she was a married woman,
even if her husband had found greener pastures.

She should be mourning the loss of her marriage and trying to atone for her shortcomings as a wife. That's what any
good Christian woman would do.

Marilee rang the doorbell and waited several minutes before the door was flung open by a harried-looking Sam
Brewer. He had shaved and combed his hair, and Marilee
could only stare dumbly at the sight of him in snug jeans
and a burgundy rugby shirt. She had not counted on him
looking so good. Lord, Lord, why had she come?

"I, uh, brought you and your family a cake," she said.

If he was surprised to see her, he didn't show it. "Thank
God you're here." He yanked her inside, almost causing her
to drop the cake. "I need a woman."

Marilee gaped at him. "Excuse me?"

"My mother has locked herself in the bathroom and she
won't let me in." He noted Marilee's blank look and went

on hurriedly, "She's taking a bath. Her eyesight isn't good, and she's pretty frail. I'm afraid she'll slip. Please see if she'll let you in." He motioned frantically toward the bathroom door.

Marilee thrust the cake at him and hurried to the door. It was locked. "Mrs. Brewer, are you in there?" she called out. "Mrs. Brewer, I'm your neighbor, Marilee Abernathy. I was wondering if you needed any help in there."

"I can pick the lock," Sam whispered.

Marilee caught a whiff of his aftershave and thought she might be dizzy. She shook her head. "Let me try to get her to open the door first. Mrs. Brewer, are you okay?"

The lock clicked and Nell Brewer peered through a slit in the door. "Marilee Abernathy? You look awfully familiar. Where do I know you from?"

"Her memory is bad," Sam said and was awarded a dark look from his mother.

"There is absolutely nothing wrong with my memory."

"I grew up next door," Marilee said.

"Oh, yes, Marilee." Nell brightened. "Hester and Will Brown's daughter. I haven't seen you since your mother's funeral. Oh, Hester was such a sweet woman. Both of your parents were lovely people."

"I miss them," Marilee said, then decided to change the subject since her emotions were running so high these days. "I just wanted to see if I could help you with your bath."

"She's kind of modest," Sam said.

Nell glared at him. "How could I possibly be modest when you've paraded me butt-naked in front of half the town?"

"They were hired to look after you."

"I don't need looking after."

"That's not what you said six months ago."

Marilee looked from one to the other. "Perhaps I've come at a bad time…"

"Now look what you've done," Nell accused her son. "You've embarrassed our guest. Sam, what's that in your hand?"

"It's a chocolate torte cake," Marilee said.

Nell looked delighted. "For me?"

"Yes."

"That's awfully nice of you, dear. We'll have a slice after my bath. Just let me grab my towel and you can come in." She closed the door.

"It'll be okay," Marilee whispered to Sam. "I've done this sort of thing before."

The door opened, and Marilee stepped inside the steamy bathroom, coming face-to-face with Sam's mother. "It's so nice to see you again, Mrs. Brewer," she said, closing the door behind her and locking it securely. She studied the woman closely, noting the cropped white hair and parchment skin. She had aged, but she looked as healthy as a horse.

"Why are you staring?" Nell asked. "Do I have spaghetti sauce on my face?"

Marilee shook her head. "Sam said you were frail. You don't look the least bit frail to me."

Nell gave a grunt. "Oh, he's full of baloney. I've never been sick a day in my life. To hear my son talk, you'd think I was about to draw my last breath." She dropped the towel and stepped inside the tub, then carefully lowered herself into the water. "Have a seat." She pointed to the toilet.

"Thank you." Marilee put the lid down and sat. If the woman was modest, she certainly didn't show it.

"This is heavenly," Nell said. "I haven't bathed in three days except to wash up at the sink."

"Why is that?"

The woman sighed as she reached for her soap and sponge. "Oh, I accidentally slipped and bruised my hip a few months ago. Sam made a big deal out of it and called 911. Here I was, without a stitch of clothing, and I had two handsome paramedics looking at my sagging behind." She grunted. "That boy is driving me crazy. Some days I feel like running away from home. But then I have to remind myself it's my own fault."

"I don't understand."

Nell lowered her voice. "Well, it's like this. I lied to get him here."

"Come again?"

"My best friend had just died, and I was so lonely and depressed I couldn't stand it. So I sort of let Sam think I was on my last legs. You know, not long for this world. Told him I was going blind and couldn't remember anything. I was just hoping for a visit, you see. Next thing I know, he moved in with me."

"With his wife and children?" Marilee couldn't help asking.

"Oh, no, he's divorced. Never had children." She paused in washing and regarded Marilee. "I suppose you think I'm a selfish old woman, only thinking of myself."

"I think you're human, Mrs. Brewer. We all get lonely." She thought of Josh, and the ache that never left.

"Sam and I have been knocking heads ever since he moved in. This place is too small for the both of us." She frowned. "Listen to me complain. I should be thankful to have him here. And I would be, if he didn't stand over me like a mother hen all the time. He keeps hiring these crazy women to take care of me. The last one stole the pearl earrings I wore on my wedding day, a gift from my dear grandmother. I couldn't convince Sam of it, he said I forgot where I put them. My memory is as sharp as a tack, and I specifically remember that woman admiring them the day before they turned up missing."

"Why don't you tell Sam the truth?" Marilee asked.

"That I faked my illness?" Nell shook her head. "He'd never forgive me. Especially after he sold his company. All I can do is pretend to get a little better each day. Not that he listens. He's already set up an interview with another woman who's supposed to look after me."

"I wish I could help, Mrs. Brewer," Marilee said.

"Call me Nell." She smiled. "And you have helped, just by listening. Now, tell me what brings you back to the neighborhood?"

Marilee sighed. "It's a long story."

"That's okay. If the bathwater gets cold, I'll just add more hot. Now, start at the beginning."

Sam was dozing on the sofa when the women exited the bathroom some time later, Nell powdered and wearing a clean gown. He rose quickly. "All finished?"

"I almost drowned," Nell said, "but Marilee performed CPR and brought me back from my grave."

Sam just looked at her.

Marilee chuckled at the woman's spunk. "Your mother is perfectly capable of bathing herself, but I enjoyed keeping her company."

Nell rubbed her hands together. "Now, how about a slice of that cake?"

"None for me," Marilee said. "I still have more cleaning to do." She thought Sam looked disappointed. Maybe she was just being hopeful, and that was downright sinful, considering her circumstances. "It was nice seeing you again, Nell, after all this time," she said and turned for the door. "You too, Sam."

Nell shot her son a dark look. "Sam, show some manners and walk the girl home."

"I was planning to," he said defensively.

"I'll be fine," Marilee told them.

Sam was already beside her. "I insist. Besides, my mother would never forgive me for not seeing you home." He opened the door and motioned her through first. He waited until he'd closed the door to say anything.

"Thanks for the help. And the cake."

Marilee looked at him. "I dropped by so I could apologize. For what happened this morning. I don't know what came over me. I was just so…low."

Their gazes locked beneath the streetlight. He looked worried. "You haven't thought of hurting yourself again, have you?"

"That's the last thing on my mind," she replied, which was the truth. Distractedly, she noted the pickup truck sitting in Sam's driveway, then looked at it more closely. "You're driving Bobby Benson's truck," she said, almost an accusation.

Sam glanced in that direction. "We're business partners. We just haven't gotten around to changing the name of the company."

"I don't believe this," she exclaimed.

"It's true. Why?"

"Our committee hired Benson Contractors to renovate Grace Blessing Home. Bobby walked off the job and went fishing."

"You're involved in that?"

"Yes. Why haven't I seen you?"

"I've been finishing up the new hardware store on the other side of town. Haven't been near Blessing Home. From what I hear, Benson wasn't getting paid."

"He's going to get his money," Marilee said tightly. "All we need is a little more time."

"The subcontractors have to be paid, Marilee. You can't expect men with families to work without pay."

"Well, the whole thing has been a disappointment. We expected a little more support from the community. You wouldn't believe how many people I've called, only to have the phone slammed in my ear."

"Everybody has problems." He sounded weary.

"You're right. Nobody has time to worry about these girls, not even their own families. I suppose they're just expected to live on the streets and have their babies on the side of the road." Obviously, Sam was no different from the rest. She turned to go.

He captured her arm. "Now, don't go running off in a huff. Surely we can work out something." He was not surprised when she pulled her arm free. "How about I run by and look at the place tomorrow. See how much more work is needed."

Marilee was surprised by his answer. "Well, okay," she said after a moment. "You don't know how much that would mean to the committee."

"I'm not doing it for the committee. I'm doing it because you were kind enough to assist my mother with her bath."

"I appreciate it regardless."

"And I'd like to make repairs at your place. That ceiling beam is going to cave in if we don't get some support up there. Won't take me long to fix it and the front door."

Marilee wondered why he was offering his help when all she'd done was sit with his mother for a few minutes while the woman had bathed. Was he trying to come on to her? She had no idea—she'd been married so long, she didn't know how men operated these days. As far as Sam was concerned, all she had to go on was his reputation, and that alone was enough reason to keep her distance. "Why don't you let me think about it?"

"I don't expect anything in return, if that's what you're thinking." Even as he spoke, Sam knew it was a lie. He'd had his eyes on Marilee for years, and the thought of spending time with her, even if he was perched on a ladder, was appealing. But first, he needed to find out what was going on between Grady and her.

"Oh, I didn't mean to imply you had ulterior motives," she said quickly, although that wasn't altogether true. This conversation was making her uncomfortable. "Well, I'd better go inside."

"You're right. You don't want Mrs. Bodine from across the street finding you in the dark with a man of my reputation."

He sounded amused, and Marilee wondered if he was making fun of her. She hitched her chin higher. "I don't much care what anyone thinks."

"Good for you." He cupped her elbow in the palm of his hand and led her toward her house. "I don't know what problems you're going through, Marilee, and the last thing I want to do is butt in. But I'm a good listener if you ever need a sounding board."

"I'm fine. Thank you, though, for your concern."

Sam suspected he would be the last one she would take her problems to. She was keeping him at arm's length, and that made him even more determined to learn more about her. "Thanks again for helping my mother. You probably think I'm overprotective, but she was in a bad way when I first moved here."

"I understand she lost her best friend."

"I meant healthwise."

"Sometimes depression can bring on physical problems," Marilee said gently. "I've spent a lot of time working with the elderly, and no matter how old a person gets they want to feel productive."

They had reached her door. Sam gazed down at her, thinking no woman had a right to look that good in sweats. She had been pretty as a young girl and still was, though the years had softened her features. "I remember how lovely you looked in the Christmas parade the year you were crowned homecoming queen," he blurted without thinking.

Marilee couldn't hide her surprise. "That was a long time ago."

"You wore a red velvet dress and tiny flowers in your hair."

"Baby's breath. I can't believe you remember."

"How could I forget? You stole the show."

Marilee had been avoiding direct eye contact until then, but when she looked up she found him studying her curiously. A light breeze ruffled his dark hair. She remembered how Grady sprayed his hair each morning with something he bought at a beauty supply house that promised extra hold. It would have taken hurricane-force winds to muss the blond mane that he was so proud of. She wondered if she would spend the rest of her life comparing men to Grady. But how could she not, after all the years she was married to him? He might be out of her life, but one did not forget sixteen years that easily. Marilee had absolutely no business staring at Sam's hair or the dark lock that had fallen onto his forehead. Or feeling flattered that he'd remembered how she'd looked in the Christmas parade all those years ago.

"Did you and Grady have children?"

"A son. He's fifteen."

"I remember being fifteen and thinking I had all the answers and everybody else was stupid." He surprised her with a sheepish grin. "I wasn't any better at sixteen and seventeen. I suppose that's why I stayed in so much trouble."

Marilee chuckled. "Yes, I remember they voted you the boy most likely to spend his life in San Quentin." He smiled at that, and she tilted her head back slightly. "Are you still bad to the bone, Sam Brewer?" She couldn't resist teasing and hoped he didn't think she was flirting.

"I must not be too bad if you're standing out here in the dark with me."

He stepped closer, and Marilee froze. She felt her breath catch in the back of her throat. His face was only inches from hers. He was too handsome for his own good, and for one wild and insane moment she thought he was going to kiss her. Instead, he reached around and opened her door.

"Good night, Marilee," he asked. "Don't forget to use the chain on your door until I can fix it."

She realized she was holding her breath, and when she let it out, hot air gushed from her lungs with such force it made her light-headed. She swayed slightly.

Sam caught her, a look of concern crossing his face. "Are you okay?"

"F-fine," she said, annoyed that she had been so taken in by his good looks that she'd almost swooned. Swooned, for heaven's sake! Nobody did that sort of thing anymore.

"You looked mighty nervous there for a moment. You didn't think I was going to kiss you, did you?" An easy smile played at the corners of his mouth.

Charm and sensuality oozed from him. Yes, he was as bad as they came, at least where women were concerned. "You're still a scoundrel, Sam Brewer."

Without another word, Marilee hurried inside and closed the door, securing the chain with trembling hands. On the other side, she heard Sam laugh softly. His morals were still lower than a gopher hole. And wasn't it just like him to *assume* he was going to make the repairs to her house? Well, he had another think coming because she wasn't about to let that…that *hellion* inside her house, much less in her life.

She came to a halt. Wait a minute. Why was she so upset? The answer came quickly. Because he'd made her feel pretty and breathless and dizzy and she didn't want to feel those things. She just wanted to feel numb, because it took the sharp edges off her emotions and made life bearable right now.

Marilee suddenly felt bone tired. She dreaded the mess that waited for her in the kitchen and longed for sleep, an escape from worrying about what she was going to do with her life. She dragged herself into the kitchen to set up the automatic coffeemaker and her mouth formed an O of surprise. The room was sparkling from top to bottom. *Winnie.*

Sam returned home and stood inside the living room, gazing about as though seeing it for the first time. Everything appeared the same, but he felt different somehow, and he knew it had everything to do with Marilee. He wondered if she knew just how close he had come to kissing her. Kissing her! He could only imagine how she would have responded. In fact, she probably would have punched him in the face. He grinned. He liked his women feisty; it was more challenging that way.

Where was her damn husband? And what about the kid?

Nell looked up from her recliner. "You've been up to no good, Samuel Brewer. I can see it in your eyes. I hope you weren't fresh with that young woman. She has enough on her hands, what with losing her husband to the town floozy."

So that was it, he thought. Marilee's husband had obviously left her for another woman and taken the kid. Is that why she'd tried to hang herself? No doubt she was feeling the sting of rejection, and Sam knew exactly what she needed. He'd known his share of widows and divorcées, and he knew how to work them.

"And you can wipe that smile right off your face. Marilee is different from the sort of women you've known."

"Mom, I'm hurt," he said. "I wouldn't think of taking advantage of her situation."

"I know you better than you know yourself, young man." Nell suddenly smiled. "Oh yes, guess who called while you were out? Shelly. Remember her? The two of you were married briefly. She promised to call back."

Sam's shoulders slumped. The last person in the world he wanted to talk to was his ex-wife, who usually called him because she needed money. As if he hadn't been generous enough, she'd already taken him to court twice to raise her alimony. He'd let her get away with it because he'd felt guilty. He should have known the difference between love and simple infatuation. He should have worked harder at the marriage. But he had taken the easy way out. He had bought back his freedom.

As if on cue, the telephone rang. Sam stared at it.

"Aren't you going to answer it?" Nell asked.

Giving a weary sigh, Sam picked up the phone. His ex spoke from the other end. "Hello, Shelly, what is it this time?"

"Sam, I'm so glad you answered," she said, sounding near tears.

He rolled his eyes heavenward. She needed something and her needs ranged from cosmetic surgery to a new Jaguar. Either way, it was going to cost him. He had offered to put her through college and pay her expenses, but Shelly wasn't interested in an education. She needed a caretaker and provider, and he'd played the part so well during their marriage that she still clung to him. He glanced at his mother and saw that she was taking it all in with a great deal of amusement.

"Sam, are you there?" Shelly asked.

"I'm here." He sank into the nearest chair and waited for what was to come, his thoughts still on Marilee. Common sense told him he had no business getting involved with her. She was probably just as needy as his mother and his ex-wife. If only he would start thinking with his brain instead of getting a hard-on every time he saw a pretty face.

But damn, Marilee Abernathy did have the best legs he'd ever seen on a female.

# *Four*

The following Monday, Marilee found herself filling out an application at the local Job Service center. She had checked the classifieds daily. Prissy's Pets was looking for someone to groom dogs, the local tavern needed a cocktail waitress, and Darnel Hines was advertising for a mechanic. Slim pickings, to say the least. She would have to look elsewhere.

"Marilee, I just want you to know how sorry I was to hear about you and Grady," Leanne Davis, who worked at the job placement center, whispered.

Marilee forced a smile to her lips as she handed the woman her job application. She and Leanne had attended high school together and had cheered the Fighting Pirates in their cutesy blue-and-gold cheerleading outfits. Her friend had since married and had three children, gaining at least ten pounds with each pregnancy. Marilee wondered if either one of them would fit in their old cheerleading skirts.

"Thank you, Leanne. You don't know how much I appreciate that. But I'm going to be just fine." She didn't believe it at the moment, but if she said it enough perhaps it would come true.

"I can't help feeling guilty. After all, I was the one who introduced you to Grady in high school."

"That was a long time ago. I certainly don't hold you responsible."

"That's why I'm going to do everything in my power to help you find a job."

With that in mind, Marilee decided to let Leanne feel

guilty a little while longer. It wasn't the Christian thing to do, but she was desperate. "Thank you. I know you'll do your best."

"Only trouble is, there aren't many jobs available in Chickpea." Leanne leaned closer. "What I want to know is, did you suspect anything?"

"Excuse me?"

"Did you know Grady was sleeping with that slut?"

Marilee shook her head. "I was the last to know." She smiled tightly. "But I'm trying to put all that behind me now and go on with my life. That's why I need a job."

"Of course you do, honey," Leanne said, patting her hand. "And we're going to find you something." She straightened in her chair and considered Marilee's application. "Hmm. You don't have a degree."

Marilee tried to look confident. "No, I don't. But I'm intelligent, quick to learn, and I'm a hard worker. There isn't much I can't do once I put my mind to it."

"Of course you can, sugar." Leanne shuffled through more papers. "Is there something you're particularly interested in? Something you're really good at?"

"I play the piano and sing. I was choir director at our church for years. But you probably already know that." She suddenly brightened. "I bake cakes."

Leanne looked up. "Do what?"

"Just ask me the ingredients of any cake you've ever heard of, and I can spout them off word for word. Red velvet, Lady Baltimore, German chocolate, you name it. I personally put together a fifty-page cookbook of my own recipes for a committee I'm on, and we sold several hundred copies." Marilee clasped her hands in her lap. She could see that it meant nothing to Leanne.

"Too bad Mitch Johnson isn't hiring over at the bakery," Leanne replied.

Marilee remained thoughtful. Surely there was something she could do. "I like being around people, for what it's worth," she said. "Folks say I have a calming effect on those who are troubled. I've spent many a night sitting with the sick in hospitals and nursing homes, and I always tried to be there when someone from the congregation lost a loved one.''

''You enjoy that sort of thing?'' Leanne asked, wrinkling her nose in distaste.

''I like helping people. Perhaps I could be a nurses' aid.''

''You'd have to take classes, and the pay is low, but it's something to keep in mind.'' She studied Marilee. ''You say you don't mind working with the bereaved?''

''Not at all. I'm used to it.''

Leanne seemed to ponder it. Finally, she reached for a file. ''Well then, Marilee, I just might have something for you after all.''

That afternoon, Marilee was waiting for Winnie when she stepped off the school bus. ''I need your help,'' she told the girl.

Winnie adjusted the shoulder strap on her book bag. ''With what?''

Marilee grinned. ''Get in the car, and I'll tell you on the way.''

''You're up to something, aren't you?''

''I want to teach somebody a lesson, and you're the perfect person to help me.''

''Who's the victim?''

''Esmerelda Cunningham. You know her?''

''The Queen Bee?'' Winnie gave a grunt. ''I know of her—rich, stingy and mean.''

''I think she needs a refresher course in manners.''

''Then I'm your girl.''

After their admittance to Esmerelda Cunningham's grand house, Marilee followed a staid-looking butler into the drawing room with Winnie on her heels, carrying the antique candelabra. Esmerelda was sipping tea from a dainty cup and listening to opera. She looked queenly, her dress crisp as new money and not a hair out of place on her white head.

''I was not expecting guests,'' she said coolly, ''but I am relieved to find my candelabra in good repair.''

"Just set it over there," Marilee told Winnie.

The girl set the candelabra on a Duncan Phyfe table with a thump as Marilee, hands on hips, faced Esmerelda. "Yes, I brought it back once I heard you'd accused me of stealing it. I have absolutely no interest in it. I don't know about you, but I have a life, and I'm not going to spend it polishing silver." She hitched her chin high and sniffed. "I prefer stainless steel myself."

Esmerelda set her cup in its saucer so hard Marilee feared it would shatter. "I beg your pardon? Do you dare come into my home and insult me after I was generous enough to donate to your cause? And who is this person with you?"

"Name's Winnie Frye," Winnie said. "Hey, I like your place. It's a bit crowded for my tastes, and I shudder to think about trying to raise a toddler around all these expensive-looking eggs you got sittin' around."

"Those aren't *eggs*," Esmerelda said. "They are original Fabergé." Winnie picked up one, and the woman gasped aloud. "Put that down immediately!"

"Don't get your panties in a wad, Mrs. C.," Winnie said. "I'm just curious by nature. I like touching things, you know?" She walked over to a Tiffany lamp. "Oh, now, I *like* this."

"Hands off!" Esmerelda almost shouted, causing Winnie to jump and almost knock over the lamp. Esmerelda sank into her chair and mopped her forehead with a handkerchief. She looked at Marilee. "What's the meaning of this?"

Marilee tried to hide her amusement. "Winnie was living at Blessing Home until it was declared unsafe. We've managed to find homes for the other girls, but we haven't had any luck placing Winnie." She stepped closer and whispered, "She has mood swings, and her pregnancy has made them worse. I guess you might say she's *hormonally challenged* right now." Marilee cut her eyes toward the girl.

Esmerelda looked from Marilee to Winnie before settling her gaze on Marilee once more. "What does that have to do with me?"

"I was sort of hoping you'd let me crash here on your

sofa for a while," Winnie said. "I'd really prefer my own bedroom, you understand, but I don't want to put you out. I reckon I could set up a bassinet over here by this window. I want my baby to have plenty of sunlight, and this place is kinda dark, if you don't mind my saying so."

"You must be out of your mind," Esmerelda said to Marilee. "No wonder your husband left you."

Marilee was surprised the remark didn't sting as much as it had in the past. "Now, now, Mrs. Cunningham, I know you're a person of good breeding, and you wouldn't think of stooping to insults, so I'm just going to state my business. We need a home for Winnie, and you have the biggest house in town. Surely you wouldn't mind having a guest around."

"I most certainly do mind," the woman said. "This is not a hotel."

"It's big enough to be a hotel," Winnie said. "I hear this place even has an elevator and swimming pool. Would it be okay if I brought some of the brothers over for a weenie roast and pool party?"

Esmerelda stared in horror. She turned to Marilee. "Don't think for one minute I don't know what's going on here. You're simply trying to embarrass me for making a fuss over the candelabra. Well, it won't work. I did my duty by donating it to your charity, it's not my fault you weren't there to hand it over at the drawing. I can only hope you've come to your senses and will see that it is delivered safely to the woman who won it."

"I don't want your dumb old candelabra," Marilee said. "We'll find another prize."

"What do you mean, you don't want it? Do you have any idea what it's worth?"

"I know what it's *not* worth, Mrs. Cunningham. It's not worth being called a thief." Esmerelda looked away. "But that's not why I'm here. Winnie needs a place to stay," she repeated.

"Is this a sleeper sofa?" Winnie asked. "I'd hate to sleep on this expensive fabric, what with my bladder problem."

Esmerelda looked as though she was about to have a seizure. "Dudley, come here this instant!" she called out loudly. The butler seemed to appear from nowhere. "Please escort these women from my home. And carry that candelabra to their car." She turned to Marilee. "My business with you is finished. I've done my part."

"Forget the candelabra, Dudley," Marilee said. "And we are more than capable of showing ourselves out." She and Winnie started for the door.

"You wait just a darned minute, young lady!" Esmerelda said. "You are *not* leaving this house without that candelabra. I insist! I'm not about to have my friends think I went back on my word." She drew herself up proudly. "I'm retiring to my bedroom now. I don't want to hear another word about it." She left in a huff.

Marilee looked at the butler. "I'll bet she's a peach to work for."

Dudley chuckled as he followed them out the door, carrying the candelabra.

Marilee pulled into her driveway twenty minutes later and found Clara and Ruby planting mums in the old cast-iron pot out front. "We thought it would cheer you up," Clara said as Marilee and Winnie climbed from the car.

Marilee was touched by her friends' thoughtfulness. "Thank you."

"How did things go with Esmerelda?" Ruby asked.

"The woman needs a beating with a big stick," Winnie said. "Imagine her not wanting to take me in. And here I am with child. I'm telling you, she can go from zero to bitch in two seconds flat."

Marilee laughed as she pulled the candelabra from her back seat. "Naturally, she insisted we take the candelabra after all. She doesn't want to look bad to her friends."

"What friends?" Winnie muttered.

"Did she apologize for what she said about you?" Ruby asked.

"What do you think?" Marilee presented the candelabra

to Clara. "I trust you'll see that this gets into the right hands."

"Yes, of course." She put it in her car.

"By the way, my next-door neighbor happens to be partners with Bobby Benson, and he has offered to take a look at Blessing Home. If he agrees to patch the roof, we'll have to come up with the money."

"How do we know he won't walk off the job like Bobby?" Ruby asked. "And how much is he thinking of charging us?" As committee treasurer, she was tightfisted when it came to doling out money.

"He's going to let me know," Marilee said. "I think that with the benefit luncheon and cookbook sales we should be able to cover it."

"There's a lot more to be done," Clara said. "We're going to have to put our heads together and come up with more moneymaking schemes."

Ruby looked thoughtful. "How about a white elephant sale?"

"That might work," Clara said. "What do you think, Marilee?"

Marilee sighed. "Maybe."

"Have you lost interest in this project?" Clara asked.

Marilee was beginning to wish she'd never gotten involved, but she couldn't let them down again. "Of course not. It's just—"

"She's got a lot on her mind," Ruby said. "And rightfully so. Honey, Clara and I need to take on more responsibility, what with all that's happened. And we need to get our other volunteers off their behinds."

Clara gave a harrumph. "What volunteers? They've all dropped out."

"Let me see what Mr. Brewer has to say, once he takes a look at the place," Marilee told them.

Winnie started for the house, and then paused. "I have a four-thirty appointment at the clinic tomorrow. I go every three weeks for my prenatal exam."

"I can drive you," Marilee said.

Clara smiled at Winnie. "Are you all settled in, dear?"

"For the time being. But I only plan on hanging around for a couple of days. My girlfriend just rented one of those luxury apartments in town, and she's having a fit for me to move in with her. Soon as she gets an extra bed, I'm outta here." She headed for the house without another word.

"She's not going anywhere," Marilee told her friends as they shot her a questioning look.

"How's the job hunting?" Ruby asked, changing the subject.

"I have an appointment with Irby Denton at the funeral home tomorrow."

"Oh my," Clara said. "You're going to work at a funeral home?"

"Irby has to hire me first," Marilee pointed out.

Both women stared back at her. Finally, Ruby smiled. "Hey, I think that's great! What exactly would you be doing there? If he hires you, I mean?"

"He needs a receptionist. It's an entry-level position, but I have to start somewhere."

"Oh my," Clara repeated.

Ruby looked at the woman. "Clara, why do you keep saying that?"

Clara stared at Marilee. "Ruby doesn't know your secret, does she?" Clara whispered.

"What secret?" Ruby asked, glancing from one to the other.

Marilee shrugged. "It's no big deal. Besides, I need this job. I just discovered Grady took a chunk of money out of our savings account."

"You need a good lawyer," Clara said.

"I've already made an appointment. Tate Radford says he can have me divorced in ninety days on grounds of adultery."

"Well, they don't come any better than Tate," Clara said, "but he's not cheap."

"I want somebody good, in case I end up with a custody battle on my hands," Marilee replied.

Clara reached for her hand and squeezed it. "Are you okay?"

Marilee offered what she hoped was a brave smile. "Better than I was. I'm not going to recover overnight and I still think of Josh constantly, but I'm definitely better."

Ruby stamped her foot on the ground. "Somebody better tell me about this secret or I'm going to throw a fit right here in Marilee's front yard."

"Oh, good grief!" Clara said. She stepped closer to Ruby. "Marilee is terrified of dead people. She has a phobia."

Ruby's eyes grew wide as saucers as she regarded Marilee. "No kidding?"

Marilee shot Clara a disgruntled look. "I'm not *terrified* of anything." Other than the future, she reminded herself.

"Marilee Abernathy, I watched you almost pass out when Sara Banks asked you to remove her husband's wedding ring from his finger at his funeral," Clara said. She looked at Ruby. "Marilee had a full-blown panic attack out in the parking lot. I almost had to bring out my smelling salts."

"I just don't like *touching* dead people," Marilee said. "I hardly think that's going to be a problem if I'm working at the front desk."

"I've touched plenty of dead people," Ruby told her proudly. "Irby sometimes calls me to do hair and makeup when his wife can't do it. Dead people can't hurt you, Marilee."

Clara looked doubtful. "Irby is never going to hire you if he finds out."

"He's not going to find out," Marilee replied. She looked long and hard at her friends. "Is he?"

Both women pretended to zip their lips, lock them shut and throw away the keys. Marilee smiled prettily. "Thank you."

"What if you have to help him embalm somebody?" Ruby whispered.

"I'm not going to go near the embalming room. You have to go to a special school for that." Both women looked skeptical. "You have to admit I'm perfect for the job. I've been comforting the bereaved for years. It's what I do best."

"You *are* perfect for the job," Clara said. "As long as you don't go near any dead people."

The following morning, Marilee watched Josh step from the bus at the high school. He was alone, his back bowed, head down. His posture said it all. He didn't fit in, never had. He paid a heavy price for being a minister's son with a weight problem. He'd never had a girlfriend, never attended a school dance or social gathering, but if he were invited, Marilee was certain he wouldn't go because he felt like an outcast. Marilee suffered as much as he did over it, but she kept quiet because Josh would have been embarrassed for her to know. But she knew. Mothers always knew. The only friends Josh had attended Chickpea Baptist, and she doubted he was spending much time there these days.

"Josh," she called out, waving at him in the crowd.

He took one look at her and turned in the opposite direction.

Her heart sank. "Josh, wait!" She pushed through the throng of students, never letting her eyes off his blond head. She caught up with him outside the gym. "Josh, please wait!"

He turned and glared at her as kids shuffled past, tossing curious looks in their direction. "What are you doing here?" he demanded.

His face was red. Marilee knew he didn't like drawing attention to himself, preferring anonymity to being noticed and risking ridicule. She often wondered why kids were so cruel. And to think she'd considered ending her life, when Josh was so completely alone in the world. "I need to talk to you, honey."

"I have class."

"Just give me five minutes, Josh. I don't think that's asking too much."

His eyes blazed. "Don't you get it, Mom? I don't *want* to talk to you. I want to be left alone."

His look wrenched her heart. "I don't deserve this, Josh."

But he was already gone, lost among the crowd. Marilee stood there, frozen, feeling as though all the air had been sucked from her lungs. She couldn't breathe, and for a moment she thought she'd be sick. Her eyes smarted as she staggered toward her car. She was only vaguely aware of the stares she received from some of the students. Don't cry, she told herself. Don't even think about it right now. The last thing she needed to do was arrive at her interview with swollen eyes.

She would cry later in the privacy of her room. In fact, she looked forward to it.


Denton Funeral Home was less than a mile from town, a massive, two-story colonial that housed the business in the basement and first floor, while the second floor served as an apartment for the family. When Irby Denton greeted Marilee on the wide porch, where ferns shuddered in the mid-September breeze, she saw that he'd changed very little since high school.

His hair was still fire-engine red, but his hairline had receded, and the laugh lines that bracketed his mouth were deeper. He wore the same mischievous look that had labeled him class clown and prankster as far back as kindergarten, where he'd swallowed one of Mrs. Finch's goldfish, sending the young teacher into a frenzy and causing one girl to throw up on her new Mary Janes. His parents had been promptly summoned to the school, and he was given a three-day suspension. Upon his return, his desk was placed at the front of the class, near Mrs. Finch, who was perturbed that he'd botched her alphabetical seating arrangements.

"Marilee, you look as pretty as you did the day they crowned you homecoming queen," Irby said, giving her a bear hug that she half feared would crack a rib. His wife, Debbie, stood beside him. They'd married right after graduation, and Marilee still recalled how the tongues had wagged when Debbie gave birth only eight months after their wedding night. Debbie's mother had declared to family and friends that the child was premature, despite the fact the newborn had weighed more than eight pounds. The couple had gone on to have a total of four children, ranging from eighteen months to sixteen years old.

"You look wonderful," Debbie said, a toddler propped on one hip. "You're going to have to give me your beauty secrets."

Marilee wondered if they were simply trying to soothe her wounded ego, now that Grady had publicly humiliated her. "Thank you. I don't believe I've met the latest addition to the Denton family."

Debbie looked proud. "This is Ben, named after Irby's grandfather. We call him Bennie."

"Nice to meet you, Bennie." She tried to shake his hand playfully, but he pulled away and buried his face against Debbie's breasts.

"He's shy," Debbie said. "And a little spoiled."

"Come on in the house," Irby said. "Would you like a cup of coffee?"

Marilee followed, stepping over a toy car as she went. "No, thanks."

Irby picked up the toy and handed it to his wife. "Honey, you're going to have to tell David to keep his toys upstairs. I can't have folks tripping over them when they come through the door."

Debbie nodded wearily. "I've tried, Irby, believe me."

He nodded sympathetically. "I know." He looked at Marilee. "It's not easy, a big family like ours living upstairs like we do, but it's cheaper this way. We have the space, mind you, but the kids still wander downstairs from time to time. Debbie, would you watch the phones while I chat with Marilee for a bit?"

"Of course."

Irby led Marilee through the reception area, passing several closed doors that she knew from experience were parlors designed for relatives to view their loved ones before burial. Antiques in dire need of polishing adorned the rooms.

"Here we are," Irby said once they'd reached a paneled

office. The furniture looked as though it had come from a garage sale. A computer sat on a battered credenza, the screen saver a scrolling marquee that read, People Are Dying to Come Here. "Have a seat, Marilee."

"Thank you." Marilee sat down and was met with what sounded like a giant fart. She leaped from the chair, and then frowned at the sight of a whoopee cushion. "Irby Denton, won't you ever grow up!"

He looked surprised. "I swear I didn't do it," he said, rounding the desk and grabbing the cushion. He tossed it aside. "David, our ten-year-old, is obviously up to his old tricks."

"And where do you suppose he learned them?" Marilee said, hands on hips.

Irby shrugged as though he hadn't a clue. "I'll tell you, the boy has no shame." He looked remorseful despite one corner of his mouth tugging as though he would burst into laughter at the slightest provocation. "I should beat all of our children, but Debbie won't permit it. That's why they're so spoiled."

Marilee knew Irby wouldn't beat a rug to rid it of dust. "Well, I hope I have no more surprises this morning."

"I'm going to be on my best behavior." He reclaimed his seat and shuffled through a mountain of papers on his desk. "I was…uh…sorry to hear about you and Grady. Debbie said I shouldn't bring it up but if there's anything we can do, please let us know."

Marilee clenched her hands in her lap. "Thank you for your concern, Irby, but don't worry."

He cleared his throat. "This place is a mess," he said, changing the subject abruptly. "My other assistant eloped two weeks ago, leaving me high and dry. Debbie and I haven't had a chance to catch up with all the paperwork. You can't imagine how thrilled I was when Leanne from the Job Service called to tell me you were interested in working here. Debbie and I both agree you're perfect for the job."

Marilee sat up straighter in her chair. "Um, Irby, before

we go on, I'd like to know exactly what duties I'm to perform.''

Irby reached for an Atlanta Braves baseball cap and plopped it on his head. "Just seein' that the place runs smoothly. Sometimes I might need you to fill in for me if I'm in the middle of something and can't let go."

"Fill in?" Her voice wavered.

"You know, hose down a body, stick 'em in the goozle and drain the good stuff. Sew a few eyelids closed."

Marilee paled instantly. She covered her mouth.

"Hey, I'm just having fun with you, Marilee." Irby looked concerned. "Are you okay, honey? You can't take things too seriously around here, know what I mean?"

"That wasn't funny, Irby. Nor was swallowing that goldfish."

"That happened a long time ago, Marilee. I've matured since then. Okay, maybe not as much as I should have, but I promise I'll be serious from now on." He put on a pair of reading glasses, as if that in itself would do the trick. "The main thing you have to do is cover the phones and know where to find me in case I have a body run."

"Body run?"

"That's not exactly how we refer to it in front of our clients. The correct term is body removal, but it means the same thing." He reached back and patted the computer. "You know how to operate one of these babies?"

Marilee nodded. "I worked in the church office long enough to learn the basics."

"Many of our clients have already made funeral preparations, and it's all listed right here, down to the last detail. We even have pictures on file so Debbie can copy their hair and makeup. We want them to look as natural as we can." He rolled his eyes. "Some of the ladies make arrangements beforehand to have their regular hairdressers come in, if you can believe it. I've never understood that, but I go along with it anyway. I reckon I ought to order some blue rinse and put a salon chair back there, only we'd have to strap 'em in. Know what I mean?"

Marilee chose to ignore the remark. She desperately needed the job. "Will I be expected to meet with the families?"

"Sometimes. This is a funny business. We have weeks where it's slower'n molasses running down a cold stovepipe, other times I don't know if I'm coming or going. But you won't have any trouble. You've helped folks through bad times before." He reached for a folder. "Our fees are listed according to the needs of individual families. You'll want to study this so you're prepared."

Marilee took the folder and glanced through it, noting the various price options. "What do you do in the event someone can't pay in advance?"

"I know this sounds harsh, Marilee, but I insist the families pay up front. It's not like I can go dig up someone if the family can't cough up the rest of the money. Although I've threatened to on a few occasions," he muttered.

"Sometimes you'll get family members who want to send off a loved one in high style, and you know just by looking at them that they can't afford it. You need to try and talk 'em down as far as costs. And they want to stick the craziest things in the coffin with the deceased. One woman had us put her husband's portable TV set in with him because she said all he ever did while he was alive was watch television." He grinned. "'Course, I had to cut off his legs to fit the damn thing in there with him."

*Ignore, ignore, ignore.* "Um, Irby?"

"Yes?"

She shifted in her chair. "Do you get many young people?"

His look sobered instantly. "Not often, thank God. They're tough. Debbie won't go near them, seein' as how we have kids and all." He paused. "That's why you can't take things so seriously, Marilee."

Marilee suddenly realized why Irby joked so much.

He opened a drawer and pulled out a sheet of paper. "We have a questionnaire we ask our new clients to fill out. Usually their minister has already been contacted, but in cases where the deceased wasn't a member of a church, we have a couple of clergy who fill in when necessary. You'll need information for the obituary.'' He paused. "You play the piano, don't you?"

Marilee nodded, wondering what one had to do with the other. "My mother insisted that all young ladies should know how to play."

"In some cases, the family decides to hold services in our small chapel. You could pick up extra money if you played for them. Anywhere from fifty to a hundred bucks."

"That's more than I made teaching piano lessons," Marilee said.

"It's entirely up to you, of course." He clasped his hands together at the back of his neck. "So, what do you say? You want the job or not?"

Marilee was surprised. "Just like that?"

"You're the perfect candidate. I can start you at eight dollars an hour, which is more than I was paying my last assistant."

It wasn't a lot of money but to Marilee, who'd done volunteer work for so long without receiving a penny, it sounded good. "I'd like to give it a try. I promise to do my best."

"I never doubted it for a minute. Now, let me show you around."

"Show me around?"

"You know, in case you need to use the ladies' room while you're here. You'll definitely want to know where the bathrooms are located."

Once again, Marilee followed Irby. They reentered the reception area, where Debbie was bouncing Bennie on her knee and talking on the phone. Irby explained Marilee's job duties, and then led her to three individual parlors, one of which held an assortment of flowers.

"This is where Mr. Elmore's family will be receiving visitors this evening," he said.

"Dan Elmore, who used to own the Plaza Theater?"

"The very same. I wish I had a dime for every time he caught me trying to sneak into the theater for free."

"He was up in age, wasn't he?"

"Almost ninety. But fit as a fiddle till the very end."

"How'd he die?"

"Fell off a ladder while painting his house. His wife went all to pieces."

"I can imagine."

"Said she had to go and hire a painter to finish the job." He glanced around the room. "Yes sir, there'll be quite a crowd tonight. That's why I'm putting Dan in room A. It's our largest parlor." He showed her the other rooms, one of which was considerably smaller. "This one is used mostly for private funerals or for those who don't have many friends."

Marilee thought of mean old Esmerelda Cunningham.

"And this," Irby said, opening a set of double doors, "is the casket room."

Marilee wasn't prepared, and she took a step back. "Oh my."

"It's okay," Irby said, cupping her elbow gently. "This is not a very pleasant room, but there'll be times you'll have to escort a family in here so they can pick out something for the deceased. Some people are very particular and want to know everything, others will leave it up to us. Just think of it as picking out an automobile."

"I suppose that's one way of looking at it," Marilee said. She pointed at a bronze-colored coffin. "That one's nice."

"That's our Cadillac of coffins, so to speak," Irby said, leading her over. "Naturally, we put the nicest ones up front, hoping our clients will choose the most expensive." He grinned. "Pretty vulgar, huh? But hey, I've got four kids to raise. Let me show you the satin lining inside." He lifted the top section.

Marilee glanced down and saw what looked like skeletal remains. She was only vaguely aware of the baseball cap and hideous smile. All the blood drained from her face, and she let out a scream. She raced from the room, praying her knees would not buckle beneath her, and slammed into Debbie, almost knocking her and Bennie over as she scrambled toward the front door.

"What in heaven's name!" Debbie said.

"There's a...dead person in that coffin," Marilee cried.

"Damn that Irby," Debbie said, her expression dark and menacing. "He's gone too far this time." She grabbed Marilee's hand. "Honey, it's okay. It's just a rubber skeleton." Marilee was sobbing. Debbie shook her slightly. "It's not real."

"What?" Marilee realized she was hysterical.

"Irby Denton, get your sorry self in here right this minute!" Debbie shouted at the top of her lungs. "Marilee, sit down before you fall down."

Marilee took a chair next to the front door in case she needed to make a quick getaway.

Irby appeared, looking sheepish. "Gee, Marilee, I'm sorry. I was just—"

"Just having a little fun, right?" Debbie snapped, causing Bennie to cry. "It's not a damn bit funny, Irby, and I wouldn't blame Marilee if she told you to shove the job up your behind." She looked at Marilee. "Honey, do you need smelling salts?"

Marilee shook her head, feeling foolish now that she realized the skeleton wasn't real. Nevertheless, it was a cruel trick on Irby's part. She tossed him a menacing look.

"I should clobber you."

"Go ahead and punch him," Debbie said. "Lord knows he deserves it." She tried to comfort the squalling child, even as she continued shouting at her husband. "This is a funeral home, not a playground!"

Irby looked contrite. "I promise it won't happen again, Marilee. Do you still want the job?"

Marilee regarded him. He truly looked pitiful standing there. "I'll take the job on a temporary basis, but if you try that sort of thing with me again you'll be looking for a new assistant."

Irby nodded, shamefaced. "How soon can you start?"

# Five

It was a well-known fact that Tate Radford was the best lawyer in Chickpea. Luckily, he'd had a cancellation; otherwise, Marilee would have had to wait three weeks to get an appointment.

She chose a smart navy suit for the occasion. It wasn't pure linen, but one would have been hard-pressed to prove it, because it certainly looked like the real McCoy. Her navy heels wore a designer label and would have cost a fortune if she hadn't found them in a consignment shop. The outfit gave her a look of sophistication—at least she hoped so, because she needed all the confidence she could muster.

She'd spent a sleepless night worrying about Josh. Marilee was sure that below his anger lay a feeling of loneliness and desolation, but how could she convince him to reach out to her? She was an emotional wreck just thinking about it. No mother wanted her child to suffer, but she couldn't allow herself to fall apart, not when she was putting plans in motion to get him back.

Later, when all this was behind her and she had a little time on her hands, she would allow herself the mother of all nervous breakdowns.

"Mrs. Abernathy, you can go in now," the young receptionist called out, startling Marilee from her thoughts. "Second door on the left."

"Thank you." Marilee stood and smoothed her skirt into place. Tucking her handbag under one arm, she proceeded down a short hall, gulping in air as she went. The door opened and a tall, angular man stepped out.

"Mrs. Abernathy, I'm Tate Radford." He offered his hand and they shook before he led her inside his office.

"Thank you for seeing me on such short notice," Marilee said, realizing she had taken in too much air and now felt dizzy. It would be just her luck to hyperventilate in the man's office.

"Please sit down," he said, motioning to a chair. Seating himself on the other side of his desk, he gave her an odd look. "Mrs. Abernathy, are you okay? You look pale."

She nodded. "I'm fine. This is my first time, you see. Not the first time I've been in a lawyer's office, of course. I had to deal with my parents' attorney after my mother passed on, but that's neither here nor there. This is my first...uh...divorce."

He looked sympathetic. "Do you think there's a chance of reconciliation?"

Marilee was surprised by the question. Even if Grady wanted her back, which wasn't likely, now that he had a woman who probably knew more positions than Dr. Ruth, how would she ever trust him again? He had betrayed her, not only as her husband, but by throwing away all they'd believed in, the very foundation of their marriage. He'd turned his back on his family and work because he'd lusted for another woman, simple as that. Worse, Grady'd taken their son into that woman's house, where he and LaFonda were living without benefit of marriage. Not that Grady was free to marry at this point, mind you, but he could have waited, instead of flaunting the affair.

"Mrs. Abernathy?"

Marilee looked up. "I'm sorry, Mr. Radford. This has been one of the most difficult decisions I've ever made, and believe me, I've spent every waking hour thinking about it. The answer to your question is no. I do not want a reconciliation. I never thought I'd say this, but I want to get out of this marriage as quickly as possible. And I want my son with me so he can live a normal life. I sense he's very troubled, and he needs guidance. He won't find it where he is presently living." She paused to catch her breath. "I guess you were just expecting a simple yes-or-no answer, huh?"

"I want my clients to feel comfortable talking to me, Mrs. Abernathy. Is your husband, by chance, Reverend Grady Abernathy from Chickpea Baptist Church?"

"He was, but he was asked to leave."

"That might prove helpful to our case." Tate pulled a yellow legal pad from his desk drawer. "I'd like to jot down a few notes if you don't mind. Now, you say your husband is living with a woman. Do you know her name?"

"LaFonda Bonaire. At least that's what she calls herself. Her real name is Betty Clump."

"So you can prove your husband is committing adultery?"

"Yes. They're living in her mobile home in Tall Pines Trailer Park."

"And he has your son? How old is the boy?"

"Fifteen. His name is Josh."

Tate sat back in his chair and regarded her. "Do you think your husband took Josh against his will?"

Marilee looked at her hands. "I don't know what to think, Mr. Radford. My son has been going through a rebellious stage for some time now. Our relationship was strained before he left. He may very well have gone on his own." It wasn't easy for her to admit that, even to herself.

"I have teenagers myself, Mrs. Abernathy. I think divorce is hard on kids at any age, but it seems to hit them hardest in the teen years. Also, the boy probably has more freedom living with his dad, and when you're a teenager that seems to matter more than anything. Have you tried talking to him?"

Marilee told him about her trip to the school. "He wouldn't even look at me."

"He's probably ashamed of what he's done. Frankly, I don't know why your husband wants the boy there in the first place. Seems like it would crowd the love nest."

Marilee shrugged. "Maybe he feels less guilty this way."

Tate folded his hands across his stomach. "I'll level with

you, Mrs. Abernathy. It won't be easy getting your son back if he prefers being with his dad. After all, he's old enough to decide with whom he wishes to live. If he were younger, you'd have no problem getting custody. As it stands, you'll have to fight, and that's going to cost money.''

Marilee shifted in her chair. ''How much?''

''First we have to prove, without a doubt, that your husband is living with this Miss Bonaire. I can hire a private investigator to spend a couple of nights watching the place, get your husband's comings and goings on video. As for your son, I'd advise you to hire a child advocate, someone who will do a home study of both residences and decide the best interests of your child. You're looking at a cost of several thousand dollars, plus my retainer, which is fifteen hundred. Now, if we get into a custody battle, my bill is going to be substantially higher. I'll need about six thousand dollars in an escrow account if we're to proceed with the child advocate.''

Marilee's heart sank. She reminded herself she was doing it for Josh, and suddenly money didn't seem to matter as much. ''I think I can put my hands on that much money. My husband and I had a modest savings account, but he's already taken out half.''

Radford arched one eyebrow. ''I suggest you get to the bank before he has a chance to clean it out completely. Once you retain me as counsel, I'll arrange for a temporary hearing and request visitation with your son. The home study will take longer.'' He pulled a sheaf of papers from a file. ''I'll need you to fill out this financial statement and give me a sworn affidavit as to what led to the breakup of your marriage. Like I said, if we can prove adultery, I can have you divorced in ninety days, but should custody become an issue, there's no telling how long it'll take.''

Marilee nodded. ''I'll have the money before you close your office this afternoon.''

Josh Abernathy stood at the entrance to Tall Pines Trailer Park and waited for the school bus. On the other side of the pockmarked road, three teenagers smoked cigarettes and watched him. Two of them were his age; one was older. He knew the older guy's reputation and decided it would be best to keep his mouth shut. Every now and then one of the younger kids would make a wisecrack, and the other would burst into laughter. Josh didn't have to be psychic to know they were talking about him. People had been making fun of him all his life. The preacher's kid, they called him, as if he didn't have a name of his own. Goody Two-shoes. Fatso.

He didn't belong, and he never had. Not with the kids who wore faded jeans with holes in the knees, and certainly not with the jocks, who ragged him in the shower because he'd put on weight over the past couple of years. He'd stopped showering, only to be made fun of in sixth period for being sweaty, so then he'd stopped participating in gym class at all. Instead, he sat on the bleachers and flunked the class each semester.

His mother claimed he wasn't fat, said he was just a big kid, but he knew he outweighed kids his own age by a good twenty-five or thirty pounds. When he wore thin T-shirts he could see the roll in his stomach, which was why he'd started wearing black, short-sleeve sweatshirts. His parents said he looked as if he was in mourning, but he didn't care. Actually, he felt as though someone or something had died. He'd had that feeling for a long time now, although he couldn't say exactly when it had begun. Probably it had started a couple of years back, when his parents had stopped talking.

Josh heard the boys snicker, but he refused to look their way. Where was the bus, anyway?

"Hey, lard-ass, you want a drag of this here cigarette?" one boy asked.

The older guy remained detached, as though his thoughts were elsewhere.

Josh ignored them. He no longer cared what people thought. When he was younger he'd go off by himself and cry. Now he just shrugged it off. He wished he'd stayed in bed. He wished he was invisible.

He *was* invisible as far as his dad was concerned. All the man could think of was his new girlfriend. Josh wondered if his dad had lost it. One minute he was this respected minister bent on saving the world, next thing Josh knew he was banging some waitress and selling used cars at the Ford dealership.

"You know, smoking speeds up your metabolism," the other kid said. "Might get rid of some of that blubber."

"Would you two shut the hell up?" the oldest kid snapped. "I've got a headache, and I'm sick of listening to you. Besides, he ain't messing with nobody."

Josh saw the bus in the distance. He hated school. Sleep was really the only thing he liked these days. As long as he was asleep he didn't have to think about how screwed up his life had become.

Sleep made him feel invisible.


Sam Brewer shook his head sadly as he and one of his crew took a tour of Blessing Home. "It would be easier to tear this place down and start from scratch," the man said.

Sam nodded. "I don't know how they managed to pass inspection all these years. The wiring is so old it's a wonder the place hasn't burned to the ground. And the plumbing is prehistoric." He shook his head. "God only knows what's holding up the roof. The house is not structurally sound."

The other man scratched his jaw. "Needs a lot of work, that's for sure. No telling how much it'd cost."

Sam sighed. He had so many jobs going on he had no idea where he'd find the time. He should never have offered to look at the place and get Marilee's hopes up, because Blessing Home looked like a lost cause, as far as he was concerned.

The last thing he needed was something else to worry about.


Ruby, Clara and Winnie were waiting for Marilee when she arrived home. A large pizza sat on the kitchen table, and

Winnie was putting out napkins and paper plates. "Congratulations on the new job, honey," Ruby said, hugging Marilee.

Marilee looked surprised. "How'd you know I was hired?"

"News travels quickly in this town," Clara said.

"That's for sure," Winnie muttered. "Can't take a leak in this town without everybody knowing about it." She eyed Marilee and propped her hands on her hips. "You look upset."

Marilee sighed. "I just left my attorney's office. I had to hand over six thousand dollars."

"For a simple divorce?" Ruby shrieked. "Hell's bells, I got one of those ninety-nine-dollar divorces. You see them all the time in the newspaper."

Marilee explained why she'd paid so much. "I had to do it. For Josh."

"Is anyone going to have some of this pizza?" Winnie asked. "I'm starving. I have to think of the baby, you know." She offered the box, and the women took a slice.

"Josh'll come around, honey," Ruby said. "He's just angry right now, and what child wouldn't be. Divorce is hard on kids."

Clara pursed her lips. "But six thousand dollars! That's highway robbery, if you ask me. Did you wipe out your entire savings account?"

Marilee shook her head. "There's still some left, but I withdrew it and moved it to my checking account so Grady can't get to it. I have the money my parents left, but I'm determined not to touch it. That's for Josh's education." She shrugged. "I'm going to have to find a night job, at least until Josh moves in, so I can try to replace the money in case of an emergency."

"Who's going clean this place and cook while you work day and night?" Winnie demanded. "I hope you don't expect me to take care of everything. This is stressing me out. That's why I hate getting involved with people who have more problems than me."

"I picked up a newspaper after I left Tate's office," Marilee said, ignoring Winnie's remark. "I just scanned it, but I think I may have found something I can do in the evenings."

"What'd you find, honey?" Ruby asked.

"They need someone to play the piano at the Pickford Inn."

"What?" Clara cried. "You're not going to work in a nightclub? Oh, Marilee, you can't be serious."

"It's a supper club," Ruby said. "Very upscale."

Clara pursed her lips. "You may call it what you like, but they still serve alcohol."

"One drink before dinner never hurt anyone," Ruby said.

Clara looked at her. "This coming from a woman who has a distillery under the front seat of her truck." She gave a harrumph. "Marilee, you simply cannot do this. What are folks going to say when they find out you're playing piano in a bar? You know they'll go straight to Grady, and he'll do anything he can to make you look bad in front of that child advocate. This could definitely work against you."

Marilee shoved her plate aside. She had not thought of that. Would the child advocate hold it against her if she took a job in a supper club? She doubted it. But if Grady found out, he'd try to make her look as bad as he could, in order to make himself look good. "Pickford is thirty miles away," she said, thinking out loud. "I wouldn't think I'd run into anyone from Chickpea."

Clara didn't look convinced. "You're still taking a chance."

"I need the money, Clara."

"You could wear a disguise," Ruby said. "I can fix you up so that your own mother wouldn't recognize you. That way you won't have to worry about any of the town gossips recognizing you. When do you plan to go for the interview?"

"Tonight. I want to get a jump-start on the other applicants."

"I'll run home and grab my supplies after I eat."

"Are you not going to eat your pizza?" Winnie asked Marilee.

"And you plan to work at the funeral home too?" Clara asked.

Marilee nodded. "I plan to do whatever's necessary to get Josh back."

"If you're not going to eat your pizza, I will," Winnie said, reaching for the untouched slice.

Clara sighed and reached into her purse, pulling out a small metal cylinder. "I know how you are when you make up your mind, so I'm not going to try and talk you out of it. But I'd feel better if you'd keep this pepper spray on you in case something unforeseen occurs."

"I don't have the job yet," Marilee said, "and I wish you'd stop worrying. The Pickford is not a sleazy beer joint."

"Oh, you'll get the job," Ruby assured her. "I don't know a single soul who can sing and play the piano as well as you."

"Take the pepper spray, Marilee."

"Thank you, Clara," she said, touched by her concern. "I know this is hard for you to accept. None of us ever suspected my life would take such a turn. I mean, Grady was a good minister. He genuinely cared about his congregation. And I just assumed all marriages had problems now and then, but I wasn't prepared for this. I have to do what I have to do. It's just…well, I'm a little overwhelmed at the moment."

"Oh, Lord, she's going to start crying again," Winnie said.

Marilee shook her head. "I'm finished crying. I have too much to do to sit around and feel sorry for myself."

Ruby patted her hand. "Good for you, honey. You're stronger than you think."

Winnie shook her head sadly. "It's not going to be that easy. You're going to need someone to look after you, make sure you eat regular meals and have clean clothes to wear.

I guess I'm going to have to hang around awhile longer. At least until you get used to working all those hours."

"That's very kind of you, Winnie," Clara said. "Ruby and I will help too."

Ruby nodded emphatically. "Darn right we will."

"Thank you," Marilee said. "I don't know what I would do without the three of you."

"You'd probably do okay," Winnie said. "You're not as weak as I thought in the beginning."

Marilee decided that was the closest Winnie would come to giving her a compliment. She pushed her chair from the table. "I need to practice a few songs on the piano," she said. "I'm sure it's dreadfully out of tune, but at least it'll help limber up my fingers."

Ruby stood. "And I need to run home and pick up a few supplies. For your disguise," she added, winking conspiratorially.

"Who's going to clean up this mess?" Winnie demanded.

"I'll do it," Clara volunteered.

Winnie shook her head. "Never mind, I'll do it. You don't know where anything goes, and I can't have you putting stuff in the wrong place, especially after I've cleaned the refrigerator and organized the cabinets."

Marilee was practicing on the old piano when Ruby returned carrying a short, platinum-colored wig, a small suitcase and a flaming-red dress. "Belonged to my ex-roommate," she said, holding the slinky outfit up for inspection. "The poor girl was a perfect size eight till her boyfriend dumped her, and she decided to eat her way through her depression. I think she was a size fourteen when she climbed on the Greyhound bus for home. Said I could do what I wanted with her clothes."

"I wear a size ten," Marilee said.

"That was before Grady ran off, honey. You've probably dropped ten pounds and don't know it. Besides, if the dress is a little snug that'll work in your favor. Now, sit down. I'm about to make a new woman out of you."

Clara and Winnie sat down as well and watched while Ruby worked her magic. When she was finished Marilee, who had never been heavy-handed with her makeup, couldn't believe the difference.

"Wow," Winnie said. "You look like a movie star. If I'd looked that good when I told my old man I was pregnant, maybe he wouldn't have walked out on me."

Clara didn't look pleased. "I think it's a bit much. Remember, less is more."

"She's going to be working under dim lighting," Ruby said. "So what do you think, honey?"

"You did a fine job, Ruby. But I'll never be able to learn how to do all this."

"I'll teach you. In the meantime, I'll plan to drop by after work each day so I can fix you up." She began pinning up Marilee's hair, and then put the wig in place. "What d'you think?" she said.

Winnie gave Ruby the thumbs-up. "Lookin' good."

"Marilee is a beautiful woman. All I did was enhance her features. Now, let's get you into that dress." She grabbed the garment and ushered Marilee into her bedroom. When they returned, Marilee's cheeks were stained the color of the dress.

Winnie's eyes almost popped out of her head. "That thing clings to you like a second skin. I didn't realize you had such a nice figure. You have to stop dressing like a librarian." Clara cleared her throat. Winnie looked at her. "Guess I shouldn't have said that, huh?"

Marilee tried not to take offense. "I think my clothes are fashionable."

"A little on the prim side," Winnie said, "but hey, I'm not exactly on the cutting edge of fashion."

Ruby preened over her handiwork. "I'll bring over a few more dresses tomorrow night."

"Just keep that pepper spray handy," Clara said, "in case some man loses control of his desires the minute he sees you."

Marilee walked them to the front door. Once they were

on their way, she closed the door and leaned against it. Her stomach was tied in knots at the thought of what she was about to do. Perhaps it was time she took a few chances in life.

The doorbell rang, startling her. Marilee figured Ruby must've forgotten some of her supplies. She opened the door and found Sam Brewer standing there.

"Marilee, is that you?" he asked, blinking several times.

She'd forgotten for a moment how she was dressed. She blushed. "Hello, Sam."

"You look...different."

"Yes, I suppose I do," she said, patting the wig self-consciously. "I'm sort of in a hurry. Is there something I can do for you?"

He handed her the iron. "I wanted to return this. I found mine." He remained standing there. He knew he was staring—gawking, actually—but he couldn't help himself.

"Thank you." He continued to stand there. "Anything else?"

"Huh?" With some difficulty, Sam managed to pry his eyes from the red dress that clung to her figure so well. Damn, but she looked good. "Oh, yeah. I stopped by Blessing Home today. I have to tell you, Marilee, it needs a lot of work. The place looks like it's ready to collapse."

"But it can be repaired, right?"

"We're talking a lot of money."

"Will three thousand dollars cover it?"

He shook his head, hoping to clear his brain. All the blood had obviously rushed to another part of his body. "It won't even come close. There's structural damage."

Marilee sighed. "We'll have to come up with more money. Can you at least start working on the roof?" she asked, wishing he had chosen another time to burden her with the news. She had enough to worrying about at the moment.

"I'm kind of backed up on my other jobs, so I'll have to do it in my spare time."

She was beginning to wonder if the girls would ever be

able to move back into the home. "Thank you, Sam, that's very thoughtful of you. I know you'll do your best. Send me an invoice for the roof, and I'll get our treasurer to write you a check right away."

As she watched him go, she wondered where on earth they would find the money to do all the work that was needed. But she couldn't worry about that now.

She had an audition.

small closet. A long bar was situated on one side, the shelf
covered in it empty hangers. Large leather furniture is placed in
the room and she wondered small comfort rather. Crisp white
cloths draped the dining tables, and candle flickered from
crystal containers. The setting was romantic, with an understated elegance. A sign that read *Please dress* in *Marilee's* as
later was belted on the fireplace. Marilee have 73
money please, you've be happier. She could buy a week a
world of groceries for what it means... for a couple of dollars.

# Six

Pickford was twice the size of Chickpea and boasted a me-
dium-size mall, which was the only reason Marilee had visited the town in the past. She drove Josh there to shop for
school clothes once a year, and she returned in December
for Christmas gifts. As soon as she arrived, she stopped at
a convenience store and asked for directions to the address
listed in the newspaper.

The Pickford Inn sat back from the road and was surrounded by a stone wall. Massive oak and magnolia trees
grew on the manicured lawn; azalea bushes skirted the building. An old carriage sat out front, and large whiskey barrels
on either side of the double front doors held an assortment
of flowers. Marilee parked near the entrance, grabbed her
stack of sheet music and climbed from the car. The wig felt
like a vise on her head and made her scalp itch. Marilee
wondered why any woman in her right mind would wear
one.

Inside, she was greeted by a slim brunette in a smart black
cocktail dress who stood near a Queen Anne desk looking
over a list of reservations. "May I help you?"

Marilee introduced herself. "I'm here about the job."

"Oh, yes. Let me find the owner, Mr. Helms. Please excuse me."

Marilee watched the woman literally glide from the room,
and she wondered if she would ever learn to walk with such
grace. She peeked inside the dining room. One wall was
dominated by a stone fireplace, in front of which sat a baby

grand piano. A long bar was situated on one side, the stools covered in a deep, hunter-green leather that was repeated in the chairs that surrounded small cocktail tables. Crisp, white cloths draped the dining tables, and candles flickered from crystal containers. The setting was intimate, with an understated elegance. A sign announced a prime rib special. A menu was posted on the wall beside it. Marilee gave it a cursory glance, noting the prices. She could buy a week's worth of groceries for what it would cost a couple to buy dinner.

"Miss Abernathy?"

Marilee turned and found herself facing a strikingly handsome man who looked to be in his mid-forties. "Mr. Helms?"

"Call me Jack."

"And I'm Marilee," she said, offering her hand, at the same time wondering if he thought she looked like a slut in her outfit. He took her hand.

"Tell me, Marilee. Can you play "I Left My Heart in San Francisco"?"

"I'm almost certain I have the sheet music."

"If you don't, I do. Come this way, please."

She followed him through the dining room to the piano, where she discovered a book opened to the sheet of music Jack Helms had requested. He sat at a table nearby and smiled.

"Anytime you're ready, Marilee."

She set her own music, as well as her pocketbook, on the floor beside the bench and took her seat, squaring her shoulders and sitting high as her piano teacher had taught. Her hands were damp and shook slightly, but after years of lessons and performing for one charity event after another, she ignored it. She placed her hands over the keys and began. She waited until she was halfway through the song before chancing a look in Jack's direction. His eyes were closed; he seemed to be drifting, as though in another time and place.

She finished the song and waited. It was a full minute

before Jack spoke. He looked as if he was trying to compose himself.

"You play beautifully, Marilee," he said, his voice choked with emotion. "I don't believe I've ever heard that song played so skillfully. It was a favorite of my late wife."

"Oh my," Marilee said. "Has she been…gone long?"

"Ten years. Died in a car accident. She was a beautiful woman."

Marilee could almost feel the sorrow emanating from him. "You've never remarried?"

He shook his head. "No. I was devoted to her."

"I'm so sorry."

"You may start this evening if you like. All that I ask is that you open and close with that song. In memory of Teresa."

Marilee had never been fond of "I Left My Heart in San Francisco," but she would have played the theme song to "Sesame Street" if it meant getting the job. "I would be honored, Jack," she said and meant it. "In memory of your wife."

He smiled, although it didn't quite reach his eyes. "Why don't we go into my office? I think you'll find my terms very generous."

Once Jack discussed the job and her pay—fifty dollars a night plus tips—she filled out the necessary forms.

"You'll have a lot of requests," Jack said, "and our customers tip generously. We cater to an older crowd. They enjoy soft dinner music. You'll only be expected to play from seven to ten Tuesday through Thursday. Monday is our slowest night, so you'll have that night off. But I'll need you until midnight on the weekends. Any questions?"

"When do you want me to start?"

"Tonight, if you could. I know this is short notice. If it's not convenient—"

"Tonight is fine. I think I'll go ahead and get started so I can warm up before the crowd comes in."

"Good idea. You can leave your purse in here if you like.

I keep the office locked.'' They shook hands once more before going their separate ways.

Marilee stopped by the ladies' room and checked her makeup. The lighting was soft, so her blush and eye shadow didn't stand out as it had at her kitchen table, and the short wig enhanced her features, even if the blond color had more silver in it than she would have liked. Perhaps she should have her own hair cut, she thought. She held her head high as she exited the bathroom and glided toward the dining area in much the same way the hostess had earlier. If only Grady could see her now.

No, the last thing she needed was for him to see her, she reminded herself. That's why she was in disguise.

Several tables had been seated in her absence. Marilee smiled at the diners and sat on the piano bench. She adjusted the microphone. ''Good evening, ladies and gentleman,'' she said, purposefully avoiding giving them her name. ''I'm going to be playing for you this evening. Please feel free to send me your requests. I'd like to dedicate this first song to Teresa.'' She began playing ''I Left My Heart in San Francisco.'' Jack, on his way to the kitchen, paused and listened, a wistful look in his eyes.

No man should be that lonely, Marilee thought as she began singing to the music. Jack looked surprised, and then delighted. Soon she lost herself in the music, as she often did. As she finished playing ''The Way We Were,'' Marilee looked up to find the hostess approaching her. She covered the microphone.

''Jack said to take a break,'' the woman whispered. ''Would you like something to drink? A cup of coffee or iced tea? Just grab it in the kitchen.''

Marilee decided a cup of coffee was just what she needed. She thanked her audience and informed them she was taking a short break. She'd already had at least a dozen requests in the two hours she'd been playing, and the crystal bowl on the piano was already half-full of dollar bills.

The kitchen bustled with activity, and the smells that had tempted her all evening sent her mouth watering the moment she walked through the swinging doors. Waitresses smiled and nodded, and a couple of them introduced themselves as they sailed past with large food trays and shoved through the door leading in to the dining room. Marilee was already beginning to feel at home. She drank her coffee, stopped by the ladies' room and returned to find a number of requests written on bar napkins, accompanied with a dollar bill or two.

By the end of her set, Marilee was beginning to get hungry, but she couldn't remember when she'd last enjoyed herself as much. The dining room was almost empty now, with the exception of a couple of tables that had come in late and were finishing up. Marilee thanked everyone for coming, and then ended her set with "I Left My Heart in San Francisco."

"Honey, you were great," one of the waitresses said as Marilee pulled her tips from the crystal container on the piano. She would count them when she got home. "My name's Gertie Johnson."

"Nice to meet you, Gertie. I'm Marilee."

"I've been here since the place opened eight years ago. You need anything, you tell me, okay?"

"Thank you."

Jack beamed as he unlocked the door to his office. "The crowd loved you," he said. "You'll be back tomorrow night, right?"

Marilee nodded as she grabbed her purse. "Seven o'clock sharp."

The drive home seemed to take forever. Marilee yawned most of the way, although it was only ten-thirty. She supposed she was tired from all the excitement.

Winnie did not look happy to see her when she walked through the door. "What's wrong?" Marilee asked, pulling the wig off and setting it on top of the piano.

"What's wrong?" Winnie echoed, hands on hips. Dressed in a purple housecoat she looked quite formidable. "Nothing, except I've been worried sick all night. Where've you been?"

Marilee could tell the girl was upset. "Working. I was

hired at the Pickford Inn, and the owner asked me to start tonight.''

"I s'pose it was too much trouble for you to inform me. I didn't know if you'd had an accident or some drunk pulled you into an alley. Clara and Ruby have been calling all night to see how the interview went. I don't mind telling you they're worried too.''

"I'm sorry, Winnie," Marilee said, noting the genuine concern on the girl's face. "I was so excited about getting the job that I never thought of calling.''

"All this fretting can't be good for the baby," Winnie said, sniffing, much like Clara did when she was annoyed. She turned for the kitchen. "I made you a sandwich since you didn't eat your pizza. I figured you'd be hungry by the time you got back from your interview. How was I to know you'd be out all night?''

The girl made it sound as though she'd been standing on a street corner picking up men until the wee hours of the morning. "Thank you, Winnie," she said. "Why don't you go to bed?''

"That's exactly where I'm going. I need my rest, what with being pregnant and all and trying to do well in school. I can't be pacing the floor and wringing my hands and wondering where you've run off too. You need to call Clara and Ruby." She climbed the stairs slowly, as though she carried the weight of the world.

Marilee called Clara and Ruby, each of whom answered on the first ring. She apologized for causing them to worry, then told them about her new job. Once she hung up, she went straight for the refrigerator where Winnie had indeed prepared her a snack. The girl had quartered a pickle and placed each wedge around a ham and cheese sandwich and covered it in plastic wrap. As Marilee ate, she counted her tips. Thirty dollars! That, plus the fifty she'd made, equaled eighty. Eighty dollars! Not bad for three hours of work. She was on her way to replenishing her savings account.

It was almost midnight by the time Marilee had showered and climbed into bed. Setting the alarm, she pulled the

covers high. She had cried a little in the shower while thinking of Josh, but now she felt calmer. Thank God she had
her friends. At least she wasn't alone.

Marilee arrived at the funeral home early for her first day
of work, where she found a frazzled Debbie still in her bathrobe, picking up toys and dusting as Bennie toddled behind
her. "There was a traffic fatality last night," she said. "Irby
picked up the body first thing this morning. The family is
coming in at ten o'clock. I wanted to make sure the place
is presentable."

Marilee helped get the reception room and parlor in order
while they took turns answering the phone and directing
calls to Irby, who was dressed in a dark suit and wearing
what Debbie referred to as his somber look.

He looked happy to see Marilee. "I'd like you to sit in
on this one and take notes," he said. "Debbie will watch
the phones."

By the time the deceased's family walked through the
front door, everything was ready. Marilee watched as Irby
welcomed them and offered his condolences. He led the
grieving family into the parlor as Debbie reappeared, dressed
in a simple black shift. Marilee grabbed a notepad and followed, sitting in a chair at the far side of the room so she
wouldn't interfere with the meeting.

Irby introduced her as his assistant, and the family nodded. Marilee could see the grief etched in the lines around
their eyes and mouths. She'd seen it before. For the next
hour she watched and listened quietly as Irby helped the
family make funeral arrangements. This was a side of Irby
she'd never seen. By the time the family left, they seemed
relieved that someone was in charge.

"I'm impressed with how you handled everything," Marilee said to Irby once the group left. "You were on your
best behavior."

He reached for his baseball cap and plopped it on his
head. He grinned. "Hey, I'm a sensitive guy. What'd you

expect me to do, tell knock-knock jokes?'' He glanced at his wristwatch. ''Well, I'd better get to work on that poor joker. The family viewing is this evening. Going to take me that long to pry the windshield off his face.''

Marilee shuddered. ''That's the Irby we know and love.''

Debbie spent a couple of hours training Marilee while Bennie napped. She hadn't realized all that was involved in running a funeral home. As she shared her lunch with Debbie, they chatted. Debbie complimented Marilee on the lavender perfume she always wore, and Marilee asked about Debbie's children.

Shortly after three, two children bounded through the front door. Debbie frowned. ''How many times have you been told to use the back door?'' She introduced them to Marilee and ushered them upstairs, leaving Marilee on her own. Marilee took calls; when the party asked for Irby, she told the caller he was tied up, but promised to have him return the call as soon as possible.

As Marilee was cleaning her desk and preparing to leave a tired-looking Irby appeared. She handed him his messages, and he thanked her for doing a good job.

''See you tomorrow,'' he said.

She nodded. ''Tomorrow.''

When Marilee came through the door, Winnie was putting dinner on the table. ''Gee, Winnie, I didn't expect this.''

''You can't go running out of here every night without your dinner,'' the girl said. ''And you need to hurry. Ruby will be here any minute to do your makeup.''

As if acting on cue, Ruby sailed through the front door with her makeup kit in tow. As Marilee gobbled her dinner, she held a handheld mirror to watch Ruby apply her eye makeup, all the while answering questions about her new job. ''You know, I think I can do this on my own next time,'' she said, once they'd put the wig in place.

''You sure?'' Ruby asked. ''I don't mind stopping by. Tell you what, I'll leave some of this stuff. If you have trouble, give me a call, and I can be here in no time.''

Thanking her, Marilee slipped into a blue sequined dress and bade Winnie and Ruby farewell as she headed out the door.

Sam could not stop thinking about Marilee. As he stood on the damaged roof of Blessing Home trying to figure out how many cartons of shingles to order, he kept seeing in his mind the way she'd looked in that red dress.

The woman was an enigma, to say the least. One minute she was trying to hang herself, next thing he knew she was caring for his mother like a loving daughter. The dress and wig didn't make sense. There could only be one reason Marilee was disguising herself: she was obviously lonely and out looking for companionship. He shook his head.

Dressed like that, he could only imagine what she'd find. Sam muttered a series of four-letter words at the possibility of Marilee checking out what he used to refer to as meat markets. And here she was, so prim and proper, and far too naive for her own good. He cursed again when he noted the rotted wood in one section of the roof. Looking through the hole, he saw the living room and several buckets that had obviously been placed there to catch the rain. Sam thought of the girls who'd had to live under such conditions and felt sorry for them.

He climbed down and sat in his truck. No matter what, he wasn't going to allow Marilee to assuage her loneliness with some no-account man who would only end up using her and breaking her heart. He would repair the damn roof. He'd do whatever necessary in order to see her.

Josh sat in a lawn chair in front of LaFonda's trailer and waited for his dad to arrive home from work. The slab of broken concrete that served as LaFonda's patio—she pronounced it paw-tio—was littered with plastic containers of dying plants. It would never occur to her to throw them away. Just let them stay there, in case she needed them for something else, she'd say, which was why the inside of her trailer was so cluttered you could barely walk through it. He thought of the house he'd lived in the past ten years. His mother, as busy as she'd been with church activities, would never let a place go. He pushed the thought aside. He didn't want to think about his mother.

Josh stood as he spied his dad's car turn into the trailer park and pull in beside LaFonda's old heap. "Hi, Dad," he said the minute the man started toward him.

"Hey, son. How was school?"

Josh shrugged. He hated school. "Okay, I guess." His dad made for the trailer.

"Uh, Dad?"

"Yes?" Grady turned.

Josh could see that he was tired. The suit he wore was crumpled, as though he'd slept in it. His dad had always been so particular before. "I don't have school tomorrow. I thought maybe we could do something tonight. Like go to a movie? There's a good action-adventure playing. Tommy Lee Jones is in it. He's cool."

Grady shook his head. "I don't know, son. My day wasn't so great. Business was slow on the car lot, so the boss put us to washing cars. Not exactly what I expected to be doing at this stage of my life." As if sensing his son's disappointment, he smiled. "Why don't we see how I feel after dinner?" he suggested. "Or maybe I can grab a nap, and we can take in the nine o'clock show."

Josh knew they wouldn't be going to a movie that night or any other. His dad was so wrapped up with the woman inside the trailer that he had little time for anything else.

Grady opened the door to the trailer. "You coming in for dinner?"

"I'm not hungry. I think I'll take a walk."

"I'll ask LaFonda to keep your plate warm, how's that?"

Wordlessly, Josh turned and started walking down the gravel road that ran through the park, hands tucked deep inside his jeans. He walked every afternoon until he was too tired to do anything more than fall asleep. At least it kept him from thinking.

The smell of food wafted through the windows of the blue-and-white mobile home two doors down. Onions frying. Josh smelled them every time he passed that trailer. Across the street, a poodle was chained to a stake in the yard. It yapped wildly as he passed. Josh hated both the smell of cooked onions and that stupid yapping dog.

He turned a corner and saw the three guys who waited with him each morning to catch the bus. He stopped, started to turn around then decided against it. He would ignore them and walk along the highway as he usually did.

"Hey, look, it's lard-ass," one of the boys called out. "Ain't you missing your supper, boy?"

"Don't look like he's ever missed a meal," another one said.

The older boy shoved them. "Why don't you two shut up?" He walked away, quickly catching up with Josh. "Ignore them, kid," he said. "They're just a couple of morons who have nothing better to do than insult people. What's your name?"

Josh stopped walking and looked at him. "Why do you want to know?"

"Hey, I'm just trying to be sociable. You don't want to tell me, that's your business."

"Josh."

"My name's Conway."

"I know who you are. I've seen you at school."

Conway lit a cigarette. "Now, there's a hellhole if ever there was one. I'd quit if I didn't think my old lady would have a bona fide conniption fit. She made me swear on a stack of bibles that I'd graduate, so I reckon I'll hang in there and do her that one favor. How come I see you walking all the time?"

"Not much else to do around here." Josh wondered why the guy was bothering with him. He was probably one of the coolest guys in school, although he seemed to be in trouble most of the time.

"Yeah, it's boring. 'Course, you gotta know where to find the action."

Josh gave a grunt. "I haven't seen much of that." He watched Conway take a long drag of his cigarette.

Conway offered him the pack of Marlboros. "You want one?"

Josh shrugged and pulled one out. Conway lit it for him. One drag and Josh went into a fit of coughing.

Conway laughed and slapped him on the back. "You ain't been smoking long, have you?"

"Not too long."

"Know what your problem is? You're too serious."

Josh considered it. "I have a lot on my mind."

"Problems at home?"

Josh looked suspicious. "Did somebody tell you something?"

"All I know is you and your old man are living with that LaFonda woman. She's a piece of work, guys moving in and out all the time. Woman has a swinging door, if you know what I mean."

"She rents out her spare room."

"Sure she does."

Josh looked at Conway. He wore a smirk. Josh would like to have known more so he could tell his dad, but he didn't want to push Conway and end up with nothing. Sometimes, the best thing to do was remain quiet and let the other person do the talking. He took a short drag from the cigarette, dropped it to the ground and stamped it out. "Thanks for the smoke," he said.

"Don't mention it." Conway looked around. "Hey, if you're so bored, maybe you'd like to go to a party later."

"What kind of party?"

"A Tupperware party," Conway said, sarcasm dripping from his tongue. "What the hell kind of party do you think I mean? There'll be women there. And cold beer. I know this cool guy named Mo. He's got an awesome place on the edge of town. Nice house, nice cars, and he's not even thirty. I work for him, detailing cars. Money's good."

Josh pondered it. He needed a job. That way he could

save his money and hopefully get the hell out of Chickpea and away from his screwed-up parents. He might even find out more about LaFonda Bonaire if he went with Conway. Boy, he'd love to get the goods on her so he could tell his dad. "You think this Mo guy would give me a job, too?" Josh asked.

The other boy shrugged. "We could talk to him."

Josh was beginning to like Conway. "Sure, I'll go."

# *Seven*

Marilee slept until ten o'clock Saturday morning. When she opened her eyes and spied the alarm clock, she almost leaped from the bed, only to remember that she didn't have to work at the funeral home that day. She let out an enormous sigh of relief. Because it was a weekend, she had worked until midnight at the Pickford Inn the night before, but it had been well worth it when she'd counted her tips. She had to work again that evening, but she had the day to herself until then.

She suddenly smelled sausages cooking in the kitchen, and her stomach growled in response. She climbed from the bed, grabbed her housecoat and made her way downstairs. There she found Nell Brewer, drinking coffee at the kitchen table.

"Good morning, Nell," she said. "What a nice surprise."

"Oh, I hope Winnie and I didn't wake you with our talking," the woman said.

"No, I never heard a thing. Good morning, Winnie. Breakfast smells delicious."

The girl nodded. "There's fresh coffee."

Marilee thanked her as she made her way to the automatic coffeemaker and poured a cup. "How've you been, Nell?"

"Just fine. I wanted to drop off your cake plate and thank you for your help the other night. And to tell you the good news," she added with a bright smile. "My son has decided not to hire anyone to take care of me right away. He said he'd hold off and see how things went."

"I'm so glad."

"He still doesn't trust me in the kitchen, and he makes me leave the bathroom door unlocked in case I fall, but I don't mind. At least I don't have a nursemaid standing over me. I don't know what you said to him, but it seems to have worked."

"I really didn't say much. Winnie, can I help you with anything? You're supposed to rest, you know."

"No, I've got it under control. And you worry too much. I feel great."

"Winnie told me you're working at Denton Funeral Home," Nell said. "How do you like it?"

"I've only been there a few days, but I think I'm going to be happy working for the Dentons. I've known them since grade school."

Nell leaned close. "You don't have to do anything with dead bodies, do you?"

Marilee shook her head. "Oh, no. Irby takes care of that."

"No way would I go near a dead body," Winnie said, turning the sausage over in the skillet. "Not after some of the things I've heard."

Nell looked intrigued. "What have you heard, dear?"

Winnie paused, one hand on her hip, still holding the spatula. "Well, my cousin once worked in a funeral home. Said he saw a dead man sit straight up one night. Claimed it was some kind of muscle reflex. I don't care what caused it, I would have made a new door getting out of that room."

Nell shuddered. "Oh my."

Marilee decided a change of subject was in order. "Winnie, are you sure there's not something I can do to help you?"

"No, I'm cool."

Nell turned to Marilee. "I don't mean to pry, dear, but have you heard anything from your son?"

Marilee told her about trying to visit Josh at school. "He's so angry."

"He's just going through a stage," Nell said. "And I should know. My son put me through the wringer while he was growing up." She paused and shook her head. "You just need to go slow. Perhaps you should send him a card, to let him know you're thinking about him."

Marilee pondered it. "I might just do that. Even though I hate sending it to that woman's house."

"Hey, you do whatcha got to do," Winnie said. "At least he'll know you still love him." She opened the oven and pulled out a pan of biscuits.

Marilee wondered if Winnie's parents had bothered to contact her, or whether they even knew where she was staying. Hearing from them would do the girl a world of good. "You've certainly gone to a lot of trouble this morning, kiddo," Marilee said, noting the biscuits had been made from scratch. "Nell, I hope you'll join us."

"I'd love to."

The women chatted while they ate. Winnie looked at Marilee. "I need to find a part-time job so I can start buying things for the baby."

"What are you interested in doing?" Nell asked.

"I don't much care as long as it doesn't interfere with my studies. I'm an honor student."

Nell smiled broadly. "Good for you!"

"You don't want it to interfere with your health, either," Marilee added.

"Oh, I feel fine and I like staying busy. Takes my mind off things."

Marilee wondered what it was that Winnie didn't want to think about. She imagined it had to do with her family.

Nell looked thoughtful. "I could use your help with the housework," she said. "Now that Sam has agreed not to hire someone to take care of me, I could use an extra hand. Nothing strenuous, you understand. You could come in for a couple of hours in the afternoon, maybe two or three times a week. I pay top wages," Nell added with a wink.

"That sounds good," Winnie said.

"And I plan to pay you for all you do around here," Marilee told her.

"I'm not taking money from you," Winnie said. "It's

only fair that I do my share around here, you giving me a place to stay and all.''

"Yes, but—''

"I'm not taking your money and that's that." She paused. "What you could do is run me over to this garage sale. It's supposed to be huge. Says in the paper they have a bassinet. I still have a little money from when I helped cook meals at Blessing Home.''

"Okay,'' Marilee said easily, deciding that if the bassinet was still available, she would buy it for the girl.

Marilee arrived home from work on Monday to find Sam on a ladder, repairing the beam in her ceiling. She came to an abrupt halt just inside her door. "Oh, Sam. I wasn't expecting you,'' she said, trying to hide the breathlessness in her voice.

He glanced down at her and smiled as she shrugged out of her jacket. The smile wavered slightly at the sight of her powder-blue sweaterdress that, while conservative, emphasized each curve. He tried not to stare. "Winnie let me in. I'm just finishing up here.''

Marilee hesitated. She had not asked him to make the repairs, but now that he was here it would be simpler to let him do the work. "I'll pay you, of course.''

"We'll see.''

From her vantage point, Marilee couldn't help noticing how good he looked in snug-fitting jeans and a navy pullover. There ought to be a law against any man looking that good, she thought, wishing her body would not react every time she saw him. But what woman, even a Christian one like herself, wouldn't get all warm and flustered around such a man? And she had no doubt Sam knew exactly what he did to women and how to work it to his advantage. The confident, almost cocky, smile on his face said it all.

"May I get you something to drink? Iced tea?''

"Winnie already gave me a glass.''

"Well, then, I'll be in the kitchen if you need me.''

She found Winnie preparing dinner. "You didn't have to

cook today. I'm off Monday nights, remember?'' she protested.

"You can set the table and do the dishes afterward. Besides, I promised Clara and Ruby I'd take care of you, and
I never go back on a promise."

"Winnie, I don't *need* you to take care of me." She kept
her voice low, hoping Sam would not overhear.

The girl faced her. "Look, Marilee, I've always pulled
my weight. I've been working since I was eleven years old.
In my daddy's grocery store," she added. "And Mrs.
Brewer and I worked out a schedule so I'm going to start
cleaning for her tomorrow after school. I plan to help out
on groceries."

"That's very noble of you, but I don't expect it, and I've
already told you I don't want you to overexert yourself, what
with the baby and all. Besides, we both agree your education
is very important."

"Working will make the time go faster while I'm waiting
for the baby to come. And it's only for a few hours a week,
just so I can have spending money." When Marilee continued to look doubtful, she went on. "If I find it's too hard
on me or it's getting in the way of my schoolwork, I'll give
it up."

Marilee knew there was no sense arguing with her. Winnie had a mind of her own, and would not be swayed once
she made a decision. It hadn't taken Marilee long to figure
that one out. "As long as you promise not to overdo
things."

The girl nodded. "Oh, I invited Sam for dinner. I hope
it's okay. He's been up on that ladder for three solid hours
now. I told him I'd fix a plate for him to take back to Nell."

"I suppose it's the least we can do," Marilee said. "But
I don't mind telling you, he makes me nervous."

"That's 'cause you're attracted to him. And I don't blame
you one bit. He's a handsome devil. You have to admit, he
certainly knows how to fill out a pair of jeans."

"He's a devil, all right," Marilee muttered. "Which is

why I plan to stay as far away from him as I can. And I'm *not* attracted to him. I'm a married woman.''

"Whatever. By the way, your lawyer called and said for you to call him back. Said he'd be in the office until six.''

Marilee glanced at the clock and saw she had only minutes to return the call. She hurried to the telephone and dialed Tate Radford's number, and was surprised when he answered.

"You've got a court date in three weeks,'' he said, giving her the day and time. "It's just a temporary hearing, but I plan to set up visitation with your son.''

"That's wonderful news!'' she exclaimed.

"Don't get your hopes up, Marilee. The judge can order it, but if the boy doesn't want to see you, you're going to have a tough time making him comply.''

"Well, it's a start. Uh, Tate, I've been wondering. Can the judge order counseling for Josh and me?''

"You can *ask* for anything. Whether you get it is a different story. I think, though, under the circumstances, the judge will feel it's in the best interests of your son. Oh, by the way, I spoke with the child advocate. He'll contact you soon. In the meantime, you might want to look into finding a good family counselor so we can present it before the court. If you go through the mental health office it'll be easier on your pocketbook.''

Marilee was grinning when she hung up. She told Winnie about the conversation.

"I told you it would work out,'' Winnie said. "But if your son's here I might be in the way.''

"Nonsense. You're part of the family.'' She looked up and found Sam standing in the doorway. Her mouth went dry.

"I'm all done out there.''

"Dinner will be ready in fifteen minutes,'' Winnie announced.

Sam looked amused. "Did you check with Marilee?''

Marilee chuckled in an attempt to hide her unease. "Winnie runs the house, Sam. If she says it's okay, then it's okay.''

"There's a half bath through that door," Winnie said, pointing. "You can wash up in there."

Sam grinned. "Yes, ma'am." He turned for the bathroom. Winnie and Marilee stared.

"Nice behind," Winnie whispered. "And don't tell me you didn't notice, because I saw you looking."

Marilee blushed as she reached into a drawer for the flatware. "Would you hush, before he hears you?"

"You think he doesn't know he's got a nice behind?"

"I'm sure he's well aware of it. That's the problem. He's full of himself." Marilee leaned closer. "Trust me, Winnie, the man is a wolf. He's sullied more than one woman's reputation in this town."

"I figure it would be worth it."

Marilee shot her a dark look as she began setting the table.

"All clean," Sam announced, stepping out of the bathroom.

"And just in time," Winnie said.

They dined on chicken-fried steak, mashed potatoes and seasoned green beans. "Where'd you learn to cook so well, Winnie?" Sam asked, once he'd tasted everything.

"I was the oldest child in my family, so I learned at an early age," she said. "And I was always cooking for our church. We had something going on all the time. Picnics on Sunday, pancake suppers, potluck dinners. Our members liked to eat more than they liked to pray."

Marilee and Sam laughed.

Marilee felt her tension ease up. "If she keeps cooking like this, I'm going to have to go into a larger-size dress. Don't forget, Winnie, I'm not eating for two."

"You look fine to me," Sam blurted, then wished he hadn't when he noted the blush that rose to her cheeks almost immediately. He turned to Winnie. "When is your baby due?" It sounded like a safe subject.

"She's due around Christmas."

"She?"

"I'm having a girl."

Sam arched one eyebrow. "Oh, yeah?"

"Don't argue with her," Marilee said. "If she says she's having a girl, then it'll be a girl."

"Do the kids at school give you a hard time about being pregnant?" he asked.

Winnie eyed him. "Do I look like the type who'd take crap off anyone?" Sam grinned and shook his head. "Actually, a bunch of my girlfriends are planning to give me a huge baby shower. And my English teacher is going through her attic looking for things."

Marilee didn't respond. If Winnie had friends, they had certainly been scarce. Not one had called or visited. She suspected the girl was just pretending to have a lot of friends so people wouldn't feel sorry for her predicament.

Sam turned his attention to Marilee. "I forgot to tell you. I've already begun work on Blessing Home. Right now I'm patching holes. I've ordered the shingles, and they should be in next week."

"Thank you, Sam," Marilee said, truly touched. She made a mental note to have Ruby contact him about the costs. "The sooner we can get those poor girls back where they belong, the better."

"Would y'all excuse me, please?" Winnie said, pushing her chair from the table. "I just remembered there's something I have to do for class tomorrow." She looked at Marilee. "Don't forget to prepare a plate for Nell before Sam leaves." The girl disappeared up the stairs.

Marilee wondered if Winnie really had something to do or was just trying to give Sam and her a little privacy. "That girl never stops," she told Sam.

"My mother says she's going to help with the housekeeping at our place."

"She claims she's up to it, but if it gets to be too much for her, I'm going to put my foot down."

"She's young and healthy. She'll be okay. She's a good cook, that's for sure."

They sat in silence for a moment, and Marilee suddenly felt uncomfortable. She wondered what he was thinking.

"How are things with your son?" Sam asked after a moment.

Marilee told him about her conversation with the attorney. "I mailed Josh a card today, inviting him out to lunch next Saturday, but I'm not getting my hopes up."

Sam nodded. "Things will work out, Marilee."

"I'm counting on it." She looked up, and their gazes locked. It was difficult not to look at him, the striking face bronzed by wind and sun that gave him a rugged, outdoorsy look. She averted her gaze, reminding herself she had no business thinking any man handsome and certainly not a rounder like Sam. She had to admit he'd been nothing but kind toward her, but with his reputation, she was certain he had ulterior motives, even if he claimed not to. She wondered what his ex-wife had been like. She imagined a woman in fishnet stockings and animal skins.

"Here, let me help you clean up this mess," he said, pushing back his own chair and grabbing several plates.

She jumped to her feet, taking the plates from him. "No, no, I'll do it."

"I don't mind—"

He seemed eager to help, but she wanted to do it herself. After all, he'd worked on her ceiling and door. "You're our guest, Sam," she said, wanting to include Winnie as well, so he wouldn't get the mistaken impression that he was there on her account. "Would you like coffee?"

"No, thanks."

"I certainly don't mind making it." Actually, she wanted to get him out of there as quickly as possible, but she didn't want to appear rude. "And we need to discuss payment for the repairs you made."

"Next time, *you* cook for me."

She looked at him. The way he said it, one would have thought he'd just made an intimate request. Her stomach did a tiny flip-flop, and she felt all aflutter. Marilee glanced away quickly. "Yes, well, I suppose that can be arranged."

Sam cocked his head to the side, studying her. "Do I make you nervous, Marilee?" he asked, thinking maybe that wasn't a bad thing. At least she wasn't indifferent toward him. That had to mean something.

Marilee wondered if he knew just how nervous he did make her. "Don't be silly," she said, trying to laugh it off. She raked the uneaten food into the trash, hands shaking as she scraped the plates vigorously. "Whatever gave you that idea?"

"Because you're scraping those plates so hard I'm afraid you're going to chip the paint."

Her hands stilled. She looked at him, and for a moment they simply gazed at one another. She should wring Winnie's neck for inviting him, then disappearing like that when she didn't know the first thing about entertaining men. Oh, she'd been a gracious hostess when Grady had invited one or two of the deacons to the house, but this was different. *Way* different. Here she was, newly separated and trying to come to terms with her new life, and she was spending the evening with a man like Sam, who left her breathless and tongue-tied and made her stomach feel like freshly churned butter.

"Sam, I am afraid you have me at a definite disadvantage," she confessed.

"Oh?" He stood and crossed the room. "How so?"

She straightened. "That should be obvious. I've been married half my life, and I am not accustomed to spending time with a single man. I'm not trying to be rude here, just honest. I don't know how to say it any other way. You're obviously more comfortable with this sort of thing than I am."

"Perhaps we can do something to remedy your, uh, discomfort," he said, taking a step closer. "I'll bet you'd enjoy my company if you got to know me better."

She saw the challenge in his eyes. "Is that so?" she asked, wondering if she was about to witness the infamous Sam Brewer make his move.

"We could spend more time together."

The plate she held slipped from her hand. Luckily, it landed in the trash can on a wad of paper towels and didn't break. She retrieved it. "You and me spend time together?" she repeated a bit more sharply than she'd meant, in an attempt to hide her embarrassment. "Like on a date? Are you serious?"

Sam was taken aback by the abrupt change in her, the rebuke in her voice, a haughtiness he'd never seen in her. The muscles in his back stiffened. Did she think she was too good for him? In his mind, he suddenly saw her on that float in the homecoming parade, the adoring crowd cheering her on. And him, the school dropout, sweeping trash from the street with a push broom, doing anything he could to make a buck because money had been so tight after his dad died. And later, sharing a pint of whiskey with his buddies and wondering what she looked like beneath that red velvet dress but knowing she would never give him a second look.

Some things never changed. He may have come up the economic ladder, but in her mind he still wasn't good enough.

"Actually, I wasn't thinking along those lines, Marilee," he said coolly. "I just figured since we're neighbors and all, it might not be a bad idea for the four of us to get together some time."

"Four of us?"

"You know, you and me, my mother and Winnie. My mother seldom gets out of the house, and I'll bet Winnie could use a break. We could all take in a movie or grab a bite to eat."

"Oh." Marilee suddenly felt like crawling beneath the kitchen table. How ridiculous she must appear to him, assuming he would want to date her when it was obvious they hadn't the first thing in common. Hadn't Winnie accused her of dressing like a librarian? Men like Sam didn't go for her type; they wanted a woman who was fresh and exciting, and…younger. And all this time she'd thought he was pursuing her, perhaps secretly hoping he was so it would take the sting out of Grady's public rejection. "Yes, that could be arranged," she said at last.

Sam would have had to be blind not to notice her embarrassment, and he felt rotten for causing it, but he was not going to let her step on his pride just because Grady Abernathy had done it to her. "I'm sorry I gave you the wrong impression. I suppose I should go."

She couldn't look at him. "Let me prepare your mother's plate." She did so in record time, wrapped the plate in aluminum foil and handed it to him. Still avoiding eye contact, she opened the back door. "Give Nell my best."

"Good night, Marilee."

She closed the door behind him and locked it. She felt like an idiot. How could she be both relieved and disappointed that Sam hadn't come on to her like she'd expected? What was wrong with her? Were her hormones out of whack or was she finally having the breakdown she'd promised herself?

Or was the man playing games with her? Marilee pondered it for a moment. That was a possibility. She'd heard Ruby mention men who were "players," and Sam Brewer was probably one of them, if not the best. Only she wasn't savvy enough to know the rules, and that made it dangerous dealing with men like him. Perhaps she was just being hopeful. It would be easier on her ego to keep thinking Sam was nothing but a scoundrel and a womanizer than to accept the notion he wasn't the least bit interested in her.

Marilee suddenly had a roaring headache. It was all too much for her poor mind to consider.

"Get a grip," she told herself as she finished cleaning the kitchen and turned off the light.

Upstairs, she passed by Winnie's room on the way to her own. Inside, the girl was lying on her bed staring at the ceiling, her expression forlorn. "Are you okay?" she asked.

Winnie mumbled something incoherent and turned over, but not before Marilee noted the red eyes. Had Winnie done the unthinkable and cried? Perhaps she was worried she would be sent back to Blessing Home once it was restored.

Marilee tried to remember what she'd said to Sam earlier when they'd discussed the renovations. Something about getting the girls back where they belonged. She groaned inwardly, knowing she'd stuck her foot in her mouth more than once that night.

She sat down beside Winnie and rubbed her back. "You know, I'd be lost if you weren't here."

"You'd manage."

"Look, Winnie, I know this probably isn't the most exciting place in the world to live, and that you'd probably rather live with one of your friends, but it would mean a lot to me if you stayed." Marilee suddenly realized she wasn't simply trying to make Winnie feel better; everything she was saying was true. "I would have been so lonely here by myself, what with trying to rebuild my life. You've made it bearable, even fun."

The girl didn't answer right away. "I've never known anyone like you, Marilee. You've been kinder to me than my own parents." She paused. "It freaked me out when they turned their backs on me. I mean, I always tried to do my best. I was a good girl."

"I have no doubt about that."

Winnie rolled over and faced her. She had been crying. "I have this sister, Darlene. She's as wild as they come, always off with some boy. She's already flunked two grades, but my parents never once gave her a hard time over it. She's lazy, too. Mama tried to teach her to cook, but Darlene can't boil water. No way could she be trusted to take care of the younger children. The phone might ring, and she'd forget all about them.

"I studied hard, Marilee, and I did everything I could to make things easier for my daddy at the store. Do you think anybody ever noticed? But if I slipped up, say I accidentally overcharged a customer or didn't charge enough tax on a purchase, boy, I caught hell."

"Oh, Winnie." Marilee knew what it was like to try to please someone, only to be criticized if she made the simplest error. "People expect a lot from those who have a lot to give. Your parents obviously had confidence in you. If they seemed to take you for granted, maybe it was because they knew you were more than capable." She paused. Is that why Grady had pushed her so hard? Because she'd actually been so good at her work that he had come to expect the best from her? When she turned the idea around and looked at the situation differently, she saw it in a whole new light. She had proven herself capable time after time. She felt a new sense of pride in herself. She didn't need a warning label on her brain. Grady had struck out at her because of his own frustrations, not her shortcomings.

"You know what, Winnie?" she said, the sudden epiphany making her feel stronger and wiser. "You and I are going to make it in this world. But it's going to be more difficult for people like Darlene."

Winnie seemed to ponder the idea. "I suppose I never looked at it that way." She met Marilee's gaze. "I've always wanted to be somebody. Ever since I was a little girl. Right now I've got my head set on being an accountant, but heck, who says I have to stop there?"

"Nobody."

"Shoot, I could be a comptroller of a big corporation or I could have my own accounting firm."

"Darn right!"

Winnie sat up. "I'd dress in snazzy business suits and carry my own briefcase—"

"You go, girl!"

"And have dental insurance for my child."

"That, too."

Without warning, Winnie slumped and her eyes misted. "I wanted so much to make Mama and Daddy proud of me. But in the end, I let them down."

Marilee shook her head sadly. "No, Winnie, they let you down."

Winnie's head snapped up, and she opened her mouth. It was obvious she was ready to defend her parents. Instead, she closed her mouth and said nothing, although it was obvious her mind was at work. The two sat quietly for a moment.

Marilee realized what a burden she had placed on Grady, always looking to him for approval. Why had she needed it so desperately? Why had it not been enough to simply approve of herself? She wondered if Winnie was asking herself the same thing.

"Thanks for talking with me," the girl said after a moment. "You helped a lot."

Marilee shrugged. "That's because I'm older and wiser."

"Definitely older."

Marilee elbowed her. "Not too old to toss you out on your butt if you make any more wisecracks about my age."

"You wouldn't last five minutes without me."

"How do I know when you won't go away?"

Winnie laughed out loud. "Hey, there's chocolate-mint ice cream in the freezer. Might not be enough for two, but plenty for one."

They looked at one another. Marilee jumped from the bed, but not before Winnie grabbed her arm and tried to hold her back. Still grasping her arm, Winnie came up off the bed like an acrobat. "Hey, I'm pregnant! I should be the one to eat it."

Marilee tried to pull free and make for the door, but Winnie blocked her. "You're on a diet!" she told the girl.

"It's low fat." Winnie made it out of the bedroom door, raced down the stairs with Marilee on her heels, trying to grab the tail of her T-shirt to keep her from getting to the refrigerator first.

"That woman is hard to figure," Sam blurted as his mother finished the dinner Marilee had sent over.

Nell looked up from her TV show. "What woman, dear?"

"You know perfectly well what woman."

Nell chuckled. "You know what your problem is, dear? You're used to women throwing themselves at you. Marilee isn't like that."

"She bends over backward for everyone but me," he grumbled.

"Perhaps that's because she knows the rest of us are sincere and don't expect anything in return."

He shot her a dark look. "I'm sincere."

"Of course you are, dear."

He didn't like his mother's tone. "I'm going to bed."

Nell chuckled. "You're going to need your rest, son. I have a feeling you're going to have to jump through hoops if you hope to catch Marilee's attention."

"What makes you think I'd bother?"

"Because she's worth it."


Jack was waiting for Marilee when she arrived for work Tuesday night. As usual, he was dressed impeccably, with not one hair out of place.

"Marilee, I'm glad you're here. I want you to be the first to sample the chef's crab cakes with lobster sauce. He's been playing with the recipe for weeks."

"I'd be honored."

He led her into his office. There, a table had been set for two, complete with fresh flowers and candlelight. Marilee was surprised, then stunned when he dimmed the light. "You've gone to an awful lot of trouble," she said, feeling uneasy with the situation. She had expected him to take her into the kitchen for a taste.

Jack looked embarrassed. "Actually, I was hoping you'd have dinner with me."

"Dinner?" She glanced from him to the table and back to him. "I don't know what to say."

"I feel like I've found a friend in you, Marilee. You seem so...understanding. About Teresa, that is."

"You don't owe me anything for listening, Jack."

"I know. That's the kind of person you are. You're a giver. Most people are takers."

He looked so sad for a moment that Marilee was at a loss

for words. "Jack, I'm sure your wife was a wonderful woman, but you need to move on," she said at last.

"I know. It's just not easy for me. Why don't we sit down?" he said, pulling out a chair for her. "Your dinner is getting cold. I asked Robert to serve everything at once. Hope you don't mind."

"I'm flattered that you invited me," she said. She took her seat and waited for him to join her. "I don't know that I can eat all this." The chef had prepared a Caesar salad, crab cakes with a white sauce, steamed asparagus and garnished new potatoes.

Marilee sighed her immense pleasure when she tasted the lobster sauce.

"This is the best thing I've ever put in my mouth," she said honestly. She tasted the rest of her dinner. Everything was perfect. No wonder the Pickford Inn charged so much.

"Would you like a glass of wine?" Jack asked, holding up a slim bottle.

Marilee chuckled. "I'm afraid I might not be able to sit up straight at the piano if I drank that. I'll just stick with water."

Jack filled his glass. "Tell me about yourself, Marilee."

She looked up quickly. "I'm afraid there's not much to tell. My life is rather...uneventful."

"Have you ever been married? You didn't specify your marital status on your application. Or is that too personal for me to ask?"

Marilee hesitated. "I'm in the process of a divorce."

"I'm sorry to hear that. Do you have children?"

"A fifteen-year-old son. He's presently living with his father."

"That must be hard for you."

"It is, but I try to stay busy so I won't think about it as much." She told him about her other job. Jack was a good listener and before long she found herself telling him about Grady and LaFonda and how Josh had refused to speak to her when she'd gone to his school. She could feel her throat thicken with emotion at the memory of her son's rejection.

"Everybody says my son will come around, but I don't know. Our relationship was strained before the breakup. I think I may have been overprotective."

"You acted out of love and concern."

"I'm afraid I may have pushed him out of my life."

"He's probably confused right now. And maybe a little angry. I hope you have a good support system. I joined a grief group after Teresa died. I think that's the only thing that pulled me through."

She told him about Clara, Ruby and Winnie.

"Good friends are hard to find."

Marilee decided a change of subject was in order. She didn't need to think about Josh and get depressed when she needed to be at her best. She asked Jack about the restaurant business, and he seemed eager to discuss it. She was surprised with how open he was. Finally, she glanced at the clock behind his desk and noted the time. "I'd better get to work." He immediately stood and pulled out her chair.

"Thanks again for joining me."

"Thank you for asking." As Marilee made her way to the ladies' room to wash up and freshen her lipstick, she couldn't help wondering why Jack had invited her, of all people, to join him. A man like that would have no trouble finding female companionship.

Gertie walked into the rest room as Marilee was finishing up. "Heard you and the boss dined together this evening."

Marilee blushed. She had not thought that a simple dinner would create gossip among the staff. "He was just being nice."

The waitress shrugged as she made for the door. "It's none of my business. I'd better check on my customers."

Marilee stood there for a moment, wondering if Gertie was angry with her. Did the waitress have feelings for Jack? If so, Marilee needed to assure her that she had no romantic interest in the man.

Marilee opened with Jack's song, and then played several of her favorites as requests filtered in. She was somewhat disturbed with Gertie's comments in the ladies' room, especially since the woman had been so friendly to her before. Marilee resolved to clarify her relationship with Jack as soon as she could. Not that Jack wasn't both handsome and charming enough, mind you. Just not handsome in a Sam Brewer sort of way. Sam was tight jeans and rippling muscle; Jack had the looks of a movie star. But as the evening wore on and Gertie became more distant, Marilee wished she'd never agreed to have dinner with him in the first place.

# *Eight*

"Okay, the first order of business today is that our new friend, Nell Brewer, wishes to become a committee member for Blessing Home," Clara said as they sat around Marilee's kitchen table the following Saturday. "All those in favor—"

"I'm so nervous," Nell blurted.

"Don't be nervous," Winnie said, glancing over her shoulder from the kitchen sink. "This group is desperate. All of the other members have quit on them."

Clara looked perturbed. "Winnie, please. We're trying to vote."

"Well, Nell has my vote, for what it's worth," the girl responded.

"You're not part of the committee," Clara pointed out.

The girl gave a snort. "There goes my reason for living."

Clara sighed and tapped her gavel on the coaster Marilee had provided. "Let's get back to business, ladies. All those in favor of having Nell join our committee say aye."

"Aye!" Ruby and Marilee said in unison.

"Aye," said Clara. "Let the record show it's unanimous."

Marilee made a note in her binder. "Welcome aboard, Nell."

The older woman shivered in delight. "I'm so excited. To think at my age I can still make a contribution to the community. That's a wonderful feeling. I can't wait to see the look on Sam's face when I tell him."

"We're proud to have you," Ruby replied.

"Welcome, Nell," Clara said, offering her hand. They

shook. "Now then, let's call the meeting to order." Once again, she tapped her gavel. "The question before us is whether to hold a white elephant sale to benefit Blessing Home."

"I can probably get us in the VFW hall," Ruby said, who often attended functions at the Veterans of Foreign Wars hall.

"I was getting to that," Clara replied, "but first we have to vote on whether or not to have the white elephant sale to begin with."

"Clara, do you have to do everything by the book?"

Clara ignored her. "Everyone in favor of having a white elephant sale to benefit Blessing Home, say aye."

"Aye," they said in unison.

"Okay, then." Clara tapped her gavel. "Once again, we have a unanimous vote."

Ruby raised her hand. "My question is where are we going to find people willing to donate to our sale? Marilee has already called about a zillion people, and nobody seems interested in helping us."

They looked at one another.

"I can talk to the ladies at my church," Nell said.

Marilee pondered the problem for a moment. "You know, it's easier for people to say no over the telephone. I think we should approach them in person. I can visit a couple of businesses on my lunch hour."

Clara tapped her pencil on her notepad. "I can talk to my editor friend at the *Gazette* once we're ready. She'll give us plenty of coverage."

"And I'll talk to my customers," Ruby said.

They discussed the matter over another cup of coffee. Once everyone was assigned a certain duty, Clara called the meeting to an end. She turned her attention to Marilee. "You look tired."

"She should be tired," Winnie said. "The woman works around the clock."

Marilee waved the remark aside. "I'm not the first person

to hold down two jobs. Besides, Winnie takes good care of me.''

"How do you like working at the Pickford Inn?'' Ruby asked.

"I like it, and the money is good.'' She told them about Jack.

Ruby made a face. "Now, don't you go getting involved in somebody else's problems,'' she said. "If he's still grieving over his wife after ten years, he needs counseling.''

"He's so sad,'' Marilee said.

"Ruby's right,'' Clara said. "It's not your problem. I know how you are, Marilee. You need to stay out of it.''

"That's what I told her,'' Winnie said. "Man needs a shrink.''

Marilee looked at them. "Don't get involved? I shudder to think where I'd be right now if I didn't have all of you.''

"That's different,'' Clara pointed out. "We're your friends. Surely this man has *someone* he can talk to.'' She pursed her lips. "People gravitate toward you because...well, because you have that look about you.''

Winnie grunted. "Yeah, sucker.''

Marilee shot her a look. "Okay, I'll stay out of it.'' But she knew that wasn't likely.

"How old is this man, anyway?'' Ruby asked.

Marilee shrugged. "Forty-something.''

"Uh-huh. Has it ever occurred to you the man is trying to hit on you?'' Marilee appeared shocked. Ruby mocked her expression. "Oh, is that so surprising? Have you glanced at yourself in the mirror lately? I swear, Marilee, you are so naive.''

"That's not the way it is between Jack and me. I tell you, the man is inconsolable.''

"Nothing that a little poontang wouldn't cure, I'll bet,'' Winnie replied.

Ruby laughed out loud and Marilee blushed as Nell tried to hide her smile behind her coffee cup.

Clara gasped. "Winnifred Frye, I'm not believing my own ears!''

"Okay, I'll shut up."

Marilee made a mental note not to discuss Jack with the girls in the future.

"Still no word from Josh?" Ruby asked.

"Nothing."

"Why don't you call him?" Clara suggested. "It's Saturday. He's probably home."

Marilee had not even thought of calling. "What if he refuses to talk to me?"

"Only one way to find out," Ruby said. "You won't get anywhere unless you try."

Nell clasped her hands together and regarded the group. "Marilee has a right to feel cautious. She's been badly hurt."

The group was silent as they pondered the dilemma.

"I don't believe this," Winnie said. "Just pick up the dang phone and call. I'll look up the number." She reached into a cabinet for the telephone book. "Now, what name should I look under?"

"Her last name is Bonaire," Marilee said, spelling it out for Winnie. "First name LaFonda."

"And if you can't find it under that, try town slut," Ruby said, earning a dark look from Clara.

"Okay, here it is." Winnie picked up the phone and stretched the cord out so Marilee could reach it.

"My palms are sweating," Marilee said. The women waited breathlessly as Winnie dialed. She waited. Grady answered on the third ring. Marilee's mouth went dry. "Grady, this is Marilee. May I speak with Josh?"

"He isn't here right now, Marilee. I'm sorry."

He should be sorry, she thought. Sorry for ruining their lives. "Do you know when to expect him?" she said, keeping all emotion out of her voice.

"No, but I'll ask him to call as soon as he gets in. How are you?"

Her heart pounded in her chest. "I'm fine. Considering." She noted the girls listening intently. "Naturally, I'm concerned about our son."

"He's fine. Still doesn't like to be told what to do. You know, teenager stuff."

"No, I wouldn't know. I haven't seen Josh since you moved him into that…that woman's home."

Grady sighed. "I've been wanting to call, Marilee, but I didn't know if you'd talk to me. I can't tell you how many times I've picked up the phone, only to put it back down because I was afraid calling would make matters worse."

"How could things be any worse, Grady?"

"I think getting lawyers involved is going to make them much worse. I was sort of hoping we could wait on that…you know, see what happens?"

"You mean wait and see if things work out with your girlfriend? And if they don't? What then, Grady? Do you expect me to take you back?"

There was silence on his end.

"Is that what you think?" she demanded.

"Marilee, I don't want to argue with you. I just think you're being hasty hiring a divorce lawyer."

"I don't wish to discuss this further," she said. "I suggest you have your attorney contact mine if you have anything to say on the matter. In the meantime, please ask Josh to return my call."

She handed the phone back to Winnie, who slammed it down on the receiver.

"Good for you, Marilee," Ruby said.

Nell and Clara looked concerned. "Are you okay, dear?" the older woman asked.

Marilee took a deep breath. She was trembling. "I will be in a minute. It's just that I haven't talked to Grady since all this happened."

"He's trash," Winnie said.

Clara patted Marilee's hand. "Josh will call. He's probably over his mad spell by now."

Marilee wasn't so sure.

Winnie sighed. "I guess this means we won't be leaving the house today. And the newspaper is full of garage sales."

"I'll run you over to a couple of them," Ruby offered.

Winnie looked pleased. "Thanks, Ruby. Hey, did I show y'all the bassinet Marilee bought me last week?" She hurried upstairs for it. When she came down she was beaming. "Marilee and I spray painted it. Looks brand-new."

The women made a fuss over it. "I can't wait," Nell said. "It's going to be so exciting having a baby around."

"And I just started my sixth month," Winnie said. "Do I look pregnant?" She offered them a side view and everyone laughed.

"Either that, or you swallowed an eighteen-wheeler," Ruby said. "Does the baby kick much?"

"All the time."

"Winnie swears it's a girl," Marilee said. "All we've bought are girl's clothes."

"Have you come up with a name?" Nell asked.

"I'm working on it. I don't want to give her just any old name. It has to be special."

Once the women left, Marilee spent the rest of the morning trying to find something to do. Leave it to Winnie to keep everything in such good order, she thought, including the laundry and ironing. Marilee sat at the kitchen table, studying the room's outdated wallpaper. If only she could afford to replace it. That wasn't in her budget, though, so she would have to leave it for now.

She watched the clock. Winnie returned with a few items, announcing everything had been picked through. "Has he called?"

Marilee shook her head. "Well, it's time for me to get ready for work."

Winnie looked sad for her. "I wish there was something I could do."

"Thanks, honey, but it's up to Josh now."


The next morning, Marilee climbed the stairs and went into one of the guest rooms, the spare Josh would occupy if he rejoined her. The drab olive walls and ugly drapes weren't the least bit welcoming, and she couldn't imagine her son sleeping in the room. Of course, she couldn't imagine him sleeping in LaFonda Bonaire's mobile home either. She pushed the thought aside.

"What are you doing?" Winnie asked.

Marilee hadn't heard her come up. "Thinking I should redecorate this room."

"For Josh?"

"Uh-huh." Marilee tried to gauge the girl's reaction, but there was none.

Winnie looked around. "First thing we need to do is burn those drapes. They are ug-a-lee!"

"My mother got them on sale."

"Sometimes it's best to walk right past those clearance tables."

"There's enough dust in here to choke a horse."

"We can handle dust. Just not the drapes."

Looking around the room, Marilee wondered where to begin.

Winnie placed her hand on her hips. "You going to just stand there like a bump on a log or do you plan to help me with this new renovation project of yours?" She reached for the drapes.

"You really feel like helping?"

"I'm here, aren't I?"

They went to work. The drapes hit the floor with a big whoosh, sending dust everywhere. They carried them to the garage and stuffed them into black garbage bags. In the utility room, Marilee grabbed a bucket of cleaning supplies, and Winnie followed her upstairs with the broom and mop. The venetian blinds were old and ended up in a garbage bag beside the drapes. Winnie opened the windows and began sweeping cobwebs from the ceiling while Marilee emptied the closet, carrying everything to the attic. She would have to go through it later. The two women stripped the beds, scrubbed walls and woodwork, swept and mopped, and in two hours the bedroom was spotless. Marilee scanned the room to make sure they'd gotten everything. She suddenly caught a glimpse of herself in the mirror and chuckled.

"Look at me, I'm a mess."

Winnie joined her in front of the mirror. "So am I. Only thing, it shows up more on you 'cause you're white." She chuckled. "Hey, we make quite a pair, don't we? You a skinny little white woman, me a big fat black woman."

"You're not fat, you're pregnant. I was as big as a barn when I carried Josh."

"I'll bet you were beautiful, just the same."

"So are you!"

Winnie looked at her. "I know what I am, Marilee. Nobody's ever going to crown me beauty queen."

Marilee felt sad for the girl, although she knew it was the last thing Winnie wanted. "Has anyone ever told you anything nice about yourself? How pretty your skin and hair are? How cute your dimples are? Or how you light up a room with your smile?"

Winnie made a sound of disgust. "Yeah, one guy did, and I was so glad to hear it I climbed in the sack with him. End of story."

Marilee suddenly felt depressed. Why hadn't someone taken the time to tell the girl how special she was? "No, Winnie, it's just the beginning."

The girl didn't speak for a minute. When she looked up, she frowned. "Don't tell me you're going to cry. You know how I hate that. It's not good for the baby."

"I am *not* crying."

Winnie grabbed a paper towel from her pocket. "Tell it to this sheet of Bounty."

Half an hour later, Marilee and Winnie had both showered and scrubbed themselves free of grime and dust. Marilee had climbed into her old sweats and Winnie had donned her maternity jeans and an oversize jersey. They stood before the refrigerator, staring inside.

"We really need to do something with this hamburger meat," Winnie said. "I was going to make spaghetti sauce but somebody talked me into scrubbing walls instead."

"You volunteered."

"Whatever."

"Let's cook it on the grill outside," Marilee suggested. "We need fresh air after being stuck in this house all day."

Marilee headed for the garage. There she found her father's barbecue grill covered in plastic. It looked new, as if her parents had seldom used it. She rolled it to the backyard and returned for the charcoal and lighter fluid. When Winnie carried the hamburger patties out, she found Marilee trying to start a fire.

"What's wrong?"

"The charcoal must be old. It won't ignite."

Winnie put the plate down and gathered sticks and pine straw, piling them on top of the charcoal. She poured a heavy dose of lighter fluid on it, struck a match, and a flame shot up. It died within seconds. Marilee gathered more sticks while Winnie poured the entire can of lighter fluid on it. Nothing. Winnie tossed the almost empty pack of matches into the grill.

"Well, this is a bust," the girl said. "How long has this stuff been sitting in the garage anyway?"

Marilee shrugged. "Not much telling. Looks like we're going to have to cook the burgers in a skillet."

Inside, Marilee put the hamburgers on while Winnie sliced a tomato and onion and washed several leaves of lettuce. "These taste great," Winnie said after biting into hers. "Not like those flat, scrawny burgers you get at the fast-food restaurants."

"Homemade burgers are best," Marilee agreed. "Josh used to love it when I cooked them." She muttered a sound of disgust. "I wonder if LaFonda cooks for him."

"Don't even go there, Marilee."

They finished the rest of their meal in silence. Marilee felt tired and out of sorts. She insisted on cleaning the kitchen and Winnie didn't argue, since she had to study for an exam. The girl climbed the stairs slowly, and Marilee heard the door close to her bedroom a moment later.

By eight o'clock Marilee had cleaned the kitchen and mopped it, and straightened the living room. She decided to make hot chocolate, then made a second cup and carried it upstairs to Winnie's room. She knocked on the door lightly. When there was no answer, she peeked inside and found Winnie already asleep, the algebra book on the bed beside her. Marilee closed the door and tiptoed downstairs.

She sat down at the kitchen table and sipped her chocolate, making a list of the businesses she would call on that week on behalf of Blessing Home. The more Marilee thought about it, the more annoyed she became that she literally had to beg people in Chickpea to help with the project. Oh, they'd been more than happy when the old courthouse and city hall building had been restored, even when a portion of the costs had come out of their pockets. They didn't want eyesores in the town and they were mighty proud of their square. The merchants hadn't minded spending money having the fronts of their buildings painted to resemble Rainbow Row along the Charleston Battery. They wanted to make the downtown attractive, so they could draw people away from the strip-shopping centers.

Those same people thought it was important that the garden club kept the flower beds tended. The historic society had no problems getting funds to renovate the old homes along Main Street, so tourists would make it a point to revisit and spend their money. But nobody cared about a group of unwed mothers, or how they were forced to live in a house where the plumbing and wiring were worthless and the house itself unsafe.

No, she wasn't just annoyed, she was mad as hell.

She was madder still that Josh hadn't called. Either Grady was pouting because she hadn't agreed to hold off on the divorce, or Josh was still punishing her for…for only heaven knew what.

The pencil snapped in her hand, and Marilee jumped. She hadn't realized how tightly she was squeezing it. In a fit of temper, she threw it across the room.

A noise outside startled her so badly Marilee knocked her hot chocolate over and it spilled across her papers. Dammit, dammit, dammit! She hated to curse, but really, she was at her limit. What now? She jumped from her chair and ran to the door, then gasped at the sight. Her barbecue grill was engulfed in flames. She wrenched the door open and found Sam dragging her garden hose toward the grill.

Marilee stood on the back stoop for a few seconds as Sam sprayed water on the fire. "Do you have a fire extinguisher?" he called out. She ran inside for it, suddenly realizing she had a splitting headache. Outside, Sam grabbed it from her and smothered the grill in white foam.

With the fire out, he stepped back and looked at her, breathing hard from the exertion. "What the hell were you trying to do, set the house on fire?"

Marilee gritted her teeth as she cut off the spigot. That sounded like something Grady would say. And here she had not thought her mood could worsen. She turned and planted her hands on her hips. "Yes, Sam, that's *exactly* what I was trying to do. Burn the damn house to the ground with Winnie and her unborn child sleeping upstairs. But *you* had to come along and stop me."

He arched both eyebrows. "Testy tonight, are we?"

She glared in response.

Sam tried a different approach. "Marilee, you should never leave a grill unattended."

She remembered his last visit to her house and became angrier. "Stop talking to me as if I were a child."

What the hell was wrong with her tonight? Sam wondered. He felt his hackles rise, but said nothing. Picking up the can of lighter fluid, he shook it. "It's empty."

"That's because we used it all." She had the sheer pleasure of seeing him gape in astonishment.

"You used an entire can to build one fire? Jesus, Marilee."

That did it! She stepped closer and pointed a finger in his face. "Do *not* use the Lord's name in vain in my backyard! I won't allow it, do you hear me?" Marilee didn't even realize she was shouting.

Sam glared back at her. She was beginning to piss him off. Here he'd been minding his own business, taking out the trash, only to find a fire blazing in her yard. He tossed the can to the ground so hard it bounced several times before coming to a rest beside a stack of burned twigs. "Gee, I'm sorry I tried to help," he said, his voice filled with sarcasm. "I should have called the fire department and let them stick you with a bill."

"And that's another thing. Stop trying to rescue me!"

"Someone has to look out for you. I never know *what* to expect when I come over."

She knew he was referring to the day she'd tried to hang herself, and she thought it sheer tastelessness to throw it in her face. She hitched her chin up and offered him a withering look. "Then why don't you stay away?"

He reacted as though she had just slapped him in the face. He sighed so deeply both shoulders heaved from the effort. "I can't."

Their gazes locked. "That's your problem."

"I'm making it your problem." All at once he reached for her and pulled her against him. She struggled, but he wrapped his arms around her waist and locked his fingers until her thighs were flush with his.

Marilee's look turned from anger to outright shock. "What do you think you're doing?" she cried. "Let me go!"

"Why? Afraid you might feel something for a change?" His voice held both a challenge and an accusation.

"What do *you* know about feelings?"

His handsome features suddenly took on a hard look. "I feel things."

"Yeah, below the belt," she blurted, regretting the words the moment they left her lips. Her face burned with shame. Her only saving grace was the moonless night that hid the extent of her embarrassment. She felt a shudder of humiliation. She had never, ever spoken to a man in such a way, not even Grady, who deserved it.

Instantly, he released her.

Her eyes stung at his reproachful look. "What kind of game are you playing with me?" she demanded. "Do you feel sorry for me, is that it? Poor Marilee Abernathy, whose husband dumped her for a cheap waitress? Or do you get some kind of perverse pleasure out of watching me claw my way through the pain and humiliation so I can try to rebuild my life?''

"I don't feel sorry for you at all," he said, his temper rising.

"Then what, Sam? Are you hoping I'll be so grateful for your attention I'll climb into bed with you?"

He clenched his mouth tight. A long brittle silence hung in the air.

Tears streamed down her cheeks. "Is that why you're working on Blessing Home? Do you even care about those girls, or are you hoping I'll be so appreciative I'll do anything to reciprocate?"

"You're way out of line, Marilee." He backed away. "Tell you what. In the future, put out your own fires." He turned and headed toward his house.

She watched him go, feeling an acute sense of loss. If ever there was a time when she needed a friend, it was now. If ever there was a moment she simply needed to be held, that moment had come.

Marilee wrapped her arms around her waist, trying to shelter herself against the night air as the tears continued to fall, but she couldn't chase away the anguish. A deep despair seemed to have attached itself to every living cell in her body.

Sam was right about one thing. She never wanted to feel again as long as she lived.

Her shoulders sagged as she walked into the house and closed the door.

An hour later, Sam sat on the edge of his bed, still trying to come to terms with all that Marilee had said. She had seen right through him, seen him for what he was—a user and a taker. He had never once done anything for anybody without expecting something in return. While she freely gave of her time and love, he took all he could get his hands on. He *had* been plotting to get her in his bed, no matter what. He had been willing, like an experienced hunter, to approach from any angle. To act like a concerned friend until he learned her vulnerabilities, then go in for the kill. To prey on loneliness or her need to feel worthwhile as a woman.

He knew what women wanted to hear, and he'd used the knowledge to his advantage more than once, without regard to whether it meant hurting them in the end.

Guilt gnawed at him now like a metal claw, hooks grasping the tender lining of his stomach, pulling, pulling. He had always taken because for some reason he felt the world owed him. But owed him for what? he wondered. Losing his father? Thrusting him into the role of an adult before he was ready? Hadn't he gotten past all those old fears and insecurities long ago? Otherwise, why would he have left the rat race in Atlanta and returned home to a simpler life?

It had not been so easy to leave the bad habits behind.

Now he'd blown it with Marilee, the kindest, most decent woman he'd ever known. He had been willing to use her like the rest, but even in her naiveté, she'd managed to find him out. He had not been good enough for her in high school, and he wasn't good enough now. It wasn't about money and success, it was about who and what he was.

Sam leaned forward, propped his elbows on his knees and raked his fingers through his hair. The worst part of it all was that Marilee, the one person he respected most in the world, had looked into his heart and found him lacking.

# Nine

Marilee's knees shook as Tate Radford escorted her inside a conference room two weeks later, where Grady and his attorney, Bruce Hicks, waited. She tried to avoid looking at Grady as the lawyers shook hands and everyone seated themselves around the table, but she felt his gaze on her. Ruby had arrived early that morning to apply Marilee's makeup—not the thick layer she wore to her night job, just something soft for daytime—but the results were more than flattering. Coupled with a new formfitting emerald-green dress that Marilee had found on sale, the total effect was meant to give her confidence and bolster her ego.

"It'll do Grady good to see what he walked away from," Ruby had told her. "He left a class act for trash."

Now Marilee tried to concentrate on what the attorneys were saying. It was their hope that they could settle the matter outside of court, instead of taking it before the judge. Marilee did not have much faith in that happening.

Tate was the first to speak. "Bruce, as I told you over the telephone, my client is suing for adultery, a claim we can substantiate. Mr. Abernathy has been residing with a Miss Bonaire for some weeks now."

Bruce Hicks cleared his voice. "Tate, Mr. Abernathy acknowledges that he and his son are residing in Miss Bonaire's home, but only as paying tenants. Mr. Abernathy has his rent receipts to prove it."

Marilee looked at Grady. "That's a lie and you know it. You clearly stated your feelings for the woman before you left."

"Marilee, if you'd bothered to call me over the past couple of weeks, we could have discussed the situation. Miss Bonaire and I are friends and nothing more." He paused to catch his breath. "When I left, you and I were not getting along, and it was obvious we needed a trial separation. LaFonda has been renting out her spare bedroom for years, and when her tenant moved I saw it as an opportunity for us to spend some time apart and decide what we're going to do about our marriage."

"Everything he's saying is a lie," she told Tate. She turned back to Grady. "Why haven't I seen my son? What hasn't he bothered to contact me?"

"Believe it or not, I've tried to convince Josh to see you, or at least return your calls, but I can't force him." Grady paused. "If it makes you feel better, he doesn't like me either right now."

Hicks cleared his voice again, in an attempt to gain everybody's attention. "If I may continue, before emotions start running high. Mr. Abernathy has no desire to pursue a divorce at this time. He feels he and his wife need more time in order to make a decision of that magnitude. He is asking for a postponement. And for the record, Mr. Abernathy absolutely refuses to agree to a divorce on grounds of adultery, if it comes to that. He hopes to take his rightful place on the pulpit once matters settle down."

"You'll never preach in this town again," Marilee said.

Tate spoke. "My client has no desire to reconcile with her husband. She wants to get this matter over with as quickly as possible. We can prove adultery, Bruce."

"You can prove I'm residing in Ms. Bonaire's home, but you can't prove there's anything going on between us," Grady said.

"As I was saying," Tate continued, "my client simply wants to get on with her life. She is willing to waive her right to alimony and divide the financial obligations and assets right down the middle, but she feels the child's best interests will be served if she retains custody."

Grady looked angry. "Josh doesn't want to see his mother at this time."

Tate ignored him. "My client has hired a child advocate in this matter. In the meantime, she is requesting visitation on Sunday and Monday, and weekly counseling with her son. She's agreed to cover the expenses."

Grady asked to speak with his attorney in private, and the two stepped outside. Tate regarded Marilee. "Are you okay?"

"I'm mad as hell," she managed to say.

If Tate was surprised with her language he didn't show it. "Stay calm, Marilee. Everything is in our favor. I take it you want to proceed with the divorce despite your husband's objections?"

"That's correct."

A few minutes later, Grady and his lawyer returned. "Mr. Abernathy still has no desire to seek a divorce at this time. He is agreeable to a temporary separation, as well as to splitting the assets and financial burdens." He paused and looked at his notes. "I believe the matter of their savings account has already been taken care of. As for your client's request for visitation and counseling, Mr. Abernathy is more than happy to cooperate, but for the moment we both feel the boy should have time to recover from the separation before determining custody. Josh is very confused at the moment and rightfully so."

"I want him out of that woman's house," Marilee said, "and I will do whatever's necessary to get him back. Josh needs guidance, and he's not going to get it living with you and your paramour."

Grady's face reddened. "Once again, you don't know the situation between Ms. Bonaire and me. As for Josh, I can't force him to visit you, Marilee."

"I think it's in your best interests to convince him, if the court orders it," Tate replied.

Hicks took notes. Finally, he spoke. "Mr. Abernathy realizes he can't stop his wife from filing for a divorce, but he will not agree to grant Mrs. Abernathy custody at this time. We have to remember, Josh chose to move from the family residence with his father, and he's old enough to decide.''

Marilee glared at Grady. She suspected he no more wanted Josh with him than LaFonda did, but that this was his way of punishing her for refusing to hold off on the divorce.

Tate began putting his papers in his briefcase. "I think we'll leave the matter of custody in the hands of the child advocate. In the meantime, my client will arrange for counseling.''

Grady was visibly not happy, but finally he nodded.

"Okay, then," Tate said. "I'll have the temporary order typed up and sent to the judge for his signature. We'll be in touch as soon as Marilee is able to secure an appointment with a family counselor.''

Hicks stood. "I'll let the judge know we've reached an agreement.''

They left the conference room a few minutes later. "Feel better?" Tate asked her as they made their way toward his car. He had insisted she ride with him to the courthouse so they could discuss the case on the way.

Marilee shook her head. "I won't rest until I get my son.''

"Be patient, Marilee. These things take time.''

Irby was in his office reading *Mortuary News* when Marilee returned to work. "May I speak with you?" she asked.

He indicated the chair in front of his desk. "How'd court go?"

"We settled everything except for the matter of custody," she said. Marilee told him of her plan to get Josh into counseling. "I'd like to arrange the sessions for when Josh gets out of school, which is around four o'clock. I'll skip my lunch hour in order to make up the time.''

"You don't have to skip lunch, silly. Debbie or I will answer the phone while you're out.''

"Thanks, Irby.''

"Now, why don't you go home? You don't look so good. In fact, if you looked any worse, I'd have to embalm you."

Marilee arrived home twenty minutes later and found Winnie studying at the kitchen table.

"How'd it go?" the girl asked.

Marilee gave her a brief rundown. "I'd like to lie down for a while. I'm beat."

"Good idea. Slip into something more comfortable and take a long nap. You have plenty of time before you have to be at your night job. When you wake up, I'll have a nice dinner waiting for you."

Marilee was too tired to argue. The meeting had drained her. "Thank you, Winnie."


The next day, Sam backed his truck into the receiving area of Felder's Building Supply and cut the engine. He found George Felder in his office, looking through invoices. "Hi, George," he called. "I came for the shingles."

George looked up. "Oh, hey there, Sam. The shingles are in the back." He suddenly looked amused. "Word has it you're working on that unwed mothers' home. What's the name of it?"

"Blessing Home."

"I can't believe you let those women talk you into it. How do they plan to pay you? Gonna give you somebody's first-born?" He laughed at his own joke.

"You have three daughters, don't you?" Sam asked.

"That's right. And they're good girls, let me tell you. Their mama raised 'em up Christian-like. They ain't likely to get knocked up like that bunch over there."

"I hope you're never faced with that decision, George. My mother used to say, it's the good girls who get into trouble because they are inexperienced and don't know much about protecting themselves. But you're right. I don't think you have to worry about that happening to your young ladies."

Felder was quiet as he escorted Grady to the back for the boxes of shingles.

Sam returned to his office and found his partner, Bobby, on the phone. Bobby was broad-shouldered and thick around the waist from the cold Budweisers he drank with the other men after work. Although he and Bobby worked well together, Sam seldom joined the guys at quitting time. He found it boring sitting on a bar stool for hours with the same men he worked with all day, and he sure as hell didn't like watching them spend their paychecks on other women when they had wives and children at home. For all his faults, Sam had never once cheated on Shelly.

Bobby was prematurely gray and that, coupled with the leathery look that he'd earned from years of working outdoors, made him look older than he was. He hung up the phone and regarded Sam.

"That was George Felder," he said. "His nose is out of joint 'cause you insinuated his daughters were sluts."

Sam shook his head. "That's bullshit." Sitting at his desk, he riffled through a stack of papers in search of an order for lighting fixtures that hadn't come in.

"What's this I hear about you getting involved in that unwed mothers' home? I walked off that job some weeks back for nonpayment."

Sam looked up. He wasn't accustomed to answering to anyone for his actions.

"The place needs a roof. They've got the money."

Bobby gave a grunt. "That place needs more than a new roof, and those women don't have two nickels to rub together. It's a losing proposition, Sam, and we've got more important things to do. Like that new shopping center you bid on last month. If we land that job we won't have time for that bunch of bleeding hearts."

Sam leaned back in his chair and regarded his partner. Bobby Benson had been his best friend in high school, but the two had lost touch when Sam moved to Atlanta. "I'm doing the work in my spare time. I don't see a problem with that, do you?" His voice held a challenge. As much as he liked Bobby, he wasn't going to take orders from the man. Besides, they were full partners, and the only reason they had a shot at the shopping center was because of Sam's expertise in handling big jobs.

"I reckon you just put me in my place," Bobby said, reaching for a cigar and biting off the tip. He tossed Sam a knowing grin as he lit it. "This got anything to do with the fact that Marilee Abernathy is on the committee?"

"I don't know what you're talking about."

"Like hell you don't. Man, you had it bad for her back in high school."

"That was a long time ago."

"You know she left her husband. He's screwing some waitress from the Tick-Tock. Moved in with her, last I heard, and took their kid with him. Sucks, if you ask me."

"That's the bad thing about small towns," Sam said. "Everybody knows your business before you do." He gave up looking for the order. It was probably stashed in the mountain of paperwork on the floor of his pickup truck. "We need a secretary."

"Won't be able to afford one if you start taking on all this charity work," Bobby chided. "You need to get laid, Brewer, so you'll stop thinking with your dick."

Sam couldn't hide his annoyance. "What I'm thinking is what a shame it is that nobody in this town gives a rat's ass about a group of young women in trouble," he said. "We haul off enough scrap lumber to rebuild the place and never miss a dime."

"Who's going to pay the subs? You expect me to send men out there for nothing? You think this company should pick up the tab?"

"I don't think it should all fall on us, no. But it certainly wouldn't hurt our image if we came up with some of the supplies and donated a little labor." Sam stood and fished his keys out of his pocket. "In the meantime, I'll do what I can, and it won't cost this company a cent." Sam started for the door.

"Hold on, Brewer," Bobby said.

Sam turned.

"You still got a chip on your shoulder, you know that?."

"So I've been told."

"You think if we help this group out a little bit it'll make us look good? A little PR never hurt anyone."

Sam chuckled. "You're right, it wouldn't hurt. Maybe we'll set a precedent for other business owners."

Bobby sucked on his cigar. "Just make sure you don't get involved with Marilee. Women like that usually go back to their husbands. They think it's the right thing to do— Christian duty, and all."

Sam felt a sudden tightness in his gut. "It's really none of my business what Mrs. Abernathy chooses to do with her personal life. I'm just doing a job."

"Yeah, yeah, yeah. This is me you're talking to, pal. You've got something at stake here or you wouldn't be spending your off time over there."

"Remind me to call on you if I ever need a personal reference," Sam said before heading out the door.


Josh spied his father sitting on LaFonda's patio when he climbed from Conway's beat-up Honda and crossed the postage-stamp lawn that had run to seed long ago. "What are you doing home from work so early?" he asked.

Grady paused for a moment, then answered bluntly. "I've been laid off. Business is bad."

Josh slumped into a battered lawn chair beside him. "What will you do now?"

His father sighed. "I haven't figured that out yet. How come you're so late getting home from school?"

"I've got a part-time job detailing cars for a guy. I've been working for him about a week now."

"You didn't tell me."

"You've been preoccupied."

Grady looked away. "I'm sorry I haven't been there for you much lately. I'm under a lot of stress right now. It hasn't helped my blood pressure, I can tell you that."

His dad didn't look the least bit sorry. Josh didn't want to hear about his problems anymore. He started to get up.

"Hold on a minute, son. I need to talk to you."

Josh stiffened. His dad must've gotten a call from school. He wasn't attending regularly. Instead, he hung out with Conway. They'd sort of become friends, although Conway sometimes pissed him off by telling him what to do or teasing him, even in front of others. But Conway had introduced him to a lot of people, and for the first time Josh felt as if he fit in. So if Conway sometimes treated him like a gofer, Josh figured it was a small price to pay for acceptance.

"I need to talk to you about your mother. We met a couple of days ago with our lawyers. She wants you to attend counseling with her. I agreed to it."

Josh shot him an angry look. "You had no right to do that without talking to me first."

"It's out of my hands, Josh. You can fight it all you want, but it's part of the temporary agreement, and the judge will probably issue a court order in the matter. You're scheduled to go to the mental health offices this Monday at four o'clock." Josh opened his mouth to respond, but Grady cut him off. "Don't be difficult, son. I have enough problems."

His dad *always* had problems. "Fine," Josh said angrily. "I'll go because I have to, but I'm not the one who screwed up our lives. Seems to me, you and Mom are the ones who need a shrink." He leaped from the chair and made his way down the road. He began to walk, faster this time, because he knew it was the only way to calm the familiar rage he felt inside.

Marilee awoke at dawn on Monday morning with her heart beating frantically. If everything went according to plan, she would see her son today. *If* Grady did as he promised and delivered the boy as planned and *if* Josh agreed to go. Of course, Grady would more than likely follow through, because it was part of the temporary agreement, but Josh might balk at the idea.

All she could do was hope and pray. In the meantime, she applied her makeup and dressed in a simple skirt and sweater. Though it was flattering, it gave her the maternal look she was hoping for.

Winnie was making her school lunch when Marilee came downstairs. She smiled, trying to hide her worry. "Good morning."

Winnie stuffed her sandwich and a diet drink into a paper sack. "You look nervous."

Marilee wondered how the girl managed to see through her so easily. "A little. But that's to be expected."

"I have something for you," Winnie said, reaching into her book bag. She pulled out something that resembled a large acorn. "It's a buckeye seed. Supposed to bring you luck."

"Thank you, Winnie." Marilee stuck it in the pocket of her skirt. A horn blew out front. Winnie jumped. "Oh, there's the bus." She hurried for the door, juggling books, which was no small feat against her ever-increasing abdomen. "I'll be thinking of you today," she called out.

Marilee opened her mouth to respond, but the girl was gone. She was sipping her coffee in silence when someone knocked on the back door. When she opened the door, there stood Nell.

"I heard about the counseling session you have with your son today. I just dropped by to give you this." She handed Marilee a worn rabbit's foot. "My daddy used to carry it with him everywhere, and said it brought him good luck. Keep it with you."

"Thank you, Nell." Marilee pocketed it. "Would you like a cup of coffee? Believe it or not, I'm running ahead of schedule."

"If you're sure you have time."

Marilee poured her a cup and was about to join her at the table when the doorbell rang. Ruby and Clara hurried in. "We can't stay," Clara said, "but we wanted to stop by and let you know we'll be rooting for you today."

"That's very sweet."

"We brought something for good luck," Ruby said, pulling a crumpled dollar bill out of her purse. "This was the first dollar I made when I opened my business. I keep it taped to the cash register. Even though I've gone through slow times, thanks to that bitch, Martha Grimes, who's always trying to steal my customers, I've managed to keep my bills and staff paid.''

"And I brought you this little cross I keep on my nightstand," Clara said. "I've derived a lot of comfort from it over the years."

Marilee was touched by her friends' thoughtfulness as she stuck the bill and rosary in her skirt pocket. "I couldn't ask for better friends," she said.

The girls bid her farewell, and Marilee rejoined Nell at the table. "Looks like I can't go wrong, with all these good-luck charms."

"I'll be praying for you all day, dear."

"I don't know if it'll do any good," Marilee said wryly. "I haven't set foot in a church since—well, since Grady was asked to leave Chickpea Baptist."

"You'll go back when you're ready."

When it was time for Marilee to leave, Nell offered to straighten the kitchen and lock up. The two women hugged. By the time Marilee stepped out her front door, she felt more confident. All at once, she spied Sam coming up her front walk, and that confidence plummeted to her feet. Marilee felt an unwelcome blush staining her cheeks.

Sam stopped dead in his tracks, his gaze riveted to her face. He couldn't help but notice how pretty and fresh she looked. She managed to appear both professional and very feminine at the same time. "Have you seen my mother?" he asked politely.

Marilee wrestled with her emotions. They had not spoken in weeks. If they happened to be leaving for work or checking their mail at the same time they only nodded. "She's inside."

"Thanks." He started up the steps to her front porch.

"Uh, Sam?"

He paused before turning in her direction. He didn't want to have to look at her and remember the words they'd exchanged the last time they'd seen one another. He didn't want to remember the shame he'd felt that night and afterward. She'd made it plain what she thought of him, and he hadn't thought too highly of himself since.

Finally, reluctantly, he turned. "What is it, Marilee?"

"I'm so very sorry."

Surprise showed on his face. "Why are you sorry? Everything you said about me was right on the money."

"I had no right to say the things I did. You've shown me nothing but kindness. And I'm the last person in the world who needs to judge." She stepped closer. "I was upset about other things that night, and I lashed out at you."

He offered her a tender smile. "Marilee, I know you've been to hell and back over this business with your husband and son, and if there was something I could do about it, I would have already done it. But you were right about me when you said all those things, and I needed to hear them. They say a true friend won't lie to you."

She smiled self-consciously. "At least you still consider me your friend."

He grinned. "That doesn't mean I'm not going to look at your legs every chance I get."

She chuckled. "Scoundrel."

"Yep."

"Rogue."

"Uh-huh."

But they were both laughing as she made her way to her car.

# *Ten*

The Chickpea Mental Health Center was less than five minutes from the funeral home. Marilee had been told to arrive early so she could fill out the necessary forms. Once she passed them to the receptionist, a lanky, red-haired man came out, introduced himself as Royce Malcolm and invited her back to his office. "I know we talked over the phone, but I'd like to look over the forms to refresh my memory." As he read, he nodded thoughtfully. "Looks like you've had quite a time of it," he said. "What do you hope to accomplish today with your son?"

Marilee fidgeted with her hands. "I want to mend our relationship and get him out of his present surroundings. I want him with me so I can offer a stable, loving home."

"Don't be too disappointed if it doesn't all happen in one session, Marilee. We're just testing the waters today."

"I don't even know if he's going to show up, Mr. Malcolm."

"Call me Royce." The phone rang and he answered it. When he hung up, he smiled. "Your son is here. Are you ready for me to bring him back?"

All at once it seemed as though the air had been sucked from Marilee's lungs. She took a deep breath. "Yes."

Royce got up. "I'll be right back."

Marilee noted the changes in Josh the minute he stepped into the room. "You've lost weight," she said. "Aren't you eating?"

He just looked at her, and she could sense his anger. He obviously didn't want to be there.

Royce pointed to a chair. "Have a seat, Josh."

Josh sat down. "Will this take long?" he asked Royce. "My dad's waiting for me in the parking lot."

"I'm sure your dad won't mind waiting," the counselor said.

Josh sank farther down in his seat.

Royce looked from Josh to Marilee and back to Josh. "Your mother has asked that we meet once a week because she thinks the two of you should work out whatever problems exist in your relationship."

Josh didn't respond.

"I know the past weeks haven't been easy for anyone concerned," Royce went on, "so we thought it might be a good idea to talk about it."

The boy grimaced but remained silent.

"I couldn't help noticing you became a little angry when you first walked into the room," Royce said. "Would you mind telling me why?"

"She asked if I was eating. If I wasn't eating I'd be dead."

"Have you lost a significant amount of weight?" the man asked him.

Josh shrugged. "A little, I guess. I haven't weighed myself."

Royce turned to Marilee with a question in his eyes. She cleared her throat. "He looks to be down about fifteen or twenty pounds. I'm concerned about his health."

Royce looked at Josh. "That's a significant amount of weight to lose in a matter of weeks."

"I walk a lot."

"Walking is a great form of exercise," Royce said, "and it reduces stress, so there are a lot of other benefits other than weight loss."

Josh looked at him coldly. "Is that why you called me here today? To discuss my weight?"

Marilee was embarrassed by her son's behavior, but she remained quiet. She assumed Royce was accustomed to dealing with angry teenagers.

"I think your physical health is important," the man said. "Especially now." Silence. "Josh, your mother requested counseling—"

"Requested?" the boy interrupted. "My dad said I had no choice. I don't want to be here."

Royce nodded. "What *do* you want?"

"I want to be left alone. I'm sick and tired of adults telling me what to do when they can't even take care of their own lives."

Marilee was shaking. "Why are you so angry with me?"

He glared at her. "Because you screwed up everything! Dad was sick, and all you did was nag him."

"I was trying to help him."

"Oh, you helped all right. Look where he is now."

"I am not responsible for your father's actions."

"And you're not going to take responsibility for what you did to chase him away, I guess. Now he's sick and out of a job." Josh looked at Royce. "I'm tired of answering questions. I showed up like I was supposed to, but I have nothing else to say."

Marilee realized she'd made a mistake by demanding Josh come for counseling. "Let him go," she told Royce.

Josh started to get up, but the counselor stopped him. "You can leave," he said, "but we have another appointment next week. Same time, same place."

Josh made a sound of disgust and left the room. Marilee was crushed.

Royce looked at her. "Try not to take it too hard."

"He blames me for everything."

"He has a right to be angry, Marilee. His life has been turned upside down, and he's looking for a place to put the blame. He's not thinking rationally, but people seldom do when they're upset. Josh is still a kid." He offered her a kind smile. "Don't lose hope."

Marilee gripped the arms of her chair, trying to absorb some of what Royce was saying. At the moment, she wasn't sure how long she could hold on. It felt as though her son had just walked out of her life—for the second time.

* * *

Sam had been pacing the floor all evening. His mother had told him about Marilee's counseling session with Josh. Nell had tried to reach Marilee by phone, but Winnie had confided the session had gone badly, and she was giving Marilee a little space.

When Sam spied her sitting on her back steps as he was taking out the garbage, he decided she had suffered alone long enough. He walked over and sat beside her. She stared straight ahead, her eyes red and puffy from crying. "Bad day?" he asked.

She nodded wordlessly.

"You can't expect a lot just from one session, Marilee."

"My son despises me," she said, trying to talk past the lump in her throat.

"Maybe." He sat there for a moment. "I hated my mother for a while after my father died."

Marilee looked at him. "Why?"

He didn't answer right away. "I've never told anybody this. I'm ashamed to admit it even now, but at the time I secretly wished she had been the one to die instead of him." He shook his head. "I still can't believe I felt that way."

"You were closer to your father?"

"Yeah. And Mom was so needy after he died. It seemed as if she couldn't do even the simplest things for herself. I suppose I was so consumed with grief I couldn't see how badly she was hurting."

"How long were you angry with her?"

"I don't remember, but I got over it after a while. Living with her gets on my nerves sometimes, because she thinks I'm still a kid. I want to buy us a bigger place so I can have more privacy, but change isn't easy for her."

"It seldom is for older people." Marilee thought about the changes in her own life, and the stress it had caused her. "I suppose the same can be said for everyone."

They were quiet for a moment. Sam glanced at her from time to time, thinking how utterly lovely she looked in the soft pool of light that spilled through the kitchen door. Watching her, he could see she was in pain. In the past, he'd always been able to distance himself from other people's problems, but with Marilee it was different. He hated watching her suffer, and he would gladly have taken it on himself rather than have her go through it. He wished he could hold her, kiss away the tears. Hell, he wished he could wave a magic wand, and her life would suddenly take a turn for the best.

Marilee swiped at a tear self-consciously. "Seems all I do these days is cry," she said.

Unable to resist touching her, Sam put his arm around her and pulled her close. He felt her stiffen, but after a few seconds, she relaxed against him. Finally, she buried her face against his throat. He knew it had not been easy for her to let down her guard like that, so he just held her quietly as she told him about her session with Josh.

Finally, Marilee raised her head, and their gazes met. "Thank you for listening."

Sam studied her beneath the porch light. She had never appeared more vulnerable. She made him think of the porcelain doll his mother kept in a glass enclosure because it was so fragile. It had belonged to his grandmother. As a child, he'd longed to take it out, touch the satin dress, stroke the black hair and trace the bone-white limbs with his fingertips. But he'd been afraid, knowing he would probably break it with his clumsy hands and now he was afraid to touch Marilee for the same reason.

Then again, Marilee was stronger than she appeared.

He looked away. "You don't have to thank me, Marilee," he said, his voice sounding thick and unsteady in his own ears. "I just…" Sam paused. "I just couldn't bear the thought of you sitting out here all alone at a time like this." He smiled. "I may be the worst kind of scoundrel, but I care what happens to you."

Marilee didn't know how to respond, so she said nothing. They sat there in a companionable silence, Marilee leaning against him, Sam stroking her hair in a comforting gesture as they listened to the night sounds. She could not remember being so tired. Waiting to see her son again and having things turn out so badly in Royce's office had taken a toll.

Time passed and Sam's arm grew numb, but he remained perfectly still as Marilee's steady breathing told him she'd fallen asleep. He suspected rest was exactly what she needed.

Winnie appeared at the back door some time later. "Is she okay?"

Sam nodded, and much to his disappointment, Marilee shifted in his arms and awoke. "Did I fall asleep?" she asked.

"Just for a minute," Sam said.

"Marilee, why don't you come on in and go to bed," Winnie said softly. "It's late."

"Winnie's right," agreed Sam, although he could have sat there all night holding her. "A good night's sleep will do you good."

Still groggy, Marilee nodded. Sam stood and helped her to her feet. "Listen," he said. "You need anything, you call me."

"Thank you, Sam." Going inside, she gave him the closest thing she had to a smile.

As he made his way across the backyard, Sam found himself wondering about the relationship between Marilee and him. Not that he could really call it a relationship, he reminded himself. Yet she trusted him, or she would never have opened up. Nor would she have fallen asleep in his arms. That meant a lot to him, and it was a new experience. He had never taken the time to really know a woman before he went after what he wanted, not even with Shelly. It was sad, considering they'd been married five years. He didn't want to make the same mistakes with Marilee, and he was determined not to push.

That meant giving up control and trusting that if it was meant to be it would happen. The thought was alien to him, Sam was accustomed to *making* things happen. He wondered what it was about Marilee that made him willing to make changes in his own life. He was still pondering that question long after he'd gone to bed. It suddenly wasn't enough that he be worthy in her eyes. Now he simply wanted to be able to look into a mirror for once and feel good about himself.

Things were tense at the funeral home the next morning when Marilee arrived. Irby did not seem his usual jovial self; in fact, he spent much of his time closed up in his office. Debbie did not appear until after lunch, and Marilee thought she looked depressed.

"How'd things go with Josh yesterday?" she asked.

"We're working on it," Marilee replied, not wanting to dump her problems on Debbie when she obviously had something else on her mind. "Is anything wrong?"

"Irby and I had an argument last night. He says he's tired of all the toys lying around when customers come in, and he's sick of seeing me in a bathrobe with curlers in my hair."

"Irby said all that?" Marilee was shocked. "What did you say?"

"I told him he was the one who wanted a shitload of kids, and I couldn't help it if it took me a little longer to get myself together in the morning." She turned away. "He accused me of looking like a rag mop. Wanted to know why I couldn't keep myself up, like you."

"Oh, I appreciate him dragging me into it," Marilee said. "I have half a mind to go in there and kick his butt right over his shoulders."

The other woman looked miserable. "How do you do it?" she asked. "How do you manage to arrive each morning looking as though you just stepped out of one of those flashy magazines?"

"You're exaggerating. But if I look halfway decent, it's because I don't have four children to contend with each morning, just me," she said, wondering if Debbie or Irby ever stopped long enough to see what they had going for them. They'd been so caught up running a business and raising a family that they had little time for themselves. Marilee had learned that lesson the hard way. She could see the sadness in the woman's eyes, and she wanted to help.

"Look, Debbie, I think it's about time you did a little less around here for everybody else and started doing more for yourself."

Debbie was prevented from answering when Irby stepped into the room. "I have to run by the dry cleaners, Marilee," he said. "There's a morticians' banquet tonight at the Holiday Inn."

Marilee gave him a look that would have killed a Brahma bull.

He turned to Debbie. "I have no idea what time I'll be home. Probably be best if I slept in my office again tonight."

Her smile was tight. "Actually, that sounds like an excellent idea."

Marilee sighed. It was going to be a long day.

Jack was waiting for Marilee when she arrived at work that night. "I hope you haven't eaten dinner."

"I brought a sandwich with me."

"A sandwich for dinner?" he said, frowning.

"I had to work late today. An emergency. I was afraid I wouldn't make it here on time so I fixed something I could bring with me." She wondered if she sounded as weary as she felt. She'd been in the process of cleaning off her desk when a distraught, middle-aged woman came in, accompanied by an EMT. She and her husband had been traveling through Chickpea on a lone highway, when a drunk driver crossed the lane and hit their car head-on, killing the man instantly. While Irby made arrangements to ship the body to her home town, Debbie and Marilee had tried to comfort the new widow, but she was inconsolable. Eventually, Debbie had called her pastor, who insisted the woman stay at his house until her daughter could come for her.

"Here, let me see that." Jack peered into the bag and sniffed. "Tuna fish? Oh, Marilee!"

"I like tuna fish."

"Why eat tuna when you can have chateaubriand? Follow me."

"Jack, I don't think—" Marilee paused just inside his

office. Once again, an elaborate dinner for two had been set up. The man had obviously gone to a lot of trouble.

"Won't you join me?" he asked, pulling out a chair for her.

Marilee was speechless. She finally found her tongue. "Jack, I appreciate all of this, but I don't feel comfortable receiving special treatment. I'm worried the other employees will resent me."

"Nonsense. Now, sit down. I can't have my star singer eating tuna fish, for heaven's sake."

Marilee took the seat he offered. The smells coming from her plate were indeed tempting, despite her not having much of an appetite these days. Winnie claimed she was nothing but skin and bones. She looked up and found Jack watching her curiously.

"I'm due to begin my set in fifteen minutes," she said.

He shrugged. "That's the advantage of dining with the boss. You start when I say you start." At her look of surprise, he went on, "I didn't mean to sound harsh. Surely you know what your presence here has meant to me. I like you, Marilee. You've only been here a short time, but I trust you. I feel I can tell you anything. A friendship like that doesn't come around often."

She was touched by his honesty and gratitude. "Thank you. But this has been a two-way street, you know. You've listened to my problems as well."

"That's what friends are for. Are you sure you won't have a small toast?" He held up a bottle of red wine.

"No, thank you."

"Well, dig in, Marilee, before the food gets cold."

Once she had eaten her fill, Marilee thanked him and excused herself, heading to the ladies' room so she could wash up before taking her place at the piano. Gertie hurried in after her, nodded curtly, checked her hair and washed her hands, then left before Marilee got a chance to speak to her. She shook her head. If it had been a long day, the night was going to be even longer. She was thankful it was her early night.

Luckily, the evening passed quickly, but by the time Marilee clocked out at shortly after ten, she was dragging.

Winnie was already in bed when Marilee arrived home. She went about turning off the lights, when the phone suddenly rang. She answered before it could ring a second time. Irby spoke from the other end.

"Marilee, I've got a big problem and I need your help," he blurted.

"Is it Debbie?" she asked.

"No, no. Debbie and the kids are fine. Something has come up. I'll be there in ten minutes."

The next sound Marilee heard was a dial tone. She stood there for a moment, wondering what could possibly be wrong that Irby had to see her at that hour. After she made a cup of instant coffee, she sat and waited. Time passed and she paced the floor, then decided to wait for Irby on the front porch. Flipping on the porch light, it flickered once and died. Well, she didn't have time to change the bulb right now. She hurried to the driveway when Irby pulled in.

"I need you to take a ride with me," he said without preamble.

"Do you know what time it is?"

"It's an emergency, Marilee." He frowned suddenly. "Why are you wearing that wig? And that sparkly dress?"

Marilee had forgotten how she was dressed. She blushed. "It's a long story." When Irby continued to stare, she went on impatiently. "I play the piano in a supper club in Pickford," she said.

"In a nightclub?"

"Sort of. And if you so much as breathe a word of it, I'll never speak to you again."

He shrugged. "Whatever you say. Just get in the truck, okay? I'll explain on the way."

"Give me a second to lock up." Marilee raced to the house, grabbed her purse and keys, debated whether to leave a note for Winnie, but decided against it. Hopefully she'd be right back. "Okay, what's going on?" she asked, the minute she climbed into Irby's truck.

"Tom Bramley suffered what appeared to be a heart attack tonight," Irby said. "He passed away about an hour ago."

"Mayor Bramley? Oh, I'm so sorry. He was a close friend, wasn't he?" She wondered if that's why he'd come by and insisted she take a ride with him, so he could talk. He and Debbie weren't doing much of that lately.

Irby looked sad. "Yeah. Tom and I go way back." He smiled fondly. "You know, he's the one who dared me to eat that goldfish. Bet me his favorite fishing pole. Anyway, we've been best friends ever since. 'Cept, now he's dead, so I'm fresh out of best friends."

"I'm sorry, Irby," she repeated. "Is there anything I can do?"

"That's why I came by. I need a big favor, Marilee. Can I trust you?"

"Of course."

He swerved close to the yellow line in the road. "Irby, watch where you're going!" she said. "Have you been drinking?"

"I had a couple of beers at the morticians' banquet, but I'm okay."

"Look, you shouldn't be behind the wheel of a car right now."

"I'm fine, Marilee. Just upset."

"You're intoxicated."

"Hell, Marilee, my best friend just died. What do you expect from me? Grab me a beer from the paper bag on the back floorboard, would you?"

Her mouth fell open. "I most certainly will not! Now, I suggest you turn this truck around and take me home. I'll make you a sandwich and a cup of coffee, and we can talk."

"Can't do it, Marilee. We got a job to do."

"What are you talking about?"

"Tom was having an affair. I only found out a couple of weeks ago when we met for lunch. He promised to cut it off, but—" Irby paused, his expression forlorn. "Well, I guess he didn't follow through."

"How do you know?"

"Because he died in his girlfriend's arms tonight. While they were, you know. *Doing it.*"

"What does that have to do with us?" Marilee asked.

"I can't let his wife, Sheila, find out. She's been seriously depressed for a couple of years now. She has some kind of chemical imbalance, and has been seeing a psychiatrist. Then, six months ago, Tom suffered his first heart attack. The woman is a mess, Marilee."

"I'm sorry to hear it, but you still haven't answered my question."

He turned to her. "What I'm about to ask from you is...well, it's against the law."

Marilee blinked several times. "You mean I could be arrested?"

"If we got caught. But we're not going to get caught."

Marilee had lost her patience. "Irby, stop beating around the bush and tell me why I'm here."

"I want you to help me get Tom's body out of his girlfriend's house."

# Eleven

Marilee gaped at him. "Are you out of your mind!" A chill crept up her spine, like a big, ugly spider climbing up her backbone, its hairy feet touching each vertebra as it went. She shuddered. "You don't mean—" She swallowed. "You're not asking me to actually...to...touch...a... body?"

"I've got it all figured out, Marilee," he said quickly. "We'll put Tom in his car and drive him out toward his house, then leave the car on the side of the road so folks'll think he had the heart attack on the way home. If we hurry, we can have it over and done with in an hour." He waited. "Please say you'll help."

Marilee realized she was holding her breath. She released it, and a gush of hot air escaped her lungs. "No way, Irby. I absolutely refuse to go along with this insane plan of yours. Now, take me home this instant!"

"Marilee, please—"

"No!" she shouted. "This is *not* part of my job description, and I'm not going to risk jail time because your friend couldn't keep his pants zipped."

"You're not going to jail. If we get caught, I'll take the rap."

"You've lost it, Irby! You need to seek help. Tonight. Right now."

"Then you give Tom's wife the news, Marilee. Tell her the man she loved died in the process of nailing his mistress."

"Don't try to make *me* feel guilty, Irby Denton! I haven't done anything wrong."

"Yes, but you know the pain and humiliation of having the whole town find out your husband is cheating on you like a dog with a younger woman."

"LaFonda isn't that much younger than me," she cut in.

"Do you want Tom's wife to have to live through the shame you've lived with? To have old women gossiping about her business over lemonade and tea cakes?"

"They are?" Marilee bristled at the thought.

"And have folks snickering behind her back that she wasn't woman enough to please her husband or he wouldn't have been out looking in the first place?"

Marilee felt her cheeks burn with indignation. "It's always the wife's fault, isn't it? Well, maybe I was too *much* woman for Grady, has anyone considered that?"

"You, of all people, should sympathize with Tom's wife, Marilee."

"I don't want to hear any more, Irby," she said, on the verge of tears. "And I refuse to be a part of this crazy scheme. Just call that man who assists you on jobs like this."

"He left earlier this evening to drive that traffic fatality up north."

"Why didn't Tom Bramley's girlfriend call an ambulance, for heaven's sake?" Marilee vaguely realized she was shouting.

"Tom told her to call me. Those were his last words, Marilee. He obviously knew he was about to die." Irby paused. "He also knew I wouldn't give him up."

Marilee covered her face with her hands. "I can't do this, Irby. It's too much, and I'm already on the verge of a nervous breakdown. In fact, I think I'm having it right now."

"I need you, Marilee," he said.

"Irby—" A sob escaped her. She was trembling all over. "You don't understand. I'm scared of dead people."

Irby stared at her. "What?"

"It's a terrible fear I have. A phobia. I just can't touch a dead body.'' There, she'd told him. Let the man fire her. She no longer cared. All she wanted to do was climb beneath the bedcovers and lie in a fetal position. Isn't that what people did when they had a breakdown?

He looked incredulous. ''But how can that be? Your husband was a minister. I would think you've seen your share of dead people.''

''Yes, but I've only touched one, and it frightened me so much I almost threw up in the church parking lot. Ask Clara Goolesby, she'll tell you.'' She shook her head as fresh tears overtook her. ''I can't do it. Go ahead and fire me if you like. I won't need my job, anyway, once I'm committed.'' Poor Josh would have to live with the knowledge his mother was insane. ''Oh, Lord,'' she cried. ''My life is S-H-I-T.''

''You're not having a breakdown, Marilee, and you can't back out on me. I've got no one else.''

She was still crying when they pulled into a neat little subdivision and parked in front of a modest brick house. They sat there for a moment. Finally, Irby reached into the paper sack in the back seat. He opened a beer and handed it to her, then opened one for himself.

''What am I supposed to do with this?''

''Drink it. Fast.''

''I don't drink.''

He pushed the can to her lips. ''You do now.''

Marilee had never touched alcohol in her life. But then, she'd never lost a husband and a son in one day, never been responsible for a young pregnant girl, never worked two jobs to make ends meet, never looked at a man like she did Sam Brewer and she was tired from having to do too many things she'd never done. ''I can't take any more, Irby.''

''Drink the beer, Marilee. It'll calm your nerves.'' As if to show her how to do it, Irby took a hefty swig of his.

Marilee looked at the can. What did it matter at this point? If they were going to drag her away in a straitjacket, she may as well be drunk. Her hands trembled as she put the can to her lips and sipped. She almost gagged. ''This tastes like horse urine!''

"Drink it quickly—that way you won't have time to taste it. It'll stop you from shaking, Marilee."

She took a huge gulp and shuddered.

Irby upended his can and sucked the beer down in a matter of seconds. He crumpled the can in his hand and belched loudly.

Marilee could barely raise the beer she held to her lips, due to her trembling, which had moved from her hands to the rest of her body. She held the can with both hands as she drained it, belching just as loudly as Irby when she finished. "I'm still shaking," she said.

"You're a wreck, Marilee. Probably take a couple of beers to calm you down." He opened another one and handed it to her.

By the time they'd polished off the second beer, Marilee was feeling woozy. "I need to go home, Irby," she said. "I have to pee."

"Not just yet, Marilee," he said, stifling a belch. "We've got to take care of business."

She looked at him. "I've already told you I'm not doing it."

He ignored her as he opened the door, climbed from the truck and came around to Marilee's side. Her door was locked.

"Open the door, Marilee," he said.

"I'm not going inside that house."

Irby took the key from his pocket, unlocked the door and reached for her. She hiccuped and scooted away. He grabbed her wrist and tugged. "Stop acting like a sissy."

"Let me go!" she cried.

He dragged her, kicking and screaming, from the truck. "Would you be quiet?" he said. "You want to wake the whole neighborhood?"

Marilee opened her mouth to scream, and he clamped a hand over it. She bit him.

"Ouch!" Irby jerked his hand away and looked stunned. "You bit me! How could you do that?"

"I'm not going in there!" she hissed. "You can't make me."

"Look at my hand, Marilee. You left teeth marks. How am I going to explain that to Debbie?"

The front door to the house swung open, and a petite brunette in a fuzzy pink bathrobe stepped out. "I thought you'd never get here," she said, dabbing her eyes with a tissue. Marilee stopped struggling with Irby and looked at the woman. She'd obviously been crying a long time; her eyes were almost swollen shut. "He's in the bedroom," she told Irby.

"Let's go, Marilee," Irby said.

"I'm outta here." Marilee turned in the opposite direction.

Irby grasped Marilee around the waist, lifted her slightly and tried to carry her through the front door, but she blocked their entrance, gripping the door frame with both hands. The brunette drew back, a horrified look on her face.

Irby smiled calmly at the woman. "This is my assistant," he said evenly. "It's her first body removal, and she's a little nervous."

"Let me go!" Marilee demanded. "I need to be hospitalized immediately."

Irby managed to get her inside the house. "Which way?" he asked the woman.

"Down the hall. Last door on the left. I, uh, managed to dress him, like you told me to."

"Thank you," Irby said, pulling Marilee toward the hall.

Marilee grabbed an overstuffed chair, thinking it would surely hold, but it wasn't as heavy as it looked. As Irby dragged her, she dragged the chair. Unfortunately, it wouldn't make it through the doorway and finally she had to let go.

In the bedroom, Irby set her down and closed the bedroom door behind them, locking it securely. He was wet with sweat. "Okay, Marilee, I've had enough of this nonsense. Here's the deal. You're going to help me or I'm going to tell everybody in town you're playing the piano in a beer joint.''

Her jaw dropped. She closed it, and her eyes became narrow slits. ''You wouldn't dare.'' She hiccuped again.

''Yes, I would.''

''And risk having me lose my son forever?'' she accused, her fear suddenly overcome by anger. ''That's low, Irby. Real low.''

''Tom was the brother I never had, Marilee.''

Marilee gazed past him, trying to make out Tom Bramley's body, but her vision was screwy because of the two beers she'd drunk. She inched closer. Tom lay on the bed, his hands folded across his chest. He looked as though he were merely asleep. Marilee waited for her heartbeat to resume normalcy. ''I can't believe you'd resort to blackmail.''

''I'm desperate.''

She looked at him. She was past the nervous breakdown stage. Now she felt catatonic. It's going to be okay, she told herself. She would check in to an asylum first thing in the morning and ask for a lobotomy. Hopefully, it would erase all her memory. ''I'm giving you my resignation now.''

''Let's just get this over with.''

He wasn't going to let her out of the bedroom, despite all her attempts to get out of doing what he'd asked. The only thing she had going for her was that she was half-drunk and feeling less fearful. Irby prodded her closer to the bed. ''Wait!'' she cried. ''First, I have to practice touching him.''

''Oh, for crying out loud!''

Marilee took a deep breath, reached down and touched the mayor's hand. The horror of it was unlike anything she'd ever experienced. She snatched her hand away, but it was too late. Marilee was suddenly overcome by a full-blown panic attack. She couldn't breathe, and felt as if a black cloak enveloped her, just like that time in the parking lot with Clara. Gulping in air, faster and faster, her heart raced and she heard a loud buzzing sound. She must be dying, she thought. She turned for the door, ready to run.

Irby grabbed her. "Marilee," he said, shaking her. "Look at me."

His voice sounded as if it was coming at her through a tunnel. "I can't! I'm dying!"

"You're not dying, you're having an anxiety attack! That was the worst of it," he said. "It's all downhill from here."

She stopped struggling. "How do you know?" she demanded.

"You think I haven't been through this?"

She looked at him. It had never occurred to her that Irby, always the jokester, had known this kind of fear. "You have?"

"Hell, yes! Try walking into an embalming room at 2:00 a.m. and finding…" He paused. "I've seen some awful things, Marilee, things I would never want my family or anyone else to see. I know fear inside out."

"What…what did you do?"

"I didn't fight it. You're fighting it, and that's only making it worse."

"I can't touch him again."

"Yes, you can, because I'm going to show you how to get through it. When you're finished, you won't ever have to worry about touching a dead person again." He paused again. "Marilee, do you trust me?"

"No." She saw the hurt look on his face. "Okay, yes."

"Then you have to do exactly as I say. It's the only way."

Some fifteen minutes later they exited the bedroom with Tom's body, Irby having slipped his arms beneath Tom's, and Marilee grasping his ankles. She tried to ignore her terror by listening to Irby's instructions. Still, tears streamed down her cheeks and the blackness felt as if it was about to swallow her up again.

"Just go with the fear," Irby said. "It'll hit you in waves. Feel them?"

She couldn't speak. The waves kept hitting.

"They can't hurt you, Marilee. Don't fight them. This is just practice, like we did in the bedroom. You're in control.

If you want to stop and put Tom's body down, you can do it anytime.''

"It's black...all around me," she managed to say.

"Close your eyes, and you won't know it's black. I'll tell you where to walk.''

She closed her eyes and followed Irby's voice, trying to hear it as her own blood roared in her ears. Let it roar, she thought. It wouldn't kill her. She had practiced touching Tom's face in the bedroom while Irby coached her. It hadn't killed her then, and it wouldn't kill her now.

Hopefully.

Some of the waves had subsided by the time they reached the garage. Together, they managed to get Tom situated on the passenger's side in his car, a Lincoln Continental, which he'd had the foresight to hide in the garage. Marilee stepped back as Irby strapped him in.

"Honey, are you okay?" the brunette asked Marilee.

Marilee could only look at her.

"Okay, that's done," Irby said once the man was secure. He closed the door and checked his wristwatch. "We need to get moving.'' He pulled his keys from his pocket. "I'll drive Tom, and you can follow in my truck. You know how to drive a stick, don't you?''

Marilee shook her head. "No, but I'm a fast learner.''

Irby sighed and banged his head against the dead mayor's car. "It's not as easy as that, Marilee.''

"So you're saying I'm supposed to drive the body," she said dully. She sucked in a deep breath. "Give me the keys.''

He looked surprised—amazed, actually. "Are you sure?''

"After what I've been through tonight, I should be able to assist in the autopsy.''


Sam continued to pace Marilee's kitchen, while Winnie drummed her fingers against the kitchen table. "Are you sure you didn't recognize the man she left with?" he asked.

"I told you, Sam, I never saw his face. It was too dark. I heard Marilee close the door, but by the time I got to the window, they were pulling out." Winnie was wringing her hands. "I'm sorry I woke you. I'm sure Marilee has a perfectly reasonable explanation for going out at this time of night."

Sam could see the girl was worried, and he knew it couldn't be good for the baby. "Of course she does, Winnie. Probably somebody she knows from the church had an illness or death in the family, and they sent for her." Sam hoped he was right, but he still couldn't figure out why Marilee hadn't left Winnie a note in case the girl woke up. He didn't like what he was thinking. Had she put on her wig and slinky dress and gone out looking for fun with some guy? Someone as inexperienced as Marilee might get more than she'd bargained for.

"You look exhausted. Why don't you go back to bed, and I'll wait on the front porch."

"I *am* tired," Winnie admitted, "but you have to promise to wake me when she comes in."

Sam patted her on the shoulder. "I'll wake you if there's a problem," he promised. He watched the girl climb the stairs slowly, as though she carried the weight of the world on her shoulders. One thing was certain; she cared for Marilee as much as he did.

Sam turned out the house lights and made his way to the front porch to wait. It was dark, and he quickly discovered the burned-out porch light. He closed the door and sat in one of the rockers, wanting to be there when she arrived with her "date," just in case the guy tried any funny business. He would give her exactly one hour before he called the police.

In the meantime, he would wait.

Marilee tried to concentrate on Irby's taillights as she followed his pickup down the dark country road, but it was difficult to ignore that there was a dead man beside her. Goose pimples prickled her flesh, and the hairs on the back of her neck stood out straight as a yardstick. Waves of panic hit her now and then, but she didn't fight them. Like Irby had briefly taught her, she simply let them come, like waves in an ocean. She felt them swell all around her and pretended she was floating on a raft beneath a summer sun, seagulls crying in the distance, a breeze ruffling her hair.

She wondered if she'd managed to overcome her phobia. What a relief that would be. Perhaps she wasn't having a nervous breakdown after all. She had simply reached her limit, and who wouldn't after all she'd been through? Her life wasn't really S-H-I-T. She had a lot to be thankful for. One thing was for sure, she was a lot stronger than she used to be. Okay, except for those few minutes when she thought she was losing her mind.

The road seemed to go on forever. They had not passed a single car since leaving the city limits, not that she would expect to at this hour. She'd known Mayor Bramley lived a good distance from town, but she'd had no idea he lived this far out. She wondered what his wife was thinking right now. Was the woman waiting up for her husband?

Marilee remembered the nights she'd waited for Grady to come home. He'd always had a reasonable explanation for where he'd been; someone was either sick or in need of counseling. Not once had she suspected him of cheating on her. She had missed all the signs. When he'd become distant, she had assumed it was stress-related. Had someone told her he was seeing another woman, she would have accused that person of lying. He was a man of God; men like that didn't cheat.

Or so she had thought.

Marilee slid her eyes to the right. Ruby had been right when she said dead people couldn't hurt you. They could give you a bad case of heebie-jeebies, but that was the extent of it. Turning back to the road once more, she did not see the raccoon until he was almost in front of her. She swerved, hit the right shoulder then overcorrected, jerking the steering wheel hard to the left. The car skidded on the gravel road as she tried to keep from running off the road. She braked, and the car gave a jolt. Tom Bramley's body fell against her, his cold limp hand landing on her thigh. Marilee screamed. The next thing she knew, she was in the ditch.

Tom Bramley fell into her lap.

She was still screaming when Irby jerked open her door.

"Marilee, are you okay?" he said, his eyes scanning her, obviously looking for blood.

"Get him off of me!" she screamed. "Get him off!"

Irby crawled across her, shoving Tom Bramley away from her. "Go with the fear, Marilee. Stop fighting it!"

"Screw you, Irby Denton!"

He looked surprised. "It's over, hon," he said. "I'll never ask you to do anything like this again. Here, let me help you out. I'll put Tom behind the steering wheel and strap him in so it'll look real. Here, take your purse."

"I have to use the bathroom."

"Go behind the car."

Marilee's jaw dropped. "Oh, hell, why not?" She'd gotten drunk and probably broken every law in the book by moving a dead body. Peeing in the bushes was nothing. She went behind the car and did her business.

"You ready?" Irby called out after he'd managed to get Tom settled.

"Yes."

Together, they scrambled up the side of the ditch, slipping and sliding on rocks and dirt. Marilee fell several times before they reached the top, but Irby pulled her up each time. They paused to catch their breath.

Irby glanced down at the car. "The lights are still on," he said. "Hopefully, somebody will see them. Let's go."

Marilee followed him to his pickup, idling on the side of the road.

They didn't speak until they were well on their way. As Marilee stared out her window, Irby kept looking at her. "Are you sure you're okay?"

"Don't speak to me," she said.

As though sensing she meant business, he remained quiet the rest of the drive. When he turned in to her subdivision, she unbuckled her seat belt. "Let me out here."

"We're almost at your house."

"I want out *now*." Marilee reached for the door handle. Irby slammed on the brakes, and she fell forward, hitting her head on the dash. Irby winced. "Are you trying to kill me?" she cried. He didn't answer. Grabbing her purse, Marilee climbed from the truck. She slammed the door behind her.

The walk to her house was less than two blocks, but to Marilee it seemed like miles. At some point her ankle had begun to throb. It'd be her luck to have broken the darn thing. Not only that, her head ached, and she didn't know if it was from the beer or banging it against Irby's dashboard. She shuddered again. The streetlights did little to alleviate her state of near hysteria, which she suspected was due to sheer exhaustion. She took deep breaths and continued on.

Marilee was surprised to find the porch light off at her house, then remembered the bulb had burned out earlier. She stumbled up the front walk to her house and hobbled up the steps to her porch. She reached the front door and groped in her purse for her keys.

"'Bout time you came home," a male voice said.

Marilee's heart stopped beating. She opened her mouth to scream, but it never came. A wave of dizziness overtook her, and she fell against the front door. Then, everything went black.

Sam bolted from the rocker and managed to catch Marilee before she hit the porch floor. Had he scared her so badly that he'd caused her to faint? She was limp as a rag doll when he lifted her in his arms. Her skin felt cold and clammy, and she smelled of beer. It wasn't like Marilee to drink, but she had obviously gone out because she was wearing a sequined dress that clung to every curve. Had she passed out? And why had she walked home? Had some jerk become fresh with her?

So many questions, not enough answers.

He shifted her in his arms and reached for the doorknob. Inside, he carried her to the sofa.

"Marilee?" he said gently, at the same time reaching for the switch on the lamp. He turned it on. She was out cold. He shook her. Nothing. Finally, he went into the kitchen for a glass of water. He tossed it in her face, and she came up sputtering.

Marilee blinked several times. "Why'd you do that?" she demanded.

"You fainted. What's wrong? You're white as a ghost, your teeth are chattering and you've been drinking."

She buried her face in her hands. "I can't...talk...about it," came her muffled reply.

"I'm not leaving you until you do. What happened to you?"

"Please—" She swallowed. "May I...have a drink of water?"

Sam hurried into the kitchen once more. He returned with a full glass and handed it to her, but she was trembling so badly she sloshed half over the side. "Here, let me help you." He held the glass to her lips so she could drink from it. "Go slow," he said as she gulped the water down. "Marilee, are you hurt? Do you need to go to the hospital?"

She answered by flopping back on the sofa. "No."

"What happened?" he repeated, this time in a stern voice. As he gazed down at her, noting her dirty dress, another thought occurred. He took a deep, shaky breath. "Were you attacked?" When she didn't answer, he grew more agitated. "Were you—?" He couldn't bring himself to say the word. "I'm calling the police."

She bolted upright. "No! No police."

"Start talking, Marilee," he ordered.

"I was in a car accident," she said quickly.

"A car accident! Are you okay?"

"I just need to clean up." She tried to stand, then cried out.

"You're injured."

"Oh, yes, I forgot. I think I twisted my ankle."

Sam took a closer look. He winced at the bluish tint and the swelling that told him she had indeed twisted it. "You need to have a doctor look at this, Marilee."

"Please—" She raked her hands through her hair. "I'm not up to it right now. Just help me to the bathroom so I can shower. I promise to tell you...everything later."

Sam swept her high in his arms and carried her toward the bathroom. She looked dazed, as if in shock. "I don't like this, Marilee. I think you need to go to the emergency room."

"No doctor. No police. Just hot water."

Sam set her down gently on the toilet and turned toward the bathtub. Once he had the water going, he helped her stand. She was unsteady. "Do you think you can manage?"

"Don't leave me, Sam."

He stood frozen to the spot. "Do you need help getting undressed?"

"Yes."

His stomach took a nosedive as he stepped behind her and reached for the zipper on her dress.

"Don't look," she said. "Please."

She was asking a lot. "Okay." He lowered the zipper and parted the fabric, slipping it off each shoulder, trying not to notice the smooth, porcelain-like skin. He slid it past her hips and let it fall to the floor. Her slip followed. He rolled his eyes and said a silent prayer when he caught sight of her in her bra and panties.

"Please turn around," she said, waiting until he'd done so. Then, grasping his shoulder for support, she slipped out of her underclothes and stepped inside the tub, trying to avoid using her bad ankle as much as possible. She slid the door closed, and checked the water before turning on the shower. She sighed her immense pleasure when the hot spray of water hit her.

"You okay?" Sam asked, feeling awkward.

"For now. Would you stay?"

"I'll stay." Sam couldn't resist looking—he was human

after all—but he could barely make out her form behind the frosted glass.

Marilee stood beneath the water for a long time, scrubbing her skin until it glowed pink. She washed her hair twice, then continued to stand there until the water grew cold. Finally, she turned it off. Sam passed her a towel, and she thanked him.

"There's a bathrobe hanging on the back of the door," she said.

Sam reached for the robe and handed it to her, taking care not to look in her direction, even though he would have given his last dime to do so. He wouldn't risk upsetting her further. "Are you dressed?" he asked.

"Yes. You can turn around now."

He found her wrapped in a white bathrobe, her hair wet and dripping. She reminded him of a lost puppy pulled in from the rain. He took the towel and dried her hair, trying to be as gentle as he could, then found her hairbrush and brushed her hair from her face. Looking at her flawless complexion, he wondered why she bothered with makeup. It was just one of those things men weren't supposed to understand, he decided. Like why women carried purses that resembled carry-on luggage, when men managed to keep everything they needed in their wallets and pockets. He noted the look in her eyes. She was definitely not herself. And she was still trembling. He wondered if she was in shock.

"I want to brush my teeth."

Sam assisted her. "You're trembling. Where would I find a blanket?"

Marilee blinked several times. "Hall closet."

"Stay put." Sam found what he was looking for and returned. He draped the blanket around her shoulders. "Let me help you into the living room."

Marilee insisted on walking, although it was more of a hobble. Once she was seated on the sofa, Sam took a closer look at her ankle. The swelling had not gone down. "I need to put ice on that."

"There should be an ice pack in the freezer."

"I'll be right back." She didn't seem to be listening. "Marilee?" He touched her arm and she jumped. "Don't go anywhere, okay?"

She nodded.

Sam returned with the ice pack. Kneeling before her, he placed it on her ankle, trying to ignore where her bathrobe had parted, showing her leg and thigh. He remembered how she'd looked in her bra and panties, and his gut tensed. He took a moment to get himself under control.

"I know you're upset, Marilee," he said gently, "but you have to talk to me. What's going on? And why were you wearing that dress?"

"I shouldn't say anything."

"I promise it won't go any further." He paused. "You trust me, don't you?"

"Yes." She didn't hesitate with her answer. "Sam, you're not going to believe this." Once she got started, Marilee couldn't stop. She told him about her night job and then paused for a reaction, but Sam said nothing. He sat on the floor in front of her, holding the ice pack to her ankle, listening. She went on to tell him about Irby's late-night call and what they'd done. Sam frowned at that. "So Tom Bramley is dead?"

She nodded. "I have always been terrified of dead people," she confessed. "When his body fell on me I just lost it. I couldn't stop screaming and crying, even though I was half-drunk at the time. I had no business behind the wheel of that car."

Sam's eyebrows arched high. Marilee drunk? At the same time, he tried to keep his emotions at bay, although he would have liked nothing better than to punch her boss in the face. "I can't believe Irby Denton would ask you to do something like that," he said. "I can't believe you went along with it."

"I did because I didn't want Tom's wife to suffer more than she already has. I know the humiliation of having your husband cheat on you." Her eyes misted. "That's why I did it." She paused. "Sam, I thought I was going to have a nervous breakdown."

He propped her ankle on a footstool and positioned the ice pack where it would not fall off. He sat next to her, holding her hand, trying to comfort her as best he could. "You're not having a breakdown, Marilee. I think most people would have reacted as you did, had they been asked to do such a thing."

"I'm just so tired, Sam."

He was surprised when she leaned her head against his shoulder.

"You can't imagine how much better I feel now that I've told you."

He squeezed her hand. "It's going to be okay, Marilee." He sat there, watching her closely. Her eyelids drooped. "Why don't you fall asleep?"

"I'm afraid to close my eyes," she confessed, although she was past exhaustion. "I'm afraid of what I might see."

"Go ahead and close them, Marilee. I won't leave you."

Finally, her eyelids fluttered closed. Sam knew the moment she had fallen asleep because her breathing became slow and steady, and the tense lines left her face. He shifted on the sofa, and she made a small sound as he reached for the lamp switch and turned it off. Holding her for a long time, inhaling her scent, wanting to protect her. She needed him right now, but it was different somehow from the neediness he'd experienced with his mother and ex-wife. In that instant, he realized that he wanted to be there for her always.

He had gone and fallen in love with Marilee Abernathy.

# Twelve

It was almost dawn. Josh was high, his first time ever, and he didn't feel so good. He'd had three beers and smoked a couple of joints at the party he and Conway had just attended. One good thing, though—he felt numb. He didn't have to think or worry or wonder what was going to happen to his life. He'd already saved almost two hundred dollars from his job at Mo Henry's place, so it was only a matter of time before he got out of Chickpea. He and Conway were already talking about moving to a place called Coconut Grove, south of Miami, where the weather was always nice and there were plenty of babes.

*If* Conway didn't change his mind and take someone else. There were times Josh sensed he got on Conway's nerves. Maybe it was because the guy was older and more experienced, but Josh was learning to keep his mouth shut instead of blurting out things that might make him look dumb in front of Conway and his friends. And he hated saying something dumb because Conway had a way of making it worse, thumping him on the head with his thumb and index finger hard enough that it stung the back of Josh's eyes. Worse than that, Conway's buddies always had a good laugh. Josh pretended to laugh, too, but it wasn't funny.

"How you hangin', Josh?" Conway asked as he swerved to miss a pothole in the road. "That was some doobie we smoked back there. You stoned?"

"Yeah." They hit another bump and Josh wondered if the tow truck had shocks on it. Still, it was a ride. Mo had lent them the truck. Seemed he was always doing favors for

Conway. Josh wished Mo would give them something sporty; he had more cars than most dealerships in town. The guy was the coolest. He always had some good-looking woman on his arm, and Conway claimed he had the best pot in town.

Now that Josh was working for Mo, Conway and another guy spent most of their time repainting cars in one of the large barns out back that had been turned into garages, then handed them over to Josh, who cleaned each car inside and out. Josh could do three or four cars on a Saturday and make good money.

"Hey, dude, what's that up ahead?" Conway said, slowing down. "See that light coming from the bushes?" He suddenly looked excited. "Maybe it's a UFO."

"You don't believe in that crap, do you?" Josh asked.

He shot Josh a dark look. "Hell, yeah, I believe in them. What d'you think, we're the only ones on this planet? You need to spend less time jerking off in the shower, man, and get some knowledge in that thick skull of yours."

Josh decided it best to remain quiet as Conway pulled over and parked. They climbed from the truck and stared down at the automobile in the ditch. Josh smiled to himself. Seemed Conway wasn't as knowledgeable as he thought.

"Somebody must've run off the road," he said. "Hey, don't just stand there, dude, grab me a flashlight from the truck."

Josh did as he was told and Conway shone the light on the car. "It's a Lincoln Continental," he said. "Brand spanking new from the looks of it. Let's go down."

Josh followed Conway down the side of the ditch, staggering as he went. He wondered how long it took for pot to wear off. He didn't like the feeling it gave him.

"Somebody paid a pretty penny for this car," Conway said once they got closer. "Doesn't look as though there's any damage that a good buff job wouldn't take care of."

Josh peered inside the window. "Oh, man," he said. "There's someone inside."

Conway shone the light at the window. "Holy shit, I wonder if the dude is injured."

Josh opened the door and shook the man. No movement. He pressed his fingers against his throat. It was cold, and there was no pulse. "He's dead," Josh said.

"Reach over and cut the lights," Conway told him.

Josh tossed him a strange look. "How come?"

"Just do it, man."

Josh turned off the lights. "We need to get to a phone," he said, "and call the EMTs."

Conway looked at him as though he'd lost his mind. "Are you crazy? They'll send the cops, and we'll end up in a detention on DUI charges. Let's take it over to Mo's. He'll know what to do. You think you can drive a Lincoln?"

Josh's eyes widened. "With a dead body in it?"

"We'll put him in the trunk."

Josh took a step back and almost slipped. "You're kidding, right? What if somebody sees me?"

"Do I look like I'm kidding? Besides, nobody is out at this hour of the morning."

The two argued for a minute, which wasn't easy for Josh since he still had a hell of a buzz going. Now he wished he'd never gone to that party. Finally, too high and tired to reason with Conway, he relented. "Okay, I'll drive."

Conway removed the seat belt, and the two of them dragged the body toward the rear of the car. Conway hurried to the front of the car, opened the passenger's door and punched a button in the glove compartment. The trunk popped open. They struggled to get the dead man inside.

Josh shuddered. "I don't like this."

Conway wasn't listening. "I'll back the tow truck closer, attach the cable, and we'll be out of here in no time."

"What if somebody drives by?"

"Like I said, nobody comes down this road this time of night. But if they do, we'll just say we found the car and decided to pull it out of the ditch like good Samaritans."

"What if they find the body in the trunk?"

"We never saw a body, you got that?"

\* \* \*

The sun was barely up by the time the boys pulled in to Mo Henry's place. Conway knocked on the door several times before Mo answered, wearing sweats and a T-shirt. A growth of stubble covered his chin and his thinning hair stood up at all angles. He did not look happy to see them. "What the hell are you doing, waking me at six o'clock in the morning?" the man demanded.

"We've got a car for you, man," Conway said. "A freakin' Lincoln Continental. Found it in a ditch."

Josh looked at Conway. Nothing he said made sense. Everything seemed electrified.

Mo looked past them. "Is it damaged?"

"Some mud and grass stains, that's all."

"Let me have a look." He started down the steps.

"Only one problem, Mo," Conway said. "There's a body in it. We moved it to the trunk."

Mo came to an abrupt halt. "What the hell are you talking about?"

"The guy was dead when we found the car. I figured you'd know what to do with him."

Mo regarded the boys with a look of disgust. "Have you guys got shit for brains? Why would you steal a car with a body in it?"

Josh looked at Conway. Steal? Who said anything about stealing a car?

Conway glanced at Josh, giving him a look that clearly told him to keep his mouth shut. He turned back to Mo. "It's a Lincoln Continental, man. Do you know how much money that would bring in?"

"I don't care if it's a fucking Concorde. I don't need the problems." He shook his head as he walked out to the car. "Pop the trunk."

Josh was growing more confused by the moment. What was going on? His head was swimming and his forehead was damp. He wiped it with an open palm that he dried on his jeans and tried to think, even in his stupor. Now all the puzzle pieces were beginning to fit: the large number of vehicles, the locked barns, the paint jobs, even when the cars didn't need them. Mo was right; he did have shit for brains.

He followed Mo and Conway to the car. Okay, so he'd only worked a couple of Saturdays. How was he supposed to know what was going on? It had never occurred to him that the cars Mo housed in the garage were stolen, and he wasn't smart enough to figure out how they got away with it. No doubt Mo had some sort of system, but Josh had no desire to find out what it was. He just wanted to walk away and never look back.

Mo looked inside the trunk. "I don't believe this," he said, shaking his head. "I've dealt with stupid people before, but you and your sidekick are the dumbest punks I've ever run into. That's what I get for letting schoolboys work for me."

Conway looked sheepish. "Mo, man, I thought you'd be pleased. I mean, we can get rid of the body—"

Mo slapped Conway hard across the face. The boy staggered backward and almost fell to the ground. "Do you know who this guy is?" he demanded.

Josh looked at him.

Conway shook his head. "It was dark. Besides, we didn't want to look."

"It's the freakin' mayor, that's who."

Josh's heart leaped to his throat. "Mayor Bramley?" he asked. He chanced a look in the man's direction, and the color drained from his face. It was the mayor, all right.

Mo slammed the trunk and regarded the boys. "Tell you what I'm going to do. I'm going to give you three seconds to get this car off my property, and if I ever see the two of you again or hear that you've been talking about this, I'm going to shoot you both, drag your bodies into my house and tell the cops you tried to rob me. Do I make myself clear?"

Conway nodded. "So you're firing us?"

Josh just looked at him. His friend had seemed so smart

in the beginning, so cool. "You're dumb as cow shit, Conway," he said.

Conway held his hands in the air as though surrendering. "Okay, we'll get it out of here. Where should we take it?"

"I don't give a damn where you take it. Just get it off my property." Mo looked at Josh. "Keep your mouth shut, kid. I mean it."

Josh nodded. "I've never laid eyes on you or this place."

Mo smiled for the first time. "Good answer. You may live to grow pubic hair." He went inside, leaving the two boys standing there.

Josh was pissed, and it showed. "So, what are we going to do now, Einstein?"

Conway looked scared for the first time. "I need time to think about it. I have a friend close by. We can take the back roads and be there in five minutes. Have breakfast, maybe take a short nap. Then I'll be able to think better."

Josh didn't like the idea of putting it off, but he had sobered up just enough to know they had no business being on the road in their present state. Maybe if they ate and slept it off, they'd figure out a solution. They unhooked the car from the tow truck, got in, and left.

"Well, now, isn't this a pretty sight?" Winnie said the next morning, standing before Sam and Marilee, who were sleeping entwined on the sofa.

Marilee's eyes popped open, and she felt a blush spread across her face. She was half sprawled across Sam's lap, and her bathrobe had climbed up her thighs during the night. "Oh, my Lord!" she said.

Sam opened one eye, took in the situation and smiled. "I tried to fight her off, Winnie, honest I did."

Marilee bolted upright and adjusted her bathrobe. "Sam Brewer, that is not a bit funny. You'll have Winnie thinking the worst."

"Don't go getting into a snit," he said. "She knows I'm teasing."

"What happened to your foot?" Winnie asked.

"She got a little rough with me," Sam said, and chuckled.

Marilee glared at him. "Have you no shame?" She looked at Winnie. "It's a long story."

Hands folded over her ample bosom, Winnie made a *tsking* sound, much like Clara when she was perturbed, but it was obvious she found the whole thing amusing. "You know, you're supposed to be providing a stable, God-fearing home for me. I just can't have you bringing stray men home with you at night. What will the neighbors think?"

Sam smiled. "A woman has needs, Winnie."

"Well, I, for one, am shocked," Winnie said. "Shocked, I tell you. I'll probably have to go in and discuss this with my guidance counselor so it won't traumatize the baby and me. Now, if you'll excuse me, I have a bus to catch. Please try to be more discreet in the future."

Marilee waited until the girl was gone. She glared at Sam. "Now look what you've done!"

He reached for her, grabbed her firmly by the hand and pulled her onto his lap, taking care with her ankle.

Marilee gaped at him. "What do you think you're doing?"

"Shut up, woman, and listen to me," he said.

"Don't tell me to shut up. I don't take orders from anyone, especially a scoundrel like yourself who has bedded half the women in town."

He chuckled. "I don't know where you get your information, Ms. Abernathy, but most of the women in this town are older than my mother. The others are either married or, how should I say it...attractively challenged? Between you and me, I don't see much action."

"It's really none of my business," she said, sniffing primly.

He grinned. He enjoyed getting her riled. "You know, I could change my sorry ways for the right woman."

"She'd have to carry a big gun."

He studied her closely. "Come on, Marilee, I know you're attracted to me. I've seen the way you've looked at me when you thought I wasn't looking."

Marilee's face flamed a bright red. "That is a bold-faced lie, Sam Brewer, and you're out of your mind if you think I'd get mixed up with the likes of you. I've already had one low-down, lying womanizer in my life. Why in heaven's name would I want another?"

A curious half smile played on his lips. "You ever had butterflies, Marilee?" he asked softly.

His question seemed to bring her up short. "Butterflies? What in heaven's name are you talking about?"

"You know, that fluttering in your stomach that happens when you wake up in the morning after a night of good loving."

Marilee's jaw dropped. She tried to get up, but he held her firm. "I don't know where you get off talking to me like that, Sam, but you are being much too familiar. I think it's time you left. Besides, I have a lot on my mind. There's a body out there waiting to be found and—"

Without warning, Sam clasped one hand at the back of her head and pulled her close, planting a solid kiss on her lips. He felt her go still in his arms, and he wondered if he'd gone too far. Perhaps she was just surprised. Stunned was probably more like it. Instead of pulling away, he tried to coax a response from her.

Nothing.

He lifted his head. "Kiss me back, Marilee," he said gently.

"No." The word came out on a gush of hot air.

"Just this once, let go," he said. She gazed at him as though mesmerized while he reclaimed her lips. He was hungry for the taste of her, but he took care not to rush her, knowing she'd only run in the opposite direction. Slowly, he felt her go limp in his arms, felt her head fall back against his shoulder as he continued kissing her. He kissed her forehead, her eyes, and ran his lip across one cheek to her neck. He pressed his mouth against the hollow of her throat. She could pretend she was indifferent, but her racing pulse told him differently.

Sam pulled back only slightly, just long enough to see

that her eyes were closed. She was beautiful. He tasted her once more. Damn, but her lips were soft.

Marilee went very still as Sam captured her lips once more. She could not think straight. All she could do was grasp his shirt with both hands and hang on for dear life.

There were kisses, and then there were *kisses*. She had to admit she liked his brand.

The kiss changed, subtly at first, but as Sam applied more pressure, she found herself kissing him back. Kissing him back! He stroked her bottom lip with his tongue, and she felt something quicken inside. Her stomach, which had been tied in knots for longer than she could remember, suddenly felt warm and liquid, and made her think of what happened to chocolate when you held it in your mouth. Her brain felt as fuzzy as it had the night before when she'd been drunk for the first time ever.

Oh, Marilee, she thought sadly. What had happened to the Christian woman she'd once been? Now she was getting drunk, dumping bodies in ditches and kissing a man who had the worst reputation in town.

All at once, she jerked back.

Sam looked at her, noted the panic in her eyes. Damn, he'd rushed her. "Are you okay?" he asked, mentally chiding himself.

She glanced away quickly. "I don't know." She shook her head. "I don't know what to say...to think."

"Sometimes it's better not to think."

She met his gaze. "I shouldn't be doing this. Sam, I'm still legally married."

"I know you are," he said, "and I know how seriously you take it, even if your husband doesn't. But what we just did wasn't wrong, Marilee. It's not wrong to need simple human affection."

She looked at him. "Is that what that was?"

"Not exactly."

She stared dumbly. "What then?"

He sighed. "Dammit, Marilee, I've had a thing for you since high school. From the first time I laid eyes on you.

But you only had eyes for Grady, the football hero. He screwed up royally when he let you go." He shook his head. "I don't know what to say. Only that I care for you. More than I've ever cared for a woman in my entire life," he added. He looked at her, the expression on his face that of a man who fears he's about to be booted out the door.

Marilee pondered it. "I like you too, Sam, but I'm not foolish enough to jump from one relationship to another. I've been married sixteen years. I know what Grady did was wrong, but that doesn't negate all the years I spent as his wife." She paused. "My whole life has changed. I don't know who I am, or where I belong. I don't know if I'll ever get my son back. I'm certainly in no position to get romantically involved with a man."

"I'm not trying to rush you, Marilee, although I know it seems that way. I couldn't help myself just now." He gazed at her. He just wanted her to tell him he had a chance with her. It was the first time in his life he'd considering begging a woman to care for him, and the experience was humbling. His voice trembled when he spoke. "I'll promise you this, Marilee. If I'm ever lucky enough to win your love, it'll be for keeps. No changing partners midstream."

She sat there for a moment, genuinely touched. "Do you know what that means to me? To hear you say those words after what Grady did to me?" Sam shook his head slightly. "It feels wonderful," she said, "to know you care for me as you do."

He nodded. "But?"

"It's scary."

"Do you think I'm not scared, Marilee? Here I am going out on a limb, and I don't know what's going to happen with you and your husband."

She frowned. "What are you talking about? I'm finished with him."

He took her hand in his. "Things could change, babe. Don't think that doesn't have me worried."

Marilee was prevented from answering when the phone

rang. Picking it up, she listened to the caller for a moment. "Irby. What do you want?"

"Are you okay?" he asked.

"No, I'm not okay. How do you *think* I am, after last night?"

"Please don't shout, Marilee."

"I'll shout if I feel like it."

"Listen, Tom's wife has been calling all morning."

"Imagine that," she said, sarcasm slipping into her voice. "Don't call me again. I don't work for you anymore, remember?" She hung up.

"Good for you," Sam whispered.

She looked at him. "Not really. Now I have to find another job. Do you know anybody who needs someone to bake cakes?"

"Are you strapped for money?" Sam asked, suspecting she would never admit to it, not even to him.

"I'm fine," she said.

The phone rang again. Marilee lifted it from the receiver and let it fall back. "I have to think," she said.

"Why don't we talk over a cup of coffee," Sam suggested. He stood, lifting her in his arms as he did so. She balked. "Hush," he said. "I need to take a look at that ankle."

He carried her into the kitchen and sat her in a chair at the table, taking a moment to check her injury. "It's still swollen," he said, "but not as bad as last night. I'll grab another ice pack from the freezer." Once he'd retrieved it, as well as a couple of paper towels, he wrapped the ice pack and very gently placed it on her ankle. "Sit tight while I make coffee."

"I don't have time to sit," Marilee told him. "I have to act."

"First, we need a plan." He thought about it while he waited for the coffee to finish dripping. Finally, he carried two steaming cups to the table.

"Thank you," Marilee said, hoping the coffee would clear her head. It was bad enough she had to worry about a dead body, a slight hangover and a bad ankle, but now she had the added stress of Sam kissing her senseless. Not to mention the embarrassment she felt for allowing Sam to witness her state of mind the evening before. She looked at him. "I'm sorry I went off the deep end last night. I really lost it there for a while."

"Don't be silly. You had every right to be upset."

Once again, the telephone rang. Marilee hobbled over to it. She was not surprised to find Irby on the other end.

"Marilee, we have to talk. The situation is desperate."

"Tell me, what part of *I quit* do you not understand?"

"You can't quit, I need you."

"You need to be locked up."

"Listen, Debbie thinks I've done something to make you quit."

"Smart woman, that Debbie. Goodbye."

"Wait! I'm willing to give you a substantial raise and a promotion," he said.

"And what will my new title be? Assistant body snatcher?"

"You'll make enough money so you don't have to dress in that silly wig and play in a nightclub."

"It's not a nightclub. Have a good life." She slammed down the phone, and then took it off the hook. Suddenly, she paled. "Oh, no!"

"What is it?"

"My wig! Was I wearing it when I came in last night?"

He shook his head. "Your hair was plastered to your scalp."

"Sam, I've lost my wig."

"You look better without it."

She shook her head. "You don't understand. I was wearing it last night when I helped Irby. It must've fallen off somewhere. Ruby gave it to me. If the police find it, they might be able to trace it to her."

Sam nodded. "You're right, we do have to find it. Could it have fallen off at the girlfriend's house?"

"I don't know. I was pretty upset at the time."

He looked thoughtful. "Here's what we'll do. You follow me out to where you left the car. Once I find it, you drive away, and I'll report the accident on my cell phone. After I look for the wig."

Marilee felt a sense of dread. As much as she didn't want to return to the scene of the accident, she knew it was the only way.

She dressed quickly. Sam decided not to take the time to go home and change clothes, although it was obvious he'd slept in his jeans and shirt; instead, he finger-combed his hair and decided it would have to do for now. He and Marilee had more pressing matters.

They were on their way out the door when a tall man with graying hair came up the front walk. "Excuse me," he said. "Are you Marilee Abernathy?"

Marilee sucked her breath in sharply. He was obviously a detective. She'd been found out. "Are you from the police department?"

The man looked surprised. "No, ma'am. I'm Ed Rogers. Your attorney asked me to do a home study with regard to your son. You were expecting me today, weren't you?"

Marilee felt her stomach tighten and feared she would have another anxiety attack on the spot. The child advocate! Of all times for him to show up. "Uh, no," she managed to say.

"Mr. Radford didn't call you? He's the one who scheduled the appointment."

"I haven't heard from my attorney."

"Have I come at a bad time?"

"Uh, well—"

Sam stuck out his hand. "Mr. Rogers, I'm Sam Brewer, Mrs. Abernathy's neighbor," he added. "Mrs. Abernathy has just learned that a dear friend of hers was in an automobile accident last night. She's too upset to drive so I'm taking her to check on him. We thought you were the police, here to notify us."

Marilee was relieved that Sam had come up with a good story on such short notice.

"I'm sorry to hear about your friend," Rogers said. "Is it serious?"

Marilee realized she was trembling. "I'm afraid so."

"We can certainly reschedule, Mrs. Abernathy." He reached into his pocket for his business card. "Why don't you call me when it's convenient." He turned toward his car.

Marilee and Sam exchanged looks. "Thank you," she whispered.

They waited until the man had pulled out of the driveway and started down the street before climbing into separate vehicles. Marilee's palms were wet as she gripped the steering wheel. She could wring Tate Radford's neck for not calling her, but she couldn't worry about that right now. She had to find her wig and do something about Tom's body.

They had driven a distance when Marilee began to wonder if she would ever find the site. Suddenly, she spied the skid marks she'd made in the gravel the night before, and the flattened weeds on the side of the road. She pulled over and parked.

"This is the place," she told Sam once he'd climbed from his truck and stepped up to her window.

"Okay, I'll have a quick look." He walked over to the side of the ditch and gazed down, looking this way and that. He climbed downward into the ditch and looked around. He saw the wig as he started up.

Marilee sighed her relief when he handed it to her. "Oh, thank goodness."

"I'm afraid I have bad news," Sam said. "The car is gone."

Marilee gaped at him. "What?"

"There's no car and no body."

Marilee climbed from her car and stood at the side of the ditch. She suddenly felt dizzy. "I have to call Irby."

Sam retrieved the cell phone from his truck and handed it to her. She dialed the number to the funeral home. Irby picked up on the first ring. "Oh, Marilee, I'm so glad you called. You wouldn't believe what's happened. Debbie's leaving me. She thinks you and I are having an affair. She smelled your perfume on me last night, but she didn't say anything until just now."

Marilee gave a snort. "You and me having an affair? That's the most ridiculous thing I've ever heard."

"Thanks, Marilee. My self-esteem just dropped another notch."

"I can't worry about your manly pride right now, Irby. We have more pressing problems. The car is gone."

"Excuse me?"

"You heard me. And Tom Bramley's body is nowhere to be found."

"My life is over," he moaned into the phone. "My wife is packing her bags as we speak, says I'll never see my children again, and when the police find out about this, my business will be ruined."

"One thing at a time," Marilee said. "We have to tell Debbie the truth."

"She'll kill me."

"At this point you have nothing to lose. I'm on my way."

"Marilee, wait—"

For the fourth time that day, she hung up on Irby.

"Want me to go with you?" Sam asked.

Marilee shook her head and handed him the cell phone. "I got myself into this, and I'm going to take care of it once and for all."

"Okay, but call me first chance you get."

Marilee arrived at the funeral home in record time, only to find Debbie carrying suitcases to her car. Marilee climbed from her own car and limped over. "Debbie, we have to talk."

"I have nothing to say to you, Marilee." She glanced down. "What happened to your foot?"

"I sprained my ankle last night."

"An acrobat, huh? Gee, how am I supposed to compete with that?"

"Please, Debbie. You need to hear the truth."

"The truth? Okay, question number one. Were you with my husband last night?"

"Yes, but—"

"And the two of you have been whispering on the phone all morning. Don't try to deny it. I picked up the extension, and I specifically heard Irby say how much he needed you. Not only that, he smelled of your perfume when he finally came home last night. How can you steal another woman's husband after what Grady did to you?"

"You've got it all wrong, and if you're any kind of friend you'll hear me out."

"Okay, Marilee, you and Irby have five minutes."

They found him in his office with his head on the desk. "Oh, Marilee, thank God you're here!"

Debbie offered her a bright smile. "Seems Irby's glad to see you. Isn't that special?" She turned for the door.

Marilee blocked her exit. "Sit down and listen, dammit!" Shocked, Debbie did as she was told. Marilee turned to Irby. "Start talking, buster."

"You don't expect me to tell her the truth."

"She's your wife, she deserves to know."

"She'll kill me."

"She'll have to take a number," Marilee said sweetly. She turned to Debbie. "Before we tell you what really happened last night, I want to say how disappointed I am in you for even thinking I'd have an affair with your husband. Puh-lease!"

Debbie seemed to take offense. She stood and planted her hands on her hips. "What's wrong with my husband?"

"That's what I want to know," Irby said.

"Shut up, Irby," his wife said.

"There is nothing wrong with your husband, I'm just not interested. For goodness' sake, Debbie, he's like a brother to me. Okay, Irby, you have the floor."

He remained quiet.

"Time's up. If you won't tell her, I will. Debbie, you'd better sit back down."

Marilee began. Five minutes later Debbie wore a look of horror. She walked over to her husband's desk and slapped his baseball cap off his head. "How could you?"

"I know it was wrong, honey, but I panicked." He retrieved his cap and put it back on his head.

"He was also a little drunk at the time." Marilee didn't bother to mention she'd drunk a couple of beers herself.

"Why did you allow him to talk you into it?" Debbie demanded.

"He blackmailed me." Marilee told her about her night job and how she was trying to make extra money to replenish her savings account after using most of it to pay her lawyer. "Irby threatened to tell everyone in town I was working in a nightclub if I didn't help him. I was afraid it might stand in the way of my getting Josh back."

Debbie slapped the cap off Irby's head once again. This time he didn't bother to pick it up off the floor. "Of all the low-down, rotten things to do to Marilee. I don't even like you anymore, Irby Denton." She turned to Marilee. "Can you ever forgive me? It's just, well, after Irby called me a rag mop—" Tears filled her eyes. "And he kept comparing me to you, and you kept coming out on top. Oh, Marilee, I am so sorry. So very sorry."

The women hugged.

Irby sighed his relief. "Thank God *that's* settled."

"Shut up, Irby," they said in unison.

"Where do you suppose the car and body are now?" Debbie asked.

Marilee shook her head. "Perhaps someone saw the car and notified the police."

"Tom's wife would have been told by now," Irby said, "and she would have called us." He shrugged. "I checked the hospital. Guy at the desk said it was a slow night, only a handful of people in the emergency room. By the way, Esmerelda Cunningham was one of them."

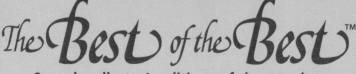
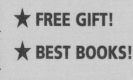

# GET 2

## HOW TO GET YOUR
## 2 FREE BOOKS AND FREE GIFT!

1. Peel off the MIRA sticker on the front cover. Place it in the space provided at right. This automatically entitles you to receive two free books and an exciting mystery gift.

2. Send back this card and you'll get 2 "The Best of the Best™" novels. These books have a combined cover price of $11.00 or more in the U.S. and $13.00 or more in Canada, but they are yours to keep absolutely FREE!

3. There's <u>no</u> catch. You're under <u>no</u> obligation to buy anything. We charge nothing – ZERO – for your first shipment. And you don't have to make any minimum number of purchases – not even one!

4. We call this line "The Best of the Best" because each month you'll receive the best books by some of today's most popular authors. These authors show up time and time again on all the major bestseller lists and their books sell out as soon as they hit the stores. You'll like the convenience of getting them delivered to your home at our special discount prices . . . and you'll love your *Heart to Heart* subscriber newsletter featuring author news, horoscopes, recipes, book reviews and much more!

**SPECIAL FREE GIFT!**

We'll send you a fabulous surprise gift, absolutely FREE, simply for accepting our no-risk offer!

5. We hope that after receiving your free books you'll want to remain a subscriber. But the choice is yours – to continue or cancel, anytime at all! So why not take us up on our invitation, with no risk of any kind. You'll be glad you did!

6. And remember...we'll send you a mystery gift ABSOLUTELY FREE just for giving "The Best of the Best" a try.

Visit us online at
www.mirabooks.com

® and TM are trademarks of Harlequin Enterprises Limited.

# BOOKS FREE!

## Hurry!

**Return this card promptly to GET 2 FREE BOOKS & A FREE GIFT!**

The Best of the Best™

◄ DETACH AND MAIL CARD TODAY! ▼

Affix peel-off MIRA sticker here

**YES!** Please send me the 2 FREE "The Best of the Best" novels and FREE gift for which I qualify. I understand that I am under no obligation to purchase anything further, as explained on the opposite page.

**385 MDL C6PJ**

(M-BB3-01)
**185 MDL C6PH**

NAME (PLEASE PRINT CLEARLY)

ADDRESS

APT.#      CITY

STATE/PROV.      ZIP/POSTAL CODE

## The Best of the Best™ — Here's How it Works:

Accepting your 2 free books and gift places you under no obligation to buy anything. You may keep the books and gift and return the shipping statement marked "cancel." If you do not cancel, about a month later we will send you 4 additional novels and bill you just $4.24 each in the U.S., or $4.74 each in Canada, plus 25¢ shipping & handling per book and applicable taxes if any.* That's the complete price and — compared to cover prices of $5.50 or more each in the U.S. and $6.50 or more each in Canada — it's quite a bargain! You may cancel at any time, but if you choose to continue, every month we'll send you 4 more books, which you may either purchase at the discount price or return to us and cancel your subscription.

*Terms and prices subject to change without notice. Sales tax applicable in N.Y. Canadian residents will be charged applicable provincial taxes and GST.

If offer card is missing write to: The Best of the Best, 3010 Walden Ave., P.O. Box 1867, Buffalo, NY 14240-1867

BUSINESS REPLY MAIL
FIRST-CLASS MAIL    PERMIT NO. 717    BUFFALO, NY

POSTAGE WILL BE PAID BY ADDRESSEE

THE BEST OF THE BEST
3010 WALDEN AVE
PO BOX 1867
BUFFALO NY 14240-9952

NO POSTAGE
NECESSARY
IF MAILED
IN THE
UNITED STATES

"Esmerelda is in the hospital?" Marilee asked. "Did anyone say what was wrong with her?"

"No, but I was told she was being a real pain in the butt. Don't worry, she's too mean to die." He paused. "I also checked with the morgue. Nothing."

Debbie sighed. "This is crazy. What are we going to do?"

"There's nothing to do," Marilee replied, "but wait."

# *Thirteen*

Marilee was pacing the floor when the telephone rang. She snatched it up, hoping it was news about Tom. Irby spoke from the other end.

"Marilee, that was a cruel thing to do to me," he said. "If you were trying to get even with me, it worked."

"Irby, what are you talking about?"

"The car isn't gone, and you know it."

"*What?*"

"It's right where we left it."

"That's ridiculous. I saw for myself it was gone."

"Well, obviously you went to the wrong spot."

"I did not go to the wrong spot, Irby Denton. The road was dug up, and the grass had been flattened from the weight of the car. Not only that, my wig was there." She paused. "Are you drinking again?"

"I'm completely sober. If you don't believe me, come see the car for yourself. I'm standing here looking at it as we speak."

"I'll be there in fifteen minutes."

When Marilee arrived, Irby was sitting in his truck smoking a cigarette. She knew he'd given up the habit years before, but under the circumstances she wasn't surprised to find him puffing away. She was about ready to take up smoking as well.

Irby climbed out of the truck, and they walked toward the ditch. He looked at her. "Well?"

"Oh, my Lord. Is Tom's body still inside?" When he

nodded gravely, she continued, "Who would take a car with a dead person in it and then return it?"

He shook his head. "I don't know. Frankly, I don't know what to think anymore, but it's time I put an end to it. I'm calling the police."

"And telling them what?"

"That I've been out looking for Tom ever since his wife called. That I saw the skid marks and checked it out. Simple as that." He looked weary. "Go home, Marilee. I'll take care of it."

She hesitated. "You'll stay until the police arrive, right? Just in case somebody else decides to take the car?"

"I'll stay." He paused. "Uh, Marilee. Have you decided whether or not you're going to come back to work?"

She tossed him an impatient look. "I'll be there tomorrow morning. We can discuss my new benefits package at that time."

Josh was quiet the next day when his dad drove him to the mental health center. He would have given anything to avoid this session with his mom. Not only did he not wish to discuss their so-called family issues, he didn't want to talk, period. He had a lot on his mind, and he knew his mom would sense something was wrong. She had a way about her.

Grady pulled in front of the mental health building and parked. "Okay, sport, we're here."

"I don't want to go in," Josh said.

Grady sighed. "We've been through this before." When Josh didn't respond, he went on. "Look, Josh, how many times have you told me you want to be treated like a man instead of a kid?" he asked. "Part of growing up is accepting responsibility. You have no choice in this matter, a judge has ordered it."

Josh grabbed the door handle and yanked it. "Don't talk to me about responsibility," he said, "or about being a man." He shoved the door open, climbed out and slammed it behind him.

Inside the waiting area, Josh found his mom sitting in a chair reading a magazine. She glanced up, saw him and smiled. He watched the smile die on her lips when he chose a seat on the other side of the room. He felt crummy about it, but he knew if he sat close she would try to make conversation. He couldn't think of one thing to say to her. All he could think about was how badly he'd screwed up by taking that car, even though he and Conway had managed to return it without getting caught. And that wasn't even the worst of it. No matter how high he'd been at the time, he would never forget stuffing Mayor Bramley's body into the trunk. He shuddered. The man hadn't deserved that, but he had wanted so badly to be accepted by Conway and his crowd that he'd been willing to do almost anything.

Conway could drop dead, for all he cared now. He'd tricked him and made a fool of him, but Josh had been so eager to get the job he'd ignored the signs that Mo Henry was doing something illegal. He was stupid. He sighed and wondered if his life would ever become normal again. It didn't look like it. He couldn't seem to stop being angry.

Only now he was angry at himself.

Royce Malcolm stepped through the doorway. Smiling, he invited them in. Josh followed the counselor and his mom down the hall and into Royce's office. He slumped into a chair and waited.

"Nice to see you again, Josh," Royce said. "How's school?"

Josh felt a sense of dread wash over him. He wasn't doing well in school, and he'd spent that morning in the principal's office for smoking in the bathroom. Another stupid move on his part; he didn't even like cigarettes. It seemed he was always doing something to get into trouble. Nobody had been able to prove anything, which was the only reason Josh hadn't been suspended, but he'd caused quite a stir. He wondered if Royce knew. "Why do you ask?" he said.

"Just curious."

Josh figured he was busted for sure. "You spying on me?"

"You have a problem with me talking to your teachers?"

"I don't like people nosing into my business. I don't go around asking questions about you, do I?"

Marilee shifted in her chair. "Josh, I'm sure Royce felt it was important."

The boy's face reddened. "I don't care *what* he feels. Or what anybody else feels, for that matter. I just want to be left alone. Why is that so hard to understand?" He looked from one to the other. "Did you question my mother's friends? Did you spy on her, too?"

Royce regarded him. "I know what it's like to want to go off somewhere by yourself, get away from it all. That's why you walk so much, isn't it?"

"I'm not answering any more of your dumb questions," Josh said.

Marilee winced. "Josh, please—"

"Why can't you leave me alone?" the boy demanded. "Why are you doing this? Don't you get it, Mom? I don't want to talk to you. When are you going to get off my back?"

Marilee sucked her breath in sharply and gripped the armrests on her chair with both hands. She gazed back at her son, and her eyes filled with tears. She swallowed hard, as if willing herself not to cry, but the tears gathered and fell to her cheeks regardless. Royce reached for a box of tissue but she ignored him, swiping the tears away with the backs of her hands.

"I am never going to 'get off your back,' if that's what you want to call it," she said. "I've done nothing to earn your disrespect, and I refuse to allow you to talk to me this way."

Josh smirked. "Then why are we here? You and Dad are the ones who screwed up. Why are you dragging me into this?"

"Because I...we don't want to see you hurt any more than you already have been."

Josh gave a snort of disgust. "You don't understand, *Mother*," he said, making a mockery of the word. "I don't want to be around you *or* Dad. The only reason I'm hanging out with him and that whore is because they're so busy nailing each other they don't care what I do." Josh saw the stricken look on his mother's face, and he felt a flash of guilt. He had never talked to her like that before. But things had changed. "I'm just biding my time until I'm old enough to get out of this town, and when I do I'm never coming back."

"You can't be serious! You're only fifteen years old. What about school?"

"I'm quitting school. And, yes, I am serious. I plan to go someplace where I never have to lay eyes on my so-called family again."

"I won't permit it."

"Marilee, calm down," Royce said.

"You have no choice," Josh told her. "If you try to stop me, I'll leave today."

She stared at her son in horror. The room began to spin wildly. Her stomach pitched, and she pressed her open palm against it. She couldn't imagine her son leaving town and ending up Lord only knew where. She had seen enough TV programs to know what happened to young runaways. They ended up on drugs and often prostituted themselves once they became hooked. "I can't take any more," she said, her voice a whimper. Tears streamed down her cheeks. The one thing that had kept her going all this time was the hope that Josh would come to his senses and move in with her, but his hate had only worsened. She slumped in her chair. "I just can't take any more," she repeated.

"Marilee?" Royce touched her hand.

"I—I think I'm going to be ill."

Royce was beside her instantly, helping her from the chair and toward the door. "I'll be back, Josh," he said. "Just stay put."

Josh turned away, not wanting to see his mother sick. He might have gone too far this time, but it was the only way he knew to get people to leave him alone. Still, the look on his mother's face tore at his gut, and he suddenly wished he'd never been born.

Royce returned a few minutes later and closed the door behind him. "Your mom won't be rejoining us, Josh," he said. "She's not feeling well."

Josh remained silent.

"I thought maybe you and I could talk for a while, at least until your dad comes for you." When the boy didn't speak, Royce went on, "Look, I don't blame you for being angry. I'd be mad as hell if I were you."

Josh looked up. "Then why is everybody trying to make me stop being pissed?"

"Your parents don't want to see you unhappy, that's all. And they're both feeling guilty over what's happened."

"They *should* feel guilty. They've ruined everything."

Royce nodded. "Things have changed," he said, "but it doesn't have to ruin your life."

"That sounds like something a psychologist would say," Josh replied. "You're exactly like everybody else. I'm just supposed to accept everything that's happened and not be mad."

"I would never tell you to do that," Royce said. "I've seen what happens to people who stuff their real feelings down deep so they don't have to deal with them. They get sick. They have heart attacks, strokes, develop cancer, all sorts of illnesses."

Josh was quiet for a moment. He felt drained, and not as angry anymore. "Some of them get high blood pressure."

"Are you talking about your dad?"

Josh nodded. "I don't think he ever wanted to be a minister."

"He was a good one, though, from what I've heard."

"Yeah, he was good. But he wasn't very happy."

"He hid it well from his congregation," Royce said.

"Like you said, he stuffed it down so deep nobody would know. It made him sick. I think some people do that with food," he added, thinking out loud. "They eat 'cause it takes away the pain."

"What kind of pain?"

Josh looked at him. "Kids making fun of you. Or not fitting in."

"You're right about that. A lot of people use food because it's comforting."

"Yeah, but the more weight you gain, the more people make fun of you. After a while, though, they don't want to be around you. You sort of become…invisible. Just another fat kid walking down the hall with no friends," he added.

"Everybody needs friends, Josh."

"I have friends from church. I just don't see them anymore."

"Maybe it's time you stopped worrying about your parents and started thinking about what you need—and what you don't need—in your life. All this anger isn't good for you. Walking helps, but you need to talk about why you're so angry."

The boy shrugged. "I'm angry with myself right now."

"It's up to you if you want to talk about it. Nothing will leave this office."

Josh's bottom lip trembled. "How do I know you're on the level?"

Royce met his gaze. "Because I know exactly what's going on at school, and I haven't given you up."

Josh considered it. For some reason, he trusted the man. "Okay," he said at last. "I'll talk. It'll be a relief to get it off my mind."

Royce leaned back in his chair. "Whenever you're ready, Josh."


Marilee found Winnie sitting at the kitchen table, doing her homework, when she walked through the door.

The girl looked up. "I take it from the expression on your face that the session didn't go well."

Marilee offered her a brave smile. "It's going to take longer than I thought."

"Anything I can do to help?"

"No, thanks. I just want to relax for a few minutes. Go on with what you were doing." She set her purse on the table and climbed the stairs to her room. Kicking off her shoes, she sat down on the edge of her bed. She had never felt so weary. Irby had been quiet at work that day; she knew he was mourning his friend's death and handling most of the funeral arrangements on his own. Although Debbie was still angry with him, she'd backed off, as if she understood her husband didn't need more problems at the moment. It had been stressful, to say the least, and this business with Josh had only made things worse.

Winnie tapped on the door a few minutes later. She opened it and peered in. "I have a question."

"Go ahead," Marilee said.

"You and Josh used to be real close, right?"

"Yes."

"What did the two of you do to get that way?"

Marilee shrugged. "I don't know. I don't know anything anymore."

Winnie sat on the edge of the bed. "There must've been some things the two of you enjoyed doing together."

"We baked cookies when he was younger. And dyed Easter eggs and decorated for the holidays. He and I did a lot of things together, Winnie, because his father was too busy to join in. I read to him a lot. Started when he was just a baby."

"Did he like it? You reading to him?"

Marilee smiled at the memory. "Oh, yes. He spent a lot of time in my lap listening to stories. Long before he understood their meaning."

"Do you remember his favorite books?"

She nodded. "I still have them. But he's too old for that now."

The girl shrugged. "Maybe. Maybe not. Try to rest now." She closed the door behind her.

Later, as she dressed for work, Marilee pondered what Winnie had said. She opened the closet and selected a pair of shoes to go with the evening dress she wore, and she

spied the box containing Josh's belongings. In it were the
books she'd saved, hoping one day to read them to her
grandchildren. As she thumbed through the pages, an enormous sadness fell over her.

She had taught Josh the sounds that farm animals made,
had taught him to count and recite his ABC's. She had
taught him the difference between the seasons, and together
they'd collected fall leaves. She had been the one who'd
watched in fascination when he'd rolled over in his crib and
taken his first steps, and she was the one who'd potty-trained
him and taught him to tie his shoe laces. She'd labored with
him over his homework, and helped him study for tests.
She'd decorated bulletin boards at school, baked cakes and
cookies for parties, and chaperoned numerous field trips.

She had read to him from a children's Bible, trying to
instill at an early age the lessons she thought were most
important in life. She had taken him into nursing homes to
visit the elderly, and they had visited hospitals where children his age were suffering from terminal illnesses. Together, they'd collected toys and canned goods for the
needy, and one Christmas Josh had spent all his savings
buying games and puzzles for children who were less fortunate. His Sunday-school teacher had been surprised when
Josh, at eleven, wanted to hold a Bible-study group for kids
his own age. That same teacher had remarked that Josh
would probably one day follow in his father's footsteps and
become a minister.

What had happened?

Where had she failed?

Jack looked delighted to see her when Marilee arrived at
work. In fact, his enthusiasm was a little embarrassing, considering there were other employees present. He leaned close
and whispered in her ear, "Dinner is waiting in my office."

"I can't tonight, Jack. I go on in five minutes." She had
purposefully been late in order to prevent him from inviting
her to share another meal.

"Don't be silly, Marilee. You're dining with the boss. It's

not like I'm going to dock your pay. Come on, it's getting cold.''

Marilee joined him, albeit reluctantly. He held her chair for her as she sat down at the small table, draped in white with fresh flowers and candlelight. She waited until he'd seated himself before saying anything. ''You know, Jack, this is very flattering, but I feel uncomfortable with all this attention. I think I've mentioned it before.''

He looked concerned. ''I never meant to make you uncomfortable, Marilee,'' he said, ''but you must realize by now that I've grown very fond of you.''

''And I you, but—''

''I felt a strong bond the first night we met.'' He took her hand. ''Marilee, I'd like to start seeing you.''

''Seeing me?''

''I know you're a married woman, and that you might feel a bit awkward. I want you to know that's one of the attributes I appreciate most about you. You have high morals. I appreciate that in a woman. So I'm merely asking you out as a friend at this time.'' When she didn't answer right away, he went on. ''This will be good for both of us, Marilee.''

Marilee picked at her salad and thought about Sam. He made her heart beat faster, and when he'd kissed her she'd felt as though she would easily melt in his arms. But Sam was a womanizer and would probably end up breaking her heart if she let him.

''Just two friends spending time together,'' Jack repeated. ''No pressure, no strings attached.''

Perhaps it wasn't such a bad idea, Marilee thought. She wouldn't have as much time to think about Josh. ''What did you have in mind?''

''How about a Broadway show in Charleston this Sunday? I have tickets for the two o'clock matinee. We can have dinner afterward.''

''I've never seen a Broadway production.''

''Well, then, it's time you did.''

She pondered his offer. Sundays were especially hard on

her. In the past, the day had centered around church and family. Without either, the day seemed to stretch out like a long road with no end. "You're right, Jack," she said. "I think it's high time."

Marilee arrived home earlier than usual and went straight to her bedroom. She stripped off her clothes and stood before the mirror for a long time. She had not done anything so silly since puberty. She studied her body. There were a couple of stretch marks on her lower abdomen, a result of gaining too much weight when she was pregnant with Josh. But the aerobics classes she'd attended over the years had kept her firm, and she was thankful for that. She turned sideways. Her stomach was slightly rounded, but her thighs and hips were firm from doing about a trillion leg lifts. She had lost weight since Grady left, despite all Winnie did to see that she ate. The main thing, she supposed, was that her complexion was still good. But she was a thirty-five-year-old woman, and she looked her age.

Not that there was anything wrong with that, mind you, but she couldn't help wondering what men like Sam and Jack saw in her, when her own husband hadn't looked twice in her direction for several years.

There was a knock at her bedroom door. Winnie peeked in, then opened the door wide. "Marilee, what in the world are you doing?"

Marilee wanted to crawl beneath the bed. Instead, she scrambled for her bathrobe. She was so startled she put her arm in the wrong sleeve and had to start over. Why hadn't she thought to lock the door? "What am I doing?" she repeated.

The girl just stood there.

"Well, Winnie, I am giving myself my monthly breast exam," she said matter-of-factly. "That's what I'm doing."

"Then how come you're staring at your butt?"

Marilee blushed. "I was...uh...checking for moles."

"Moles?"

"Yes. Once a month I do my breast exam, then I check

for unusual moles." She arched one eyebrow at Winnie. "Don't you?"

"You think I want to see my butt in the mirror right now?" the girl asked.

"Any doctor will tell you how important it is to do a monthly exam. It's just part of my routine now." The girl nodded, and Marilee wondered if she'd been able to pull it off.

"I just wanted to let you know I made a snack for you. It's in the fridge."

"Thank you."

The girl started to close the door. "Uh, Marilee?"

"Yes?"

"I won't mention this little incident if you won't."

# *Fourteen*

Clara, Ruby and Nell arrived at Marilee's the next morning at ten o'clock for their weekly meeting to discuss Blessing Home. "The roof is finished," Ruby announced. "As we've received no bill, I plan to drive over to Benson Contractors personally to pay for the job."

"I hope we have enough money," Clara said.

"Sam isn't in a hurry for that money, girls," Nell said.

"Your son has already donated his time, honey," Ruby said. "Besides, we don't want Bobby Benson telling everyone in town we don't pay our bills. Now we have to come up with the money for plumbing and electrical work."

"I make a motion to discuss the white elephant sale now," Clara said.

Nell looked excited and raised her hand.

"You have the floor, Nell."

"Well," the woman said, wearing a bright smile. "I've hardly been able to contain myself, I'm so excited, but I wanted to wait until the meeting." She paused. "I checked with every church in town, including my own, and they've promised to help with donations." She looked at Clara. "All we need is a date."

The group clapped for her as Winnie walked in to the room. She stopped short. "Does this mean y'all are happy to see me?"

Marilee chuckled. "The applause was for Nell." She told Winnie what the woman had accomplished in just a week's time. Winnie gave her a high five.

"Marilee, do you have anything to report?"

She sighed. "I'm afraid this has been a bad week for me, but I plan to spend part of the day going by some of the businesses in town. See if I can generate any interest. I'm also baking cakes in my spare time. I should have plenty to donate to the bake sale."

"Good luck finding people in this town to help," Ruby said. "I believe you've been down that road before."

"Yes, but like I told you, it's harder for people to say no in person."

"I could never say no to you, dear," Nell said to Marilee, squeezing her hand.

"Ask her for fifty grand and watch how quickly she changes her tune," Winnie said. Nell smacked the girl on the behind.

Clara tapped her gavel. "Ladies, please, we're having a serious meeting here."

"That's the problem with you, Clara," Winnie said. "You're always so serious. When was the last time you had a little fun?"

"I don't have time for fun. Ruby, do you have anything for us?"

"We should plan on doing something one night," Winnie said. "Just us girls. All we do is sit at this kitchen table and talk about committee stuff."

Clara arched one eyebrow. "Have you forgotten that Ruby and I are taking you to garage sales tomorrow?"

"Winnie's right," Ruby said. "We never do anything fun. We could all go to dinner one night, maybe catch a movie afterward."

"I know what we could do," Nell said, a twinkle in her eye. "We could drive over to the Pickford Inn and listen to Marilee play the piano."

Marilee blushed. She would feel funny with her friends watching her entertain. "The Pickford is very expensive," she reminded them.

"They have soups and salads, don't they?" Ruby asked. "We can afford something like that, right, girls?"

"Why don't we go tonight?" Nell suggested. "It's more fun when you do things spontaneously."

Clara wore a pinched look and began tugging at her short hair, giving it the tufted look that clearly indicated she was uncomfortable or annoyed. "They serve alcohol in that place," she said. "Besides, I have a previous commitment."

Ruby scoffed. "I'll just bet you do," she said. "What are your big plans for the evening, Clara? You plan to sit around in that shaggy old bathrobe and watch Elvis videos? And what if they do serve alcohol? You don't have to drink anything."

"It just so happens I *do* have plans for the evening," Clara insisted. "The Friends of the Library is having a book sale this evening, and I'm in charge of it. Don't you read the newspaper?"

"Maybe we can go one night next week," Ruby said. They looked at Clara.

"Okay, I'll go," she finally said in exasperation. "Now, do you think we can finish our meeting? I'm sure we all have things to do." She turned to Ruby. "You haven't even given your treasurer's report. That's supposed to be one of the first things we take care of during each meeting."

"I've given my report," Ruby said.

"You said you were going to Benson Contractors to pay the bill, that's all. We don't know how much money we have, nor have we discussed what, if any, expenses we've had to pay out."

Ruby glared at Clara, then looked at the others. "Would somebody shoot me if I agree to join a different committee after this is over?" She gave her report, and Clara seemed happy for the moment. "I've also checked out a couple of locations where we might hold our white elephant sale, and every place wants to charge except the VFW hall." She patted the back of her hair. "It just so happens I have a very nice friend there and—"

Clara tapped her gavel on a book. "Thank you, Ruby, but we don't need a rundown on your personal life."

Ruby slammed her folder closed. "Now, you listen to me,

Clara Goolesby. I don't know what bug crawled up your behind, but I've had enough of your ill-mannered ways. As of right now, I'm resigning. And I will never, do you hear me, *never* agree to be on another committee with you. You've already run off most of our other members, so if I'm not doing a good job, take care of it yourself.''

Clara sniffed. ''I suppose we'll have to find another treasurer.''

Ruby smiled at the others. ''Would you ladies excuse me? I have a perm in fifteen minutes.'' She thanked Marilee for the coffee and left.

''What's wrong, Clara?'' Marilee asked gently.

The woman looked as if she might cry. ''I'm just out of sorts,'' she confessed. ''My bad moods are driving everybody crazy at work. And this stupid Blessing Home project is taking forever. We told the families they would only have the girls a few weeks, but it's been going on for two months now. Some of the girls have had their babies, and their caretakers spend half the night walking the floor with them because the girls don't know the first thing about being mothers.'' She sighed. ''It's just one big headache, Marilee, and I wish I'd never gotten involved in the first place.''

''All the more reason for us to go out and enjoy ourselves,'' Nell said. She patted Clara's hand. ''Things are starting to move along. We'll have this place restored in no time, just wait and see.''

Clara sighed. ''I just wish these girls would have thought about the consequences before they made their decision to have unprotected sex, because it's very stressful for those they're staying with.''

''Excuse me, Clara,'' Marilee said, as Winnie stalked off and made her way up the stairs. ''You just hurt Winnie's feelings, and she doesn't deserve it.''

Clara covered her mouth. ''Oh, my word! I was so upset I didn't realize what I was saying. I would never intentionally hurt her feelings. I mean, she's like one of us.''

''She *is* one of us,'' Marilee said coolly. ''Now, if you'll excuse me, I'm going upstairs to speak with her.''

Clara rose from the table. "I have to pick up Ruby. She may be in a huff, but she obviously forgot I drove us over." She sighed again. "I guess I owe everyone an apology."

Nell stood as well. It was obvious she was uncomfortable. "I'd better be getting home. I have a lot to do if we're going to get this bazaar off the ground."

Marilee found Winnie sitting on her bed reading a book. "Okay, I know your feelings are hurt, but you're just going to have to get over it. Clara is stressed to her limit right now, and she wasn't thinking."

Winnie looked up. "I don't want the baby and me to be a burden on you."

"I'm sure it's going to be an adjustment at first," Marilee said, "but we've handled tougher stuff than this." The girl remained quiet. Marilee planted her hands on her hips. "Listen, kiddo, I'm not going to sit around and watch you feel sorry for yourself. It's not good for me, and it's not good for your baby. This world isn't going to stop turning just because you've had a bad day."

Winnie looked up. "Where've I heard that before?"

"So what's it going to be? You plan to sit here feeling crummy or do you want to go with me and try to guilt-trip this town into helping us with Blessing Home?"

Winnie brightened. "I'm going with you. I love making people feel guilty."

L&M Printing was located between the Honey Bee Candy Store and Elvin Purdy's Hardware. Most of the stores in the little square boasted new green and white striped canopies. A salesman from New Jersey had sold a canopy to Shipley's Art Gallery and Supplies, and suddenly the whole town had to have one. Folks laughingly called it Canopy Row. And when the Honey Bee set two massive clay pots of flowers on either side of their door, the other merchants began doing the same, as though each had to outdo the rest.

When Winnie and Marilee walked into L&M Printing, Marilee was glad to see the place was filled with customers. It would certainly make hers and Winnie's job easier.

"You're on," she whispered to Winnie.

"Oh, my, look at these nice message pads!" Winnie called out loudly, attracting the attention of everyone in the store. Several people craned their necks this way and that as they tried to see who had spoken. As Winnie hurried up to the display table sitting in the center of the room, she bumped it, turning the table on its side and dumping what looked to be a thousand pads with L&M's logo and phone number at the top. They flew in every direction.

"Oh, I am so embarrassed!" the girl said, bending over to pick them up. But her round belly got in the way, causing her to get down on her knees in order to retrieve them.

Marilee rushed over to her. "Winnie, you shouldn't be doing that," she cried out. "You're in no condition. Here, let me help. "

Larry and Marge Mosely, the owners, rushed out from behind the counter. "Marilee, is the girl all right?" Marge asked. Several customers also tried to assist.

"I don't know, Marge. Winnie, honey, are you hurt?"

"I think I wrenched my back," Winnie said, grimacing.

"Should I drive you to the emergency room?"

"Maybe I should just go home and sit in a hot tub."

Larry looked concerned. "If you think you need to go to the hospital—"

"No, no, I'll be okay. I'd move that table if I were you, though. It's in the way."

"How far along are you, dear?" a customer asked as Larry slid the table from the center of the room and straightened the cloth.

"Almost seven months. If I get any bigger I'm going to have to ride in the back of Flick Rhodes's meat truck."

"You're so young," the woman said. "I'll bet it's stressful for you."

"Heck, you think this is stressful, you should have seen me the day my folks kicked me out for getting in the family way and not having a husband."

"No!"

Larry, Marge and Marilee were picking up notepads and stacking them on the table as another customer tried to assist.

"Said they weren't going to have an unwed mother living in their house. And them being Christians and all."

"Sometimes those are the worst," another woman, who was holding a small Yorkie, added, "I couldn't imagine putting my poor pooch out on the street, much less my own child. Where did you go?"

"You ever heard of Blessing Home?"

Larry looked up sharply and caught Marilee's eye, but she glanced away quickly and continued stacking the pads onto the table.

"The unwed mothers' home? Why, yes, I have, as a matter of fact. It's great that there's a place for young girls to go when they need a helping hand."

"Well, actually, ma'am, the city closed it down because it was unsafe."

Larry paused and looked at Marilee again. "Are you the one who called me for a donation?" he demanded. "The answer is still no. Kids today need to learn to accept responsibility for their own actions."

The woman holding the Yorkie gasped. "Why, Larry Mosely, I'm not believing what I just heard. You'd refuse to help a young girl in trouble? What if your daughter got into trouble? And here you are, deacon of the Methodist church, not to mention one of the most successful merchants in town. Are you planning to take your profits with you when you go to your Maker?"

"Mrs. Framer, you don't understand," he said.

"I understand greed, Mr. Mosely."

Marilee suddenly recognized the woman. Della Framer owned almost all the convenience stores in town and surrounding areas. When her husband passed away ten years ago, she'd been devastated. Although she'd only owned a couple of stores at the time, she'd managed to acquire several more since then, including Chickpea's only fashionable boutique, and she'd proved herself a formidable business-woman.

Larry blushed. "I can't afford to give to every charity in this town, Mrs. Framer, much as I'd like to."

Mrs. Framer smiled. "Marge, honey, would you please cancel my order? I think I'll have to take my business elsewhere. I know Ross's Print Shop on the other side of town would love to have my business, and Mr. Ross is a generous man."

Marge blanched. "Oh, Mrs. Framer, I know we can work out something."

Larry shot Marilee a dark look. "Are you trying to ruin my business?" he hissed.

"No," Marilee said just as softly, feeling genuinely sorry for the man. She and Winnie had gone too far. "Mrs. Framer, please don't cancel your order on account of us. I'm sure we'll find the funds to renovate the home."

"Hey, we meant no harm," Winnie said. She looked at Larry Mosely. "We were just going to get a price on flyers announcing our white elephant sale. The proceeds will go directly to Blessing Home, of course. Like Mrs. Abernathy said, I'm sure we'll get what we need. The Lord always provides."

Mrs. Framer pulled out her checkbook. "You're darn right you'll get what you need. I'm writing you a check right now for five hundred dollars, twice the amount I just saved by canceling my order with L&M. Tell you what else I'm going to do. I'll put donation boxes in all my stores. We've done this sort of thing before, and you can bet we collect plenty of money."

Marge Mosely glared at her husband, then flashed a sweet smile at Marilee. "Mrs. Abernathy, of course we'll help. We can certainly give you an excellent rate on flyers." She suddenly snapped her fingers. "Tell you what, if you'll just settle for black and white on inexpensive paper, we'll donate the flyers and even stick them in the Wednesday newspaper for free. Everybody in town will see them."

"Oh, Mrs. Mosely, we don't expect you to just give them to us," Marilee said. "We have money."

"That's right," Winnie replied. "And I'm willing to do-

nate my time here after school in order to pay you back.''
She turned to Marilee. ''That's okay with you, isn't it?''

''I don't know, Winnie. You get so light-headed these
days that I worry about you. But if it would make you feel
better—''

''No!'' Larry replied, almost knocking the table over
again in his nervousness. His forehead was wet with per-
spiration. ''We don't expect anything in return. Why don't
you call me when I'm not so busy?''

''Same number as before?'' Marilee asked sweetly. He
looked embarrassed, but nodded.

''Well, now, that's much better,'' Mrs. Framer said.
''Marge, honey, don't bother canceling my order. I'm proud
to do business with people who care about the less fortunate.''

''Excuse me, but I couldn't help overhearing your dilemma,'' Fred Bean, owner of Bean Electrical, joined the
discussion. ''I heard Blessing Home was in need of electrical
work. I'll be glad to donate a few supplies and labor. Seems
only right that folks should pitch in as much as they can,
when it benefits our community. Here, take my business
card. When you call, ask to speak directly to me.'' He
handed it to Marilee, who thanked him profusely.

Mrs. Framer motioned for Marilee and Winnie to follow
her outside. ''You're both very good,'' she said.

Marilee blushed. ''I don't understand.''

''Sure you do, honey,'' she said, giving her a hearty wink.
She looked at Winnie. ''Are you in school, child?''

Winnie drew herself up to her full height. ''Not only am
I in school, I'm on the honor roll. I'm going to study ac-
counting at the junior college once I graduate high school.
I plan to have my own accounting firm.''

Della Framer smiled. ''You did an excellent job in there,
although I half expected Larry Mosely to have a stroke. He
can be such a tightwad at times.''

''I think Mrs. Framer is on to us,'' Marilee said to Winnie,
giving a small chuckle. ''Were we that conspicuous?''

''You were superb. Not the pro I am, of course, but I've

had many years of practice, which is how I got where I am today." She looked at Winnie. "So you're an honor student, and you plan to open your own firm one day? You seem to be a very determined young woman. Many women in your condition might give up."

"I know what I want, and I'm going after it," Winnie told her.

Mrs. Framer nodded. "My name is in the phone book. Call me when you get your accounting degree. I could use a live wire like you working for me, and I'll be happy to pass your name on to my friends."

Winnie and Marilee looked at one another.

"In the meantime, I happen to know a few people in this town who owe me favors. I'm sure they'd be more than willing to help with your cause."

Wearing looks of amazement, Marilee and Winnie followed the woman down the sidewalk. Soon they'd been promised donations from a variety of shops, including Betsy's Florist. There Marilee purchased a small bouquet. "For Esmerelda Cunningham," she told Winnie. "She's been in the hospital."

Winnie looked astounded. "You're taking her flowers after the way she talked to you?" When Marilee nodded, Winnie shook her head. "You know, it's people like you that make the rest of us look bad."

That evening when Marilee arrived at work, she headed straight to Jack's office to drop off her purse. Jack looked up from his desk and greeted her warmly. "What time should I pick you up tomorrow?"

"How about I just meet you here, say, around noon?" Marilee said. "It's on the way." He nodded, and she turned, almost bumping into Gertie, who had come into the room carrying her own purse. The woman didn't speak, just turned around and left.

Marilee looked at Jack. "I have one question to ask. Is there anything going on between you and Gertie Johnson?"

"I tried to be friends with Gertie," Jack said, looking

surprised, ''but she wanted more than I was willing to give. I suppose she'll hold a grudge for the rest of her life.''

''Thank you for telling me, Jack. I needed to know.'' She smiled. ''See you tomorrow.''

# *Fifteen*

On Sunday, Marilee rose at dawn and started baking. By the time Winnie came downstairs in her maternity jeans and a white cotton shirt, Marilee had managed to get a half-dozen cakes baked and cooling on racks.

"Smells good in here," the girl said.

"I figured I'd better get started, so we have enough cakes and pies for the bake sale." She poured chocolate chips into a large bowl of cookie dough. She had tripled the recipe, so it was difficult to stir.

"You're going to freeze them, right? I don't need any sweets sitting around."

Marilee grinned. "Yes, I'm going to freeze them. I don't need the temptation either."

"Are you going with us to the garage sales this morning?" Winnie asked.

"I can't. I already have plans." Marilee held her breath.

Winnie stuck her finger in the cookie dough and tasted it. "What plans?"

"I'm attending a play in Charleston."

"That's nice. Will you be home for dinner?"

"No."

"Okay."

Marilee waited for more questions and was surprised when they didn't come.

Winnie faced her. "I have a favor to ask, but I don't expect you to answer right away, and if you don't want to do it, I'll understand."

"I'm listening," Marilee said, wondering what it could be.

"On my last doctor's visit, he asked if I planned to take childbirth classes."

"And?"

"I'd really like to, but I need a coach."

Marilee smiled. "Are you asking me to go into the delivery room with you?"

Winnie nodded. "Only if you want to."

Marilee threw her arms around the girl's neck. "I'd love to! When do we start the classes?"

"Gee, Marilee, I wasn't sure you'd want to do it."

"Of course I do. I'm going to be her aunt, after all."

Winnie looked touched. "The classes won't begin until the end of November. We've still got about six weeks, but I have to go ahead and sign up. We can take one class a week for six weeks or go to two full Saturdays. I was sort of hoping to do it on Saturday if you can manage, to get it over with sooner, you know? You'd still have plenty of time to get ready for work."

"Saturday will be fine." Marilee smiled again. "This is going to be so exciting."

"I plan to have my baby naturally. No pain medication whatsoever. I don't even want them to give me an aspirin."

"It's entirely up to you, Winnie, but you certainly don't have to decide right now." The doorbell rang. "They're here."

Marilee wondered if Clara would show up.

Clara and Ruby came into the kitchen. Marilee stood there, a smile frozen in place as she tried to assess if the two had made up.

"You've started baking," Ruby said, sniffing the air.

"She's not going with us to the garage sales," Winnie said. "She's going to a play in Charleston."

Ruby and Clara looked at Marilee. "A play?" Ruby asked. "In Charleston?"

"That's right."

All three continued to stare as Marilee dropped dough

onto cookie sheets. When it was obvious that no information was forthcoming, Clara spoke. "Winnie, may I have a word with you?"

The girl shrugged. "Sure." They went into the living room.

"I hope you don't mind if I help myself to a cup of coffee," Ruby said. "My old percolator is on the blink this morning."

"Of course I don't mind." Marilee eyed her closely. As Ruby passed by Marilee, she formed an *O* with her thumb and forefinger to let her know everything was okay with Clara.

Clara and Winnie returned to the kitchen a few minutes later, just as Nell walked through the back door. She glanced at the cakes. "You've been busy this morning."

"Marilee's going to a play in Charleston," Ruby blurted.

"Good for you!" Nell said. If she was curious, she didn't show it. Instead, she looked at the others. "Is everybody ready?"

Clara stood there with her hands folded primly. "Before we go, I would like to apologize to everyone. I've been such a grouch lately."

"Oh, don't be silly, dear," Nell said. "We all have bad days."

Winnie patted Clara on the back. "I've already told you everything's cool. I know you didn't mean what you said yesterday."

Marilee gave Clara a hug. "You're among friends. We've all been through hard times, and we're always going to be there for one another."

"Tell them the rest, Clara," Ruby prodded gently.

Clara looked down at her feet. "Well, I've been having a few problems. *Female* problems," she added. "My doctor says I'm in full-blown menopause. I'm on estrogen, but I have awful mood swings."

"Aren't you a little young for that?" Nell asked.

"My mother went through menopause in her late thirties.

The doctor said that's probably why I'm going through it early."

Marilee gave her a sympathetic smile. "I wish you had shared this with us earlier, instead of keeping it to yourself."

"It's not easy for me to talk about things," Clara said, "but I feel better now that it's out in the open. I just feel so tense and irritable all the time, but I promise I'll try not to take it out on everybody."

"Now, you just listen to me, dear," Nell said, reaching for a piece of paper and scribbling on it. "There's absolutely nothing I don't know about menopause, and I've probably got a few books on the subject since I never throw out anything. Here's my phone number. You call me, and we'll talk it out over coffee. I'll look for my books in the meantime."

"Thank you, Nell," Clara said. "I'd love to talk to someone about it." She paused. "Now that I've gotten that out of the way, I have a little bit of good news. I drove by Blessing Home yesterday after Ruby dropped me off at my house, and you'll never believe what I found. Seems some of the citizens have decided to help out after all. There's a whole stack of lumber out front, and Fred Bean left his business card taped to the front door, saying he would be glad to look at the electrical work. Not only that, there's a truckload of bricks and plywood from Benson Contractors."

Nell beamed with pleasure. "I knew my Sam would come through for us. I overheard a telephone conversation he had with Bobby Benson on the telephone. Not that I was eavesdropping, you understand. 'Course, Bobby doesn't do anything unless he benefits. He'll expect us to list him as a contributor in the newspaper."

"We have no problem with that." Clara said. "It may encourage other donations." She paused. "Once I saw all that lumber, I just started crying when I thought of how discouraged I'd been over the whole thing."

Marilee continued dropping dough on a cookie sheet. "That's understandable. We've been working on this for several months now. I'm just as antsy as you are."

"It still doesn't excuse my behavior, but I decided I'd

like to join all of you when you go to the Pickford Inn. It *is* time I learned to loosen up and have a little fun in my life. We can go in my car, if you'd like.''

''That's wonderful,'' Nell exclaimed.

Winnie looked impatient. ''Okay, now that that's settled, let's get out of here. If we don't hit the garage sales early all the good stuff will be gone.''

They filed out the door a few minutes later. Marilee was still thinking about Clara when the telephone rang. Esmerelda Cunningham spoke from the other end.

''What do you want now?'' the woman demanded.

Marilee blinked. ''I beg your pardon?''

''Why did you bring me flowers? Are you trying to soften me up so I'll give you something else for your charity event?''

Marilee wondered why the woman was so suspicious. ''You've already given us a very nice donation, Mrs. Cunningham. We don't expect anything else. I dropped the flowers off because I'd heard you were in the emergency room the other night. I hope it's nothing serious.''

The woman grunted. ''Simple indigestion, but Dudley insisted I have a doctor look at me. He gets worked up over the smallest things. And I don't trust this hospital one iota, let me tell you.'' She paused. ''Well, thank you for the flowers, but it really wasn't necessary.'' She hung up without another word.

Marilee hung up as well. She wondered why it was so difficult for Esmerelda Cunningham to accept gifts, and why the woman had so much trouble being friendly. She glanced at the clock. Seven-thirty. She had plenty of time before she had to meet Jack at the Pickford. She finished the cookies, cleaned the kitchen and considered making a couple of pound cakes. Instead, she decided to sit down with a pen and paper and start planning Winnie's surprise baby shower.

She'd been tossing the idea around the last couple of days, considering what she would serve, whom she would invite. She would love to have invited Winnie's friends, but she had no idea who they were or if they existed. Surely one of them would have called the house by now. The whole thing was strange, but Marilee would never ask the girl and risk embarrassing her. Nevertheless, Marilee often wondered if Winnie's friends had backed off when they'd discovered she was pregnant. No matter what, she was determined to see that the girl had her baby shower.

At eight o'clock the doorbell rang. Marilee wiped her hands on a dish towel and made for the door. She found Sam standing on the other side. He looked too good for words.

"I'm here to take you to breakfast."

"Breakfast?"

"You know, the first meal of the day. Actually, it's the most important meal."

"Well, I—" She glanced around the living room and fidgeted with her hands.

He grinned. "You can't think of a good reason to turn me down, can you?"

She blushed. "Actually, I was in the middle of something."

"From the smell, I'd say you've been busy in the kitchen. But you can still take time for breakfast, right?"

Marilee told herself she was flirting with disaster. She had absolutely no business going anywhere with Sam Brewer. But he *had* done a lot for her, sitting up half the night when she'd had her mini-breakdown, driving out to the scene of the accident. And he'd been kind enough to call and check on her a couple of times since.

"I suppose I could spare a few minutes," she said. "I probably need to change clothes first."

"You look fine. Let's go."

"Would you mind if we stopped by Esmerelda Cunningham's house on the way? I'd like to drop off a batch of cookies."

Sam smiled. "Always the Good Samaritan."

Marilee wrapped a dozen cookies in foil and followed

Sam out the door, where a late-model town car she'd never seen waited. "Did you borrow someone's car?"

"This is my car," he said. "I keep it in the garage since I mostly drive my truck." He saw her hesitate. "We can take the truck if you'd be more comfortable."

"No, this is fine."

He walked her around to the passenger's side and helped her in. She was amazed by how clean it was compared to his truck, which he seldom washed and which was always crammed full of construction equipment. He pulled into Esmerelda's driveway a few minutes later, and Marilee grabbed her cookies. Dudley answered the door. "These are for you and Mrs. Cunningham."

Dudley looked surprised. "How kind of you, Mrs. Abernathy. I'll be sure she gets them."

"Tell her she has to share them with you." Marilee said goodbye, crossed the driveway and rejoined Sam. "Okay, I'm ready."

The last—the *absolute* last—place Marilee would have chosen for breakfast would have been the Mockingbird Café, where everybody in town congregated on Sunday mornings, either before or after church.

Flora Bigsby, the owner, greeted them at the door. "Hi, Marilee, Sam," she said, as though it were an everyday occurrence for the two to come in together. "You want a booth or a table?"

"A booth, if you have it," Marilee said. "Preferably in the back."

Sam grinned. "Ashamed to be seen with me?"

"Of course not."

Marilee was conscious of the eyes that followed them as she and Sam followed Flora toward the back of the restaurant. Sam waited until Marilee sat down before sliding in next to her. "What do you think you're doing?" she asked.

"What?" he said innocently.

Marilee wanted to duck beneath the table. "There is a perfectly fine seat across from here. I suggest you take it."

Sam handed her a menu. "Why should I move when I'm

perfectly comfortable right where I am? I like facing the room.''

"I'll be happy to sit on the other side.''

"No way. I want the whole world to know you're my girl.''

Marilee saw that he was grinning like a rooster in a hen-house. "I am *not* your girl.''

"It's just a matter of time. Now, what'll you have?''

"Just coffee, please.'' The sooner she got out of there the better.

"Well, I'm as hungry as a bear, and you look like you could use a little meat on your bones.''

Flora's daughter, Bea, appeared bearing two cups of coffee. "'Mornin' Sam. Hi, Marilee, haven't seen you in a while. What can I get you?''

"Coffee is fine,'' Marilee said.

Sam smiled. "Don't listen to her, Bea, she's on another one of those crazy diets. We'll have the Hearty Man's Special.'' He looked at Marilee. "How do you like your eggs cooked?''

Marilee wasn't about to argue and draw more attention to them. "Scrambled.''

"Me too,'' Sam said. "Oh, and we want sausage with it, right, Marilee?''

She nodded.

Bea jotted down their order on her pad. "Be just a jiffy.'' She hurried away.

"There now,'' Sam said, raising his cup of coffee to his lips. "Nothing like a good breakfast to start the day.'' He looked at her. "Why are you still holding that menu? Are you hiding?''

"Of course not.''

"You're so worried what others might think. Has it crossed your mind that people have other things on their minds besides what Marilee Abernathy is up to these days?'' She didn't answer. "Okay, go ahead and hide. As for me, I'm going to enjoy myself. I'm with the prettiest girl in town, and I feel like one lucky man." He grinned as Marilee closed her menu and put it aside.

"Do you know how many women would love to be in your shoes right now, sitting with a handsome, successful guy like myself?"

She knew he was teasing and laughed in spite of herself. "You certainly have a lofty opinion of yourself."

"And you love every minute of it. You know, if you play your cards right I might spring for lunch as well. We could take a long drive and—"

"Sorry, but I have plans."

"Oh?" When she didn't volunteer information, he pressed. "So what are they?"

She looked at him. She wondered how she could find him so attractive one minute, only to tell herself the next she was crazy for being involved. Not that she was really involved, mind you, but she did feel a sense of obligation toward him for recently helping her out.

"I just like knowing how my girl spends her time when she's not with me."

Marilee sighed. "Would you please stop calling me your girl? I'm nobody's girl."

He studied her for a minute. "You don't have a date, do you?"

Marilee regarded him. "If you must know, I *do* have a date. I'm attending a Broadway production in Charleston this afternoon."

He clasped his hands together on the table. He didn't look very happy with the news. "Do I know him?"

Marilee studied his hands. They were large and tanned from the sun, his nails clipped short, scrubbed clean. "I doubt it."

Sam smiled, but it was forced. He didn't like the idea of Marilee seeing another man, but there wasn't anything he could do about it. "A Broadway production, huh? I suppose you go for that sort of thing."

"I've never been to one, to tell you the truth."

"I would gladly have taken you if you'd told me, but

you've dodged all my invitations. This must be a special guy." When she didn't say anything, he went on. "I hope he's a gentleman. He's not the pushy sort, or anything like that?"

"Pushy?"

Sam shifted in his seat and looked her directly in the eyes. "You have to be careful with men, Marilee."

She tried to keep a straight face. "I do?"

He glanced around quickly before leaning closer. "You've lived somewhat of a sheltered life, Marilee. Heck, you were no more than a baby when you married, and, well, now that you're on your own—" He paused, as though trying to come up with the right words. "You're a little on the naive side, if you don't mind me saying so. Dating is not like it used to be."

"I'll try to remember that," she said.

"So, who's the lucky fellow?"

Marilee sighed. "If you must know, he's my boss at the Pickford Inn, and I've already had dinner with him several times. He's a perfect gentleman, so you needn't worry."

"You've had dinner with him. You never mentioned it."

"I didn't think it necessary."

"You've had dinner with another man? How come you've never had dinner with me?" He looked none too pleased at the thought.

"I'm having breakfast with you right now," she said.

He was prevented from answering when a woman suddenly appeared at the table.

"Marilee, is that you?"

Marilee smiled. Jenny Rawlings was a member of Chickpea Baptist Church and had been a good friend who'd often volunteered for jobs that nobody else wanted. "Jenny, how nice to see you again." Marilee held out her hand, and they shook.

"I thought I saw you come in. I didn't mean to interrupt, but I just had to find out how you're doing. I would have called, but I had no idea where you were, or if you'd left town."

"I'm in my parents' old house," Marilee said. "And I'm fine, Jenny. Doing just fine."

Jenny smiled pleasantly at Sam and went on, as if a strange man sitting beside the ex-preacher's soon-to-be ex-wife was of little consequence to her. "We have missed you so much, Marilee. Things just aren't the same without you. The new minister and his wife are very kind, and they try hard, but, well, everything is so different now."

"I'm sorry to hear it."

"Not only that, most of the volunteers dropped out, and we had to close down some of the programs."

Marilee couldn't hide her disappointment. "What about the senior citizens' hot lunch program?"

"Oh, we're still doing that, but we had to cancel Mother's Day Out, and the Wednesday-night potluck dinners. Seems nobody has time for anything these days. We can't even get people to visit the nursing home."

"Is the church holding their annual bazaar this year?" Marilee asked.

Jenny shook her head. "I think a lot of folks lost their enthusiasm after what happened with, well, you know." She seemed embarrassed to have mentioned it.

Bea appeared with their food, and Jenny stepped out of the way. "Oh, I shouldn't have interrupted your breakfast," Jenny said. "I just wanted to stop by and say hello. I wish you'd consider coming back to Chickpea Baptist, Marilee. Maybe convince Clara and Ruby to rejoin us as well. We could certainly use the help." She smiled and left.

Marilee was quiet once Jenny left, and Bea refilled their coffee cups. Sam picked up on it right away.

"You okay?" he asked.

She shrugged. "Just disappointed. We all worked so hard to get those programs started."

"Maybe you *should* go back," he said.

Marilee stirred her grits. "I would feel uncomfortable."

"You didn't do anything wrong."

"All the members know my business."

"You're going to have to stop worrying about what other people think. Except for me. You know what I think?"

She was curious. "What?"

"I think you're one of the strongest women I know. You've dealt with a lot lately, but you keep right on going. I admire you for that."

"Thank you, Sam."

"You haven't touched your food."

Marilee nibbled on a piece of toast. Finally, she tasted her eggs. "And thank you for asking me to breakfast."

"Are you having a good time?"

"As a matter of fact, I am."

He was pleased. "So cancel the date with your boss and spend the day with me."

She met his gaze. It was tempting. Even more so than getting all dressed up and seeing her first Broadway play. Sam Brewer made her heart beat faster, and when he looked at her that way she had trouble breathing. Which is precisely why she shouldn't cancel her date with Jack, she reminded herself. "I don't think so," she said softly, "but I appreciate the thought."

Sam tried to hide his disappointment. "Maybe some other time," he said.

# *Sixteen*

Jack was waiting for Marilee when she pulled into the parking lot of the Pickford Inn. She wore a simple, ankle-length, black dress with tiny white dots, and a matching jacket. She'd purchased it from her favorite consignment shop months ago for a fraction of what it would have cost off the rack.

Jack seemed impressed as he helped her into his white Mercedes, which looked as though it had just rolled off the showroom floor. "Marilee, you look absolutely stunning. And I much prefer your hair to the wig."

She blushed, wondering if Jack thought her silly for working in disguise. He was the only one at the Pickford Inn who knew anything about her personal life; she hoped he understood why she went out of her way to look different.

"Thank you, Jack. You look very nice yourself." It was true. He wore crisp beige slacks, a knit shirt and a navy jacket. His shoes shone like a new appliance. She could not imagine him in faded jeans and rugby shirts.

The ride to Charleston took little more than an hour, but the time passed quickly as Jack described the show they were about to see. "I promise you'll enjoy yourself, Marilee," he said. "I think I told you it's a musical. The troupe will be doing songs from *Cats, Les Misérables, Rent* and *Miss Saigon,* to name only a few."

"You've already seen this production, haven't you?" she asked.

"Not this particular one. I saw numerous plays when I lived in New York, but that seems like another lifetime."

"Do you ever visit?"

"Oh, no. The memories are too painful. That's where…where Teresa died. Upstate New York," he added. "We were visiting our country home at the time." He turned to her and smiled, although it didn't reach his eyes. "After her death, I figured a change of scenery would help, so I moved to Pickford and bought the inn, and the rest is history. But let's talk of something else. Tell me about Chickpea. I've only driven through it a couple of times."

Marilee told him about the town in which she lived, told him about Winnie and her friends, and their attempts to raise money for Blessing Home. "We have our own little theater, but everyone involved, even the actors, donates their time. I've seen a few of their plays, and several of us from church saw the *Nutcracker* when they put it on at the high school."

"I'll have to take you to a professional ballet," Jack said. "Perhaps at Christmas."

Marilee was surprised he was making plans for the future, but she was not in a hurry for the holidays to begin. She needed time to prepare herself in the event Josh refused to visit. If he didn't show up, she would simply have to make the best of it. Besides, she wanted Winnie to have a nice holiday. She'd learned long ago the quickest way to forget one's troubles was to help someone else.

Marilee forgot about everything else once they arrived at the theater. They were early so Jack purchased a program, and they studied it in the lobby as they waited for the show to begin. Once the curtain rose, Marilee found herself mesmerized, and she wondered what Sam would think of the show. She couldn't imagine him sitting through a musical, any more than she could visualize Jack sitting in a booth at the Mockingbird Café.

"Enjoying yourself?" Jack asked at intermission.

Marilee smiled. "Oh, yes! Thank you for inviting me."

He smiled. "Are you kidding? Watching you have this much fun makes it more pleasurable for me." He nudged her. "I noticed you got a little teary-eyed when they sang the theme song from *Cats*."

"It was very moving."

"I'm surprised your husband didn't take you to these events."

Marilee's smile faltered. "We never had the time," she said. "When you're involved with a big church there's always something going on, or somebody in need." She wouldn't mention that she and Grady could never have afforded to attend such events on a minister's salary, at least not on a regular basis.

"I think it's time people started doing nice things for you, Marilee." Jack took her hand and squeezed it gently. "You're a beautiful woman. You'll have men standing in line before you know it, and the one who wins your heart will be the luckiest man in the world."

The compliment was so nice and unexpected it caught Marilee off guard. "What a lovely thing to say."

"I'm merely being honest. I feel you've been taken for granted far too long."

Marilee pondered his words as they went back in to see the second half of the performance. She was not surprised when the cast received a standing ovation, and she and Jack applauded as eagerly as the rest of the audience. She felt as if she were on a cloud as they left the auditorium. Afterward, Jack drove to an exclusive French restaurant that he claimed had received glowing reviews. He pulled into valet parking, and a man in a white jacket hurried up.

As Jack led her into the restaurant, Marilee forgot about everything else that was on her mind. Chickpea had a couple of elegant restaurants, but nothing of this caliber. Jack ordered a bottle of wine that was so expensive she allowed him to pour just a smidgeon into her glass, which she sipped cautiously. The veal dish he'd recommended tasted better than anything she'd ever put in her mouth. They were coddled and pampered by the staff, and when Marilee visited the ladies' room, she found a woman waiting for her with linen hand towels and various perfumes so she could freshen up. The woman even used a lint brush on Marilee's dress, taking time to compliment her on her outfit. Marilee noted a basket of tips by the door, and she placed a dollar bill inside on her way out. She felt like a queen.

Nevertheless, as the evening progressed, her thoughts kept returning to Sam, and she found herself comparing Jack to him constantly. It wasn't quite fair, seeing as how Jack had gone to so much trouble for her. As they drove back to Pickford, she couldn't keep her mind from drifting toward Sam, even as Jack entertained her with amusing stories about the restaurant business.

"I owned a very successful bistro in New York," he told her, "right in the heart of Manhattan. That's where I met Teresa. She and her friends lunched there often. Naturally, she insisted I sell the restaurant once we married. She traveled abroad extensively, and she wanted me right beside her. You might say I became a gentleman of leisure," he added with a smile, "but I missed the hustle and bustle of restaurant life. I've always had a strong work ethic, and I didn't quite know what to do with myself at first. That's why, after her death, I decided to get back into the business."

Marilee wondered if Teresa had been a demanding woman. Surely it would have been difficult for Jack to give up his thriving business in order to accompany her in her travels. But, knowing Jack as she did, he would have done it for the woman he loved and wouldn't have complained.

"Tell me more about yourself, Marilee. I want to know everything about you."

She could see that he was sincere. "I'm afraid my life has been dull compared to yours," she said. "Other than a few vacations Grady and I took, I've spent my entire life in Chickpea."

Jack smiled at that. "A small-town girl. I like that."

Marilee was disappointed to see they had arrived back at the Pickford Inn so soon. "I had a wonderful evening, Jack," she said as he walked her to her car.

"That makes two of us." He unlocked her door, kissed her on the cheek and waited for her to climb in. "Drive safely."

It was after nine o'clock when a still-smiling Marilee arrived home to find a slew of baby clothes folded neatly on the kitchen table. A note from Winnie bragged about the deals she'd found at the garage sales that day. The girl had obviously washed everything, ironed some of them, and Marilee couldn't help smiling as she reminisced about all the cute things she'd bought Josh when he was a baby.

She sighed happily and thought of going to bed, but she knew she was too wound up to sleep. She put water on to boil for hot chocolate and wished Winnie was awake to hear about her evening. She was still curious why none of her friends had questioned her about her plans. Perhaps they hadn't wanted to pry.

Marilee had just pulled a mug from the cabinet when someone knocked lightly on the back door. She turned on the back porch light and found Sam standing there, looking rumpled in his jeans and pullover shirt.

"I saw your car pull up," Sam said as she let him in. His eyes seemed to drink in the sight of her. "Marilee, you look beautiful."

"Thank you, Sam." She felt beautiful.

He stood there for a moment, still staring. "You got any more of that hot chocolate?"

"How did you know I was making hot chocolate?" she asked.

"Just a wild guess."

"Sure. Have a seat." She made her way to the stove where she found the water boiling. After pulling out another mug and filling two cups, she started to sit down. "Oops, almost forgot." She reached for the napkins, folded them into neat squares and placed them beneath each cup, just as the waiter had done in the restaurant. She sat down, her back ramrod straight and head held high, much the way Jack had sat through the evening. She would have to take care to remember her manners, now that she would be going to nice places.

Sam arched one eyebrow as he took it all in. Was she trying to impress him? "Well? Aren't you going to tell me about your evening?" She'd obviously enjoyed herself very much; she hadn't stopped smiling since he'd walked into the house.

"I had a wonderful time," she said. "The production was stupendous," she added, using a word Jack had used earlier. "I've never heard such melodious voices or seen dancers move so gracefully and with so much fluidity, yet with a fine-tuned precision."

Sam arched one eyebrow. "That good, huh?"

"Stupendous," she repeated.

He looked at her. Smile, smile, smile. "Glad you had a good time." He tried to sound sincere. He would have been happier if she'd done something fun with him. "You know, I've been to a couple of plays, myself," he said.

Marilee realized she was slouching. Not much, not really enough to notice, and she was tired. That had to count for something. Once again, she sat tall. A yawn escaped her, but she patted her mouth gracefully. "That's nice."

She sounded as if she didn't believe him. Sam started to tell her the names of some of the plays he'd seen, but decided against it. He wasn't going to brag just to make himself sound good in comparison to another man. If that's what it took to impress her then she was no different from the other women he'd known.

Perhaps he was trying too hard. He'd never had to work at winning a woman's favor in the past, and it was beginning to irk him that Marilee was oblivious to what other women saw in him.

"More hot cocoa?" Marilee asked, deciding cocoa sounded classier than hot chocolate.

"No, thanks." Sam frowned. "Is something wrong with your back?"

"My back?" She blushed and relaxed her muscles. Maybe she was overdoing it. "No, it's fine."

Sam stood. He was in no better a mood than when he'd first come over. In fact, he was jealous, and it wasn't an emotion he was used to dealing with. "I'd better get back," he said. "I have an early day tomorrow." He surprised her by leaning over and dropping a kiss on the top of her head.

"Sleep well, Marilee." He started for the door and turned. "Hey, I'm glad you had a good time. I'm sorry for teasing you at the restaurant this morning, you know, asking all those dumb questions. Every woman needs to be able to dress up and go to nice places. And you do look beautiful."

He smiled and left, leaving Marilee confused. One minute he acted jealous, the next minute he acted as though he couldn't care less if she'd spent the evening with another man. She finished her hot chocolate slouched over her chair, because there was nobody to see.

When Marilee looked at her paycheck on Monday, she discovered Irby had given her both a raise and a new job title. Her check had been tucked into a white envelope and attached to a note of thanks for all she'd done. Irby seemed a little more upbeat than he'd been the previous week, but the somber air remained. He didn't quite meet her gaze as he discussed the business of the day.

"I picked up a nursing-home patient last night," he said in a monotone. "Mr. Raymond Kellet. Died in his sleep. His relatives are scattered all over the country, but they're flying in, should be here late this afternoon. There will be a viewing tonight, so I'd better get busy."

Marilee nodded. He sounded as though he'd rather be anywhere but there.

"Oh, by the way, Kellet's daughter has requested a small service in the chapel here, tomorrow at 9:00 a.m. I wanted to see if you were interested in making a few extra bucks playing the organ. She's only asked for a couple of songs, so it shouldn't take long."

"I'll be glad to do it," Marilee said. "Nine is pretty early."

"Yeah. Seems his son has a busy schedule and has to return home immediately."

"Gee, that's too bad," Marilee said. "Poor Mr. Kellet should have chosen a more convenient time to pass on."

Irby nodded. "You can bet he'll find time to drop by the

attorney's office for the reading of the will, the selfish bastard."

Marilee looked up in surprise. She had never heard Irby use such strong language before. The man was definitely not himself these days, and she had no idea what to say or do. "Where's Debbie?" she asked, thinking a change of subject was in order.

"At the beauty parlor. She called our baby-sitter first thing this morning and made arrangements to be away all day."

"I'm glad to hear it," Marilee said. "She seldom takes time for herself."

"I should probably help out more."

"I'm sure Debbie would appreciate it."

Irby looked thoughtful as he turned toward his office.

The day seemed to drag, and Marilee realized she missed the old Irby—his jokes, his irreverent sense of humor that made working at Denton Funeral Home an enjoyable time. She hoped that once Irby got over the loss of his friend, things would return to normal.

Shortly before Marilee closed for the day, Debbie walked in, wrestling an armful of bags from Belks, the only store in Chickpea where designer fashions were sold, if one could afford it. "Oh, my gosh, Debbie, you look wonderful!"

Debbie patted her hair, which had been tinted, cut and styled. "Your friend Ruby works wonders. She even showed me a new way to apply my makeup."

"Yes, she's pretty good at that," Marilee said, mildly amused.

"I figure, if I can make dead people look good, I should be able to do something with my own looks." She paused. "How's Irby?"

"Not so good."

"Still moping around?"

Irby picked that moment to come in. He came to an abrupt halt and stared at his wife. "Wow, Debbie! You're beautiful."

"Thank you, Irby. It's been a long time since you've told

me that. As much as I appreciate it, though, Marilee and I need to talk to you about something serious.''

"You're both walking out after all," he said, more to himself.

"No, we're not going anywhere. But you've got to snap out of this. I know you're depressed over losing Tom, and all that transpired afterward, but Marilee and I miss the old Irby."

"I thought you wanted me to act...you know...more responsible."

"You *are* a responsible person. Our business is doing very well."

"That's nice." He didn't sound very excited about it.

"This is a serious business, Irby. It can be depressing at times. I know it gets to you from time to time, because it gets to me as well. But the reason we're successful, at least partially, is because you have a great attitude."

"I do?"

Both women nodded. "Attitude is everything," Marilee said.

Debbie walked over to her husband and slipped her arms around his waist. "I want the old Irby back."

He seemed to ponder the idea. "I guess I'm still feeling guilty over Tom."

"Don't," Debbie said. "You gave him a funeral fit for a king. His family was genuinely touched." Debbie paused. "And because of you, Sheila will never know her husband died in another woman's bed."

Irby looked surprised. "You're not still mad at me for that?"

"I'm not saying what you did was right, I'm saying I understand *why* you did it. I've visited and talked with Sheila a number of times, and she is distraught enough over Tom's death. I can't imagine the devastation and betrayal she would have felt had she known the truth. I know you had her best interests at heart when you made the decision to move the body."

"I could have lost my license," Irby said.

"But you didn't."

"I think we should try to put the incident out of our minds," Marilee said, "and go on from here."

Irby studied his wife for a few seconds. "Is that a new dress?"

"Yes, as a matter of fact, it is."

"It's awfully pretty. You look...very nice, Debbie. Maybe you and I can get that sitter to come back again so we can have a night out. Just the two of us." His face suddenly reddened, as though he'd only just realized Marilee was still in the room. He checked his wristwatch as if to cover his embarrassment. "Well, I have a few calls to make." He disappeared into his office and closed the door.

"What do you think?" Marilee asked.

Debbie shrugged. "Hopefully he'll snap out of it soon. He gets like this from time to time, though not very often, thank goodness. I don't have to tell you this is a tough business," she said. "We don't always get old people who die in their sleep in nursing homes. So my husband makes sick jokes and plays silly pranks, and somehow that gets him through."

Marilee nodded. She understood tough times. She knew what it was like to ache so deep inside that it was all she could do to function. Irby had found a way to deal with that ache, and because of it she had a new respect for the man.

"One good thing," Debbie said, suddenly brightening. "He noticed me."

"And he suggested dinner out."

"I can't tell you the last time Irby and I did something without the kids."

Marilee hitched her purse over her shoulders and grinned. "I'd say the two of you are long overdue."

Marilee was still smiling when she climbed into her car a couple of minutes later. It looked as if things were working out for her friends. She wondered why couples often took one another for granted, so much so that the romance often flew right out the window. When had she and Grady begun taking each other for granted? Probably long before she started wearing those flannel gowns and floppy socks.

If she ever had a second chance at love, she would never forget how important it was to keep the romance alive.

Marilee found a dozen long-stemmed yellow roses waiting for her when she arrived home from work. Attached was a thank-you note from Jack. "Oh, how lovely," she said, feeling like a young girl.

Winnie nodded. "I need to meet a man who'll send me yellow roses. They don't come any prettier than that."

Marilee saw the wistful look on her face. "You will meet someone one day. He'll be a wonderful husband, and a good father to your baby."

"Yeah, but will he send me yellow roses?"

"Once he finds out how much you like them." She set the vase on the kitchen table.

Marilee found Jack in his office when she arrived at the Pickford Inn. "I just wanted to leave my purse in here and to thank you for the roses. They're beautiful."

"Thank *you*," he said, giving her a broad smile. "I had a wonderful time Sunday. Let's do it again soon."

She smiled and floated toward the piano.

Marilee opened with her usual song, then played from her list as customers filtered in. Tuesday was not a busy night, but the Pickford had its regular customers, so business was steady. She was coming back from her break when she looked up and found the hostess seating Clara, Ruby, Nell and Winnie. The girls had obviously decided to surprise her. She walked over to the table.

"I thought y'all were coming in Saturday night," she said, giving them a stern look.

"Clara noticed you had a Tuesday-night special," Winnie said. "Surf and turf for twelve ninety-five. We're going to order two dinners and split them."

"Also, I figured there'd be less drinking if we came during the week," Clara whispered as Ruby rolled her eyes.

Nell looked excited. "We're going to eat slowly so we can stay late and hear all your songs. We can drive back together."

Marilee nodded. "Okay. Don't forget I take requests. Only I don't expect any of you to tip me. Behave yourselves."

Marilee stopped by the hostess desk before she returned to the piano. She hadn't gotten to know Andrea well, but the woman was always polite. "Andrea, those ladies you just seated are friends of mine," she said. "Please don't give them a check, no matter how much they insist otherwise. I'll pay it tomorrow night. Oh, and they'll be staying until closing."

"No problem. I'll take good care of them," she promised.

Marilee took her place at the piano and began playing while requests drifted in, accompanied by the usual dollar bills. Ruby, Nell and Winnie each had a request and insisted on tipping her, despite the dark look she shot them. From time to time, Marilee glanced up and found her friends chatting among themselves as they shared their dinners. She was glad to see them having a good time.

It was near closing when Andrea seated two men near the front. Only a couple of tables remained, but they were finishing up. Andrea handed the newcomers a menu and walked over to Marilee.

"Jack asked me to see if you could play a little longer tonight to accommodate these big shots from Atlanta," she said, nodding toward the men. "Gertie is going to serve them since most of the others have clocked out, but she's not too happy about it."

Marilee nodded. "Sure, I can stay awhile longer. Would you please tell my friends, in case they want to go ahead and leave?" The woman nodded and made her way toward their table.

"Your friends are here for the duration," Andrea said when Marilee finished her next song. "I asked Gertie to make a fresh pot of coffee and feed them dessert. On the house,'' she added, and winked.

Marilee was touched by her generosity. "Thank you." She smiled at her friends and began playing a Barbra Streisand number. Gertie appeared at the newcomers' table and took a drink order, forgoing her usual smile. The waitress obviously did not want to be there. She served their drinks and one of the men handed her a bill. She nodded and walked over to Marilee.

"Do you believe these jerks say they need a few minutes to decide on what they want?" she whispered. "The chef is fit to be tied. Why do people wait this late to eat? Don't they know it's bad for digestion? Oh, they asked me to see if you know 'You Are So Beautiful.'" Gertie stuffed a ten-dollar bill into the tip bowl and walked away as Marilee began playing the requested song.

Jack joined the men as they were eating their appetizers. He smiled at Marilee, and she immediately began playing his favorite, "I Left My Heart in San Francisco." He and the men seemed deep in conversation; they pointed to the wine list as Gertie served their salads. They'd obviously selected an expensive wine because Jack, who'd already sent the bartender and the others home, excused himself to unlock the wine cabinet.

Marilee wondered how long she would be expected to play, but the men kept sending requests, accompanied by hefty tips, so she stayed. Once again she sent the hostess over to tell her friends to go on home, but they continued to wait it out. It was nearing midnight by the time Gertie handed the men their check. They paid, then got up and followed Jack into his office.

"Jeez, I thought they'd never finish eating," Gertie said as she stripped the table of the remaining glasses and silverware. "At least they tipped well. I'm going to walk out with you and your friends, if you don't mind. That new security guard didn't show up tonight, and I don't like going out into the parking lot this time of night. I'll grab our purses from the office."

Marilee was surprised the woman was being nice to her, but she wasn't about to complain. "Thanks, Gertie."

"You guys ready to leave?" Marilee asked once she'd gathered her music and joined her friends.

"Marilee, I had the best time tonight," Clara surprised her by saying.

"We all had a ball," Ruby said, and Nell nodded vigorously.

Winnie looked tired. "I had a good time too, but I don't care for old-fart music."

"We cater to an older crowd," Marilee said.

"I pretty much figured that one out on my own."

"Come on, let's go home," Marilee said. "I'm just waiting for Gertie to grab my purse from the office."

The women stood and walked in the direction of Jack's office. After waiting several minutes, Marilee tapped lightly on the door.

One of the men opened it. He smiled. "Come on in, ladies," he said, stepping aside. "We're having a little party."

"I just came for my purse," Marilee said.

"Besides, we can't stay," Winnie said. "I'm with child, and I need my rest."

"Oh, but I insist." He pulled a gun from the waistband of his slacks.

The women froze.

"On second thought, I think I can spare a few minutes," Winnie said, going inside. "How about you ladies?" she called over her shoulder.

They exchanged looks as they followed Winnie into the room, where Jack and Gertie waited, both of them bound and gagged.

# *Seventeen*

"Shit," Ruby said once the man had closed the door behind them and locked it.

Marilee gasped, noting the open wall safe above Jack's head. "Are you okay?" she asked, looking from Jack to Gertie, neither of whom could speak at the moment. Jack had been taped to his desk chair, and Gertie bound from shoulder to ankle to another chair.

"Please," the man said, motioning to the sofa. "Sit down and join us."

"Are you asking us or telling us?" Winnie asked.

He waved the gun in her face. "Guess."

The four of them scrunched together on the sofa. "This just beats all," Ruby said. "We finally convince Clara to go somewhere and look what happens."

"Shut up," the man told her.

Marilee gazed about, dazed, as if she were watching the whole thing in a movie but not really participating. Seconds passed before she realized she was trembling. Suddenly, all she could think of was Josh, and the possibility that she may never see him again. And Nell. The woman was too old to have to go through something like this. And what about Winnie and the baby? And Clara and Ruby? Oh, how she wished they had never come for dinner.

"Look, if you're going to pop us just do it and get it over with," Winnie said. "I'm too tired to plead for my life, and I've already got a killer backache."

"Why don't you just keep your fat mouth shut?" the other man said, showing his pistol for the first time.

"Don't touch her," Marilee said, forgetting her fear for a moment. "You've got your money, why don't you go?"

"And I'm not fat," Winnie said. "I'm pregnant. And dealing with a little edema at the moment because—" He put the gun to Winnie's nose and her eyes crossed as she stared down the barrel, while the others barely allowed themselves to breathe. "Guess edema isn't a real attention grabber for you, is it?" she said.

"Lady, if you don't keep your mouth shut, you're going to be sorry you ran into me."

She opened her mouth to speak, but seemed to think better of it.

He looked at his partner. "Check the place," he told the other man, "just in case."

"I know you," Marilee said to the first man. "You're the new security guard. Frank, isn't it? What happened to your beard? And your hair? It used to be dark."

"He must've been wearing a disguise at the time," Ruby whispered.

The man smiled. "Hey, you two are pretty smart for a couple of blond chicks. Not to mention good-looking." He looked from one to the other. "Could be me and my friend might want to have a little fun with you girls before we go." Frank stepped close to Marilee. "I'm gettin' hard just thinking about it."

"What's wrong, can't you get a real date?" Winnie asked.

"Shut up, you black bitch." He raised his hand to slap her.

Nell cried out. "Please don't do that. I could have a heart attack, and you'd have that on your conscience the rest of your life."

Frank paused and looked at her, but before he could say anything his partner returned, bearing more duct tape. "Found this in the pantry. Coast is clear. Let's bind 'em up and get the hell out of here."

They began taping the women's arms and legs together, then strapped them to the furniture and to one another so there was no possibility of them moving. Frank made a move to tape Marilee's mouth, and she turned her head.

"There's no need for that," she said. "You've tied us so we can't escape. Nobody is going to hear us."

"She's right, man," Frank's partner said. "Besides, we don't have enough tape." He looked at them. "They ain't goin' nowheres."

Frank shrugged and tossed the rolls to the floor.

"Please—" Nell began. "Please remove the tape from their mouths," she said, nodding toward Gertie and Jack. "I...I can't breathe looking at them," she said, "and I feel light-headed. If I end up having a stroke and die, you could be charged with that."

"I thought you said you had a bad heart."

"I'm old. Everything's gone to hell."

"You're a pain in the ass, lady."

Frank shook his head as he yanked the tape off Gertie's mouth. She mouthed an obscenity, which he ignored as he pulled the tape from Jack's mouth as well. "Are you satisfied, old lady? Is there anything else I can do to assure your comfort? A can of Ensure, maybe?"

"I could use a pillow behind my back," Winnie said.

"Stop pushing them," Clara ordered. "What do you think this is, a dinner party? These guys mean business."

Frank smiled at her. "You're a very intelligent lady. Why can't I rob more people like you?"

"Thank you," Clara said, lifting her chin and giving the others a haughty look.

Once the men left, locking the door securely, Marilee looked at Gertie and Jack. "Are either of you hurt?"

"Just my pride," the waitress said, still smacking her lips where the tape had pulled at the tender skin.

"I'm okay," Jack managed to say.

Gertie looked at him. "I thought you had a buzzer beneath your desk," she said, "to call that security company if something happened. I specifically remember how you complained for weeks when you got the bill for it."

"I was afraid they'd see me reach for it," he said.

"So you did nothing?" She gave a grunt of disgust. "You just sat there and allowed them to pull all of us in here? They could have raped or killed us. You're the man here, Jack. A real man would have tried to protect us."

"I don't know why you keep all your money in that safe, anyway," Nell told him. "I bury all my valuables in my flower bed. Safest place in the world. 'Course, my son thinks I'm crazy."

Gertie continued to glare at Jack. "You could have prevented this, but you were more concerned with your own hide. You've always cared more about yourself than anyone else. It took me a long time to see it, because I was in love with you and saw only what I wanted to."

The women on the sofa looked at one another, eyebrows raised high.

"Gertie, must we air our dirty laundry in front of everyone?" Jack asked wearily.

"Hey, I'm enjoying it," Winnie said. "You have what you might call a captive audience."

Gertie regarded Marilee. "It's true, honey. All Jack cares about is what Jack wants, and he usually gets it. I'll bet you've heard that song-and-dance routine about his poor wife, Teresa," she said. "It's just a ruse to make you feel sorry for him, and it usually works. He used it on me too."

"I'm sure the memories are painful for him," Marilee said.

"Painful, my ass. Teresa died in a car accident. She was in the process of leaving him because he'd slept with all her friends, including the housekeeper. Hell, the man will sleep with anybody who has a pulse. He's a user and a womanizer."

"Shut up, Gertie!" Jack snapped.

"And that's not the half of it," Gertie said. "His wife was worth millions. Not only that, her car had been tampered with."

Jack's face became bloodred. "I was cleared of any wrongdoing. Now, shut up or I'll—"

The room grew silent.

Gertie laughed at him. "You plan on tampering with my car, too?" Once again, she looked at Marilee. "He was a young, strapping stud, washing dishes in some bistro, when Teresa took one look and fell in love with him, just like I did. She groomed him to be the man he is today, and he took advantage of her. The poor woman never suspected a thing until the very end, but she died before she could change her will. Jack got everything. Her friends were outraged. Why do you think Jack left New York? I'll tell you—because he became an outcast. Teresa had seen to it that he was accepted by polite society, so to speak, but after her death those doors were slammed in his face."

Jack was silent, but anger literally seethed from him.

Marilee was speechless. "How do you know all this, Gertie?"

"Because he used me just like he's trying to use you." She sniffed. "Oh, I was heartbroken, let me tell you. I kept blaming myself. Fortunately, I have a cousin who does a little private-detective work on the side. He came back with enough info on Jack to write a book and its sequel."

"How long have you had this so-called information?" Jack demanded.

"Two months," she said. She turned to Marilee and smiled prettily. "See, I'm four months pregnant with Jack's child. He gave me five thousand bucks, told me to get rid of the problem and take a vacation. I gave a portion of the money to my cousin instead." She hitched her chin high. "My child is going to have everything his or her little heart desires."

"Oh, Gertie, you should have told me," Marilee said, wishing she could reach out and comfort the woman. "But Teresa had money, I don't. What could Jack possibly hope to get from me?"

"He doesn't need money, sweetie. He just wants to get you in bed. And as long as you hold out, he'll wine and dine you and take you to every play in Charleston."

Marilee blushed profusely.

Clara looked at Ruby. "I *told* you Marilee was going with him to see that Broadway production."

"Yes, and I told *you* it was none of our business. If Marilee had wanted us to know she would have said something."

"I knew it too," Nell said. "Sam pouted for two whole days."

"You girls need to get a life," Winnie told them before turning her attention back to Jack and Gertie, who'd stopped arguing long enough to stare at the group.

Marilee shook her head, embarrassed. Now her closest friends knew she'd gone to Charleston with a lowlife womanizer. Wasn't it bad enough she'd been married to one? "I'm going to have to move to a foreign country," she said.

Jack looked at her. "What I feel for you is real, Marilee. You're different from the rest."

Marilee's voice was calm when she spoke. "You'll have to find another piano player, Mr. Helms."

Gertie smiled. "Good for you, Marilee. I, on the other hand, plan to hang around."

"Aren't you afraid?" Nell whispered, eyeing Jack.

"I've got a copy of Jack's file with my cousin, my attorney and in my safe-deposit box," Gertie replied, "with instructions to hand it over to the newspaper if anything happens to me. Believe me, Jack likes being a respectable businessman and hobnobbing with the rich. He doesn't want the truth to get out." She smiled. "Besides, I like it here."

"You know what they call that, don't you?" Winnie said. "Job security."

Sam awoke on the sofa with a start, having fallen asleep watching the eleven o'clock news. He'd spent three hours that evening working at Blessing Home, only to arrive home to a dark house and a note from his mother that she and her friends were having dinner at the Pickford Inn so they could watch Marilee perform. He'd grabbed a sandwich and struggled to stay awake, but obviously he had lost the battle.

He glanced at the wall clock and frowned. It was

4:00 a.m., and he hadn't heard his mother come in. Rising, he went and checked her bedroom. The room was neat, as always, and the old quilt on her bed bore not a single wrinkle. The only thing out of place was her bathrobe, which was lying across an old rocker that had been in his family for generations.

Where the hell was she?

He retraced his steps to the living room and stepped out the back door. Marilee's house was dark. He vaguely noticed that it was raining.

Sam found the telephone book beneath the wall phone in the kitchen and looked up the number to the Pickford Inn. No answer. He grabbed his cell phone and ran for the truck.

Five minutes later, Sam turned onto the highway leading to Pickford. The rain was coming down harder. He picked up his phone and dialed 911 and proceeded to explain the situation to a dispatcher, who checked to see if there had been any accidents reported.

"Nothing here," he said. "I'll ring the police in Pickford and have them call you."

Sam hung up and drove, ignoring the speed limit as he pressed his foot on the accelerator.

The parking lot was dark when Sam pulled up in front of the Pickford Inn, but he spotted Marilee's car right away, sitting next to another car he thought belonged to one of her friends. A Mercedes was parked out front. He climbed from the truck and hurried toward the double glass doors. They were locked tight. He knocked hard and waited. The muscles in his jaws tensed. He didn't like it. He pounded on the door.

Nothing.

The loud ringing of the cell phone sent him running back to his truck. It was the dispatcher from the Pickford Police Department, informing him there'd been no accidents. Sam briefly described the situation.

"I'll send a couple of cars over right away," the dispatcher said.

"I'm going in," Sam informed her.

"You can't do that. You'll get picked up for breaking and entering."

"My mother might be in there," Sam said. As well as the woman he was growing to love more than life itself, he added silently. "I'll take my chances." Sam hung up and raced to the double doors where an oversize flowerpot stood. He grabbed the pot and tossed it through a door, covering his face as glass shattered and flew in every direction. He reached inside and turned the lock.

Sam found himself standing in a long carpeted hallway beside a hostess desk. He glanced in both directions. Everything was dark. Hearing a shout, he took off in that direction. "Hello?" he called out loudly. "Is anybody here? Mom? Marilee?"

Marilee recognized Sam's voice instantly. "We're back here, Sam," she called loudly. "Turn left at the end of the hall."

Sam went weak with relief at the sound of her voice, but didn't stop. She and his mother could be injured. And what about Winnie? He had to find them. A group of voices called out, and he followed the sound to a door right off the hall. It was locked. He cursed. Damned if he wasn't always breaking down doors to save Marilee's neck. He stepped back and threw himself forward, hitting the door with his shoulder. It didn't budge, but he was certain he'd broken every bone in his body above his waist. He shoved a stack of menus off a small round table and slammed it into the door with all he had. It seemed to burst before his very eyes.

Breathing heavily, he stepped inside and found the group bound with duct tape. His eyes immediately sought out Marilee, who sat beside Winnie and his mother. He sighed and wiped sweat from his face, trying to stop the flow of adrenaline rushing through his veins. "Is everybody okay?" he asked, looking for wounds, blood, anything.

"We are now, dear," Nell said cheerfully. "Except I really need to use the ladies' room."

# *Eighteen*

It was almost eight-thirty in the morning by the time the women had finished answering the police's questions. Sam had kept the coffee coming and offered moral support to everyone but Jack, at whom he tossed a dark look each chance he got. So that was his competition, he thought. Marilee obviously went for the polished, sophisticated type. Sam suspected right away that Jack Helms was not the man he pretended to be. There was something about him that Sam couldn't quite put his finger on, but if Jack and Marilee were close, it didn't show. She seemed to be avoiding the man, as did most of the women. Sam made a point to stay as close to Marilee as he could.

"Oh, my Lord, I have to go!" Marilee cried, suddenly remembering she had to play for the Kellet funeral. She jumped up from the dining-room chair, where she'd been sitting for more than two hours. "I'm late for work!"

Sam, standing only a few feet away, looked at her incredulously. "Work!" he said. "You're in no condition to work. You need to go home and sleep."

She handed him her empty coffee cup. "I have no choice," she said, explaining the situation.

"You'll never make it."

"I have to." She looked at the officer. "Are you finished questioning me? I've told you everything I know."

The chief of police, who'd arrived on the scene shortly after the officers had stormed the restaurant and then had spent much of his time on a cell phone, hurried over to the group. Don Harris was a big man, with a balding head and meaty features, who'd done all he could to make the ladies feel at ease after the night they'd spent.

"Good news," he told the group. "A couple of guys fitting the description were arrested about a hundred miles from here earlier this morning on a DUI charge. An officer searched their vehicle and found a large amount of cash under the seats. He also found a security-guard uniform wadded up in the trunk of the car." Harris gave Sam a satisfied smile.

Nell looked up wearily. "Oh my, I wonder if it could be the same men who robbed us?" she asked.

Sam nodded appreciatively at the chief as he patted Nell's hand. "My mother needs her rest."

"I understand," Harris said, giving the woman a sympathetic look. "It'll take a while to get these guys back over here, but I'm going to have to ask everybody to come into the station later so you can have a look at them. Won't take long, but we just need to see if you recognize them in a lineup."

Marilee sighed. She was so tired she wasn't sure she could pick out her own mother in a lineup. "I have to be somewhere at nine," she said, "but I can come in after that."

"Why don't we schedule it for eleven-thirty, then?" he suggested. "I'll tell the others." He pulled Sam aside. "Don't worry about bringing your mother. She's tired, and we'll have enough witnesses."

"I'll be there," Marilee said. She started down the hall. Sam went after her.

"I can't believe you're going to work," he said as he helped her into her car, both of them trying to dodge the rain. "Why don't you let me drive you? I don't like the idea of you driving in this weather."

Marilee shivered as the cold rain hit the back of her neck. She could read his concern in the white lines that bracketed his mouth. "Thanks, Sam, but I'll be okay. You need to see to your mother." She closed the door, cranked the engine and took off.

Sam shook his head as she pulled away, tires squealing on the wet pavement.

"I don't believe what I just saw," Winnie said, joining him with an umbrella.

Sam looked at her. "What do you mean?"

"Marilee's on her way to play for a funeral in a red sequined dress and platinum wig."

It was all Marilee could do to keep her eyes open as she raced to the funeral home, almost running into a dump truck at one point. Slow down and think, she told herself, trying to clear the fog from her brain. Although she was exhausted beyond belief, she was wired from having drunk so much caffeine. She arrived at the funeral home at nine-fifteen. Squealing to a stop, she cut the engine and raced inside the back door of the chapel, almost running into Debbie and Irby in the small hallway just outside.

"Marilee, where on earth have you been?" Irby demanded. "Everybody's here, and they're waiting for you. I don't mind telling you, some of them are quite irritated."

Marilee did not see the strange look he gave her as she brushed past him. "I'll explain later."

Debbie followed, a frown marring her forehead. "Uh, Marilee, wait! You can't possibly—"

"No time, Debbie," she said, racing inside the chapel.

Marilee was only vaguely aware of the small crowd that had already gathered inside the chapel. She made straight for the piano and sat down. Without thinking, she automatically began to play "I Left My Heart In San Francisco."

"Marilee, what were you thinking?" Irby said, once she'd played for the service. She hadn't realized until she was halfway through the opening song that she was supposed to be playing "How Great Thou Art." When her brain had finally kicked in, it suddenly occurred to her that she hadn't thought to change clothes before taking her place in front of the solemn-faced crowd. By then it was too late. She had been mortified beyond belief, but there had been nothing she could do except keep playing. She'd slipped from the chapel as soon as she'd finished, only to find Irby and Debbie waiting with a look of pure stupefaction on their faces.

"Are you okay, honey?" Debbie asked.

With tears in her eyes, Marilee told them how she'd spent the evening and much of the morning.

Debbie gaped at her. "Oh, you poor thing!" she said, closing her arms around Marilee immediately. "Why didn't you call us? We could have found a replacement."

Marilee sniffed. "I didn't want to let you down." She also needed the extra money since she'd quit her night job.

The service ended, and a tall brunette exited the chapel and made straight for the three of them. Linda Kellet, the deceased's daughter, looked mad enough to spit nails.

"How dare you!" she said, giving them all a scathing look. "How dare you make a mockery of my father's funeral."

Irby cleared his throat. "Was there a problem, Miss Kellet?" he asked innocently.

"Problem?" she repeated, her voice ripe with sarcasm. "Only that you hired a trollop to handle my father's service. If you think for one minute I'm going to pay this bill, you're out of your mind. Not only am I not going to pay this bill, I plan to contact an attorney immediately."

"Miss Kellet, I'm afraid there's been some misunderstanding," Irby said. "Your father left specific instructions on how he wished his funeral to be handled, and we did everything to accommodate him."

Marilee and Debbie exchanged anxious looks.

"What the hell are you talking about?" the woman demanded.

"He didn't discuss it with you beforehand?"

"Discuss what?"

"Your father had a great sense of humor," Irby said. "I was fortunate to know him well."

"You knew my father?"

"Yes. I met him while visiting another patient at the nursing home. I'm surprised he never mentioned it. Well, that's not important," Irby went on, "but your father told me several times that when he died he didn't want folks playing sad music. Mrs. Abernathy only played those religious tunes because you requested it."

The woman stared at him. She crossed her arms. "What exactly did my father say he wanted?" she asked.

Irby smiled. "He said, 'Irby, when I go, I want you to hire dancing girls and play my favorite song, "I Left My Heart In San Francisco."'" Irby dropped the smile. "That was his favorite song, you know."

"I had no idea," she said meekly.

"We were just doing as we were told, Miss Kellet. I'm sorry if you were embarrassed, but we have to take the deceased's wants into consideration."

"I feel so silly," the woman replied.

The chapel door opened and another man stalked out. "Are you the owner?" he demanded.

Irby offered his hand. "Irby Denton. Very nice to meet you. You must be Raymond's son, Garth. He spoke highly of you."

The man was obviously taken off guard. He composed himself quickly. "I hope you know you're in a shitload of trouble, Mr. Denton, for turning my father's funeral into a circus act. I'd like to know where you found this broad," he said, pointing to Marilee.

Irby smiled. "First of all, Mr. Kellet, we do not refer to ladies as broads around here. Second, this sweet woman is Reverend Grady Abernathy's wife. Meet Marilee."

Garth glared at Marilee. "I don't care if she's married to the pope. She had no business showing up for my father's service dressed like that."

Linda Kellet turned to her brother. "Don't use that tone with Mr. Denton," she said. "He was only doing as Father requested."

"What are you talking about?" Garth demanded.

"Daddy gave Mr. Denton specific instructions on how he

wanted his service to be handled. You should be glad that Mr. Denton was kind enough to honor them.''

''You're saying Father asked for someone to dress up like a call girl and play that stupid song?''

''Daddy had a very funny sense of humor,'' Linda told her brother, ''and you would have known that, had you visited him more often while he was in the nursing home. It just so happens ''I Left My Heart in San Francisco'' was his favorite song.'' She glanced at her wristwatch. ''We need to leave for the graveside service,'' she said. ''I believe you have a plane to catch.''

''We're supposed to meet with Father's attorney before that,'' Garth said.

Marilee and Irby exchanged looks.

Linda Kellet stiffened. ''Oh, yes, we wouldn't want to miss that, now, would we?'' She marched off without another word.

Garth started after her, then turned. ''I hope we don't have any more surprises waiting for us at the grave site,'' he said to Irby.

''Depends,'' Irby said, ''on whether you like dogs and ponies.''

''That's not a damn bit funny,'' Garth said, and walked away.

Debbie looked at her husband. ''Honey, I didn't know you knew Mr. Kellet or that you visited him in the nursing home.''

''I never met the man in my life,'' Irby said. ''Now, if you ladies will excuse me, I have to stuff old man Kellet in a hole so his son will get out of my face. Marilee, go home and rest.''

Debbie looked at Marilee as her husband hurried away. ''Well, I guess the old Irby is back.''

Marilee found Sam waiting in her kitchen when she arrived home. ''Where's your mother?''

''Resting. She's in no condition to face a lineup after having stayed up all night.''

Nell picked that moment to walk in the back door. "Everybody ready to go? I want to put those scoundrels behind bars before they terrorize more innocent people."

"Mom, I asked you to rest."

"I'll rest when this is over." She looked determined.

Sam shrugged, knowing it was useless to argue. His mother had become even more feisty than usual the past couple of months; he assumed Marilee and her friends had something to do with it, and he knew his mother had never been happier. He owed a debt of gratitude to Marilee and the others.

Marilee showered and dressed in record time, woke Winnie, and they were on their way in a matter of minutes. Sam had chosen to drive his car, since it would accommodate everybody. Marilee didn't care that her hair was wet and that she wore no makeup. She just wanted to get this business out of the way and rest. The rain looked as though it would continue through the day.

"Marilee, I've been thinking," Sam said. "You're one of the strongest women I've ever met, but you need an equally strong man in your life. That Jack fellow doesn't look all that capable."

Marilee glanced over her shoulder at the back seat and was relieved to find Winnie and Nell sleeping. "I don't work at the Pickford Inn anymore," she replied, "so I won't be seeing much of Mr. Helms."

Sam was relieved. "Well, that's too bad," he said. But he was grinning. His smile faded after a moment. "Are you going to be okay financially?"

"I'll be fine." She patted his hand, and he captured it, letting it rest on his thigh as he drove. Somehow, it felt natural to Marilee. "By the way, you were a real hero last night, you know that?"

"I did what I had to do. It's only natural to want to protect those you love."

Marilee's insides warmed at the thought, and her hand remained on his thigh until they reached the town of Pickford.

Chief Harris was waiting for them when they arrived. "Jack Helms and Gertie Johnson have already come and gone," the chief said. He looked surprised to see Nell. "You okay, Mrs. Brewer?"

"Of course I'm okay," she said. "Why wouldn't I be?"

"This won't take long," he said. He explained the procedure before escorting Marilee into a room that shared a large window with an adjoining room. Six men appeared in a lineup. She had no trouble spotting the two who had robbed the Pickford.

Sam paced the floor as the others took their turn.

When it was over, Harris looked satisfied, although he didn't comment on the women's choices. He handed each of them his card. "I'll be in touch." He looked at Sam. "These lovely ladies need to go home and rest now."

Marilee found herself nodding off several times as Sam drove them home. The rain had let up, but the roads were slick. Once they arrived at Sam's place, the weary group parted, and Sam escorted his mother inside their house as Marilee and Winnie crossed the lawn to theirs. Sam ushered his mother into her room, helped her out of her coat and pulled off her shoes once she sat on the edge of the bed.

"Are you sure you don't want anything to eat?" he asked.

"Not now," she said. "I'll get something later. You need to check on Winnie and Marilee."

Sam had already planned to do just that. He found the two eating a sandwich at the kitchen table. "Do either of you need anything?" he asked.

"A little shut-eye, and I'll be okay," Winnie said.

Sam stared at Winnie. "You're not having any pains or anything?"

"I'm fine," the girl assured him. "Stop worrying." She carried her plate to the sink and trudged upstairs.

Marilee offered Sam half her sandwich, but he shook his head. "Is your mother okay?" she asked.

"She was sleeping like a baby when I left. You've barely touched your sandwich," he said.

"I guess I'm not hungry."

He saw her shiver. "Are you cold?"

"A little."

"Come on." He stood and held out his hand.

Marilee didn't question him. She took his hand and let him lead her up the stairs and into her bedroom. She supposed she was just too tired to argue. He released her hand and pulled back the covers. "Climb in," he ordered as he took her phone off the hook and tucked it into a drawer on her nightstand. He covered it with a throw pillow and closed the drawer.

"Sam, what on earth are you doing?"

He chuckled. "I learned that little trick in my partying days."

"Among other things," she said drolly.

"Yes, but those days are behind me."

She sighed. "I'll never be able to fall asleep. I'm too wound up." Nevertheless, she kicked off her shoes and crawled beneath the covers. Sam sat on the bed beside her and began removing his own shoes.

She looked at him, mouth agape. "*Now* what are you doing?"

"I didn't get much sleep myself last night. I thought I'd lie down beside you for a minute if you don't mind." When she merely stared at him, he smiled. "Don't worry, I trust you completely. Now, scoot over."

For some crazy reason, that's exactly what she did. She didn't stiffen when Sam joined her beneath the covers and pulled her close so that her head rested on his shoulder; instead, she relaxed against the contours of his body, seeking out his warmth, which soon chased the chill away and soothed her frazzled nerves.

"Go to sleep now, Marilee," he said, his voice lulling her. "You're safe."

She did feel safe, for the first time in months, and it was only then that she realized the enormous amount of stress she'd been under, even long before Grady had walked out on her.

How strange that she'd found sanctuary for her tired soul in the arms of a scoundrel like Sam Brewer.

It was some time before Marilee awoke. When she did, she noticed the rain had stopped. Sam was still sleeping beside her, holding her close, his body comforting and reassuring. She studied him, wondered if he was capable of being faithful to a woman.

She knew he cared for her, but was he the type of man who could love a woman for the rest of his life?

Marilee stared at the ceiling, trying to pull her thoughts together. Would Grady have risked his life for those he loved, as Sam had done? She could see Grady ordering the police about, using his influence to get things done, but she could not envision Grady actually putting himself in danger if there was somebody else to do it.

Marilee wondered if she was falling for Sam. The thought terrified her. How could it have happened so quickly? She had only been separated from Grady a couple of months; surely she needed more time to recover from the loss of her marriage. Yes, but she now knew she had not loved Grady for the past couple of years they'd lived together, at least not the way a woman should love her husband.

Grady had known, and deep down she had suspected it.

Leaving him had not crossed her mind because, as a team, they did well together, and their life was so full that she seldom had time to think about it. But there were times she realized just how lonely her life had become. Like when Grady sat up late watching TV or reading as he did each night, and she climbed into a cold empty bed. And that feeling of loneliness that never went away. Although his leaving had devastated her at the time, she admitted now it was a relief. He had done what she was incapable of doing.

Marilee knew the moment Sam opened his eyes. She looked up and found him watching her, curiously at first. Instead of feeling shy or uncomfortable after having shared a nap with him, she felt a sense of renewal, as if everything was going to be okay.

He grinned. "What would the ladies at Chickpea Baptist Church have to say about you now?" he asked.

Marilee stretched. "Frankly, I think they'd be jealous that I was in bed with the town stud."

He winced. "What does a man have to do to live down a bad reputation in this town?" He snapped his fingers. "I know. Hang out with the town's finest lady."

She smiled. "Know what I think?"

"What?"

"I think I like napping beside you."

He smiled back. "It was pretty nice, wasn't it? At least I got one of my wishes."

"What was that?"

"Waking up next to you. Of course, in my fantasy it would have been after a night of mad, passionate lovemaking."

Marilee shivered.

"Cold?" he asked, giving her a knowing look. "Or warm?"

She blushed. Sam was beginning to know her better than she knew herself. He leaned forward to kiss her, but was interrupted by a knock at the door.

Winnie and Nell peeked in. Winnie grinned; Nell's hands flew to her breasts. "Samuel Brewer, this sort of thing is simply not done! There's a young girl living in this house. Close your eyes, Winnie."

"No way," the girl said. "I like the looks of this."

Marilee blushed. "I'm afraid it's my fault, Nell," she said. "I was so shaken when I came home that Sam decided to stay with me for a while. I guess we both dozed off. I promise it was completely innocent."

Nell didn't look placated. "Well, I'm not about to have my son jeopardizing your good reputation in this town. Samuel, if you're going to share a bed with Marilee, I insist you do the decent thing and marry her."

Sam looked amused. "Marilee isn't exactly in a position to marry anyone right now, and besides, I'm not sure she'd have me."

"Maybe if you changed your sorry ways," Nell replied.

Sam frowned as he looked at Marilee. "And to think only a few hours ago she was so proud of me for rescuing her."

"Look, I don't care what anybody does as long as it doesn't involve guns and duct tape," Winnie said. "We just wanted to tell you dinner is ready."

"And I helped," Nell said proudly. "Now, you come on out of this bedroom, Sam, so Marilee can freshen up."

"Yes, ma'am." He stood and grabbed his shoes, tossing Marilee a boyish grin. "See you downstairs."

Ruby and Clara popped in as the four were finishing their meal. "Did any of you watch the six o'clock news?" Clara asked. "They have coverage of us leaving the Pickford Inn. We wanted to call, but the line was busy."

"Oh, the phone is off the hook in my bedroom," Marilee said.

"I'll put it back on," Sam said, and hurried up the stairs as Clara's and Ruby's gaze followed. They looked at one another, then at Marilee.

"I'm not going to say anything," Ruby replied. "And neither are you, Clara."

"We were really on the news?" Winnie asked excitedly. "Boy, the kids at school will love it. Maybe my old friends will start speaking to me again." As if realizing she'd said too much, she busied herself clearing the table.

"They'll probably show it again at eleven," Ruby said.

Marilee only vaguely remembered the television crew parked outside the Pickford Inn. She had been so intent on getting to the funeral home that she'd ignored the flash of cameras. But her thoughts were centered on Winnie at the moment. She had suspected the girl's friends had abandoned her when she became pregnant, just as her parents had. Marilee's heart ached for her.

Ruby went on. "The only reason we weren't bombarded with reporters was because Chief Harris had the officers surround the place with crime-scene tape. Frankly, I wouldn't have minded talking to those reporters. I could have put in a good word about my salon." She frowned. "Naturally, my hair was a mess, and my dress was as wrinkled as a duck's tail."

"How'd I look?" Winnie asked.

Ruby looked at her. "Pregnant as all get-out."

"Janie, from the *Gazette,* wants to interview us," Clara said. "I told her I'd let her know."

Marilee suddenly remembered her manners. "Clara, Ruby, get a plate. Looks like Nell and Winnie fried enough chicken for an army."

"We can't stay," Ruby said. "My friend from the VFW called to say they were cooking steaks on the grill tonight and wanted to invite us over so we could tell them our harrowing adventure. We came over to invite y'all."

"I can't believe I'm going to a VFW function," Clara muttered, rolling her eyes.

"Oh, hush, Clara, it'll be good for you. And stop tugging at your hair, I went to a lot of trouble to fix it up nicely." Ruby glanced at Sam as he was coming down the stairs. "They want to meet you too," she said, "now that you're a hero."

"I'm really not up to it," he said. "Maybe some other time."

Ruby looked around. "Anybody else?"

"I have to study," Winnie told them.

Marilee yawned. "Maybe some other time, Ruby. I'm still tired."

"I'll go," Nell said, surprising them all. "Maybe I'll meet a man. Am I dressed okay?"

"Sure you are," Ruby said. "Let's go."

Sam was amused at the thought of his mother looking for men. "Please be home early. I can't spend another night sitting up waiting for her to come home."

# Nineteen

Marilee walked into the Mockingbird Café as though it were an everyday occurrence for her to lunch alone. In the past, she would have felt nervous and self-conscious doing so. To avoid it, she would have grabbed a hamburger at a drive-through window or waited until she arrived home to prepare something. She didn't know why it was so important to do something so insignificant that other people did all the time, but it *was* important. She waited while Flora, the owner, seated couples and groups of women. Marilee saw that she was the only one in the entire place eating alone, unless you counted the busboy standing near the back, who was eating a bag of chips while waiting to clean the next table.

She hitched her chin high. She could do this. Why, she could go to the theater alone if she wanted. She could order a large buttered popcorn and eat the whole bucket by herself if she liked. She could attend a play by herself, instead of staying home because nobody else wanted to go.

Marilee had purposefully chosen a time when the café would be busiest because she wanted to prove to herself that there was nothing she couldn't do if she put her mind to it, no matter how uncomfortable it made her at first. Look what she'd already done! She had survived Grady's leaving, her son's anger and her phobia of dead people, although she still preferred not touching them. She had even survived a robbery. She had found a job—*two* jobs, actually, although she'd quit one of them. She kept her bills paid, had learned to check her car for oil and transmission fluid, she'd even caulked around the windows and checked the attic for insulation when her power bill had shown a slight increase. She'd learned, with Winnie's help, how to replace that rubber bulb inside the tank of her toilet, and she had repaired a leaky faucet. To some people it might sound silly that she was so proud of her accomplishments, but each one was a small victory to her.

Flora greeted her warmly. "You waiting for somebody, Marilee?"

Marilee smiled. "No, I'm alone today." She said it proudly.

"You want a booth?"

"I think I'll take that small table in the center of the room if you don't mind."

"Certainly." Flora led her over and handed her a menu. "Our special today is Salisbury steak." She hurried away.

Flora's daughter Bea appeared a few minutes later. "Hi, Marilee. Are you by yourself today?"

Once again, Marilee smiled. Why did people naturally assume one could not dine alone? Of course they could. "Yes, Bea, and I'd like the special."

"Coming right up."

Marilee sat there wondering what she should do while she waited for her food. She chanced a look around, nodded at several people she knew then pulled a paperback from her purse, a book on positive thinking she'd purchased at the local used bookstore.

Marilee's lunch arrived. She ate and read, only vaguely aware of the people around her.

Bea stopped by to refill her iced tea. "So where's that handsome devil you came in with the other day?" she asked.

"I'm sure he's at work," Marilee said. "I don't really keep up with his comings and goings."

"You on your lunch hour?"

"Yes. I decided I was tired of eating at my desk. You can bring me the check next chance you get."

"Sure, honey."

Well, now, Marilee thought. She had asked for her own

check. She pulled money from her wallet. She would not be chintzy about tipping like Grady; she would leave Bea twenty percent.

Marilee paid her bill and walked out of the Mockingbird still holding her head high. She climbed into her car and drove to the funeral home, feeling pretty good about what she'd done. Such a small thing really, but once you tackled the small problems it made the bigger ones easier to handle.

Josh was sitting in the waiting room at the mental health center when Marilee arrived, pausing at the door long enough to close her umbrella. It seemed the rain would never let up. He glanced up, their gazes locked for an instant before he returned to the magazine he was reading. Marilee selected a magazine and thumbed through the pages calmly as she waited for Royce Malcom, who was running late. If her son wished to ignore her, fine.

Royce finally appeared, wearing a smile. "Can you believe this rain? Somebody needs to think about building an ark. At least it's dry in my office." Mother and son rose from their seats and followed him down the hall.

Once seated, Royce glanced from Marilee to Josh. "So, how'd your week go?"

"Fine," Marilee said. "Just fine, thank you."

Josh shrugged. "Okay, I guess."

A moment's silence. "Josh, do you feel like talking today?" Royce asked.

The boy shook his head. "Not especially."

Royce regarded him. "I was hoping after our last session you might feel more comfortable talking with your mom."

"I have nothing to say," Josh replied, sliding down in his chair.

"Okay," the counselor said. "But we're scheduled for an entire hour."

Marilee straightened in her chair. "Since I'm paying for this session, I refuse to waste the next hour," she said, "so I've brought one of Josh's favorite books. I'll just read it aloud, if you don't mind." Royce looked amused.

Josh frowned at her. "I'm not interested in listening to some dumb story," he said.

Marilee smiled. "Well, Joshua, next time you can pay for the session, and we'll spend the hour doing what you want to do, which up to now has been pouting and smart-mouthing Royce and me. I don't mind telling you, I've grown mighty bored watching it. At least this story will make the time pass more quickly."

"Your mother's right, Josh," Royce said. "She *is* footing the bill. The least we can do is cooperate. Besides, I wouldn't mind hearing the story."

Josh didn't respond. His eyes were fastened to the toe of his sneakers. Marilee noted they were wet but she didn't say anything, lest he accuse her of treating him like a baby or trying to smother him. If Josh wanted to walk around in wet sneakers that was his business.

She opened the book to the first page and began reading a story about a girl named Fern, who was desperately trying to convince her father not to kill a newborn pig by the name of Wilbur. Fern promised to raise the pig herself, feeding him from a bottle, cuddling him like a baby. As she read on, she heard a sniff and looked up. Josh, so angry and resentful in the beginning, was now slumped in his chair covering his face with both hands. Marilee stopped reading.

"Are you okay, Josh?" Royce asked.

The boy shook his head. "Why did you bring that book?" he asked his mother. He dropped his hands. Tears streamed down his cheeks.

Marilee felt her son's pain tug at her heart. "Because at one time it was your favorite," she said softly.

Josh leaned his head back against the chair, staring at the ceiling. "It was," he confessed.

Marilee looked to Royce for guidance. She felt she had finally reached her son, and now that she had, she was paralyzed with fear. Should she continue reading?

Royce reached for several tissues and handed them to Josh. "It's okay to cry," he told the boy. "You've been in pain a long time."

The boy continued to weep silently. "I'm all screwed up," he said. "I don't know where I belong anymore." He paused, trying to regain his composure. "I don't know what to do."

"About what?" Royce asked. "School? Friends?"

"I don't have any friends," Josh replied. "But you already know that."

"You made that choice," Royce said. "Besides, you *do* have friends at church."

"I don't see them anymore."

Marilee's heart ached for her son. "I'm sorry, Josh."

The boy looked at her. "Why are you sorry? I let you down. You should be mad at me. I'm mad at myself. I hate living with Dad and LaFonda. I only went with him because I wanted to hurt you. I thought it was your fault he left. I thought you'd chased him away." Fresh tears filled his eyes. "But it wasn't your fault. I know that now." He paused to catch his breath and mop his eyes. "Mom—" he choked on a sob "—I'm sorry."

Marilee was at his side instantly, and Josh stood and fell into her arms. She held him while he cried. "It's okay, Son," she said, holding him tight. "Everything's going to be okay."

He didn't look convinced. "I don't like it there. I don't like the people who live around us. Dad has changed, and I don't even like him anymore."

Marilee felt tears, hot on her cheek. "Your father is going through something we don't understand," she said. "That doesn't make him a bad person. He's just confused."

Josh looked at her. "You don't hate him?"

She smiled. "No, Josh. I don't hate your father. I'm just disappointed in him."

Josh pulled away, as if suddenly embarrassed by his outpouring of tears. He reclaimed his seat, but instead of returning to her own chair, Marilee took the one next to his.

"I'm glad the two of you finally cleared the air," Royce said. "Feel better, Josh?"

The boy nodded. "Yeah. But it still doesn't change things."

"What would you like to change?" Royce asked.

"I'd like to see my parents get back together and everything become normal again, but I know that's not going to happen. I just—" his voice broke once more "—I wish I could get out of that place."

Marilee's heart leaped with joy. "You can, Josh. I have plenty of room. I would love nothing better than to have you."

The boy pondered the idea for a long time. "I'd like that," he said after a while, "but I need to talk to Dad first. He hasn't been feeling well, and he lost his job. I don't want him to think I'm turning my back on him." He paused, and it was obvious he was struggling with his emotions. "Would it be okay if I moved in sometime next week?"

Marilee tried to contain her excitement. She didn't want to appear overly anxious. She was ready to take her son home now. But she wouldn't push and risk alienating him again. "Take your time, Josh," she said. "You're old enough to make your own decisions."

The boy looked surprised, but he didn't say anything.

Marilee called Tate the minute she got home. "I don't need the child advocate," she said when he answered. "My son is coming home."

"I'm happy for you," Tate said. "I know how important this is to you." He paused. "By the way, I'm sorry I forgot to call about the appointment with Ed Rogers. Since you don't need him anyway, I'll reimburse you the two thousand dollars."

When Marilee hung up, she was smiling. Her friends had told her Josh would come around, but she hadn't believed them. Now she was on the way to rebuilding their relationship. And the money from Tate would certainly come in handy.

Winnie chose that moment to come downstairs. "Well, well, you look mighty pleased about something."

Marilee felt as though she were on a cloud. "Josh is coming home."

"Oh, thank the Lord!" Winnie rushed over and hugged her. "You know what that means, don't you? We've got to work like crazy to get that room in order."

"We'll never get it done by the weekend."

"Oh yes, we will." As she finished speaking, the phone rang and Winnie answered it. "Oh. Hi, Julie," she said. "Been a while since I talked to you." She was quiet as she listened. "This weekend? Sorry, but I have to help my best friend do some work to her house. See you at school."

"What was that all about?" Marilee asked.

"My old girlfriend is having a party, and she wants me to come. The kids are all excited over me being on the news and doing that article for the newspaper."

"You should go," Marilee insisted.

"No way. I'm busy this weekend."

"So I'm your best friend?" Marilee asked, grinning at the girl.

Winnie gave her a bored look. "Don't get cocky. That could change now that I'm the center of attention at school."

Marilee was thrilled for her.

"We've got a lot of work to do," Winnie said. "May as well call Clara and Ruby."

Marilee made the calls, and the girls were delighted with the news. "I'll have to redecorate the extra bedroom," she told each of them. "Something a teenage boy will like."

"We need to go to Wal-Mart," Winnie said once Marilee had hung up, "to look at paint. Won't take me long to get ready, since I only have one pair of pants I can fit into now."

The two were about to walk out the door when the doorbell rang. Marilee found Clara and Ruby standing on the other side. They both congratulated Marilee and hugged her. "We're here to help," Clara said in her no-nonsense tone.

"First, we need to buy paint for Josh's bedroom," Winnie said. "Actually, this whole place could use a paint job."

"Something a little brighter," Ruby said. "And this kitchen wallpaper has to go." She looked at Marilee.

"Lucky for you I know all about wallpaper. I also know where we can get the best deal."

Nell knocked on the back door. "Oh, good, everybody's here," she said. "I baked a nice peach cobbler."

"We don't have time to eat right now," Winnie said. She gave Nell the news.

Nell threw her arms around Marilee. "I knew he would come around after a while."

It was all Marilee could do to keep from crying. "How will we ever be able to get all this done before Josh moves in?"

"We're women," Ruby said. "We can do anything we put our minds to."

"We need to go to Wal-Mart," Winnie said for the second time.

"The wallpaper place is just down the street," Ruby said. "Clara and I can swing by there and meet you at Wal-Mart." She looked at Marilee. "Listen to us. Here we are making plans, and we haven't even asked if you can afford to do all this."

"My lawyer is reimbursing me two thousand dollars now that I don't need a child advocate, and I've saved every dime of my tips from the Pickford Inn. Besides, I don't care what it costs. I want this place to feel like home when Josh arrives."

"What are we waiting for?" Nell said.

The women were out the door in a matter of seconds. A light mist fell, but nobody seemed to notice. Winnie, Nell and Marilee rode in her car, Clara and Ruby in Ruby's truck. When they arrived at the store, they hurried inside, each woman grabbing a shopping cart.

"Where should we go first?" Nell asked.

"Paint department," Ruby said, already headed in that direction. They followed one another caravan-style and pored over the wide selection of paint charts.

"May I help you?" a young salesman asked. His name tag read Mike.

"How old are you, Mike?" Marilee asked.

He looked embarrassed. "Nineteen. Why?"

"What's your favorite color?"

He didn't hesitate. "Navy blue."

"Never mind," Winnie said, waving him aside. "The room is not big enough. It'd look like a shoebox if we painted it that color."

"Would you like to hear my second favorite color?" he said.

All five women looked his way. "Okay, dear," Nell said. "What is it?"

He reached for a paint chart and pointed to a color. "Khaki."

"Khaki?" Clara said.

"That's a boring color," Winnie said. She crossed her arms over her breasts. "Whoever heard of painting a bedroom khaki?"

"You wouldn't believe how many people buy it," the young man said, sounding defensive. "It's clean-looking, and it goes with everything. Doesn't show fingerprints." He paused and smiled. "And it goes excellent with navy blue. You could have a navy bedspread and curtains."

Winnie looked him up and down. "Are you Wal-Mart's personal interior decorator?"

Mike looked surprised at her bluntness. "No, but a lot of people ask my opinion. Is this for a man or woman?"

Marilee wondered why Winnie was acting so rude. "It's for my son's room."

"Thank you for your help," Winnie said. "We'll take it from here."

"Are you expecting a baby?" he asked.

She gaped at him. "Do I *look* like I'm expecting a baby?"

"Well, yes. My sister is expecting. She's due in December."

"So am I."

"Are you taking childbirth classes?"

"Yes. Any more personal questions you'd like to ask?"

Mike smiled as if he was enjoying himself. "You and

your husband will enjoy it. I know my sister and brother-in-law do."

"I don't have a husband, okay? My baby's father left town the minute he heard I was pregnant. And you can stop feeling sorry for me right now, because I don't need a husband. I have my friends and that's enough."

"I don't feel sorry for you, and I wasn't trying to be nosy. I guess I'm just excited about my sister having her baby." He grinned. "It means I'm going to be an uncle."

Winnie seemed to soften. "Oh, well, I can understand that, but we don't have time for small talk, we have to buy paint."

The four other women followed the exchange, turning to Winnie then back to Mike. Marilee felt like shaking the girl.

"Excuse me," Winnie told them. "I need to find the ladies' room."

Mike smiled. "My sister goes to the bathroom constantly. I'll be glad to show you where it is."

"I know where the bathroom is located, thank you very much."

He grinned. "Yes, but somebody needs to press the buzzer to let you in. That could take time, since the woman who presses the buzzer works in layaway."

Winnie sighed. "Okay." They headed toward the back of the store.

Marilee smiled at the others. "I think she likes him."

"His choice of colors isn't bad," Ruby pointed out. "I think they'd be perfect for a boy's room."

"Look at this," Clara said. "Robin's-egg blue. That would look beautiful in your living room, and since your sofa is a neutral color it would work. Unfortunately, that would mean getting rid of those lovely draperies your mother bought."

"Who said anything about painting the living room?" Marilee asked, although she liked the idea. The house needed a face-lift in the worst way. And she could replace the drapes with inexpensive miniblinds. They continued to search through colors.

Winnie returned. "Do y'all believe that man asked me for my telephone number and address?"

"Did you give it to him?"

"Do I have the word *stupid* written all over my face?" She gave a grunt. "Of course I gave it to him."

Nell chuckled. "He's cute, don't you think?"

"And smart," Winnie said. "He's attending the community college, working on an accounting degree, just like I plan to do."

Ruby patted Winnie on the back. "He *is* cute."

"So why's he flirting with me?" Winnie said.

Marilee made a sound of disgust. "Now, what kind of question is that?"

"Look at me." Winnie pointed to her stomach. "I'm as big as a house."

"You're pregnant, for heaven's sake!" they chorused.

The young man appeared a few minutes later. "Sorry, but somebody needed me in hardware. Have y'all decided on a paint color?"

"We'll take two gallons of khaki," Marilee said.

"And a couple of gallons of robin's-egg blue," Ruby told him. She checked her wristwatch and looked at Marilee. "While he mixes the paint, Clara and I will run by the wallpaper store and pizza place then meet you back at your house. We have to study wallpaper samples for the kitchen."

"Get me a salad," Winnie said, "with low-fat dressing." She looked at Mike. "I have to keep my weight down."

"You know where I hide the spare house key, right?" Marilee said, reaching into her purse for money. "I'm paying this time. Besides, I have a coupon. Buy one, and you get a second one for half price."

They argued for a moment while Mike mixed the paint. Finally, Clara and Ruby agreed and hurried off.

Marilee smiled at the young man, who was looking at Winnie. "Excuse me, but would you like to join us? You've been so helpful, and we'd love to have you."

He looked surprised. "I don't get off until nine."

"We can save you a couple of slices," Marilee offered.

He looked at Winnie and smiled. "Sure, if it's okay with you."

Winnie shrugged. "I suppose so."

"We'll look forward to it," Marilee said.

Marilee, Nell and Winnie arrived back at the house an hour later, having purchased the paint and two twin navy bedspreads with matching curtains. Clara and Ruby arrived shortly thereafter, bearing two pizzas and a stack of wallpaper books. Winnie grabbed a large pitcher of tea from the refrigerator while Nell filled glasses with ice. They scanned books and samples that Ruby had managed to get from the store. "It would be best if you select from one of these samples," Ruby said. "Not only have they been reduced, they're in stock."

"Oh, look at this," Winnie said, picking up one. "Clouds."

"I don't know where that sample came from," Ruby said. "Anyway, that won't work for a kitchen."

"But it would work for a nursery," Winnie replied.

Marilee smiled. "It most certainly would."

"For a boy or girl," Clara pointed out.

"I already know it's a girl," Winnie said.

Ruby nodded. "So you've had a sonogram."

Winnie nodded. "They did one, but I wouldn't let them tell me the baby's sex. They don't have to. It's a girl." Winnie eyed the pizza as she ate her salad. The women insisted she take a piece.

"Just a small one," she said. "For the baby."

Together, they pored over wallpaper samples for an hour, until they were distracted by the ring of the doorbell.

Winnie froze. "Do you think that's him? He's not due for a while."

"Only one way to find out," Marilee said.

Winnie jumped from the chair and hurried to the door. She opened it then slumped when she found Sam on the other side. "Oh, it's you," she said dully.

Sam stepped inside. He looked amused. "I'm happy to see you too, Winnie. Is my mother here, by chance?"

"I'm in the kitchen, Sammy," Nell called out.

Sam filled the doorway as he stood there taking in the scene. "Well, now, what have we here?" He moved over to let Winnie squeeze by, but his eyes remained fastened on Marilee.

"You tell him, Marilee," Nell said.

She looked at Sam and smiled. "Josh is coming to live with me."

Sam broke into a broad grin. "Oh, Marilee, that's great! That's just great. I know you must be relieved."

"We're going to redecorate the house before he moves in," Ruby said.

Sam nodded. "When's he moving in?"

"Less than a week," Winnie replied, taking a bite of pizza. "We plan to work this weekend."

"I'm so excited I can't stop smiling," Marilee confessed.

Sam looked stunned. "You're going to redecorate this entire house in a weekend?"

"I'll do as much as I can after work," Marilee said.

Sam scratched his jaw. There was no way in hell they could do it in two days. "The weatherman is calling for rain over the next couple of days, so I'm going to have some time on my hands." He looked at Winnie. "Where are you going to stay while all this painting is going on?"

"Huh?" The girl looked up.

Marilee slapped her forehead with her palm. "What was I thinking?" She looked at Winnie. "Honey, you don't need to be around paint fumes right now."

"She can stay with us," Nell said.

Winnie looked crestfallen. "I want to help."

"Don't worry, we'll keep you busy," Marilee said. "Somebody has to make sandwiches and prepare dinner. We won't have time."

"Winnie and I will be glad to do it," Nell said. "Won't we, dear?"

The girl nodded. "As long as I can do something."

"I'll see you ladies later," Sam said. His and Marilee's

gazes met and locked, and she held her breath. He smiled then, almost tenderly. "Congratulations on getting your son back."

"Let me see you to the door," she offered.

"Don't bother. Looks like you have a lot of planning to do." He turned for the living room but paused. "Have you already bought the paint?"

"Two gallons for Josh's room and two for the living room."

"I could've gotten you a discount. Don't buy paintbrushes or anything like that. I can supply everything you need."

"Thank you," Marilee said.

"Well, I never," Ruby said once Sam was gone. "Nell, did you see the way your son was looking at Marilee?"

"Yes, dear. It's gotten to be old hat."

"Did you see the way Marilee was looking at *him?*" Clara said.

Winnie gave a grunt. "Okay, so they're hot for one another. What's the big deal?"

Marilee blushed. "Sam and I are just friends. That's all. Friends. Now, let's get busy. We have to make a lot of decisions tonight."

Once the girls left, Winnie and Marilee cleaned the kitchen. Marilee noted the teenager was quiet. "Are you okay?" she asked.

Winnie didn't look at her as she wiped the kitchen table. "I knew he wouldn't show."

"It's still early."

"It's almost ten o'clock. He got off work an hour ago."

"I'm sure he has a perfectly reasonable explanation."

"Yeah, like maybe he doesn't want to become involved with a woman carrying another man's child. Doesn't take a rocket scientist to figure that one out. I was stupid to get my hopes up. I'm crazy for letting it bother me. It's not like it's the first time I've been rejected."

Marilee turned to her. "So you think because one man

rejected you it's going to be that way forever?'' When Winnie didn't answer, Marilee took the girl's hands in hers. ''Listen to me, Winnie. You have everything going for you. You're kind and loving, and you're very bright. Sure, this baby is coming at a time in your life when it's a bit inconvenient, but you're not the type to let that stop you. Any man would be lucky to have you as a friend.''

''Don't worry about me. You need to think about Josh,'' the girl said. ''I'll only be in the way, now that he's coming home.''

''We've been through this before. You're family.''

Winnie looked relieved. ''Thanks, Marilee.''

They turned off the lights and started upstairs, just as the doorbell rang. ''That's probably for you,'' Marilee said.

''I doubt it. Anyway, it's late, and I'm tired.''

''Answer the door.'' Marilee was firm.

Winnie sighed and started down the stairs. With the chain intact, she unlocked the door and opened it an inch. ''Oh, it's you,'' she said when she spied the young man standing on the other side.

''I'm sorry I'm late, Winnie,'' he said. ''My dumb car wouldn't start, so I had to call someone with jumper cables.''

''Yes, well, thanks for stopping by, but I have to go to bed now.''

''Wait, this is for you.'' He passed a single red rose through the door. ''I picked it up at a convenience store. Didn't dare turn off my engine. Please accept my apology.''

''I prefer yellow roses,'' she said.

He chuckled. ''Work with me here, okay?''

''You're just doing this to get free pizza.''

''You're right. Did you save me any?''

''It's cold.''

''I like cold pizza.''

Winnie sighed, closed the door and pulled the chain free. ''You'll have to eat fast because I'm tired.''

He laughed. "I'll have to eat fast because I left my car running."

Having heard the entire exchange, Marilee smiled as she quietly climbed the stairs for bed.

A New Author 279

his husband. "I'll have to call his lawyers I let him off tonight."

Having heard the entire exchange, Marilee settled in as quietly catfooed the stairs for bed.

# *Twenty*

Marilee was still in her bathrobe when Sam appeared the following morning with two men and a woman named Lori. Winnie had already left for school, grumbling about the rain.

Marilee blinked at the sight of the people behind him. "What's going on?"

"This is part of my crew," Sam said. "We're going to get this place in shape. Why aren't you dressed for work?"

She was too stunned to speak at first. "I was just about to put on my clothes." She smiled at the group and invited them inside. "Sam, would you mind coming into the kitchen for a moment?"

He followed.

"What are you doing?" she whispered.

"I told you I'd help you redecorate your house."

"I didn't expect you to bring in all these workers."

"Look, Marilee, I'm good, but I'm not that good. I'll need a little help."

"I don't expect you to do everything. The girls and I plan to work on it all weekend. Besides, I can't afford to hire professionals."

He put his hand on her shoulder. "These people are on the payroll. They can't work in the rain. Now, tell me which color goes where." She shook her head to clear it, but it was no use. Sam had obviously decided to take matters into his own hands. She showed him the paint.

"You selected wallpaper for your kitchen, right? What about the bathrooms? I noticed the paper was outdated."

Marilee was insulted. "They don't look *that* bad. Besides, I really can't afford to do the bathrooms right now."

"We'll worry about that later. Did you choose any samples?"

"Yes, but—"

"Let's see them. Lori, would you please come in here? And the rest of you can begin bringing in your supplies."

Marilee was growing more annoyed by the moment. How typical of Sam to bring strangers into her house when she wasn't dressed. It wasn't that she didn't appreciate his good intentions, but it was a little embarrassing standing there in her kitchen in her pink and white polka-dot house slippers.

"Marilee, this is Lori. She could wallpaper the Chickpea water tower and you'd never find a seam."

The two women nodded. "Show me what you've got," Lori said.

Marilee handed her a sample. "This is what I've selected for the kitchen. They're half price at the Wall Covering Shop on Main Street. I understand they're in stock."

Sam pointed to another stack. "What are these?"

"They're for later, when I can afford to do the bathrooms. And this—" she held up the paper Winnie had wanted for a nursery "—I was thinking I might turn the small room next to Winnie's into a nursery. My mother used it as her sewing room. It's not much bigger than a walk-in closet, but it would hold a crib and changing table and maybe a small dresser. I have plenty of time for that, but I should probably go ahead and buy the paper, since it's on sale."

Sam's men brought in ladders and laid drop cloths on the floor as Marilee talked. Lori took each sample and noted on the backs which room the paper was to be used in. "Okay, I'll get the measurements and head to the wallpaper store," she said.

"You need to get ready for work," Sam told Marilee.

She pulled him aside. "Should I give Lori a blank check?"

He shook his head. "She'll charge it to my account. We'll settle up later." He checked his wristwatch. "Do you have time to show me the room where Josh will be sleeping?"

Marilee led him upstairs and opened the door. Sam looked around.

"What do you think?" Marilee asked.

"This will be easy enough. I see you've already cleaned it thoroughly."

Marilee stared at him, noting the way the early-morning light shone in his dark hair. She had no reason to be irritated. He was simply trying to help in an impossible situation. "Sam, I don't know how to thank you. You've been so kind."

"Your son is arriving in less than a week. We have to move on this right away."

"I'll have to cook you five hundred meals to pay you back."

"That'll work. Now, get out of here." She turned for the door. "Wait," he said. He caught her wrist and kissed her soundly. "*Now* you may go."

Marilee arrived at the funeral home twenty minutes later. Debbie was waiting for her, dressed in an olive suit with a matching scarf. She looked quite pretty.

"Are you okay?" Debbie asked. "I heard those men who robbed the Pickford Inn confessed to everything."

"Yes, thank goodness," Marilee said. She gave her a big smile. "And I'm better than okay. Josh is moving in early next week. My entire house is being renovated as we speak."

Debbie hugged her. "I'm so happy for you, Marilee. Would you prefer taking a couple of days off? Things are kind of slow right now."

"I've been ordered out of my house so the painters can do their job. I guess I'd better hang around here. Where's Irby?"

"In his office. He's working with an older couple making future funeral arrangements. I wish more people thought ahead like that. It's much easier when we have everything on file. Of course, not everyone gets a chance to make arrangements," she added ruefully as she checked her wristwatch. "I have to run a couple of errands and meet a friend for an early lunch. The baby-sitter is already here. I'll be back in time for you to go to lunch at one, if that's okay."

"Fine."

Marilee spent much of the morning filing and adding information into the computer. As she worked, she thought about how lucky she was to have such wonderful friends who were so willing to help her prepare for Josh's homecoming. Debbie returned precisely at one. "Go ahead and take as long as you like," she said.

On a whim Marilee drove to the local Dairy Queen where she ordered three foot-long hot dogs with onion rings and soft drinks. She drove to Esmerelda Cunningham's house, wondering if the woman would turn her out the moment she saw her. Oh, well, she'd just have to risk it. She suspected Esmerelda needed a friend, even though the woman would be the last to admit it. She rang the bell, and Dudley answered promptly. He smiled when he saw her. "Have you and Mrs. Cunningham had lunch yet?"

He eyed the sacks in her arms. "Actually, I was just about to prepare something."

"I brought foot-long hot dogs with all the fixings," she said.

He looked amused. "I'll tell Mrs. Cunningham right away."

Five minutes later, Esmerelda stepped off the elevator that led from the third floor. "Really, Marilee, you've made quite a nuisance of yourself dropping by unannounced." But the woman didn't look as annoyed as she sounded.

"I know, but I was never taught good manners, so it can't be helped. Where should I unpack our lunches? I'm on my lunch hour so I can't stay long."

Esmerelda sighed. "Let's just eat in the kitchen. It'll take Dudley forever to set up the dining room."

"In the kitchen, ma'am?" Dudley said, obviously surprised.

"That's what I said," Esmerelda replied. "Move along, Dudley, Marilee doesn't have long."

While Dudley prepared three glasses of iced tea, Marilee unwrapped their hot dogs. "Oh my," Esmerelda said. "I can't remember when I last ate one of these. And onion rings? It's certainly not on my diet, but I suppose this one time won't hurt."

Marilee noticed the woman ate with gusto, as if she hadn't had a meal in days. She even ate half of Marilee's onion rings.

"I understand you work at Denton Funeral Home," the woman said. "What a ghastly job that must be."

"It's not so bad," Marilee said. "Irby and Debbie are old high-school friends, so we get along well."

"What is your job description?"

"I'm a receptionist. I was recently given a nice raise and promoted to administrative assistant." Marilee wasn't about to tell her what she'd had to do to earn it.

"It must be awfully depressing," Esmerelda said.

Marilee shrugged. "I suppose it's all in how you look at it. I have to meet with distraught families, some worse than others, but I've had a lot of experience dealing with those who've lost loved ones. And I've learned that the more you help people, the more it takes your mind off your own worries."

"What about those that don't have family?" Esmerelda asked.

"Doesn't matter. Everybody has someone who loves them."

Esmerelda seemed to ponder that as they finished their meal.

Marilee noted the time. "I have to run." She pushed her chair from the table before Dudley could pull it out for her.

"Dudley, get my purse so I can pay Marilee for lunch," Esmerelda said.

Marilee shook her head as she made for the door. "This one's on me."

The rest of the day dragged for Marilee as she wondered what was taking place at home. She couldn't help feeling guilty for being annoyed with Sam that morning, but she'd been so shocked. She hadn't forgotten his kiss, though. It had stayed with her all day.

She looked at the calendar, willing the time to pass quickly so she and her son could be reunited soon.

Unless he changed his mind.

Her stomach did a little flip-flop at the thought. No, she couldn't start thinking like that or she'd drive herself and everyone else crazy in the process.

Ruby called to let her know she and Clara would be right over after work.

"I don't think it's necessary," Marilee said. "Sam came in first thing this morning with part of his crew. Everything seems to be under control."

"Oh, Marilee, that man has it bad for you."

"I haven't really noticed," she lied.

"Honey, this is me you're talking to, remember? I saw the way you looked at him last night. Listen, I know you need more time, but just don't let a good thing pass you by."

"The man is a womanizer, for Pete's sake!" Marilee said.

"That was high school. Do you know how much testosterone young men have at that age? Now that Sam's older, his level has probably dropped considerably."

"Ruby, I don't have time to worry about Sam's testosterone level."

"Okay, okay, but before I go I have something to tell you. You can't breathe a word of it."

"What is it?" Marilee asked.

"Clara met a man at the VFW."

"No kidding?"

"I've been dying to tell you, but I haven't been able to get a minute alone with you. His name is Melvin. He was in Vietnam. Lost an arm, bless his heart, but he's the sweetest thing. He asked for her phone number before we left. You should have seen the look on Clara's face. She got all flustered, started tugging at her hair. I had to jerk her into the ladies' room for one of our girl-to-girl talks. Finally, she agreed to let him call her."

"Well, now, that *is* something," Marilee said.

"And Nell danced with a man, can you imagine that? She made us swear not to tell Sam. Oops, gotta run. My shampoo and set just walked in."

There was a click from the other end. Marilee hung up the phone, but she was smiling. Clara had met a man, and Nell had danced with one. Imagine that.

Marilee arrived home after work and found several trucks still parked outside her house. She stepped inside the front door and came to an abrupt halt. For a moment she thought she was in the wrong house.

Sam appeared out of nowhere. "What do you think?"

"I'm speechless," she said. "It doesn't look like the same room. And you had the trim painted. Everything looks so clean."

"I like the color you picked out," Sam said. "It's a nice shade of blue. It seems to work okay with your furniture. Except for those drapes. Luckily we had to take them down to paint."

"I'm replacing them anyway," Marilee told him.

Sam looked relieved. "Come take a look at Josh's room."

She followed Sam through the house. She paused in the kitchen, where she found Lori using some kind of steam device to remove the old wallpaper. "The paper has already been stripped from the bathrooms, and I've got a man prepping the walls now. Lori should be able to start putting up the new stuff in the morning. I think you should let the men go ahead and paint the whole house, Marilee. May as well get it all done while they're here. Lori recommended a soft beige."

Marilee nodded dumbly as she followed Sam upstairs. He opened the door to Josh's room, where she found the room, including the trim, already painted. "Oh my," she said.

"I think it turned out well," Sam said. "Come look what we're doing to the nursery."

"Sam, I wasn't expecting all this," she said.

"I wanted to do it for you, Marilee. I know how excited you are about Josh coming home."

The room that was to be the nursery had been papered in clouds, and Marilee could not hide her surprise. "Has Winnie seen this?" she asked.

"Not yet," Sam said. "I don't want her to see it until it's finished."

Marilee stepped inside the room. A man was at work nailing a cabinet to the wall next to a set of shelves. "Oh, Sam, she's going to love it." Marilee turned to him, and her eyes glistened. "I don't know what to say, except thank you." She hugged him, and he held her for a long moment.

On Sunday, Winnie insisted on seeing the house, which had been painted and papered throughout. A proud Marilee personally escorted her to the nursery and opened the door. The girl gasped. "Is this for the baby?" she asked.

"Yes. All we need is a crib. I know you're going to keep her in the bassinet in your room in the beginning, so we have plenty of time to find one." Marilee paused when she spied tears streaming down the girl's cheek. "You're crying, Winnie."

"Nobody has never done anything this nice for me," the girl said. "Nobody. I am just beside myself."

Marilee put her arms around her. "I'd say it's about time somebody did something nice for you."

"I have to call Clara and Ruby. Oh, and Mike."

"Mike?"

Winnie looked slightly embarrassed. "He called me a few times while I was staying next door. He has the day off. We're going out for burgers."

"Well, well—"

"Don't give me that look. We're just friends."

"Go ahead and call," Marilee said. "I'd better get downstairs. I have cakes in the oven."

"More cakes?"

"Yes. Good thing my mother's old freezer in the garage still works."

Clara and Ruby arrived first. There was much oohing and aahing over the place as Winnie led them through the house.

When they joined Marilee downstairs, she was in the process of putting two pecan pies in the oven.

"How many pies and cakes have you baked so far?" Clara asked.

Marilee shrugged. "I've lost count. I bake every time I have a few minutes on my hands."

"Don't knock yourself out," Ruby said. "We've got women all over town baking."

"Not as good as mine," she replied.

The doorbell rang, and Winnie hurried off to answer it. Mike came into the room, smiling shyly. "Your place looks real nice, Mrs. Abernathy," he said.

"Call me Marilee."

"Let's go upstairs," Winnie said. "You have to see the nursery."

"Mind if I call Nell over?" Clara asked. "We need to have a brief meeting."

Marilee shrugged. "As long as I can keep doing what I'm doing."

Nell arrived a few minutes later. She had already toured the house with Sam and was delighted to see Winnie so pleased with the nursery. "I just knew she'd love it."

"Okay, let's get started with the meeting," Clara said. "I have a lunch appointment."

Ruby and Marilee exchanged looks but didn't say anything. Marilee noticed Clara was wearing makeup.

"I'm thinking we should hold the bazaar two weeks from now," she said. "Saturday, November seventh. Everybody's going to be concentrating on Halloween this coming Saturday, and I'm afraid we'll be pushed for time." She glanced at Ruby. "The VFW hall has been gracious enough to allow us to hold the bazaar inside in case the weather turns bad. They've also agreed to run a concession stand and cook hamburgers and hot dogs out back."

"We already have donations pouring in like crazy," Ruby said, "thanks to Clara's friend at the *Gazette*. And Della Framer has been more than generous. Thank goodness you ran into her."

"Speaking of the *Gazette,* Janie is going to write an article early next week and give us a free advertisement," Clara said.

"L&M Printing called yesterday," Marilee told them. "We have about a thousand flyers."

Clara sighed her relief. "Things are finally beginning to happen."

Nell ran through her list. "The ladies from my church have agreed to help. I've assigned someone to the hospitality booth, handcrafts and quilts, the good junk, as we call it, and the toys and games. We thought it would be a good idea to have something for the children. Which reminds me, they're lending us their dunking booth—and someone to man it." The girls chuckled at this.

She paused and scanned her list. "I figured Marilee and another lady from my church could take care of the baked goods, and Clara might enjoy running the books and magazines table, since she knows more about that than anyone else."

Clara nodded. "I'll be happy to."

"Ruby, would you be interested in handling records, cassette tapes and videos?"

"Sure."

Nell looked up. "What do you think?"

Clara and Ruby stared at the woman. Marilee had paused in her work to stare, too.

"Is anything wrong?" Nell asked. Her face reddened. "Perhaps I shouldn't have just assumed everyone would want to take on the tasks I assigned them."

"Oh, no, that's not a problem at all," Ruby said. "It's just—" She looked at Clara and Marilee and saw her amazement mirrored in their expressions. "When did you have time to do all this?"

"I worked on it all last week," Nell said. "And since Winnie's been helping out, I've had even more time on my hands the past few days."

"You've gotten more done in the past couple of weeks than we've managed to do in months," Marilee pointed out.

Nell blushed. "I don't work full-time like the rest of you, remember? Besides, I've done this sort of thing all my life."

Clara sat up straight in her chair and smacked a book with her gavel. She beamed. "Looks like we've got ourselves a bazaar, ladies!" She smiled prettily as she packed her folders away. "Now, if you'll excuse me, I have to be somewhere." She almost slammed into Winnie and Mike as they exited the stairs.

"Where's Clara going in such a hurry?" Winnie asked. "Is her house on fire?"

Ruby made a production of zipping her lip.

Grady pulled into Marilee's driveway Monday evening, but neither he nor Josh got out of the car right away. Marilee peered at them from behind the curtain, wishing her son would hurry and get out of the car. Should she go out to meet him? she wondered.

"What's taking so long?" Clara whispered, glimpsing a look over Marilee's shoulder.

"I suppose that good-for-nothing Grady is giving Josh one of those father-son talks," Ruby said. "Like how to protect yourself against genital herpes."

"I still don't think this surprise party is a good idea," Winnie muttered.

"Why not, dear?" Nell asked. "Marilee wants to make her son feel welcome."

"The kid is dealing with a lot right now," Winnie replied. "He might be embarrassed with all the attention."

Marilee wondered if the surprise party would indeed be too much for her son. Josh had always been on the shy side. He might very well take one look at the women and run right back to his father's car.

It was too late to worry about that now, though. Everything was in place. The house had been decorated with Welcome Home, Josh signs, streamers and balloons. Snacks and a large cake that Marilee had baked waited on the table. "I hope we're not making a mistake," she said.

Grady and Josh climbed from the car. The boy followed

his father to the trunk, and they pulled out several suitcases and boxes. Marilee closed her eyes and gave a silent word of thanks. Looked as if Josh planned on staying awhile. He and Grady carried the items to the front porch. His father gave him a brief hug before climbing into the car and pulling away.

The doorbell rang, and Marilee froze on the spot.

"Don't just stand there," Winnie hissed. "Open the door!"

Taking a deep breath, Marilee walked over and opened it. Josh stepped into the room holding two of his suitcases.

"Surprise!" the women shouted at the top of their lungs.

Josh simply stood there, blinking in confusion.

Marilee knew instantly she'd made the wrong decision. "Hello, Son. The girls and I wanted to throw you a welcoming party."

He nodded. "Thanks," he said, but his look admonished her.

Marilee's smiled faded. The party was too much too soon, and she would have given anything to be able to take it back.

"Is anyone going to invite the poor kid inside?" Winnie demanded. "Here, Josh, let me help you with your bags."

"Who are you?" he asked.

"I'm an unmarried, pregnant, black girl," she said. "I'll bet you figured out the black-and-pregnant part all by yourself. Anyway, I live here. Your mama probably forgot to mention it." She picked up his other suitcase. "Let me show you to your room, m'lord. You're going to love it."

Josh followed her upstairs as the women watched from below. Winnie opened the door. "Ta-da!" she said, stepping aside so he could get a clear view. "What do you think?"

"Sure beats where I've been living." He slumped onto one of the beds.

"Hey, don't get too excited," Winnie said, setting the bag on the floor. "Listen, I know this isn't easy, walking into a house full of women, but your mama thought it would be nice to have a little party for you. I disagreed, of course, but nobody around here listens to me. So, if you need anything, you let me know.''

"Maybe you could show me the escape hatch."

Winnie grinned. "We could tie your bedsheets together, and I could lower you to the ground through that window."

He smiled for the first time. "When is your baby due?"

"Not until around Christmas."

"Where's the father?"

"Who knows? Probably off poking some other unsuspecting girl."

"He just split on you?"

"Yep. Some men are like that."

"My dad ran out on my mom."

"I know. Life can be a real bitch."

"I've never lived in a house with a black person."

"I'd never lived with white folks until I got knocked up and my parents kicked me out," Winnie said matter-of-factly. "And I can tell you, it's different. For one thing, y'all don't eat like black people."

"What do you mean?"

"Well, we eat things like chicken gizzards and pig's knuckles. You ever had pig's knuckles?"

"Nope. Don't plan to either."

"You haven't lived until you've tried them. And polk salat and chitterlings, which is a highfalutin way of saying hog's intestines."

Josh grimaced. "That's disgusting."

"Hey, I know white folks who eat chocolate-covered ants. Now, *that's* disgusting. I'd much rather eat hog's intestines than bugs." She studied him. "So, what do you do for fun?"

Josh shrugged. "Well, lately I've been stealing cars."

"No kidding! I have an uncle who used to do that. Made good money, till he was caught and sent to the big house."

"You don't believe me, do you?"

"'Course I do. Which makes me glad I don't own a car. I travel by bus. You haven't stolen any buses, have you? I'd imagine it would be tough hiding them."

"What do you do? For fun, I mean?"

"Mostly I study. I'm an honor-roll student."

"You play chess?"

"Not only do I play, I kick butt at it."

"I have an awesome chess set. Got it for my birthday. Haven't found anybody who can beat me."

"I can beat you blindfolded and with one hand behind my back." Winnie glanced toward the door. "Look, your mom went to a lot of trouble for this party. Why don't we go down and have some of that food?"

Josh hesitated.

"I swear, you won't find one hog intestine on the table."

"Okay, but I don't really feel like being around a bunch of old ladies."

"These are nice old ladies, and they'd do anything for your mom. You promise not to act like a jerk, I'll let you beat me in a game of chess."

Finally, Josh nodded. "Okay, might as well get this over with." They started from the room. "You won't rat on me about stealing cars, will you?"

"No, I figure that's your business. But if you get busted, don't come to me. I don't have the money to bail you out of jail."

"I don't do it anymore."

"I guess that makes you an ex-car thief, huh?"

He followed her downstairs. Marilee met them at the bottom. "What do you think of your room?"

"It's nice," Josh said. "I like the colors you picked out."

"May we eat now?" Winnie asked, eyeing the party platters of food on the table. "I've been starving myself all day so I could have a piece of cake."

Ruby opened the refrigerator and began pulling out soft drinks. Once they'd filled their plates, everyone found a place to sit. Marilee noticed Josh was sticking close to Winnie, and she saw the two had made friends quickly. After they'd eaten, Marilee carried in an armload of gifts. Josh looked embarrassed. "We didn't spend a lot of money on them, honey. We just thought it would be nice to get you something. I hope you don't mind."

Josh opened Winnie's gift first and saw that she'd bought him a T-shirt.

"Look at the back," the girl urged.

Josh turned it around and saw the name Phish printed on the back. "Cool," he said.

Marilee had found a pair of Nike Air Jordans on sale, and when he opened them he looked pleased. Nell, Ruby and Clara had pooled their money and purchased a small boom box.

"Gee, thanks, everybody," Josh said, loosening up for the first time. "This was really nice of you."

Someone knocked on the back door, but before anyone could answer, Sam stepped inside. "Am I too late for the party? I just got off work."

Marilee was happy to see him. "Come on in," she said. "There's still plenty of food." She introduced him to Josh, and they shook hands.

Josh started for the back door. "Where are you going?" Marilee asked anxiously.

"I just want to grab some fresh air," he said, closing the door behind him.

"I'll go out and sit with him," Sam said, noting the worry in her eyes. He filled his plate and stepped outside. Sure enough, he found Josh sitting on the back steps. "You couldn't take it either, could you?" Sam said.

Josh looked up. "Too many women. They haven't shut up since I walked through the door."

Sam shrugged. "They mean well. The one with white hair is my mother."

"You still live with your mom?"

"I recently moved back because she wasn't well."

"Oh. Do you live in the neighborhood?"

"Next door," Sam said. When the boy didn't respond, he added, "Think you'll like living here?"

"It's different."

Sam figured the boy felt lost at the moment. "You like to fish?"

"I haven't been since my grandfather died. He used to take me a lot."

"If you like, we can go next weekend. It'll get you out of the house."

"Yeah, okay."

"What do you say we get up early Sunday morning and go? Make a day of it?"

"That'd be cool. But I don't have a fishing rod."

"I've got plenty. I'm sure we can find someone to pack us some food, and we'll take off as soon as the sun comes up. In the meantime, if things get to be too much over here, you can always stop by my place. I've got a big-screen TV and plenty of videos."

"You got any Jim Carrey movies?"

Sam wasn't a Jim Carrey fan, but he'd buy every movie the man had made, if it would help Josh become acclimated to his new home. "I'm sure I can find a couple. What do you think of Winnie?"

"She's cool."

"She tells it like it is."

Nell stepped out the back door a few minutes later. "Hello, boys," she said. "I see you're hiding out here. Don't let me interrupt you, I'm on my way home and wanted to say good-night to Josh."

Josh stood. "Thanks again for the gift, Mrs. Brewer."

"Call me Nell. And you're welcome." She patted Josh's cheek. "You sure are a handsome fellow. I'll bet every girl in school is after you."

Josh blushed. "I don't know about that."

"You need any tips on women, you ask my son," she said, motioning to Sam. "He used to be quite a ladies' man."

"Josh doesn't want to hear all that, Mother," Sam said. "I'll be home after a while."

Nell said goodbye and picked her way across the lawn.

Josh chuckled. "Sounds like you were pretty hot with the chicks when you were young."

Sam grinned. "I did okay."

"I've never even had a girlfriend."

"Don't be in too big of a hurry. Women have a way of making you crazy. You like dogs?" he asked.

"Yeah, but I could never have one. My dad's allergic to pet fur."

"My friend has a female golden retriever. She had puppies some weeks back. They're not full-blooded, they're half Lab. I was going to ride over and look at them, if you want to go."

"Sure, but I need to ask my mom." Josh disappeared inside. When he returned, Marilee was with him.

"What's this I hear about puppies?" She gave Sam a disapproving look.

Sam told her about his friend's dog. "I just thought Josh might like to have a look at them."

Marilee could see the boy wanted to go. It was on the tip of her tongue to ask what time they'd be back, but she didn't. "Sure. Just don't bring them all home."

"Give me fifteen minutes to clean up," Sam told the boy.

Josh nodded and went back inside. "Oh, there you are," Clara said. "Ruby and I are on our way out and wanted to say goodbye to you."

"Josh, you sure are a good-looking fellow," Ruby said. "Did you have a growth spurt? You look different from when I last saw you at church."

"I've lost a little weight."

"He's lost a lot of weight," Marilee said.

Josh thanked them for his gift, and they were on their way.

Winnie surveyed the kitchen. "I want to know who made this mess. I suppose you expect me to help you clean it up," she said to Marilee.

"I'll clear the table," Josh said.

"The guest of honor never cleans up," Winnie said. "Would you look at all this food? Marilee, I told you we prepared too much."

"Sam and I can eat it Sunday," Josh said. "We're going fishing, so we'll need to pack a lunch."

Marilee looked surprised. "You and Sam are going fishing?"

"It's okay, isn't it?"

"Sure, honey. I'm glad you made a new friend." She would thank Sam later for offering to take him.

The sound of a horn out front sent Josh in the direction of the front door. "Gotta go now." He paused and looked at his mom, hurried over for a hug and left.

Marilee stood there, speechless.

"Don't you dare cry," Winnie said. "If you start crying, I'm not going to help you clean up." She automatically reached for a paper towel and handed it to Marilee.

"I won't cry," Marilee said as she dabbed at a stray tear.

# Twenty-One

"Josh, what on earth would we do with a dog?" Marilee asked as she sipped her coffee the next morning.

The boy looked up from his bowl of cereal. "You wouldn't have to do anything, I'd do it."

"Who's going to pick up the dog poop?" Winnie said, coming downstairs, her book bag slung over one shoulder. "Puppies do that sort of thing, you know. Matter of fact, it's what they do best. I'll do a lot of things, but I won't pick up dog poop."

"It wouldn't be so bad if somebody was here during the day to look after him," Marilee said, "but we can't very well train him when we're away so much of the time."

A horn blew. "The bus!" Winnie cried, hurrying for the door.

Josh leaped from the table, grabbed his bag, kissed his mom on the cheek and followed the girl. "Just think about it, okay?" he called over his shoulder.

Marilee pondered the dog issue as she finished her coffee. A dog might be just what Josh needed in his life right now. He'd never been able to have a pet before because of Grady's allergies. Somehow, she'd have to see that he got one. She would talk to Sam about it.

Josh appeared restless at dinner that evening. "Is everything okay, Son?" Marilee asked, noting he'd barely touched his food.

"I should probably call Dad," he said.

Marilee nodded. "That would be nice."

Josh left the table and picked up the telephone. He dialed the number and waited. "Hi, Dad," he said a moment later. "Did I wake you?" He was quiet for a moment. "That's too bad. Are you taking your medicine?"

Marilee tried not to eavesdrop, but she couldn't help it.

"Yeah, I'm doing okay," Josh said. "Mom fixed up a room for me, it's pretty cool. And our neighbor, Sam, is taking me fishing Sunday. Maybe you and I could grab a hamburger Saturday." After a minute, the boy went on, "Yeah, I understand. No, really, I do." He hung up.

Marilee saw the look of dejection on his face. "Everything okay?"

"Dad's not feeling well. His blood pressure is up."

"I'm sorry to hear it," Marilee said.

"He's probably just stressed out over losing his job."

"You're having lunch with him on Saturday?"

The boy shook his head. "He doesn't think he'll be up to it." He glanced around the kitchen. "Unless you need help with the dishes, I'd really like to go to my room for a while."

Marilee felt badly for him. Damn Grady for not being there when the boy needed his father. And where was Sam? Of all times for him to be late. "I made a special dessert for you," she said, trying to keep the boy downstairs a little longer.

"I'm not really hungry, but thanks." He started for the stairs.

There was a knock at the back door. Marilee sighed her relief. "Josh, would you get that before you go up?"

"It's Sam," he said, peering through the window. He sounded happy to see him. He unlocked the door and pulled it open. A reddish-blond puppy rushed into the kitchen, wearing a bright red bow. Sam followed with a bag of food. "Oh, man!" the boy said, dumbfounded. He glanced at his mother. "Is he for me?"

Marilee nodded. "He's all yours."

"Awesome!" Josh got down on his knees and petted the puppy. He looked from Sam to Marilee. "Thanks."

Sam smiled and winked at Marilee as he set the bag of puppy food on the table.

The animal licked Josh in the face and raced around the kitchen, sniffing everyone's feet. Without warning, he stopped and peed on the kitchen floor.

"Uh-oh," Josh said.

Winnie pointed a finger. "See that! I told you what would happen if you brought a puppy into this house. Don't think for one minute I'm going to clean it up."

Marilee reached beneath the sink for a disinfectant spray and a wad of paper towels. In the past, she would have become upset having an animal make a mess of her kitchen floor, but right now she wanted Josh to enjoy the moment. They would discuss the rules later. "Here," she said, handing them to her son. "You may as well get used to it."

Josh cleaned up the mess and carried the dog to the door. "I'm going to take him outside."

Marilee smiled at Sam. "Thank you," she said. "Did you have to pay much for him?"

Sam shook his head. "Actually, my friend was glad to get rid of him. He's running an ad in the newspaper tomorrow. He sent this bag of food so you'd know what to feed the puppy."

"You can see Josh is thrilled."

"A boy needs a dog." The two stared at one another for a long moment. They weren't even aware Winnie was in the room.

The girl looked from one to the other and shook her head. "I'm going upstairs to set my hair on fire. If y'all need me, just holler."

"Huh?" Marilee looked up, but Winnie was already gone. "Did she say something about a fire?" she asked Sam.

He shrugged. "Sorry, I wasn't listening. Oh, while I'm thinking about it, I borrowed a large cage from a guy at work. "

"A cage?"

"It's probably best if you confine the pup while you're gone during the day. You don't want to come home and spend an hour cleaning up after him. He's young, he'll sleep most of the day anyway."

"Good idea," she said, never taking her eyes off Sam's face.

"Well, I should be going." He looked reluctant to leave. "I'll bring the cage over after dinner. But first, I'd like to see how Josh and the puppy are getting along."

Marilee grabbed a sweater and joined Sam on the back steps. The night air was cold, and Josh wasn't wearing a sweater. For a brief moment, she longed to say something or go get one for him but decided against it. Instead, she just enjoyed watching Josh and the puppy chase each other across the backyard, laughing as the boy tossed a stick and told the puppy to retrieve it, only to watch the dog run in the opposite direction. The animal was obviously more interested in playing.

"Don't worry, you'll have plenty of time to teach him tricks," Sam said. "Right now, he's just happy to be here."

"You think he likes me?" Josh asked.

Marilee laughed. "Looks that way." She couldn't help noticing how happy and relaxed her son looked. The hardness she'd seen in his eyes was gone, as was the bitter twist around his mouth that he'd worn for months. Had his parents' bickering and separation stolen Josh's boyish smile? Had living with Grady and LaFonda changed him in some way? It would have been easy to let herself feel guilty over the past, and in the past Marilee might have given in to it. But guilt and blame had never gotten a person anywhere. All she could do was concentrate on the here and now. And Josh *did* seem happier the last few days.

"What are you going to name him?" Sam asked.

"Rascal. I thought of that the minute I saw him."

Marilee rubbed her arms, trying to chase away the night chill. "He looks like a rascal." She suspected the dog could get into all kinds of mischief if left to his own devices. Presently, he was trying to dig a hole in the backyard while

Josh tried to get him interested in something else. Marilee knew she had things to do, but she was reluctant to leave. "I'm so glad you thought of the dog," she whispered to Sam.

He took her hand and squeezed it. "Whatever helps, babe," he said.

She was so warmed by the endearment that the night air suddenly didn't seem so cold anymore.

On Halloween, Josh and Winnie helped Marilee pass out flyers. Because it was Saturday, the grocery stores and shopping centers were full, so they took advantage of it by putting the flyers beneath the windshield wipers of parked cars. They hit several big apartment complexes and stuffed flyers beneath the doors.

By three o'clock, Winnie was complaining of a backache and Josh was sorely concerned about his dog. Marilee decided they had passed out enough flyers for one afternoon. They headed home, had dinner and prepared for trick-or-treaters. Rascal followed Josh around as he and Winnie took turns passing out Halloween candy, while Marilee baked and touched base with Clara.

The woman on the other end of the line sounded tired but excited "Ruby and I posted flyers in shop windows, stapled them to telephone poles and any other standing object we could find. And Della Framer, bless her heart, had L&M Printing make hundreds of copies for her convenience stores, and she's instructed her cashiers to give one to every customer who comes in the door. And get this. Ruby talked to her friend at the VFW this afternoon. Donations have been pouring in for two days now, thanks to Janie at the *Gazette*. I'll tell you, Marilee, this thing is going to be big!"

Marilee heard Josh get up before 6:00 a.m. the following morning. She joined him downstairs and began preparing an enormous lunch as he popped two waffles into the toaster.

Rascal was eating food from his new dish, his tail wagging furiously.

"I've already taken him out once," Josh said, "and I'll take him out before I go. But I'm going to be gone all day."

Marilee read the concern in his eyes. "I'll look after him."

Winnie came downstairs rubbing her eyes. She wore pink and blue kitty-cat pajamas. The top stretched across her growing abdomen, and it looked as though the buttons would pop off any minute. "What's all this racket down here? Is somebody sick?"

"Josh and Sam are going fishing," Marilee said.

Winnie blinked. "At this hour?"

Josh pulled his waffles from the toaster and poured syrup on them. "That's when the fish are usually biting."

Sam knocked on the back door and sent Rascal into a fit of barking. Josh smiled. "At least we know he's a good watchdog." He let Sam in.

"You almost ready?" Sam asked, his eyes immediately falling on Marilee. She was wearing her white terry-cloth bathrobe and thick socks, one of which had fallen around her ankle. Her hair was pulled into a short ponytail, and she'd flung a dish towel over one shoulder. He grinned. There were so many sides to her, and he loved every one of them. To keep from staring, he walked over to the coffee-maker and helped himself to a cup.

"I have to take Rascal out real quick," Josh said. "I'm going to miss him today."

Marilee's gaze rested on Sam, who looked quite at home in her kitchen. He wore jeans and a heavy sweatshirt. There was something about Sam Brewer in jeans that made her mouth go bone dry the minute she saw him.

Sam took a cautious sip of his coffee. "We're going to catch so many fish you won't have time to worry about Rascal. You'd better grab a jacket," he added. "It's nippy out there this morning."

Josh pulled his jacket from a hook beside the back door and hurried out.

"I'm going back to bed," Winnie said, trudging up the stairs without another word.

Sam continued to eye Marilee over the rim of his coffee cup. "You wearing anything under that?"

She blushed profusely. "Sam Brewer, what a thing to ask!"

He looked amused as he drained his cup.

Clara arrived later that morning. "You won't believe what's happened."

"I hope it's good news," Marilee said.

"Better than good. A-1 Rentals is supplying one of those rubber houses for the children, and Edith-Ann LeCroy is bringing in two ponies so we can offer pony rides. Also, A-1 Rentals has offered to lend us canopy tents in case we run out of room inside the VFW hall. The way it looks, we'll probably end up using it."

"That *is* good news," Marilee said. "Your friend at the *Gazette* has certainly been a big help to us. People are finally getting involved."

"That's not all. I've saved the best for last. Late yesterday afternoon, a man pulled up in a delivery truck and began unloading cartons of silver and china and a whole slew of antiques. When I inquired about the donor, I was told everything came from Esmerelda Cunningham. Marilee, we're talking a fortune in donations!"

Marilee was stunned. "Why would Esmerelda Cunningham get rid of all her prized possessions?"

"I was hoping you'd have the answer to that. Not that we don't appreciate her generosity, of course, but I wanted to come to you before I did anything with her belongings."

"Where are they now?"

"In a locked room."

"Keep them locked up for the time being," Marilee said. "I'll talk to Esmerelda and get back to you."

"Let me know as soon as possible so I can run by the library and advertise over the Internet."

Marilee arrived at Esmerelda Cunningham's house an

hour later. She found the woman sitting in her library, sipping tea and reading a book of poetry.

"I was just told that you sent an entire truckload of very expensive items to be sold at our bazaar," Marilee said without preamble.

"And a fine good morning to you, Mrs. Abernathy," Esmerelda said.

Marilee's shoulders slumped. Leave it to Esmerelda to put her in her place. "Good morning, Mrs. Cunningham. Now, about your donation—"

"Are you complaining?"

"Not at all," Marilee assured her. "I can't begin to thank you for your generosity. It's more than we ever hoped for. But the committee never expected you to part with family heirlooms."

"Mrs. Abernathy, I have no family. I'm the end of the line. And with all the fuss over the bazaar, it seemed only right that I donate something. Everything came from my attic, and frankly, I have no need for it." She paused and drew herself up. "Besides, I've grown weary of people in this town referring to me as mean old Mrs. Cunningham, the stingiest woman in town. Don't think for one minute that I don't know what's being said behind my back. I have my pride, you know."

Marilee blushed. She had been as guilty as the rest of them. "It's very kind of you," she said. "More than any of us expected. But we have no idea how to price the items."

Esmerelda waved aside the remark. "I have an old friend who used to work for Sotheby's. He's retired now, but I'm sure he'd be happy to help you. Perhaps he could arrange a silent auction. I'll call him." She paused. "Be sure someone from the *Gazette* mentions these items in the newspaper. She'd be wise to send the information to several other papers as well. That way you'll draw people from all over. People who appreciate the *finer* things in life," she added, as though she couldn't imagine anyone in Chickpea having enough sense to know real quality.

"That's an excellent idea."

"Now that that's settled, I'm sure you have a million things to do before Saturday. I won't keep you."

Marilee smiled, knowing she had just been dismissed.

Sam and Josh arrived home late afternoon. Josh immediately grabbed Rascal from his cage. "Hi, boy, did you miss me?"

"I just took him out," Marilee said. She looked at them. "So where are the fish?"

Josh looked up. "We only caught a few little ones so we threw them back. We still had a good time, though, didn't we, Sam?"

"Yes, we did."

"Sam taught me to play poker."

Marilee's mouth dropped open. "Poker!"

"Now, Marilee, don't get all huffy. We weren't playing for money."

"We used pebbles," Josh said. "It's a good thing Sam brought cards or we'd have been bored."

Marilee could tell her son had enjoyed himself, so she decided to let the poker-playing slide. "Well, take off your coats, and I'll fix you some hot chocolate. Guess this means I'll have to cook you guys cheeseburgers for dinner, although my heart was set on a nice fish dinner."

"You're going to cook burgers?" Sam said, sounding worried. "You didn't buy a new grill, did you?" When Marilee shook her head, he looked relieved. "Josh, allow me to tell you about the last time your mother cooked hamburgers."

"That's not necessary," Marilee said.

"I gotta hear this," Josh said. By the time Sam had finished the story, the boy was doubled over with laughter and the dog was thumping his tail in delight.

"Very funny," Marilee muttered from the stove. But she didn't mind being the brunt of the joke as long as Josh found something to laugh about.

* * *

Marilee took the day before the bazaar off from work. She iced cakes, packed them in boxes donated by the local bakery and made several trips to the VFW hall where Clara, Ruby and Nell, as well as a dozen other women were setting up. Sam showed up to do whatever lifting was necessary and spent much of his time flirting. Marilee, despite the butterflies in her stomach, told him she had absolutely no time for such nonsense.

Finally, he grabbed her hand and pulled her into a room where signs had been painted and were in the process of drying. "How about a little kiss for all my hard work?"

"Okay," she relented. "One small kiss, and we get back to work." She primly offered her lips.

He chuckled and pulled her into his arms, capturing her mouth with his and kissing her until she was breathless and dizzy.

When he released her, her head was spinning. "You cheated," she said, trying to catch her breath and keep her heart from flying out of her chest.

"You're right, I'm downright worthless. By the way, are you wearing panties under that skirt?"

A shiver raced up her spine as Marilee gaped at him in disbelief. "Well, I have never, *ever*—"

"That's your problem, Marilee. Maybe it's time you did."

"There's no hope for you, Sam Brewer."

"You're right. I'm a lost cause. You'd better git while the gittin' is good."

Marilee opened the door and almost bumped into Josh. "Have you seen Sam?" he asked.

She knew her face was the color of a red delicious apple. "Yes, we were just looking over the signs. They're dry now. You may want to help Sam put them in place."

"Hey, buddy," Sam said. "I could use your help."

Marilee hurried from the room, realizing she was holding her breath. The last thing she wanted Josh to see was her kissing Sam Brewer.

"Excuse me, madam," a small man, wearing thick-framed glasses, said. "I'm Mr. Dill. I used to work for

Sotheby's. Mrs. Esmerelda Cunningham has asked me to oversee a silent auction for your bazaar.''

Marilee escorted him to the room where Esmerelda's donations were stored and unlocked the door. "We haven't moved the items out as of yet," she said.

He glanced around the room. "This will be fine. I'll need a couple of large folding tables to display some of the smaller pieces, but I should have more than enough space. I'll also need someone to move the furniture around. And of course there should be a sign above the door, so people will know where the silent auction is to be held."

Marilee found Sam and Josh posting signs. "Sam, we need more men."

"Okay," he said. "I'll call a few guys and see if they can help out."

"Just so happens I have two strong men with me," Winnie said, coming up behind her.

Marilee turned and found Mike and another teenager beside him. "We're here to help," Mike asked. "This is my friend Jo-Jo. Just tell us what you need."

She thanked them and told them where they could find Mr. Dill.

Within an hour, Sam had enlisted the help of several more able-bodied men, including Bobby Benson.

The day passed quickly as everyone worked, setting up tables, unloading boxes. Clara had to request several more tables for her books and magazines. Marilee and Ruby carried one over for her.

"How come it's taking you so long to get your tables in order?" Ruby asked. "You're not using the Dewey decimal system, are you?"

Clara looked perturbed. "Of course not. But I've had to place the books in categories. Fiction, nonfiction, romance, adventure, science fiction—"

"Is this a menopause thing?"

"It's called organization, Ruby. Perhaps there's a lesson in it for you."

"Well, you can obsess over it as long as you like, but I'm grabbing something to eat."

"Perhaps when you've had a bite, I can help you arrange your table," Clara said.

Ruby looked at Marilee, who was doing her best not to laugh. "I think Clara is low on estrogen today, if you ask me. Either that or she needs to get laid."

"Oh my," Marilee said, not knowing how else to reply.

The VFW members had supplied hot dogs and drinks, but nobody lingered over lunch because there was too much to do. Fortunately, Nell had made a diagram of where everything was to be placed, but they were quickly running out of space.

"I'm glad A-1 Rental is letting us use their tents," Marilee told the woman. "We're going to have to move the tools and lawn mowers outside."

"May as well move the exercise equipment out there too," Nell replied, making adjustments to her diagram. "We'll have to do that first thing in the morning."

It was after nine o'clock when an exhausted Marilee and her group finally left. Nell, who'd been driven home by Bobby Benson earlier, had promised to make submarine sandwiches. The girls ate at the kitchen table while Sam and Josh chowed down at the coffee table in the den.

"I'm too tired to live," Ruby said. "Somebody just shoot me and put me out of my misery."

Winnie grunted. "Don't talk to me about tired."

The weary group finished their sandwiches, thanked Nell and said good-night. It was obvious Sam wanted to spend time with Marilee, but it was impossible under the circumstances. "Try to rest," he said as he walked Josh and her to the door. "Tomorrow's going to be another hectic day."

Marilee, Nell and Winnie arrived at the bazaar early the next morning, only to find a long line at the door. "Oh my goodness!" Nell said. "This is a good sign."

"We'd better go through the back," Marilee told them.

Clara and Ruby were already inside, as was Mr. Dill who

was still going through Mrs. Cunningham's donations. "I've listed the absolute minimum bid we'll accept on these items," he said. "I've also supplied a large box that will remain locked during the auction. Those who participate will be assured that nobody will see their bid until the auction is officially over. At that time, I'll announce the names of the highest bidder."

"That sounds perfect, Mr. Dill," Marilee said. "We are so lucky to have you with us today."

The man preened.

Clara pulled Marilee aside. "We have a small problem," she said. "The fellow who was supposed to sit in the dunking booth came down with a bad cold. We have no one to man it."

"I'll work on that," Marilee promised.

Sam and Josh arrived shortly afterward. "Are you ready for us to start carrying things out to the tents?" Sam asked.

"Yes. Your mother has a diagram of where everything is to be placed."

"Okay, let's go," Sam told Josh.

"One more thing," Marilee said. "Our volunteer from the dunking booth took ill. We need someone to fill his place."

Sam and Josh exchanged a look. "I guess that means us," Sam said.

The boy shrugged. "We can take turns."

Sam shook his head. "We'll have to run home and grab bathing suits as soon as we get set up."

"Thank you," Marilee said.

Once the bazaar officially opened, people rushed through as though they couldn't get inside quickly enough. Marilee took her place at the baked goods table. A woman named Hilda had been assigned to help her, which was a good thing, because people swarmed the table and Marilee knew she would never have been able to keep up. Before Marilee knew it, lunchtime had rolled around. She sent Hilda to grab something to eat, and the woman returned with hot dogs and colas.

"You *have* to see the hunk in the dunking booth," Hilda said. "Why, if I were a single woman and twenty years younger, I'd hog-tie him and take him home with me." She blushed. "Listen to me talk, and me being a fine Christian woman."

Marilee was almost ashamed of herself, but she hurried outside the minute things slowed down at their table. The lawn was packed with activity: a horseshoe toss, a fishing booth and a big board holding numerous balloons where children took turns trying to burst one with a dart. There was a long line at the rubber house and the pony rides. She spied the dunking booth and hurried over.

Sam was standing beside it wearing a bathing suit, with a towel draped over his shoulder. Marilee could only stare at the broad, hair-roughened chest, and the way the hair thinned over his stomach and formed a line that disappeared beneath his bathing suit. Lord, Lord, she thought. Her gaze dropped to his legs, lean but muscular, covered with the same black hair. She swallowed, and it felt like one of Winnie's favorite pickled eggs going down her throat.

If Sam noticed her staring he was polite enough not to mention it. He simply smiled. "Have you come to relieve us?" he asked.

Marilee tried to keep her eyes shoulder level. "I just wanted to see how things are going out here." she managed to say.

"Hi, Mom."

Marilee glanced over and saw Josh in the dunking booth. "Aren't you cold?" she asked him.

"Naw, I'm having too much fun to be cold." An elderly gentleman stepped up to the booth and threw a ball. He missed the target completely. Josh laughed. "Give it up, mister," he said. "You couldn't hit the broad side of a barn." The man took another ball, tossed it hard at the target and Josh was dumped unceremoniously into the water. He came up sputtering.

Marilee and Sam laughed. "That'll teach you to talk back to your elders," Sam shouted to the boy.

Marilee hurried back inside, where she tried to concentrate on selling baked items, despite the mental picture she had of Sam in his bathing suit. The crowd was still thick, and she noted a number of people going into the silent auction room.

By three o'clock, Marilee and Hilda had sold almost all of the baked items and were getting ready to break down their table. From the looks of it, she and Hilda weren't the only ones selling out, Marilee noticed. The surrounding tables had cleared considerably as had the large appliances and furniture.

By five o'clock, the crowd had thinned, although a number of people had gathered at the door where the silent auction was still going on. Marilee wondered how Mr. Dill had done as she and Hilda began to assist the others in packing away the items that hadn't sold. Sam and Josh appeared, this time fully dressed, and they immediately began breaking down tables and stacking boxes along one wall so the Salvation Army could pick up the leftovers on Monday.

"Have you seen Mom and Winnie?" Sam asked Marilee.

"One of the volunteers drove them home a couple of hours ago," Marilee said. "They were exhausted."

Marilee headed to the silent-auction room and found Mr. Dill standing at the back door with a checklist as people carried out boxes of china and antiques.

"The auction went very well," he whispered to Marilee. "I haven't tallied up the figures yet, but I've sold completely out. I'll call Ruby Ledbetter first thing in the morning and give her the numbers."

"Thank you, Mr. Dill," Marilee said. "I don't know what we would have done without you."

"My pleasure. Besides, Esmerelda would have wrung my neck if I'd said no."

It was after nine o'clock by the time the VFW building had been cleared, swept and mopped. A number of men had already taken down the tents and cleaned up the debris outside. A tired Marilee thanked the volunteers, said goodbye to Clara and Ruby and climbed into her car with Josh. Sam followed and turned into his driveway, waving to them before going inside his house.

Winnie was lying on the sofa watching TV when Marilee and Josh came through the front door. "I made sandwiches," she said.

"Did you take Rascal out?" Josh asked.

"Three times. You owe me. Once I get my figure back and start dating, you'll be the first one I ask to baby-sit."

"Seems Mike likes your figure just fine," the boy countered.

Winnie grunted. "What do you know about romance? You're just a kid."

"I'm taking lessons from Sam. I hear he's got a way with the ladies."

Marilee arched one eyebrow. "Oh, yeah?"

Winnie shook her head sadly. "Josh, there are some things better left unsaid."

Ruby called at ten o'clock the following morning. "Marilee, I hope you're sitting down," she said, "because I have the final figures."

"I'm listening," Marilee said.

"Well, after expenses, we personally brought in more than twelve thousand dollars on the bazaar."

"I'm impressed," Marilee said. "What about the silent auction?"

"I just got off the telephone with Mr. Dill. You're going to love this. He came about four hundred dollars short of fifty grand. We have a grand total of sixty-two thousand, one hundred dollars and seventy-eight cents."

Marilee dropped the telephone. She picked it up. "Ruby, are you sure?" she asked, fearing her heart would give out on her.

"I've been going through the figures since five o'clock this morning."

Marilee was beside herself with happiness. "Have you told Clara?"

"I've been trying to reach her but her line is busy. She's probably talking with her new beau. I'll try her again."

Marilee hung up. She realized she was trembling. Sixty-two thousand dollars! It was more than enough money to renovate Blessing Home. She could only think of one person she wanted to share the news with. She hurried out the front door and across her lawn and spied Sam cleaning out the back of his truck.

"Sam!" she shouted. "You won't believe it!" She jumped the hedges, but her foot caught in a root, and she fell face first on the ground.

"Marilee!" Sam dropped his shovel and raced to her side. He knelt beside her and pulled her into his arms. "Marilee, are you hurt?"

She laughed. "Only my pride. Was my fall at least graceful?"

"No, honey. You looked like a one-legged gazelle going over those hedges." His look sobered. "You could have broken your neck. Are you sure you're okay?"

She saw the love and concern in his eyes, and her insides grew soft. "Oh, Sam," she said, his name sounding like a sigh.

His gaze fell to her lips. "What, baby?"

"Would it shock you terribly if I told you—"

"Told me what, sweetheart?"

Marilee gazed up at him, longing to tell him the truth about how she felt about him, that she thought she had fallen in love with him, but she was afraid. "Well, I—" She was prevented from saying anything more when Nell stepped out the front door.

"Sam," the woman called out. She glanced around the yard and frowned. "Sam, what are you doing to Marilee?" She hurried over.

Marilee was almost thankful for the interruption. The last thing she wanted was to have Sam think her forward. "I fell over the hedges," Marilee confessed.

"Oh my!"

"But I'm okay."

"Then why is my son still holding you?"

Sam grinned. "Because she feels so good, Mom."

Nell looked fretful. "I'll bet Edna-Lee Bodine is getting an eyeful. Sam, dear, please get off poor Marilee this instant. You'll have the neighbors thinking she's a loose woman."

"Aw, Mom, can't we stay like this for a few more minutes?"

"I insist you stop this nonsense, Samuel Brewer. Marilee has a son to think about."

Sam got up reluctantly and helped Marilee to her feet. Once she'd brushed herself off, she remembered why she was there. Her face lit up. "You'll never believe this," she said, "but the bazaar brought in sixty-two thousand dollars. And that doesn't even count all the other donations we've received."

Nell and Sam both gave a shout of joy and took turns hugging one another. "That'll be more than enough to get Blessing Home in shape," Sam said. "You girls should be proud of yourselves."

"I think the dunking booth brought in the most money," Marilee teased. "All those women couldn't wait to get a look at you in your bathing suit." Marilee chuckled. She was almost sure he'd blushed.

"Oh, goodness, I forgot," Nell said. "You have a telephone call, Sam."

"Who is it?"

"Shelly."

Sam's smile disappeared from his face. "Tell her—" He turned away from Marilee. "Never mind, I'll tell her." He stalked toward the house.

"Shelly is Sam's ex-wife, right?" Marilee said, feeling a bit uncomfortable that the woman was calling him.

Nell nodded. "Moneygrubbing female," she muttered. "Always looking for a handout. Good thing Sam has a lot of money."

Marilee arched one eyebrow. "He does?"

"Didn't you know? He sold his Atlanta business for big bucks."

"He doesn't act or dress like he has money," Marilee said.

"Oh, that's just Sam. Besides, money doesn't mean anything to him. He's not afraid of hard work. Do you want to come inside for coffee?"

Marilee was strangely disturbed by the news. Did Sam think she was after his money like his ex-wife? she wondered. "No, I'd better get back to the house. I just wanted to give you the news."

Inside, Sam snatched up the telephone. "Okay, Shelly, what is it *now?*" he demanded.

The woman on the other end hesitated. "What's wrong with you?" she asked.

"I'm tired, that's what's wrong. I'm tired of you calling me every time you chip a fingernail or need money for a new car. I have my own life now."

"Sam, I—"

"Listen to me, Shelly," he interrupted. "If you don't stop hassling me I'm going to call my attorney. I am not sending you any more money, you got that?"

"Yes, Sam," she said, "but that's not why I'm calling. I just wanted to let you know I'm getting married."

Sam sighed his relief, feeling as though a giant boulder had just been lifted from his shoulders. No more phone calls from Shelly, crying and asking for help. He laughed. "Well, why didn't you say so?"

# Twenty-Two

The following Saturday, Winnie and Marilee attended their first childbirth class. "I don't know why I need this class," Winnie said, carrying the pillow they were told to bring. "I watched my mother have two babies right in her bed, and there was nothing to it. This is a waste of time, if you ask me. I wouldn't bother if my doctor weren't so insistent."

"Well, I certainly need it," Marilee said, "if you plan on having me in the delivery room with you."

"Did Grady go in when you had Josh?"

"Are you kidding? Grady passes out at the sight of blood. My mother went in his place, and she claimed it was the most rewarding experience of her life." She smiled. "I'm glad she and I were able to share it."

Ellen Moore, the class instructor, greeted the couples and asked that they introduce themselves. She spent the first hour going over a handout, which described the changes that they could expect to take place when they went into labor. After a brief question-and-answer session, she discussed the three stages of labor. More questions followed before she had the couples move to the floor so they could practice various breathing exercises.

"What do you think?" Marilee asked Winnie once they broke for lunch.

Winnie shrugged. "I'm not worried."

They returned to the classroom after lunch and watched three videos of women giving birth. Afterward, Mrs. Moore discussed what type of pain medications were available, should the expectant moms become too uncomfortable during the labor process. "I would suggest you discuss your options with your doctor before you go in," the woman said.

Winnie looked relieved when the class ended. "I'm not attending the next class," she told Marilee as they walked to the car. "I know all I need to know."

"Did you get nervous watching the videos?" Marilee asked.

"Heck, no," she said. "Those women didn't so much as break into a sweat. I'm telling you, Marilee, this is going to be a piece of cake."

Marilee decided it was best to keep her mouth shut.

Thanksgiving and winter arrived on the same day, coating the ground with a thin layer of ice that sent Rascal slipping and sliding across the back lawn when Josh took him outside. Marilee watched from the kitchen window, chuckling to herself.

"Don't tell me you're cooking already," Winnie said, coming down the stairs. "It's not even eight o'clock. Besides, Nell specifically asked you not to bring anything. That's why she hired a caterer, remember?"

"I don't want to show up empty-handed," Marilee said. "I figured it wouldn't hurt to bake a few pies."

"A few?" Winnie looked at the pies cooling on the counter. "Two pecan, one apple and three pumpkin pies?" She arched both eyebrows.

"Okay, so I get carried away when it comes to baking."

Josh came through the door with Rascal in his arms. He was still laughing. "I saw the whole thing," Marilee said.

"I don't think he likes cold weather," Josh told her. He set the dog down and shrugged out of his coat. "Hold on, Rascal, and I'll feed you in a minute." He draped the coat over the chair and grabbed the dog's bowl.

"Josh, you're feeding him too much," Winnie said. "Look how fat he's getting. He's a regular roly-poly."

"All puppies are fat in the beginning," Josh said. He patted Winnie on the stomach. "And who are you to call my dog roly-poly? Looks like you're about to give birth to Hulk Hogan."

Winnie frowned. "I'm going to pretend I didn't hear that."

"I think I'll call Dad," Josh said, "and wish him a happy Thanksgiving." He went into the living room.

Marilee noted the sad expression on her son's face when he returned. "Everything okay?" she asked.

The boy shrugged. "Dad's not having Thanksgiving dinner."

"Oh?"

"LaFonda split. Packed her bags and moved to Tennessee to be closer to her family. Said she couldn't live with a man who was sick all the time and had no job. I knew it wouldn't last."

"I'm sorry to hear it." Marilee didn't like to think of anyone spending the holidays alone, not even Grady. Nevertheless, it irked her that he'd shared the information with Josh and put a damper on the boy's Thanksgiving.

"Yeah." The boy went upstairs to his room.

Marilee and Winnie exchanged looks but didn't say anything.

The group arrived at the Brewer household at precisely one o'clock. Sam met them at the door wearing charcoal slacks, a light blue dress shirt, and tie. Marilee smiled. "Well, now, you look nice," she said, realizing it was the first time she'd seen him when he wasn't wearing jeans.

Sam simply stared back at her, noting how pretty she looked in a pleated, dove-gray skirt and light pink sweater. "You look pretty good yourself," he said.

"May we come in?" Winnie asked. "It's cold out here."

Sam gave an embarrassed cough, realizing he'd forgotten the others because he was so happy to see Marilee. "Yes, please do." He stepped back so they could enter. "I see everybody's dressed up today. Winnie, I must say you look ravishing. Is that a new dress?"

She preened. "As a matter of fact it is. Marilee bought it for me since I was about to bust out of everything I own."

Marilee headed straight for the kitchen, where she found

Nell all aflutter. "You won't believe what happened," the woman said. "I ordered enough food for six people, and the caterer got it all wrong and brought enough for ten. Marilee, why on earth did you bake those pies? I told you not to bring anything."

"She didn't want to come empty-handed," Winnie said, setting one of the pies on the counter.

"Well, I'm glad you're on time," Nell said. "Sam and I just put everything on the table." She led them into the dining room. "Sam, why don't you sit at this end and Josh can sit at the other." She looked around. "And Marilee, you can sit there," she said, pointing to the chair next to Sam. "Winnie and I will sit on the other side."

Marilee hid her smile. It was obvious Nell wanted her close to Sam. Once they were seated, Winnie said the blessing.

"Everything looks wonderful," Marilee said. "And you're right. There's enough food here for a small army."

"Which is why I'm sending you home with leftovers," the woman said. "Sam and I can't possibly eat all this food." She smiled. "Sam, would you like to carve this beautiful, twenty-five-pound turkey?"

"Mom, you know I'm no good at that sort of thing. Let Josh do it."

"Me?" Josh looked surprised. "I've never carved a turkey before."

Sam carried the turkey around to Josh's side. "It's time you learn."

Marilee was certain Sam knew how to carve the bird, but she was touched that he was doing what he could to make Josh feel at home.

"I'll help you, dear," Nell said. She showed him how to slice the breast. "The rest of you can start passing the food around if you like."

Josh began to slice the breast from the bone while Nell guided him through it. "Anyone prefer dark meat?" he asked.

"I like the drumstick," Winnie informed them.

"So do I," Josh said.

"Good thing there are two of them," Winnie replied, "because I know with you being a gentleman and all you'd insist on giving it to me."

Josh grinned. "Not necessarily. Especially since you cheated yesterday when we played chess."

"I never cheat. You're just a lousy player."

"Okay, everyone dig in," Nell said once the food had been served. "And don't be shy, there's more than enough for seconds."

Despite Nell's prompting Josh ate very little. "May I be excused?" he asked as soon as everyone finished eating. "I need to check on Rascal."

"Sure, honey," Marilee said.

"Just get back in time for dessert," Nell said.

The boy slipped out the back door. Nobody said anything for a minute. Finally, Sam pushed his chair away from the table. "I think I'll run over and check on Josh. He seems awfully quiet today."

Nell waited until Sam closed the door. "Josh looks upset. Is he okay?"

Marilee folded her napkin in her lap. "He misses his father. Grady is ill today and his girlfriend walked out on him, so he's spending the holidays alone."

"Grady deserves it, if you ask me," Winnie said.

"Yes, but our son is suffering over it," Marilee said. "What Grady does is his business, but I don't like to see Josh upset."

"Josh just needs more time," Nell said, patting Marilee's hand. "After all, he's trying to adjust. But he seems happy enough to me."

Winnie looked thoughtful. "This is the first Thanksgiving I've spent without my family," she said. "It hurts a little, but I'm thankful I have y'all in my life. I think it would be terrible to spend the holiday alone."

Marilee looked at Nell. "Would you mind if I fix a plate for Grady before I leave?"

"Are you kidding? I'm sending half of this stuff home with you."

Marilee and Winnie began clearing the table. Marilee filled a sink with warm, sudsy water and began washing the china, while Winnie loaded the other dishes into the dishwasher.

Sam waited on Marilee's back steps while Josh let Rascal out. The boy looked troubled, but the dog was obviously glad to see his young master because he stayed by Josh's side the entire time. After Rascal had gone to the bathroom, Josh sank onto the steps next to Sam.

"What's wrong, Josh? You look preoccupied," Sam said.

Josh nodded but he didn't meet Sam's gaze. "I'm sort of worried about my dad," he said. "It just doesn't feel right, him going without Thanksgiving dinner."

Sam nodded. "At least he won't have to wash dishes." He nudged Josh. "And neither will we, if we stay over here long enough."

Josh didn't seem to be listening. "This is the first time my parents haven't been together for the holidays. It feels weird, you know?"

"I know, Josh, believe me. My dad died when I was in high school. I was angry at first, because he was my best friend. I didn't get a chance to say goodbye. He had always been in excellent health. Nobody knew he had a bad heart until one day he just slumped over in his chair and was gone." He patted Josh on the shoulder. "It's hard at first, but I promise it gets easier as time goes on."

Josh was quiet for a moment. "Do you like my mom?"

Sam wondered how to respond. He was crazy about Marilee, but he didn't think Josh was ready to hear that. "Your mother is one of the finest people I've ever met, and I consider her my friend. My mother thinks the world of her."

Josh looked as though he wanted to ask more questions but didn't. "Sam?"

"Yeah?"

"Thanks for getting me Rascal," he said, rubbing his fingers across the puppy's silky ears.

"You're welcome."

"You think they're finished cleaning the kitchen yet?"

"Yeah, and if we don't get back they'll eat all the dessert."

"I'm going straight to bed," Winnie announced once they returned home. "All that food made me sleepy." She went upstairs.

"I'm going to take Rascal out again," Josh said.

Marilee was already loading food onto three plates. "I was thinking we should probably take some of this food to your dad," she said. "No sense wasting it."

Josh smiled for the first time since his phone call to his father. "Thanks, Mom."

Marilee had packed the food into a box by the time Josh returned with Rascal. "Ready?"

"Sure." Josh carried the box to the car for her. "This is a lot of food for one person."

"I have another stop to make after we drop a plate off at your dad's," she said.

Marilee had never seen where Grady lived, and she was shocked at the sight of the old mobile home with its peeling paint and the clutter surrounding it. Grady had always been so particular. A large cat was curled on a lawn chair, and Marilee wondered how Grady could tolerate an animal, given his allergies. She kept her feelings to herself, though, as she reached into the box for the plate of food and a pumpkin pie.

Josh carried them to the door and knocked several times before Grady answered. If Marilee had been shocked to find him living in squalor, she was doubly so when she saw the man's appearance. He looked surprised at the food and disappeared inside for a few seconds before walking out to the car. As if sensing his parents needed privacy, Josh picked up the cat and sat in the chair, stroking the animal. Marilee had not expected Grady to come out and talk to her, but she put her window down.

"Thank you for dropping off the food, Marilee," he said. "You shouldn't have gone to the trouble."

"It was no trouble. Besides, Josh was worried about you."

Grady seemed to be studying her. "You look very nice," he said. "All dressed up for the holidays, I see." He paused. "I was sorry to hear about your ordeal at the Pickford Inn," he said. "I had no idea you'd taken a second job. You must have been scared to death."

"No harm done." She couldn't help feeling concerned about his appearance. "Grady, are you okay? You don't look so well."

"I haven't been responding to the blood pressure medication, so my doctor put me on something else. Maybe this one will work. Uh, Marilee? Do you think we could sit down and talk sometime?"

She looked at him. She couldn't imagine what he wanted to discuss with her. "We'll see," she said, not wanting to commit herself. "I'd better get going. I have another errand to run." She started the engine. Josh stood and returned the cat to his resting place. He hugged his dad and rounded the car, climbing in the passenger's side.

The drive to Esmerelda Cunningham's house didn't take long. Marilee carried the box of food to the door and rang the bell. Dudly answered. "Mrs. Abernathy, what a pleasant surprise. Would you like to come in?"

"I can't stay," she said. "I just wanted to drop off a few leftovers from Thanksgiving dinner. There's enough for both of you."

Dudley peered into the box. "And pecan pie to boot. You're too kind, Mrs. Abernathy."

"Please, call me Marilee," she said. "Happy Thanksgiving, Dudley. Please give Mrs. Cunningham my best." She walked to her car and pulled away.

"That's old lady Cunningham's house, isn't it?" Josh said.

"Yes, it is."

"Why did you take her food? She's the meanest person in town."

"Yes, she can be cranky at times, but I think it's all an act."

"A very good act," the boy replied.

Night came, and Winnie trudged down the stairs. "I'm hungry," she announced.

"There are still plenty of leftovers in the refrigerator," Marilee said.

"Where's Josh?"

"He took Rascal out."

"Is he feeling any better?"

"Much better."

Josh returned and put Rascal in his cage for the night. "I'm tired. I think I'll go to bed early." He hugged Marilee. "Thanks for taking that plate to Dad."

Winnie looked at Marilee. "You took a plate of food to Grady?" When Marilee nodded, Winnie shook her head.

"I did it for Josh."

Marilee joined her at the kitchen table and gazed down at Rascal. The poor dog looked lost. Feeling sorry for him, she opened the cage door and pulled him out. He was so thankful he began licking her ear. Marilee laughed softly as she made her way up the stairs to Josh's room.

His bedroom door was open. "You forgot something," Marilee said.

Josh looked up and brightened when he saw his dog. "What do you mean?" he asked.

"You can't just leave poor Rascal in his cage on Thanksgiving night."

Josh looked surprised. "You mean I can sleep with him?"

"He's your dog." Marilee would never have permitted such a thing in the past, but Josh needed cheering up.

He took the puppy in his arms and received a wet kiss on his nose. He laughed. "I think he likes me."

"Well, you're a pretty likable person."

Winnie was finishing up her snack when Marilee came

downstairs. She washed and dried her plate. "I can't believe how tired I am," she said.

Marilee looked at her. "Speaking of which, I want you to stop doing so much around here. I can take care of things now that I'm not working a second job. You just need to concentrate on school and your baby."

"I'll admit I'm starting to slow down." She walked over to Marilee and surprised her with a hug. "You're too good to me. Happy Thanksgiving, Marilee."

Marilee hugged her back. "Same to you, Winnie. Now, why don't you go upstairs and rest?"

"I think I will. Good night, Marilee."

Sam felt restless. He missed Marilee. It was torture being away from her and she was all he could think about. This falling-in-love business was hard on a man.

Nell looked up from her TV program. "Why don't you go on over and see her?" she said.

Sam looked at her. "Am I that obvious?"

"Yes, and you're driving me crazy."

Sam grinned and let himself out the back door. A moment later he knocked on Marilee's door. She looked happy to see him, Sam thought as he stepped inside. "Where is everybody?"

"They went to bed early."

"So we're alone?" When she nodded, he slipped his arms around her waist. "Come here, woman, and kiss me." He pulled her closer and kissed her. When he lifted his head, he grinned. "That was so good I'm coming back for more."

This time the kiss was slow and lingering, and when he prodded her lips with his tongue, Marilee opened her mouth to receive him, slipping her arms around his neck. He moaned deep in his throat and pressed his body against hers, wanting more.

Marilee's body responded instantly. Her belly warmed, and her nerve endings tingled with pleasure. She couldn't get close enough to him. She raised her hands to his hair and let it slip through her fingers. She had wanted to touch his hair for a long time.

A noise on the stairs made them jump. Marilee looked up to find Josh standing there, staring, his face masked in disappointment. "Excuse me for interrupting," he said, "but I figured I should take Rascal out one more time." He carried the dog outside.

"Damn," Sam muttered. "I wish he hadn't seen that."

Marilee was stricken. "I thought he was asleep. I'm so embarrassed. Should I talk to him?"

"I'll do it." Sam walked out the back door. Marilee sat at the table and waited.

He found Josh sitting on the back steps, wearing a glum expression. "I'm sorry, Josh," he said. "What you saw in the kitchen just now was all my fault."

"My mother was kissing you back." He looked at Sam. "You told me you were my mother's friend, not her lover."

"I'm not her lover, Josh, but I care deeply for her."

"You'd like to be, though, wouldn't you? What's stopping you? Is it me? Am I in the way here?"

"Of course not."

"Looks like I showed up at the wrong time."

"That's not true."

"That's why you bought me this dog, isn't it? And why you took me fishing. Because you have the hots for my mom."

"Josh, you've got it all wrong. Please listen to me."

"I know the routine," the boy said. "My dad's girlfriend acted like she was crazy about me in the beginning because she knew it would make my dad happy. You're no different than she is."

"That's not fair, Josh. I'm your friend."

"You're no friend of mine. You're just using me to get to my mom." He grabbed his dog, went inside and hurried up the stairs without a word to Marilee.

Sam came through the door a moment later. Marilee was sitting at the kitchen table. "I heard the whole thing," she said. "You didn't have to accept the blame. I had as much to do with it as you."

Sam could see she was near tears. He took the chair beside her and put his hand over hers. "I can try to talk to him again after he cools off. Your kid means a lot to me, and I don't want him thinking I don't value his friendship or that I was using him to get to you."

"Maybe it's best if we don't see one another for a while," she said, although it was not a pleasant thought.

Sam gave a deep sigh. "Is that what you really want? It sure as hell isn't what I want."

"You know how important it is to me that my son be happy."

"What about us?" he asked gently. "Don't we deserve happiness?"

"Josh is my first priority, Sam. You know what I went through to get him back, and I'm not going to risk losing him again." She swallowed hard. "Not for you or anyone else."

Sam was afraid to ask the question. "Are you saying you don't want to see me anymore?"

"All I'm saying is I think we should back off for now."

"My life is worthless if I don't have you to share it," he confessed. "I've never said those words to another woman, Marilee."

She felt the same. But Josh had already been through so much, and he was still a kid. He needed time to heal from all that had happened. She would have to put her feelings for Sam on hold until she was certain Josh would be okay. "If you care about me, you'll go along with this for now."

He sat there for a long moment. She was asking a lot, but Sam was beginning to realize that loving someone often meant making sacrifices. It meant giving. "Okay, Marilee." He squeezed her hand before releasing it. He stood and made for the door, glancing over his shoulder before he stepped out. "But you know where I am if you need me."

Marilee locked the back door and turned out the lights. She climbed the stairs and knocked on Josh's bedroom door.

No response. Finally, she went into her own bedroom and closed the door.

Josh barely spoke to Marilee all week, grabbing a bite to eat when he came home then going straight up to his room. He called his dad several times, but the conversations seemed to depress him.

"Josh is just pouting," Winnie said one evening when she and Marilee were alone. "He'll get over it."

"I'm not so sure," Marilee said.

"So Sam kissed you. So what? You ask me, it's about time the two of you got together."

"I'm married to Josh's father, Winnie. Josh loves his dad, and he's concerned about Grady's health."

Winnie pointed to the calendar. "You're going to be a divorced woman in exactly one week. Or have you forgotten?"

Marilee looked at the calendar. She *had* forgotten. "You're right, Winnie. In one week, I'll be a free woman." She whispered the rest of her sentence. "Don't say anything to Josh. I'd rather he not know."

Winnie muttered a sound of disgust. "When are you going to stop trying to protect your son from every little thing and allow him to grow up?"

"He's been through enough."

"That's life, Marilee, and the more you try to shield him from it, the harder it's going to be on him when he has to make it on his own. In the meantime, you're going to lose the best thing you've ever had."

Marilee hoped that was not the case.

# Twenty-Three

Josh was quiet the following week, and it was all Marilee could do to act cheerful while she was at work. When Debbie put up a few Christmas decorations, Marilee realized she hadn't given much thought to the holidays. On Friday, she knocked on Irby's door. "I have to leave at three-thirty today."

He looked concerned. "Everything okay?"

"I have divorce court at four."

His look softened. "Okay, Marilee. If there's anything Debbie and I can do, please let us know."

She smiled. "I'm okay, Irby, really. I just want to get it behind me."

Marilee arrived at the courthouse shortly before four and found Clara and Ruby waiting for her. "We thought you might need a little moral support," Ruby said.

Marilee thanked them and sat down. Nell arrived a few minutes later. "Sorry I'm late. I had to take a cab."

"That's very sweet of you, Nell."

"Winnie was worried about you. She called me this afternoon from school and asked if I would check on you."

Marilee was deeply touched that her friends cared so much. She sniffed and wiped her eyes.

"Don't cry," Ruby said. "Grady will think you're sad over losing him."

Marilee took the handkerchief Nell offered her. "I don't think he's going to be here."

Tate Radford arrived, briefcase in hand. If he was surprised to see her surrounded by her support group, he didn't mention it. "This will go fast, Marilee," he said. "As I told you, Grady and his attorney won't be present today because they're not contesting. Why don't we go on in?''

"I'll be praying for you," Nell said.

"Hold your head high," Ruby said.

"Be tough," Clara added.

Marilee nodded and followed her attorney inside. She was trembling, but he took her hand and squeezed it. "Everything will be fine.''

The bailiff appeared and asked that everyone stand. Marilee felt her knees quake as she stood beside Tate. The judge cleared his throat. "Let's begin," he said.

Marilee concentrated on remaining calm as the judge read her petition and asked questions. Finally, he slammed his gavel, and the matter was over. Marilee couldn't help feeling sad. Sixteen years of marriage, and it was over as quickly as most people could scramble an egg.

The women looked surprised when Marilee and her lawyer walked out of the courtroom a short time later. "I'll file the decree," Tate said, "and mail it to you." He smiled, patted her shoulder and left her standing with her friends.

"Well, that's that," Marilee said. "It's a done deal."

"How do you feel, honey?" Nell asked.

"Sad and relieved at the same time."

Clara pulled Marilee aside. "Winnie is going to spend the weekend with me since the other girl is no longer with me. We thought it would give you and Josh some time together.''

Marilee drove Nell home. "Do you need anything?" the older woman asked when Marilee pulled in front of her house. "I can make you a pot of soup."

Marilee shook her head. "I'm fine, Nell. Go inside and get out of this cold."

Josh met Marilee at the front door. His eyes were wide, his breathing fast. "Mom, we have to go to the hospital."

Panic seized her. "Are you hurt?" she asked, looking him up and down.

"It's Dad. He's in the emergency room. They think he had a stroke. Where were you? I called you at work, but they said you'd left early. I even called Sam's cell phone and left a message.''

Marilee was surprised he'd tried to reach Sam. "I had things to do," she said, being deliberately vague. Now was not the time to discuss how she'd spent her afternoon.

They were on their way in minutes. Marilee broke the speed limit getting to the hospital. Once they arrived, she let a white-faced Josh out at the emergency-room entrance and searched for a parking place. When she entered the hospital she found Josh arguing with the receptionist.

"They won't let me in," Josh complained loudly.

Marilee tried to quiet him as she appealed to the woman at the window. "I'm sorry to bother you, miss, but my son is very upset about his father."

"I know," the woman said, "but as I tried to explain to him, the doctor has ordered several tests for your husband, and no one is allowed back there at the moment." She looked sympathetic. "I promise to notify you as soon as I hear something."

Josh turned, walked to a chair and fell into it. "This is all my fault," he said when Marilee took the chair beside him. "I should have been there for Dad. I should have been there for him once that slut LaFonda walked out."

Marilee was taken back by her son's language, but she didn't say anything. He was upset. "This is not your fault, Josh. Your dad is a grown man. He's obviously not following his doctor's orders." She paused. "Stop making excuses for him."

Josh tossed her an angry look and moved to the chair across from her. Marilee wondered if she'd been too harsh, but Winnie was right. Josh had to face facts or he would never grow up. A shadow fell over her, and she looked up to find Sam. Relief flooded her. She had never been so happy to see someone.

"I came as soon as I got the message," he said. He sat beside Josh. "You okay?"

The boy shrugged.

"Your dad's going to be fine," Sam said, patting him on the knee. "Just have faith."

"I lost that a long time ago," the boy muttered.

Marilee looked away. It hurt to see her son so bitter. Had he turned away from all he'd once believed in?

"You can't lose faith, Josh," Sam said. "That's what gets us through the tough times."

Sam's comments surprised Marilee. She had never thought of him as a spiritual man. Apparently, there was more to him than she knew. Their gazes met, but she glanced away quickly, fearing he might read the pain in her eyes. She had missed him terribly.

They waited for almost two hours while Josh paced the room. Sam tried to concentrate on the magazine he was reading, but his thoughts were centered on Marilee. He wondered if she had thought about him at all in the past weeks. He hadn't been able to get her out of his mind since he'd agreed to back off.

The receptionist finally called them, and Josh hurried over. "You can see your father now. He's in room three."

Josh paused and looked at his mom. "Aren't you coming in with me?"

She stood. She had no desire to see Grady but Josh seemed to expect it. "Of course," she said.

They found Grady lying on a gurney. "Hi, Dad," Josh said. "How are you feeling?"

"Not so good, Son. The doctor says I'm not responding to the medication he put me on. Hello, Marilee. Thanks for coming."

She nodded and took a chair beside his bed. The door opened, and a young doctor walked through, looking as if he was in a great hurry. "Mrs. Abernathy?"

Marilee looked up. Her divorce had become final that very day, yet people were still referring to her as Grady's wife. It was of little significance at the moment.

"Yes?"

The doctor introduced himself. "Your husband is okay for the moment. He had a very mild stroke and only lost consciousness for a few seconds. We're going to try a new medication, but there's little we can do if Mr. Abernathy refuses to cooperate. He knows what he has to do.'' He scribbled something on his clipboard. ''We've decided to keep him overnight so we can observe him.'' He looked at Grady. ''I suggest you see the doctor I recommended earlier.''

Grady sighed. ''If you think it'll help.''

''Can I stay with my dad?'' Josh asked.

The doctor looked at him and smiled. ''Sure. We'll move him to a private room shortly, but he has to remain quiet. There's a recliner in the room, Mrs. Abernathy, if you'd like to stay for a while. It'll be at least another hour before we get your husband settled in.''

Marilee nodded. ''Where should we wait?''

''I'm sending him to the third floor. You can wait in the visitors' lounge.''

Josh took his dad's hand. ''I won't leave you,'' he promised. ''I'll be waiting when they take you up.''

''Thanks, Son. I just want to rest now.''

Marilee and Josh exited the room. Sam stood the minute they returned to the waiting area. ''It was a mild stroke,'' Marilee said, ''but they're keeping Grady overnight.''

''I have to go,'' Josh said. ''I promised Dad I'd be waiting for him upstairs. You don't have to stay. I'll call you in the morning.''

''You plan to spend the night?'' Marilee asked, unable to hide her disappointment.

''Yeah, Mom. I'm not leaving him.'' She opened her mouth to protest, but Josh cut her off. ''Dad has nobody, don't you get it? Just me. I'm going to stay with him until he's better.'' He paused. ''Even if I have to move back in with him.''

Marilee was stricken. ''Josh, please think this over carefully.''

''Nobody else seems to care what happens to him,'' he replied. He turned to Sam. ''Tell her what it's like to lose your father. Tell her what it's like for your dad to be fine one minute and dead the next. Tell her.''

''I don't think your dad's condition is that bad,'' Sam said.

Josh looked impatient. ''Look, I just want to be alone right now, okay?''

Sam cupped Marilee's elbow in his palm. ''Let's go.''

She handed Josh a twenty-dollar bill. ''Why don't you grab something to eat from the cafeteria while you're waiting. The doctor said it would be at least an hour before you can see your father.'' Josh mumbled his thanks and pocketed the money. With tears shining in her eyes, Marilee followed Sam out of the emergency room.

''Where'd you park?'' he asked.

She looked around the parking lot. ''Over there.''

He led her in the direction of her car. ''Give me your keys.''

''I'm okay.''

''Don't argue with me, Marilee, you're in no condition to drive.''

''What about your truck?''

''I'll have someone drive me over tomorrow.''

He helped her into her car, and they were on their way. Marilee stared at the passing scenery without seeing it. ''I've lost him again,'' she said.

''Josh is just scared right now.''

''I should have stayed with him.''

''That's not what he wanted.'' Sam stopped at a red light and looked at her. ''You need to get used to the fact that Josh is not a little boy anymore, Marilee. He's becoming a man.''

Marilee leaned her head back against the seat and closed her eyes. It had been a long day. She glanced at her wrist-watch and saw that it was only seven o'clock. It seemed later, somehow.

Sam pulled into her driveway and cut the engine. ''Sit tight, I'll get your door.''

Inside, he helped Marilee off with her coat and hung it in the closet. "Can I get you something? Have you eaten?"

"I'm not hungry."

The phone rang. "That's probably my mom. I'm sure she's been watching for us out the window." Sam answered it. Nell spoke from the other end. "Grady's fine," he told her. "Josh is with him." He explained the situation further. "Marilee's doing okay, but I'm going to sit with her for a while."

When he hung up he found Marilee slumped in a chair in the living room. "How 'bout I make you a cup of coffee? Or hot chocolate?"

"I'm fine."

"You look dead on your feet, Marilee. You've been through a lot today, from what my mom said."

So he knew about the divorce. "I'm really okay, Sam," she said, wishing people would stop worrying about her. Maybe she wasn't okay at the moment, but she would get through it, because that's the way she was.

Sam disappeared into the kitchen, and Marilee could hear him rummaging about in the cabinets and refrigerator. She closed her eyes and thought of Josh. Perhaps everybody was right. Maybe it *was* time she allowed him to grow up. She had tried to remind herself of that fact daily. She'd even reminded herself at the hospital, but somehow she kept slipping back into her old habit of wanting to take care of everything for him.

"Marilee?"

She opened her eyes and found Sam standing there. "I'm sorry, I must've dozed off. What time is it?"

"After eight. I fixed a little something. I hope you like bacon and eggs for dinner."

"That's very thoughtful of you, Sam." He held out his hand, and she took it and let him lead her into the kitchen where he'd already prepared their plates. He pulled her chair out for her, and she sat. Once she'd tasted her scrambled eggs, she looked up in surprise. "You're a good cook."

"I had to learn," he said with a smile. "My ex-wife wasn't real handy in the kitchen."

"Your mother said she's always trying to get money from you."

"That's in the past," he replied. "Shelly is getting married."

Marilee took a bite of her toast. "Your mother also said you had a lot of money. Said you'd sold your business in Atlanta and made a huge profit."

"My mother has a big mouth."

"Why were you keeping it from me?"

"I wasn't keeping it from you, the subject just never came up." He looked at her. "Does it bother you?"

She shrugged. "It's just you seem to know so much about me, and I know almost nothing about you after you left Chickpea."

He looked thoughtful. "I'm not sure I want you to know all of it. I did some things I'm not very proud of." He clasped his hands on the table. "I have always taken from people, Marilee. I've used them at times. So you were right about me on that account. I never loved my ex-wife. I guess that's why it was just easier to give her money than live with the guilt."

"Why did you marry her?"

He was thoughtful. "Maybe I was infatuated. She's a beautiful woman. Once I became financially secure it suddenly became important that I have something to show for it. A lovely wife, a nice home, a family."

"But you never had children."

He shook his head. "Shelly and I never quite saw eye-to-eye on that one. She had too many things she wanted to do first. Tour Europe, attend every social event in town, see the best plays. Whatever was going on, no matter where it was, she wanted to be part of it." He smiled. "I guess I was selfish. I had no interest in being on the go all the time, so I stayed home. We grew apart until I realized I preferred being alone to living with someone with whom I had nothing in common. I figured she felt pretty much the same, but she took the split hard. I think she feared being alone more than anything, so I tried to be there for her as much as I could. Not that I was doing her any favors. The more I did for her, the less she did for herself.''

Marilee pondered it. ''Maybe you've given more than you think, and you're not taking credit for it.'' He shrugged. Finally, she smiled. ''If I'd known you were so well off I would never have let you drink coffee from a chipped souvenir mug.''

''The one from Florida with the alligator on it? That's my favorite.'' He leaned forward on his elbows. ''I don't care about things like that, Marilee. I don't place much emphasis on money, but I worked hard for many years to get where I am today. I know what it's like to live from hand-to-mouth, to buy my clothes from secondhand stores. I don't have to worry about that anymore. If my mother gets sick, I can afford to see that she gets the best medical attention. I'm proud of that fact.''

''I'm proud of you too, Sam.''

His look turned tender. ''That means a lot to me. I never really cared about what anyone thought of me until I met you. I've missed you, Marilee. I never knew I could miss someone as much.''

''I've missed you too, Sam.''

He reached for her hand and squeezed it. Marilee looked into his eyes and saw her own love mirrored there.

Finally, he sat back in his chair and grinned. ''I've made coffee for us, and if you don't mind, I'm going to drink mine out of that chipped mug.''

She chuckled. ''Whatever it takes to make you happy, Brewer.''

''You make me happy.''

They stared at one another for a moment. His look was so intense that Marilee found it difficult to breathe. She wondered if he knew what he did to her. He only had to look at her in a certain way to turn her inside out. Her pulse raced, every nerve in her body came alive. It was as if she had suddenly awakened from a deep sleep. Unable to stand his scrutiny a moment later, she stood up.

Sam caught her wrist. "I'm cleaning the kitchen tonight. Just relax in the living room, and I'll bring in your coffee shortly."

"You're spoiling me."

"You need spoiling."

Once Sam finished the kitchen he carried their coffee into the living room. There he found Marilee in the recliner. "Come sit beside me on the sofa," he said.

She joined him, and they sipped in silence for a moment. Marilee realized she and Sam had not spent much time alone, and she was glad for the opportunity. They began talking. Sam told her more about his life in Atlanta; she told him about hers in Chickpea. They talked about their favorite foods and movies. When Marilee glanced at the clock she saw it was almost eleven. Where had the time gone?

"I think it's time you got to bed," Sam said. "Come with me."

Marilee followed him upstairs, pausing at the door as he switched on the lamp beside her bed. "Where are your pajamas?"

"Huh?" She gave him a blank look. "Oh, I should have a clean gown in that laundry basket on the dresser."

Sam found a gauzy, powder-blue gown on top. He handed it to her. "Why don't you get out of those clothes? I'll cut off the lights and lock up on my way out." He turned for the door.

"Sam?" He paused and looked at her. "Please don't leave me."

He met her gaze, and the love in her eyes took his breath away. "Are you sure?"

"I've never been more certain of anything in my life."

"Okay, babe, I'll stay. Go ahead and get undressed. I'll be right back."

Marilee waited until he was gone to begin undressing. She folded her clothes neatly and placed them on a chair, then pulled the gown over her head. She walked to the window, moved the curtain aside and stared out into the night.

Sam stepped into the room and found Marilee at the window. He pulled the covers aside on the bed. "Come lie down, Marilee," he said softly.

She did so. Once he'd tucked her in, Sam kicked off his shoes and pulled his shirt off. Marilee merely looked at him. He reached over her and switched off the lamp, and pulled her close.

"Try to sleep," he said softly.

Marilee awoke several times during the night feeling disoriented. Sam must've sensed it, because he moved closer.

"It's okay, sweetheart. Go back to sleep."

At dawn, Marilee opened her eyes. Sam was snoring softly beside her. She pulled from his grasp, and he awoke. "I need to use the bathroom," she said.

He released her and closed his eyes. Marilee slipped from the room and made her way downstairs. She found the number to the hospital and dialed it. A nurse on the third floor assured her that Grady was resting, and his blood pressure had gone down during the night.

"Have you seen our son?" Marilee asked.

"He's fine," the nurse said. "He's sleeping in the recliner next to his father's bed. I'll make sure he gets a breakfast tray when we start serving."

"Thank you." Marilee climbed the stairs once more and went into the bathroom, where she took a hot shower. She dried and reached for her bathrobe. The house carried an early-morning chill, and she shivered. Sam was still sleeping when she reentered the bedroom and climbed in beside him. She studied him, the olive-skinned, sun-toughened face, the strong jaw. She had come to love that face, and the man who wore it.

He opened his eyes. They were gentle and contemplative as he regarded her in the soft morning light. "Your teeth are chattering," he said. "Are you cold?"

"A little."

"Come here." He opened his arms to embrace her, and

she snuggled against him, taking in his scent and body heat. "Better?" he asked.

"Much." She looked up and met his gaze. His eyes were dark, compelling, magnetic. She felt drawn to him, a curious longing that was as wonderful as it was frightening. "You make me feel…" She paused, thinking he might find her words silly.

"What?" he said.

"Safe."

He kissed her forehead. "I can't prevent bad things from happening, Marilee, but I can be there for you, if you'll let me."

"Sam?"

"Yeah?"

"I love you."

He looked deeply into her eyes. "I love you too, Marilee. I was afraid I'd never hear those words from you." He kissed her softly, tenderly. When he pulled back, he struggled with his emotions, and his face took on a look of pure vulnerability. "I'm laying my heart at your feet, Marilee."

Her own heart swelled. Marilee scooted closer and tucked her forehead beneath his chin, feeling the stubble on his jaw. "Do you think it's too soon for us to feel this way?"

He rolled onto his back, and she lay in the crook of his arm, feeling him stroke her hair. "We're not kids, sweetheart. We know what's real and what isn't. I think we both want the same things out of life. I know I'm a better man for knowing you."

Marilee could not remember when anyone had said something that kind to her. She placed her hand on his bare chest, allowing the black hair that grew there to curl around her fingers. In just a few months Sam had filled a void in her that had been with her for as long as she could remember. Not even Josh or her charity work had been able to touch that part of her. Nor had Grady. It had taken her sixteen years to discover the difference between loving someone and being in love, to experience a feeling of such closeness that it was difficult to tell when one left off and the other began.

Suddenly, Marilee could not get close enough to the man beside her. The yearning she felt for him filled her heart and made her long for more, his scent, his touch. His skin was warm as she ran her hand lightly down his chest to his stomach. She heard him suck in his breath, and she became still, though her heart beat a frantic message to her brain that what was happening between them was right.

Sam turned his head on the pillow and his dark eyes searched her face. ''Marilee?''

His voice seemed to come to her through a fog. She touched his nipple, watched it contract and was fascinated. Just the very thought that her touch could affect him made her giddy. Her stomach fluttered, and she felt warm. Sam lay very still, his body tense, as though waiting. She almost smiled. Sam Brewer, town stud, was afraid to make a move. Well, if Sam wouldn't, by golly, she would.

She raised her head slightly and touched the very tip of his nipple with her tongue. He drew in another shaky breath.

''Oh, Marilee.'' Her name was a soft sigh on his lips, but his eyes gave her a subtle warning. ''Be careful.''

She slipped her hands beneath the covers and touched him. He was hard inside his jeans.

''Marilee, wait—'' His voice was strained as he raised up on one elbow and gazed down at her. ''Please don't start something you can't finish.''

She felt a strange surge of excitement, knowing he wanted her as much as she did him. ''I want to make love with you, Sam,'' she said softly, almost shyly. ''I hope you don't think it's wrong of me.''

''Oh, Marilee.'' He wondered if she had any idea what her words meant to him. Sam cupped her face in his hands and kissed her, his lips grazing hers, giving her time to adjust. He had wanted her from the first time he saw her, but now that she had finally voiced the words he'd ached to hear, he was almost afraid. She was so different from the other women he'd known in his life. Beautiful and sexy, but filled with such sweetness that he didn't know how to proceed.

Go slow, he warned himself.

He saw the need in her eyes, her full lips wet from his kiss. "I love you, Marilee, but we haven't discussed birth control."

She was touched by his concern. "I just finished my cycle. I'm safe right now."

He kissed her again, slowly, feather light. She responded as he'd hoped she would, parting her lips. He raised his head a fraction, and she followed, as though half-afraid he would stop. He had to know in his heart that she had no reservations about being with him. He slipped one arm around her, pressing his hand against the small of her back. She arched against him, running her fingers through his hair and bringing his face yet closer. She kissed him fully, her shy tongue darting inside his mouth. It was his undoing. Once again he cautioned himself against rushing her, although his own need was great. He pressed his lips against her throat and felt her racing pulse. He nibbled her earlobes, and she shivered. He cupped her breasts and flicked his thumbs against the fabric of her gown, teasing her nipples.

Marilee closed her eyes and gave in to the sensations, and when he pulled the straps down and gazed at her breasts for the first time, she felt no shyness, no reservations whatsoever.

Sam tongued her nipples until her breathing became rapid. He pressed a thigh between her own, and she parted her legs every so slightly. He applied a gentle pressure where he knew she would enjoy it most. She moaned softly and opened herself to him fully. His heart soared.

Marilee's head spun at the pleasure of Sam's touch. How did he know exactly what she needed, when she had no idea what he desired from her? All she could do was cling to him and respond. He pulled her gown off and removed her panties, skimming her outer thighs and hips with big hands that hard work had toughened. Marilee was lost in a world of sensations as he acquainted himself with her body, his eyes and hands eager to know her. Another time, she might have shrunk away in modesty, but as his fingers trickled across her belly she forgot everything. The gentle massage sent a current of desire through her, spreading heat from deep inside, making her soft and liquid.

He cupped her hips and pulled her closer as he kissed her deeply, his thigh moving ever so gently, a seesawing motion that took her breath away.

All at once, Sam couldn't get enough of her. The very air they breathed seemed charged. His clothes became a hindrance, and he pulled away long enough to discard them. Marilee reached for him, stroked him. He gritted his teeth and touched her for the first time. She was wet. His body flamed. He kissed her belly, circled her navel with his tongue and pressed his lips against the downy growth between her thighs. He felt her stiffen, and he pulled back. He would not take more than she could give at the moment, even though her scent was intoxicating. He longed to touch her with his tongue, stroke her until she cried out, but he would wait until the time was right.

He gazed at her, drinking in the sight of her naked body. His eyes worshiped her unblemished skin and every curve. "I knew you would be beautiful," he said, his voice raspy, "but I had no idea just how much." Moving over her, he swept her thighs wider apart and hovered only a second before he entered her slowly. Marilee cried out, surrendering to him. He thrust deeply, urging her to move with him until they found their pace. Her body seemed to vibrate as she was filled with a white-hot heat that made her grasp his hips and hold him tight against her. Her thoughts ceased as she abandoned herself to the uncontrollable burst of sensation. She could no more control her outcry of passion than she could her next breath.

Sam thrust once more. His desire peaked and his body shuddered violently. He emptied himself inside of her and collapsed.

They lay side by side for a long time, gazing at one another as though seeing for the first time. Marilee touched his lips with her fingers, her insides glowing with love.

Sam kissed the tip of her finger. "Next time I want to taste you," he said.

Marilee's stomach did a little flip-flop. "Well, I—"

"There'll be no holding back, Marilee. I want to know all of you."

She shivered.

The phone rang, startling her, but she was thankful for the interruption. She snatched it up. Her son spoke from the other end. "How's your father?" she asked.

"Not so good," Josh said. He sighed. "His doctor is planning to release him today, but only if Dad will agree to bed rest. He has no place to go. He's been evicted from his place."

"I'm sure he can find an apartment."

"He's too sick right now to look for one." The boy paused. "I need a favor, Mom. I know this is an imposition, but would you mind if he stayed in my room for a couple of days?"

Marilee sat up. Sam seemed to realize something was going on and he sat up as well. She glanced at him and found a question in his eyes. "I don't know, Josh. That would be a bit awkward, don't you think?"

"Just for a couple of days," he said. "Three at the most. You won't have to do anything. You won't even know he's there."

Marilee pressed one hand against her forehead. The thought of Grady coming into her house almost made her ill. "Can't he stay with a friend?"

"All his friends have deserted him." His voice was filled with scorn. "I wouldn't ask you if it weren't an emergency."

She sighed. "You're asking a lot."

"I know."

A long silence ensued. "Oh, Josh," she said. "I don't know what to say."

"He doesn't have much money or I'd call a cab and put him in a motel. He called Uncle Charles, who promised to send some, but it'll take a couple of days."

"How long before they release him?" she asked.

"Probably this afternoon."

Marilee's brain seemed to stop functioning. "I'll need to think about this, Josh."

"I'll call you back in an hour," he said.

She hung up.

Sam looked at her. "I only heard one side of the conversation, but I didn't like the sound of it. What's going on?"

She didn't want to tell him, didn't want to spoil the mood from their lovemaking. "Grady has no money and no place to live."

"What does that have to do with you?"

"He needs a place to stay for a few days."

"You're not thinking of letting him come here?"

She looked at him. "What else can I do?"

"Dammit, Marilee, that's Grady's problem!"

"It's Josh's problem too. That makes it mine."

Sam raked his hands through his hair. "I don't know what to say, Marilee. I mean, how am I supposed to feel?"

"How do you think *I* feel?"

He met her gaze. "What if I said no? What if I told you that I don't feel comfortable with your ex-husband in this house?"

She looked away. "Please don't make this more difficult."

"You're going to let him stay here, aren't you?" He held his breath, but he already knew the answer. He reached for his clothes.

"Sam?"

He looked at her.

"I'm not doing it for Grady."

"I know that." He stood and dressed quietly. Neither of them spoke. Finally, he sat on the edge of the bed, just sat there, shaking his head.

"Please don't be angry with me," she said.

Sam stood and tucked in his shirt. He saw the pain in her eyes, and he ached for her. "I'm not mad, Marilee. I'm just confused as hell." He walked around to her side of the bed, dropped a kiss on the top of her head and was gone.

# *Twenty-Four*

Marilee picked up Josh and Grady later that day. Josh climbed into the back, and Grady took the passenger's seat next to Marilee. "I appreciate what you're doing for me, Marilee," he said, strapping on his seat belt.

She looked straight ahead. "I trust you'll find a place right away."

"Yes, of course."

The ride home seemed to take forever. Josh and Grady exchanged a few words, but Marilee remained quiet. She was livid at both Grady and herself. She had hurt Sam with her decision and who could blame him? She was allowing her ex-husband, a man who had done the despicable, to use their son to gain entrance into her home. Still, it was for Josh's sake she was permitting it.

Once inside, Grady commented favorably on the changes. "Looks like you've done okay for yourself, Marilee."

She ignored him. "Josh, please show your father where he'll be sleeping. I've put clean linens on the other twin bed." She looked at Grady. "Since you're not well, I'll have Josh bring your meals to you on a tray."

"I hate to put you to the trouble, Marilee."

"Oh, but I insist. Besides, it's only for a couple of days."

He nodded. "Whatever you feel is best." He followed Josh upstairs.

Nell called a few minutes later. "Sam gave me the news. I'm so sorry you've been put in such an awkward position. You're a saint, Marilee, a true saint. If you need anything, you know you can call on me."

"Thank you, Nell." Marilee only wished Sam had been as understanding.

Clara brought Winnie home Sunday night. Marilee decided to give them the news up front. "Grady has been in the hospital," she said. "He will be staying in Josh's room for a couple of days. I don't want to discuss it, I'm just telling you so you'll know."

Winnie started to open her mouth, seemed to think better of it and went upstairs.

"I'd better go," Clara said. She looked sad for Marilee. "You'll call if I can help?"

"Thank you, Clara. You don't know how much I appreciate that right now."

Marilee prepared a simple dinner that evening and asked Josh to carry Grady's meal upstairs on a tray. "I'm sorry I was rude to you at the hospital, Mom. I know this isn't easy for you. I promise to make it all up to you."

Marilee had no reply.

He started for the stairs and turned. "Do you realize Christmas is only three weeks away? We don't have a tree."

She nodded. "You and I can look for one." And she needed to finish her Christmas shopping now that Tate had returned her money.

"Just say when."

Ruby called that evening. "I heard the news," she said. "How about I make a meat loaf one night and bring it by? Save you a little time in the kitchen."

"That would be nice, Ruby. Thank you." They chatted for a moment. Marilee hung up and wondered how she would ever manage with her ex-husband living under her roof. She would just have to make the best of it and get him out as fast as she could.

Grady was still living there after a week, and Marilee's nerves were growing taut, although she didn't say as much to Josh, who seemed to feel guilty about the whole thing.

She'd taken him to pick out a Christmas tree, but it was still on the front porch where they'd left it.

"I think Dad's depressed," he said, as he fed Rascal. "He doesn't want to get out of bed. All he does is sleep. And when he isn't sleeping he's complaining."

Marilee remained quiet.

Josh sighed. "I guess I never realized how unhappy he was, because you always tried to smooth things over."

Marilee handed Josh the newspaper. "I've circled the rental section. Ask your dad to look at it."

"I'll try, Mom."

She looked at her son. "Your father is not staying indefinitely, Josh. He's well enough to move now. It's time."

Josh nodded. Suddenly, he brightened. "Mom, when are we going to decorate the tree?"

"As soon as I bring the ornaments down from the attic," she said. "I've just been tired lately." Her energy was at an all-time low, and she knew it had to do with the stress of Grady living there. Winnie hadn't said much about the situation. She seemed to be tolerating it for Josh's sake, but it was obvious she didn't want Grady there. The baby was due in a couple of weeks, and Marilee had not even had time to write out the invitations to her baby shower.

"You're not thinking of putting all those artificial doves and satin bows on it again this year, are you?" Josh asked, interrupting her thoughts.

"I thought you liked them."

"That's sissified, Mom."

Later that evening, Nell dropped by. "Guess what?"

Marilee saw that she was excited and smiled. "What?"

"Sam and I haven't decorated our tree yet, and I understand you haven't trimmed yours, either."

"I'm afraid I haven't been in the mood, but I have managed to pick up a few gifts on my lunch hour."

"Well, Sam and Josh were talking and—"

Marilee was surprised. "They're speaking again?"

"Yes, thank goodness. And guess what they've come up with? They think we should have a girl tree and a guy tree."

"Come again?"

"Well, Josh was complaining about how you put all these goofy decorations on the tree, so Sam came up with a cute idea. He thinks us women should get together and decorate your tree as we like, and he and Josh will decorate the one at our house. I think that sounds like fun."

"That'll do Josh good," Marilee said. "By the way, how is Sam?"

"Miserable. Working too hard. I think he prefers it that way right now. I understand he's got a full crew out at Blessing Home." She paused. "I've never seen Sam like this, Marilee. He's never loved anyone like he does you. You've made a difference in his life and I will never be able to thank you enough for that."

Tears stung the backs of Marilee's eyes. Lord, she missed Sam. "I'm sorry this had to happen, Nell. I'm doing my best to get Grady out of here. Sometimes it seems so hopeless."

"I know, dear. You do what you have to do and let me worry about Sam. The problem with my son is that he's used to getting what he wants when he wants it. He's never had to learn patience. This is good for him. So, when do you want to start decorating?" she asked, changing the subject. "I think us girls should have a little party. Nothing big. I'll bring plenty of snacks."

"Is tomorrow night too soon?" Marilee decided it was about time she got in the spirit of things and she figured it would do Josh good to have a little fun after waiting on his father all the time.

"I'll go home and phone Clara and Ruby right now," Nell said.

"Call me as soon as you talk to them. I'll be glad to pick up a few things from the grocery store when I go out. Oh, Nell, I wonder if you'd help me plan a baby shower for Winnie."

"I'd be delighted. When would you like to have it?"

"How about some time next week?" Hopefully, by then, Grady would be gone and things would be back to normal.

"I've already bought the invitations, and I've been picking up decorations and snacks at the store. But I don't know who any of her friends are at school. I might ask Josh."

"You know, what she needs more than anything is a crib. I'll try to find one that's reasonable, and maybe we can all chip in." Nell winked. "You just leave it up to me."

Marilee spent the following day getting ready for the tree-trimming party, although there wasn't much to do, since Winnie had spent the previous day cleaning like a mad-woman. Marilee had protested, but Winnie claimed she was tired of sitting around. She had even scrubbed the tile in the bathrooms.

Josh helped Marilee drag the tree into the house and carry decorations down from the attic. Winnie had remained in bed, complaining of flu symptoms. "Don't let Grady hear you're not feeling well," Marilee whispered. "He'll auto-matically think he's got it too."

"I'm going to take it easy today," the girl said, "so I'll be up to attending the little party tonight."

Once Josh had managed to get the tree into the metal holder, he glanced at his wristwatch. "I almost forgot. Sam and I are going Christmas shopping."

"Oh?" Marilee couldn't hide her surprise. "That's nice. Do you want to eat lunch first?"

"Naw, we'll grab something while we're out." The boy paused. "Would you mind taking Dad's tray up? I'm sorry to ask, but—"

"I'll take care of it," she said.

"Mom, is there anything in particular you want for Christmas this year? That doesn't costs more than ten dollars?" he added.

She looked at him. "What's the going price for hugs?"

He looked embarrassed as he hugged her quickly. "This one's on the house."

"Oh, Josh, I need to ask you something. Do you know who any of Winnie's friends are?"

"How come you want to know?"

Marilee was surprised that he seemed defensive. She

knew Josh and Winnie were close. They played chess from time to time, and she'd heard them talking on occasion. "I'm not trying to pry," Marilee said quickly. She told him about the surprise baby shower they were planning.

"Her friends dumped her when she got pregnant, Mom. Even her best friend, and they grew up together."

Marilee nodded. "I sort of suspected as much. But they started calling after the robbery at the Pickford Inn."

"All I can tell you is she pretty much keeps to herself at school. I think she prefers it that way. We kid around a lot when we see each other, but she spends most of her free time studying. If I were you, I'd just invite Clara, Ruby and Nell. But don't invite me, okay? I don't want to attend a baby shower." He looked at the clock. "I'd better go next door before Sam leaves without me."

"Thanks for telling me, Josh."

Marilee prepared soup and sandwiches. Winnie came downstairs, and they made small talk as they ate, although the girl didn't have much of an appetite. "Does *he* have to be fed?" the girl asked, motioning toward the stairs.

"I'll take him a tray in a minute."

"I'd take it up and raise hell with him if I weren't feeling so crummy. Bet I could get his sorry butt out of that bed."

Marilee chuckled. "If anybody could do it, you could." She became serious. "I'm going to have a talk with him when I go up."

Marilee knocked on Josh's bedroom door a few minutes later. Grady called out from the other side and she carried in the tray. "Here's your lunch," she said, setting it on his lap.

"Thank you. I understand Josh is out shopping with his friend Sam." She nodded. "Uh, Marilee, why is that pregnant, black girl living here?"

His question annoyed her. After all, it was her house, and she could do as she pleased. "Winnie is living here because I invited her. Do you have a problem with that?"

He shook his head emphatically. "No, of course not. Josh says she has the flu."

"Oh, no, nothing like that," Marilee said quickly. "She's fit as a fiddle. Just tired, that's all, which is understandable since her baby is due in a couple of weeks." She sat on the opposite bed. "Grady, we have to talk."

He put his tray aside. "I've been wanting to talk to you, too, Marilee."

"Okay," she said, hoping he was about to tell her he'd finally found a place of his own. "You go first."

He sighed. "Marilee, I know I've been a burden on you, and I'm sorry. I've been depressed. I saw a staff psychiatrist while I was in the hospital, and he wrote me a prescription for an antidepressant. I have a follow-up visit this week, but I'm already beginning to feel better." He paused. "I guess I've been depressed a long time, and I just hadn't realized."

She pondered it. She had dealt with depressed people at the church, and she knew the symptoms well. Why hadn't she noticed them in her own husband? "I'm glad you're feeling better. Once you get your own place and go back to work you'll be fine."

"That's what I wanted to talk to you about." He clasped his hands together and leaned on his knees. "Marilee, I've had a lot of time to think while I've been recuperating. I've made so many mistakes these past few months. I don't know how I'll ever make it up to you and Josh."

"You owe me nothing, Grady. Just try to be a father your son can be proud of."

"I destroyed our family," he said. "I've done nothing but pray since they rushed me to the hospital, and I think I'm right with the Lord now, because He's opening doors for me at last."

"I'm glad to hear it. Now, tell me your plans."

"I called my brother, Charles, from the hospital, and we've spoken a few times since I've been here. He knows of a church in Georgia that's in desperate need of a minister."

Marilee's jaw dropped.

"I know what you're thinking," he went on quickly. "After what I've done, I don't deserve to be on the pulpit, but I'm a changed man, Marilee. We could start afresh.''

She arched both eyebrows. ''We?''

''Marilee, the Lord has given me a second chance, I'm asking you to do the same.''

She felt as though she'd been punched in the chest. ''You're not serious.''

''At least hear me out. I know I don't deserve it, but I think you and I could make it work if we tried. Not only for our sake, but for Josh's.''

''Grady, I couldn't possibly—''

''We would have to remarry, of course, but I promise you wouldn't regret it. I'll do everything I can to make you happy. I still love you, Marilee.'' He reached out and touched her hand. ''That's why I wanted to call you all those times. That's why I wanted to hold off on the divorce. It didn't take me long to realize what a mistake I'd made moving in with that woman. I was so glad when she left because it saved me the trouble of having to break it off.''

Marilee pulled her hand away. She suddenly felt ill. She did not wish to rehash their marital woes, and she certainly didn't want to hear about Grady and LaFonda's relationship problems.

''We're not the first couple to have problems,'' he insisted. ''We can use this experience to help others. I believe things happen for a reason. Maybe the Lord felt we'd grown complacent in our marriage and the Church. I'm not the first minister to fall from grace, but the Lord has worked a miracle in me.''

Marilee felt the room swim before her eyes. ''I can't talk to you about this right now,'' she said, rising from the bed on unsteady feet. She had come in hoping to discover he'd finally found a place to live, but all this time he'd been planning how to get her back.

He stood as well. ''Are you okay?''

''I have to lie down.''

"Would you at least think about what I've said? Your forgiveness means everything to me."

She *was* thinking. And wondering how she would ever get him out of her life. She paused at the door. "I forgave you a long time ago. I think you should take that job in Georgia," she said.

He was smiling when she left the room. "Thank you, Lord!" he whispered.

Josh arrived at Sam's at precisely seven o'clock carrying a large, brown paper sack. "I brought a few items I thought we might need for the tree," he said.

Sam looked into the bag. "Oh, this is good." He grinned. "First, let's have some eggnog and snacks."

"What kind of sandwiches are these?" Josh asked, staring at the food on the coffee table.

Sam gave a grunt. "We're getting the surplus from the girls' party. These are called pinwheels. We also have chicken salad with pineapple and almonds. And this is Brie with some kind of strawberry sauce."

"Yuck!"

Sam grinned. "Don't worry, I ordered a pizza. It should be here any minute."

"Won't your mom's feelings be hurt?"

"Naw, she knows I don't go for this sort of thing. Although I used to have to eat it on a regular basis."

"How come?"

"I attended a lot of parties in Atlanta. My ex-wife was into that sort of thing. Social climber and all that."

"Too bad for you."

"Yeah, but that's in the past." He wouldn't tell Josh how much it had cost him to be free of Shelly. "Remember this, Josh. Just because a woman is beautiful doesn't mean you should marry her."

"I don't think I want to get married anyway," the boy said. "It's such a hassle, living with parents who don't like each other."

"How are things going over there?"

Josh looked sad. "My parents are getting back together."

Sam went still. He felt as though a giant fishhook had just ripped through his gut. "Are you sure about that?"

"My dad told me when we got back from Christmas shopping. My mom's not talking. She's been locked in her room all day." The boy sank onto the sofa. "I don't really want to talk about it, if you don't mind."

"Then we won't."

The doorbell rang. "Here's our pizza." Sam was thankful for the reprieve. The thought that Marilee was reuniting with her ex-husband was more than he could take, especially after her confession of love the other night. Grady must have guilt-tripped her into going back to him. That was the only explanation Sam could think of. The man had spent enough years in the pulpit to know how to make people see things his way and no doubt he knew all of Marilee's buttons and how to push them. Sam longed to punch the man in the face. If Marilee couldn't see through him she was blind.

Sam returned with the hot pizza and a forced smile. Although the last thing on his mind was eating and trying to be a good host, he couldn't very well back out now. He would see that Josh enjoyed himself no matter what. "Let's eat," he said. "Then we'll decorate this tree the way it ought to be."

"I'm with you," Josh said, but he wasn't smiling.


"Okay, here's the plan," Nell said once the girls had gathered in the living room. "I have a gift pack of nuts, a giant assortment. Cashews, pecans, walnuts, Brazil nuts, you name it. This is the prize for the best tree."

"How are we going to decide who has the better tree?" Clara asked. "We need a judge. Someone who can be impartial."

"I can be impartial," Winnie told them, "because I'm not decorating *any* tree."

Nell looked hurt. "Are you not feeling well, dear?"

"I think she's come down with something," Marilee said. "She overexerted herself yesterday, what with all the cleaning she did. I tried to stop her, but Winnie has a mind of her own."

Nell felt her forehead. "Well, you don't have a fever."

"I'm not surprised she's tired," Ruby said. "The baby's already dropped. I noticed it the minute I walked into the house tonight."

"What do you mean the baby has dropped?" Winnie asked. "She's not going to fall out, is she?"

"It means your time is getting closer," Ruby said. "She's positioning herself."

"We should have taken that second childbirth class," Marilee said.

"You just stay put, Winnie," Clara ordered, a stern look on her face. "If you need anything we'll get it for you."

Winnie did as she was told, then gave an enormous sigh of disgust. "Would y'all please get on with decorating this tree? I can't sit here all night."

Ruby looked at the others. "Yes, I think she can be impartial."

"Oh, Marilee, what beautiful white doves," Nell said once Marilee had opened one of the boxes marked Christmas Decorations.

Marilee smiled proudly. "These were given to me by my mother years ago."

"Marilee always has a beautiful tree," Clara said, opening another box. "Look at these ribbons and bows. They'll add a Victorian flair."

The women made a fuss over each box they opened. "Ah, here are the lights," Ruby said. "All white. Frankly, I prefer white to those tacky colored lights."

Winnie shifted in her chair. "Y'all have been here for an hour and haven't put up the first decoration. Why not just throw some tinsel on it and be done with the whole thing."

Marilee and Ruby began stringing the lights. When they plugged them in, the tree lit up like something out of a fairytale. "I'm surprised they all work," Ruby said. "I usually spend the first couple of hours replacing bulbs."

Marilee nodded her satisfaction. "I do all that when I take

down the tree so that when it's time to decorate everything's ready.''

"Good thinking," Nell said. "I wonder how Sam and Josh are coming along."

"Okay," Sam said once he and Josh had strung the tree with red lights. "What we want to do here is hang these fishing lures every six or eight inches. Be careful not to stick yourself with the hooks. Then we'll hang these cigars and poker chips from the fishing twine."

"I can't believe you actually drilled holes into each chip. That must have taken forever."

"The hard part was drilling holes in these fake fish."

"They look real." Josh grinned for the first time. "Man, this is going to be the best tree ever." He went back to decorating. "Oh, I almost forgot. I brought over empty Vienna sausage and pork-and-beans cans."

Sam gave him a thumbs-up. "Perfect."

After a few minutes, he turned to Sam. "Are you in love with my mom?"

Sam didn't know how to respond. He finally decided to be honest. "Yes, I am."

"Then why don't you fight for her? I'd fight for the woman I loved."

Sam was surprised. "You don't fight for someone's love, Josh. When you care about another person, you just want them to be happy."

"She was happier before my dad came back into our lives."

"It's lovely," Nell said. "The prettiest tree I've ever seen."

"Beautiful," Clara added.

Marilee beamed. "You really think so?"

"Marilee always does a fine job when it comes to decorating a tree," a male voice said. The women looked up to find Grady standing in the doorway.

Marilee was surprised to find him dressed. "What are you doing out of bed?"

"I heard all the laughter down here and decided to investigate. Hello, Clara. Ruby." He looked at Nell. "I don't believe we've met. I'm Grady Abernathy." He didn't bother to speak to Winnie.

Nell offered him a polite smile. "Nell Brewer," she said. "I believe you attended Chickpea High with my son, Sam."

Grady looked taken aback. "Sam Brewer?" He regarded Marilee. "Not the infamous Sam Brewer?" he teased, but his look reprimanded her.

Marilee had to bite her tongue to keep from saying something that would embarrass the group further. A long silence followed.

"We're having a little contest," Nell finally said, as though trying to make everyone comfortable. "My son and Josh are decorating our tree next door and—"

"Josh told me about the contest," Grady interrupted. "Would you like me to be the judge?"

Winnie spoke up. "I've already been selected as judge, thank you very much." She looked at the others. "But I can't very well make a decision without seeing the other tree."

"I'm sure Sam and Josh have finished by now," Nell said. "Why don't we go over and take a look?"

"That sounds like a great idea," Grady said. The women looked at him. "It's okay if I go, isn't it? I'd like to say hello to Sam."

Marilee felt a flush of heat creeping up her neck. How like Grady to put her in an awkward position in front of her friends. She was not looking forward to seeing Sam after the way they'd left things, and she was certain Sam had no desire to see her ex-husband. She would have preferred staying home, but she knew Josh would be disappointed. "I don't know, Grady."

"Of course he can come," Nell said, although she didn't seem pleased about it.

Winnie struggled to get out of the chair. "This'll be great," she muttered. "Just great."

The group didn't bother with their jackets as they hurried out the door. Clara, Ruby and Nell kept tossing Marilee anxious looks, but Winnie remained silent. It was obvious the girl was angry. They reached the front porch and Nell peeped in. "It's us, Sam. We're here to see the tree. Are you ready?"

"Come on in," he called out.

They stepped inside, and the women burst into hearty laughter at the sight of the guys' tree. An Atlanta Braves baseball cap was perched at the top where the angel would normally appear. Winnie laughed so hard tears filled her eyes. She held her stomach. "I'm sorry, girls, but I have to give it to these guys, this is pretty original."

Clara sniffed as though she was highly insulted. "You like this tree better than ours?"

Sam had not seen Grady come into the room, but the minute his eyes caught sight of him, his smile faded into a grimace.

Josh looked at his father, and his face seemed to drain of color. "What are you doing out of bed?"

"I thought I'd join the merriment," he replied. He stepped forward and held his hand out to Sam. "Been a long time, Sam. I haven't seen you since you dropped out of high school." When Sam didn't bother to shake hands with him, Grady gave an embarrassed cough and let his own fall to his side. "I can't tell you how much I appreciate your befriending our son," he said. "I know I speak for Marilee as well. You've done more than your share to make this time easier for him."

Sam just looked at him, his eyes dark and filled with loathing. Once again, an uncomfortable silence ensued.

"Dad, you need to go home and lie down," Josh said.

"I feel fine, son. This is a special occasion indeed. Not only are we celebrating the birth of our Lord, your mother and I are celebrating the rebirth of our life together."

Marilee snapped her head around and stared at him in

horror. It was as though all the oxygen had been sucked out of her. She could feel the stares, but given how angry she was, she knew it would be best to handle the matter at home. "I think it's time we left, Grady."

"And miss the party?" he asked.

Marilee met Sam's gaze, and the hurt and disappointment she saw in his eyes was unbearable. She turned to Grady, but before she could say anything, Josh cut in.

"Dad, you don't look so well. You need to lie down."

Grady put his arm around Marilee's shoulder and pulled her against him. She automatically stiffened and tried to pull away. He looked surprised. "I'm sorry if I let the cat out of the bag before you were ready," he said, "but I would think this is something you'd want to share with our friends. After all, they've been there for you through this grievous time. Even Sam here," he added. "Surely a single man like Sam has better things to do with his time than baby-sit our child."

"I am not believing what I'm hearing," Winnie muttered.

Marilee's face flamed. Somehow Grady had gotten the impression that she was going back to him. "Grady, we need to talk," she said between gritted teeth.

Josh stepped forward. "Dad, you're embarrassing Mom."

"Let me handle this, Josh," Sam said. He stepped up to Grady until they were nose to nose. "You're way out of line, Abernathy. I don't baby-sit, and you don't come into my house and embarrass my friends."

Grady looked taken aback. "I apologize if I've offended you, Sam. I had no right to assume you had ulterior motives for spending so much time with Josh." He gave Sam a good-old-boy nudge. "I'm just remembering our high-school days. You were quite the ladies' man even then. Nevertheless, I'm sure you'll be the first to congratulate Marilee and me now that we've patched things up."

Sam looked from Marilee to Josh. Their faces were white; they looked stricken. The blood roared in his ears. Grady had just hurt and embarrassed the woman Sam loved more than life itself, as well as Josh, who was the closest thing he'd ever had to a son. "Yeah, I'll congratulate you," he said. He reared one fist back and punched the man in the face. Grady fell to the floor with a loud thump.

The women screamed and jumped back. Josh leaned over his dad and shook him. He looked at Sam. "He's out cold."

Winnie burst into hearty laughter that earned her a dark look from Marilee. "Hey, I'm sorry, but he had it coming. If Sam hadn't done it I would have."

Sam covered his fist with his other hand. He saw the horror and disbelief in Marilee's eyes as she gazed in his direction. "I'm sorry, Marilee," he said. "I just couldn't stand there and let him go on like that."

"So you knocked him out?" she cried. She knelt beside Grady and shook him. "Grady, are you okay? Open your eyes, speak to me."

Winnie was still laughing hysterically. "You come with me," Ruby said, pulling her toward the front door. "You're out of control."

Clara plucked at her hair nervously. "Should I call an ambulance?"

Nell shook her head. "No, dear, I rather like looking at Mr. Abernathy from this angle."

Outside, Ruby shook Winnie. "Get a grip on yourself, young lady!"

"I can't help it," the girl said, holding her sides. "You don't know what it has been like having that man under the same roof." She tried to swallow her laughter. She'd almost succeeded, when Ruby let a chuckle slip. Before long, they were both doubled over on the porch laughing. They looked up and saw Clara standing at the door.

"This is not funny," Clara said. "A man is unconscious in there. Your behavior is—well, it's downright vulgar."

Ruby and Winnie paused, trying to affect a sober expression. "What did you do to your hair, Clara?" Winnie asked.

"Looks like you stuck your finger in a light socket," Ruby said. "You've got to stop doing that or your new beau will think you have head lice." She slapped her hand over her mouth the minute the words came out.

Winnie looked surprised. "Clara has a boyfriend?"

"Thank you very much for putting my business on the street, Ruby Ledbetter," Clara said. "I will never tell you another secret as long as I live." She stalked inside.

"Clara has a boyfriend?" Winnie insisted.

Ruby removed her hand. "I wasn't supposed to tell."

Winnie shook her head. "Oh, girl, you know what this means? You'll never be able to check out a book from the library again."

They burst into fresh laughter. "That's not funny," Ruby said. "I've betrayed a friend's trust. Lord, she'll pull all her hair out over this."

Winnie guffawed, sending Ruby into another fit of laughter. They turned away, determined not to look at one another as they tried to get their laughter under control. Finally, they settled down, but the moment they looked at each other, all was lost and they began again. Winnie gasped. "Oh!" she cried and grabbed her abdomen.

"What?" Ruby managed to ask.

"Oh, Jesus!" Winnie cried. "Oh, Lord!"

"What's wrong with you?" Ruby demanded.

"I think my water just broke."

Both women looked down at the small puddle forming around Winnie's feet.

# *Twenty-Five*

"**S**omebody help us!" Ruby cried, peering inside the door.

Marilee, in the process of helping a dazed Grady to his feet, looked up to find Ruby standing in the front doorway. "What *now?*"

All at once, Winnie yowled with pain.

"We have to get Winnie to the hospital," Ruby said. "She's in labor!"

Marilee's eyes widened in disbelief. "But she's not due for two weeks."

Hands on hips, Ruby looked from Marilee to Winnie and back to Marilee. "Okay, I'll tell her to stop it this instant. Dammit, Winnie, stop it this instant!"

Nell and Clara hurried to the door and gaped at Winnie, who was clutching her stomach. "Oh my goodness, let me get some towels," Nell said.

"We can take my truck," Sam said, grabbing his jacket.

Marilee touched Winnie gently. "Okay, try to remain calm. Are you having a contraction?" The girl nodded. "Just relax," Marilee repeated as Nell handed her several towels. She and Sam ushered her to his truck. They managed to get the girl inside, despite her distress.

"We'll follow you in my car," Clara said.

"I'm going, too," Josh told them.

"Do you have room for me?" Nell asked.

Ruby nodded. "Of course we do. Come on, honey."

The entire house emptied in a matter of seconds. Nobody

gave a second thought to Grady, who was standing near the Christmas tree rubbing his jaw.

"She's already dilated three centimeters," a sweet-looking nurse named Peggy said once they had Winnie situated in a bed in labor and delivery. "She's moving right along."

"My mother had all her babies quickly," Winnie replied. "Said she didn't have time to lie around in bed all day 'cause the laundry and ironing would pile up." She winced as another contraction hit.

"Okay, start breathing from your mouth," Marilee said.

The girl grunted. "Where else am I going to breathe from, my ears?"

"You know what I mean. Like this." Marilee began breathing the way they'd been taught in class, and Winnie followed. She watched the monitor. "The contraction is almost over, honey, just hang in there."

"You're doing very well," Peggy said.

"I want to see my doctor," Winnie told her. "I need something for pain."

"I've already spoken to Dr. Johnson," Peggy said, "and he instructed me to give you something to help you relax. That's what I just put in your IV. It's a little too early to give you something stronger."

"What do I have to do to get it," Winnie asked, "foam from the mouth?"

Peggy patted her on the hand. "Just keep up with your breathing, hon. You're doing fine. Just fine. Your doctor will be here shortly."

"He's probably on the golf course," Winnie muttered after the woman had left the room.

An hour passed. Marilee could see Winnie's contractions were getting stronger and lasting longer. The girl moaned aloud and gripped the handle on the bed. "My back is killing me. Somebody better give me some drugs or I'm going to throw that monitor through the window."

Marilee tried to comfort her. "You're in the active phase,

Winnie. Remember what Mrs. Moore taught us? We need to go to shallow breathing.''

''I don't want to breathe, I want you to shoot me.''

''Oh, my word!'' Nell said once they'd seated themselves in the waiting area, except for Sam, who'd chosen not to come in. ''I forgot to lock the door before we left the house.''

''Honey, that ain't all,'' Ruby said. ''We left Grady standing in your living room.''

Josh looked up. ''He probably locked up before he left.''

Nell took his hand. ''Honey, I'm sorry Sam hit your father. Sam's not a violent man, but I guess he reached his limit.''

''I don't blame him,'' Josh said. ''I respect him for taking up for my mom. I felt pretty awful for her.'' He looked around. ''I need to talk to him.''

Sam was sitting in his truck in the parking lot when Josh found him. The boy wrenched the passenger door open and climbed in beside him. They both sat in silence for a moment.

''Anything happening in there?'' Sam asked.

''The nurse said Winnie's labor is going fast.''

''That's good.'' Sam looked at Josh. ''I'm sorry for what I did back there. I don't know what came over me.''

''You were defending my mom and me,'' Josh said. ''Nobody has ever stood up to my dad like that, they thought he was this great man of God and all, so he pretty much did and said what he wanted. Even if he was wrong. You put him in his place.''

Sam looked surprised. ''You're not angry with me?''

''I don't like seeing my dad punched in the face, but like Winnie said, he had it coming.'' Josh sighed and leaned his head back against the seat. ''I just wish he'd go to Georgia without us.''

''I'm leaving,'' Winnie announced.

''What?'' Marilee looked up from the monitor. They had

been panting and blowing for some time, and her doctor still hadn't shown up.

The girl made to get out of the bed as a contraction hit, and her entire body went rigid.

"You *can't* get out of bed right now," Marilee said frantically. "Now, three pants and blow. Three pants and blow."

The door opened. "Hello, Winnie," a gray-haired man dressed in hospital attire said as he stepped into the room. "I see you've decided to prove me wrong and have this baby early."

Winnie stopped panting. "Do you think she'll be big enough?" the girl asked worriedly. "What with her coming before her time and all?"

"She'll be fine," he assured her, looking at the monitor. "She's got a healthy heartbeat." He turned to Marilee. "I'm Dr. Johnson," he said as he washed his hands at the sink. "Sorry it took me so long to get here. I just came out of delivery. But I've been keeping up with Winnie's progress."

"She's been having a rough time of it for about an hour," Marilee replied.

Peggy stepped through the door. "I checked the patient about an hour ago," she said. "As I told you, she was dilated five centimeters."

"Let me have a look." He smiled at Winnie as he took a look. "Goodness, girl! You must be in a hurry." He turned to the nurse. "She's dilated to eight." He looked at Winnie. "We're going to give you something for pain. You hang in there, and I'll check on you in a bit."

"Somebody needs to tell us something," Ruby said once midnight rolled around. "At least give us an update."

Nell was dozing in the chair next to her and opened her eyes. "Yes, we need an update."

"I'll ask this time," Clara said, leaving the visitors' area.

"I'll come with you," Ruby offered.

Clara's look was cool. "That's not necessary."

Ruby grabbed her arm and prodded her along. "Look, I'm

sorry I told Winnie you had a boyfriend. It just slipped out. Give me a break for being human, Clara.''

The other woman sniffed. ''Well, I guess there was no harm done. I just don't want to appear silly in front of the others, you know, carrying on about a man like I'm some teenager.''

Ruby stopped walking and looked at her. ''Listen to me, Clara. I've been around the block so many times they've named street signs after me. If you've found someone kind and decent in this world, someone who thinks you're as great as the rest of us do, you shouldn't care what other people think. You just go for it, girl. We were put on this earth to love. What greater gift is there?''

Clara looked surprised. ''Why, Ruby, what a nice thing to say.''

They started walking. ''So have the two of you *done it* yet?''

Clara almost tripped over her own two feet. A blush spread across her cheeks. ''Why, Ruby Ledbetter, I can't believe you asked me such a question! Melvin and I have only dated a few times. He's a gentleman, and I'm a lady.'' She shot her friend a sidelong glance. ''Of course we've done it, and guess what?'' she whispered. ''He found my G-spot.''

''You go, Clara!'' Ruby was still grinning when they stepped up to the long counter leading to delivery.

Winnie and Marilee were hard at work. Sweat beaded both their foreheads. ''Two cleansing breaths,'' Marilee reminded her. ''You're doing great.''

''Okay,'' Dr. Johnson said. ''Let's push.''

Winnie grabbed the bedrail and pushed with all her might. Once the contraction ended, she collapsed on the bed.

''Lookin' good,'' the doctor said. ''Only a couple more.''

When the next contraction hit, Winnie and Marilee began the breathing pattern once again.

''The baby is crowning,'' the doctor said. ''Get ready to push again.''

Winnie, who had been too caught up in her labor to show any interest, paused and gazed into the overhead mirror. "There's my baby," she said. "Look, Marilee, there's my baby's head." Another contraction hit, and they automatically went into their routine. A couple of contractions later, the baby slipped from Winnie's womb.

"You have a new daughter," Dr. Johnson said, holding the baby up for inspection.

Winnie smiled broadly through her exhaustion as he placed the newborn on her stomach.

Warm tears streamed down Marilee's cheeks as she took in the scene. "She's beautiful, Winnie. Just like her mother. What are you going to name her?"

Winnie had tears in her eyes as well as she met Marilee's gaze. "Her name will be Marilee Elizabeth Frye," she said softly. "After you and my grandmother."

Marilee was deeply touched. "Oh, Winnie, I never expected—"

"I know." A nurse reached for the baby and Winnie closed her eyes.

It was a weary but excited group that left the hospital shortly before 2:00 a.m. Marilee rode with the women, Josh with Sam. Once they'd said a quick good-night, Marilee and Josh went into the house. After taking Rascal out, Josh trudged up the stairs, but Marilee grabbed the phone book, looked up a number and dialed.

"Is this the Frye residence?" she asked when a sleepy-sounding woman answered. "I'm looking for the parents of Winnie Frye."

After a brief pause, the woman on the other end answered, "This is her mother."

"Mrs. Frye, I'm Marilee Abernathy, Winnie's friend. I thought you might like to know you have a new granddaughter. She was born at 12:38 this morning."

"A granddaughter?" the woman said. "How's Winnie?"

"Both are fine. I just thought—" Marilee gave an exhausted sigh. "I thought you should know."

"Thank you."

Marilee hung up the phone. When she turned she found Grady standing at the bottom of the stairs.

"You okay?" he asked.

"Fine." She noted his bruised jaw. "And you?" Her words were clipped.

He tried to smile but winced. "I'm a little sore. I guess I made a fool of myself."

She tried to keep her anger at bay. "You guessed right."

"Josh wouldn't even speak to me when he came into the room just now."

Marilee sat in the chair. Her feet ached from standing beside Winnie's bed all night. "You were way out of line saying what you did tonight. I never once agreed to go back to you."

"You told me you'd forgiven me. You said I should take the job in Georgia. I thought—"

"You thought wrong. That's the trouble with you, Grady. You hear what you want to hear. Now hear this. I want you out of here by noon tomorrow or I'll have you escorted out by the police."

"Does this have anything to do with that Sam fellow?"

"It has to do with us."

He looked at her long and hard. "You've changed, Marilee."

"Thank God for that." She stood and made her way upstairs, pausing at the bottom step. "Noon, Grady."

It was late when Marilee awoke. She went down into the kitchen to make coffee and found Josh sitting at the table eating a bowl of cereal. She mumbled a good-morning.

"Dad left in a taxi about an hour ago."

Marilee leaned against the counter. "I'm sorry."

He looked up. "I know you've already divorced him, Mom. He told me."

Marilee hung her head. "I shouldn't have kept it from you. Are you okay?"

He nodded.

"I've made a lot of excuses for Dad over the years. I did it at the hospital, too, and I hurt you. Again," he added, hanging his head. "You were right. It's up to him to see that he gets better." He sighed heavily. It was obvious he was struggling with his emotions. "I just want us to be happy, Mom."

Marilee walked over and hugged him. "We will be. And you can see your dad whenever you like."

He remained quiet.

"How do you feel about going back to Chickpea Baptist?"

He shrugged. "It'll feel funny at first, but I'd like to see my friends."

"We'll start next Sunday."


Marilee and Josh visited Winnie after lunch. Marilee brought flowers and a new car seat for the baby's ride home, and Josh carried an enormous teddy bear. Winnie looked touched. Marilee noted a vase of yellow roses on the girl's night table.

"Mike brought them," she said.

Marilee gave her a knowing look. "I told you it would happen one day."

"Not only that, several of my girlfriends called. They plan on visiting later." She looked at Josh. "That's some teddy bear you got there. Did you break into a toy store?"

"I bought it with my own money." He passed it to her. "Consider it your Christmas gift as well, because I wasn't counting on spending that much on you."

"I love gifts that come straight from the heart," she said. "Wait till you see my baby."

"Does she look like you?"

"Darn right she does."

"That's too bad."

"Don't mess with me, Joshua. I may be sore, but I can still kick butt."

Someone knocked on the door. Clara and Ruby came into

the room, both carrying flowers and gifts. "We just saw the baby!" they announced.

"She's beautiful!" Clara said. "And Winnie, how sweet of you to name her after Marilee."

"Get this," Ruby said. "Clara and I are standing at the window looking for your baby. Of course, she's the only black baby in the room, yet Clara still read all the names on the bassinets, trying to find one with the last name of Frye." Ruby shook her head sadly. "So I took a chance and told her I thought it was the dark-skinned baby."

Clara laughed self-consciously. "I guess I was caught up in the excitement." She looked at Ruby. "Besides, I don't think of Winnie as being black or white, I just think of her as my friend."

Josh rolled his eyes at Winnie. "I can't handle all these women," he said. "I'm going to grab something to eat in the cafeteria."

Nell came into the room some twenty minutes later. "Sam and I just saw the baby. Oh, Winnie, she looks like a little doll. So beautiful. She has your eyes." She turned to Marilee. "How are you? I've been so concerned."

"I'm better now that Grady's gone."

"For good?" Winnie asked. When Marilee nodded, the girl looked relieved. "How's Josh taking it?"

"Surprisingly well."

"Well, we certainly have plenty of things to celebrate once we bust Winnie out of here," Ruby said. She looked at Clara. "Don't we?"

Clara blushed. "I have a little announcement to make."

All eyes were on her. "Tell us, dear," Nell said.

"I've fallen in love. After all this time, I've finally met the man of my dreams."

The women gave a whoop and took turns hugging her.

"I can't believe it happened so quickly," Clara said. "I mean, I don't believe in love at first sight or anything like that, but Melvin Benefield is the kindest, most loving man I've ever met. So when he told me he was in love with me this morning, I confessed feeling the same about him."

Marilee couldn't stop smiling. "Clara, I am so happy for you."

"As are we all," Ruby said.

Winnie looked perturbed. "Okay, I'm thrilled that Clara has found a man, but does anyone want a blow-by-blow description of my labor?" Without waiting for an answer, she began. The women stepped closer to the bed and listened attentively, grimacing when Winnie told them the pain she had survived, and smiling when she described holding the baby for the first time. She looked at Marilee. "I couldn't have done it without you."

"Nonsense," Marilee said. "You have already proven you can do anything you set your mind to."

"You serve as a pretty good example," Winnie replied, and the two smiled at one another.

The door opened. A middle-aged couple peeked in. "Winnie?" the woman said.

The girl went very still. "Mama? Daddy? What are you doing here?"

Winnie's mother stepped inside while her father remained at the door. "We just saw our new granddaughter. Why, she's beautiful! Just like you."

"How did you know?"

Marilee cleared her throat. "I thought your family should be notified," she said. "I hope that's okay."

The woman stepped up to the bed. Tears streamed down her cheeks. "You don't know how many times I've wanted to pick up the telephone and call you. We, I mean your daddy and I, have spoken to Reverend Bishop a number of times regarding the matter, but we were too embarrassed to call you after what happened. Can you ever forgive us?"

Winnie glanced away quickly and swiped at her cheeks. "Why don't we talk about it later?"

Clara and Ruby started for the door. "We're going to have a bite to eat in the cafeteria," they said. "Anybody want to join us?"

"I will," Nell said. She started for the door, then turned. "Marilee, are you coming?"

"I might be along later."

Nell nodded and followed the others out.

Marilee walked to the bed and kissed the girl on the forehead. "I'll be back this evening." She looked at Winnie's parents. "You have a wonderful daughter. You should be very proud of her."

Winnie's father spoke for the first time, with a great deal of emotion. "We are proud of her. Always have been. We're just not very proud of ourselves right now."

Marilee found Sam standing at the nursery window, his broad shoulders hunched, his hands stuffed into the pockets of his jacket. He looked as though the weight of the world had landed on him, and the burden was more than he could bear. She joined him and stared through the window wordlessly as a nurse visited each bassinet. She caught the clean scent of Sam's aftershave.

"Where are the others?" he asked without looking at her.

"Having lunch in the cafeteria."

He nodded, but his gaze remained fixed on Winnie's baby. "Isn't she lovely?" Marilee said.

"Yes." He turned to her, taking in the face he'd come to love. Her hair gleamed beneath the lights. She looked so delicate and fragile standing there in her simple skirt and sweater, but he knew she was one of the strongest, most determined women he'd ever met. "I'm surprised you're speaking to me after last night."

"Why don't we try to put it behind us?" she said softly. Marilee's heart ached at the raw hurt she saw in his dark eyes. His handsome face was drawn, and there were lines on either side of his mouth. "You look tired, Sam."

"I couldn't sleep after I got home last night. Just sat on the edge of my bed thinking."

Marilee had not slept well herself. She had spent the entire night thinking about all that had occurred these past months. She felt as though she'd come through a bad storm, and although she'd survived it, she was still picking through the rubble, trying to find her place in the world. She hoped that place was with Sam. She looked away, not wanting him to see the yearning in her eyes.

"Look at them," she said, gazing at the newborns instead. She was surprised to find her maternal instincts perfectly intact. She wondered if other women longed for a baby every time they found themselves looking through a nursery window. "They're all brand spanking new."

Sam nodded. "Yeah, they're starting out fresh. They haven't had time to make mistakes or know the meaning of regret or loss."

"I don't like seeing you this way, Sam."

"How do you expect me to feel? I'm in love with you, Marilee. How do you think it feels knowing the woman I love is going back to her ex-husband?"

"Oh, Sam." She touched his cheek and watched his jaw harden. "I never told Grady I was going to Georgia with him. He just assumed it, because I've always done what was expected of me. I don't have to live like that anymore." Her eyes misted. "Besides, why would I leave Chickpea when everything I want and love is right here?"

Sam was afraid to get his hopes up. "You're not going back to him?"

She shook her head. "Grady left this morning. At my insistence, I might add."

All Sam's fears and doubts drained from his body, leaving him with a feeling of renewal, as full of hope as the newborns on the other side of the window. "I thought I'd lost you, Marilee. I can't tell you what it did to me."

She smiled. "You're going to have a tough time getting rid of me, Sam Brewer."

He looked at her for a long moment. "Are you sure?"

"I'm in love with you, too, Sam. You give me butterflies."

His heart swelled with love. "Oh, Marilee—" He started to say something, then paused when a nurse walked by.

Finally, Sam pulled his hands from his pockets, raised one to her face and caressed her cheek with his knuckles. Her skin felt like satin. He wondered if she knew how much

power she had over him, over his heart, his very soul, for
that matter. He had felt hopeless and helpless without her;
now he felt like a king. His body vibrated with life when,
only moments before, he'd thought his life was over. He
slipped his arms around her, pulling her close, inhaling her
sweet scent, made even sweeter by the knowledge that she
was his.

"You know, if we get married," he said, "we'll have to
buy a big house to accommodate everybody. The Edgerton
place is for sale. It has five bedrooms and a two-bedroom
guest house. Mother and Winnie could share the guest house
since they get along so well. Mom would be a big help with
the baby. She's come a long way, thanks to you and your
friends."

Marilee knew the house well. It was beautiful, despite
needing some TLC. "You've been giving this a lot of
thought, haven't you?"

"I was hopeful, Marilee, until I feared I might lose you.
By the way, the house is big enough in case we decide to
add to our family. Of course, it would take me several
months to renovate it, so we could have a long engagement,
say, three or four months, if you feel you need more time.
Or we could get married tomorrow," he added with a grin.

Marilee stared at him. "Is this is a marriage proposal?"

He pulled her closer. "I adore you, Marilee, and I want
you with me, always. I want you to be my wife, if you'll
have me. I swear I'll be a good husband and father. And I'll
set the best example I can for Josh. I already think of him
as a son."

Marilee nuzzled her face against him. She was only
vaguely aware of passersby, of the scene they were creating
in the maternity ward. The storm had passed, and she was
a stronger person because of it. There would be others, because life was like that. But she knew who she was and
where she belonged.

In Sam's arms, she could weather anything.

**Everybody's in the mood for romance...except the bride.**

MIRA®

# Robyn Carr

## The Wedding Party

Charlene Dugan started her day as usual—single. But her decision to utter those three little words—*let's get married*—has everyone around her in a tailspin. The maid of honor is in a tempest over a man fifteen years her junior. Her daughter, the official bridesmaid, has decided to reinvent herself. The groom is spending all of his free time with the wedding consultant. And her ex-husband, a man who still drives her crazy, is making some pretty convincing arguments for a second chance.

The wedding party is out of control, they're calling for rain and the bride has cold feet. This isn't *exactly* what Charlene had in mind.

> **"Carr offers a well-written, warm-hearted story and a genuinely fun read."**
> —*Publishers Weekly* on *The House on Olive Street*

*On sale October 2001 wherever paperbacks are sold!*

# CHRISTIANE HEGGAN

---

66577   ENEMY WITHIN         ___ $5.99 U.S. ___ $6.99 CAN.
                  *(limited quantities available)*

TOTAL AMOUNT                                    $_____
POSTAGE & HANDLING                              $_____
($1.00 for one book; 50¢ for each additional)
APPLICABLE TAXES*                               $_____
<u>TOTAL PAYABLE</u>                            $_____
(check or money order—please do not send cash)

---

To order, complete this form and send it, along with a check
or money order for the total above, payable to MIRA Books®,
to: **In the U.S.:** 3010 Walden Avenue, P.O. Box 9077, Buffalo,
NY 14269-9077; **In Canada:** P.O. Box 636, Fort Erie, Ontario,
L2A 5X3.

Name:_____
Address:_____ City:_____
State/Prov.:_____ Zip/Postal Code:_____
Account Number (if applicable):_____
075 CSAS

   *New York residents remit applicable sales taxes.
    Canadian residents remit applicable GST and provincial taxes.

MIRA®